The Duke Conspiracy

WENDY MAY ANDREWS

Sparrow Ink
www.sparrowdeck.com

ISBN - 978-1-9994932-6-4

www.wendymayandrews.com

Anything is possible with a spying debutante, a duke, and a conspiracy.

Growing up, Rose and Alex were the best of friends until their families became embroiled in a feud. Now, the Season is throwing them into each other's company. Despite the spark of attraction they might feel for one another, they each want very different things in life, besides needing to support their own family's side in the dispute.

Miss Rosamund Smythe is finding the Season to be a dead bore after spying with her father, a baron diplomat, in Vienna. She wants more out of life than just being some nobleman's wife. When she overhears a plot to entrap Alex into a marriage of convenience, her intrigue and some last vestige of loyalty causes them to overcome the feud.

His Grace, Alexander Milton, the Duke of Wrentham, wants a quiet life with a "proper" wife after his tumultuous childhood. His parents had fought viciously, lied often, and Alex had hated it all.

Rose's meddling puts her in danger. Alex will have to leave the simple peace he craves to claim a love he never could have imagined. Can they claim their happily ever after despite the turmoil?

Dedication

My books have a recurring theme of friendship. In this book, the hero and heroine were childhood friends before a family feud ruins their relationship. They can't help their loyalty to their old friendship, though when they are each threatened from outside sources. I loved writing about their loyalty to one another. So this book is dedicated to all the loyal friends who stick to one another through thick and thin.

My parents are my biggest fans in life. Without them I would be nothing.

My husband is my greatest support.

My cover artist, JB Designs, did an outstanding job with this series, thank you Josephine!

And last but most definitely not least, my editor, Julie Sherwood. Thank you for tightening things up for me.

Table of Contents

Chapter One

Their eyes met across the crowded ballroom. Rose's stomach tumbled and a wave of heat swept her as she took in his rugged good looks. He had changed since she saw him last, three years ago. She had always thought Alex's beautiful sea-green eyes were his best feature, but the sight of them had never caused goose bumps to skitter up her spine as they did now. Previously, it had always been her opinion that girls who sighed over handsome men were silly widgeons, but now she had an unforeseen empathy for them. The air of maturity that emanated from him suited him, she thought absently, as she struggled to breathe through the uncharacteristic fluttering of her heart.

He had not yet descended the stairs so he was clearly visible, but she was surprised that he even noticed her, tucked away in the corner of obscurity such as she was. Her surprise turned to shock when she recognized the look of appreciation warming his eyes as his gaze remained on her for what felt like eons, but was undoubtedly a couple of seconds. She was torn by a whirlwind of conflicted feelings. A part of her preened under the admiration of the handsome nobleman, while another part bristled with indignation that he would even dare to look at her, considering their history. She could feel her mother's resentment smoldering behind her, but Rose was unable to tear her eyes from Alex's gaze. She almost wished she could go back to how she had been feeling just a couple moments before.

Moments earlier…

Rose tapped her foot with impatience. Glancing around the room at the crowd of glittering High Society, she wished fervently that she could be elsewhere. Even though this was the so-called "Little Season," there were an uncomfortable number of people crowded into the fashionable ballroom. Despite the multitudes, or maybe because of them, a sense of loneliness was stealing over her.

"Stop that tapping, Rosamund," her mother hissed.

Rose twitched in surprise. She had quite forgotten that Mama was nearby.

Her silent sigh puffed past her lips with a disconsolate gust. "We most certainly are not in Vienna anymore," she muttered to herself, careful that Mama didn't hear.

Mama was so rarely nearby in Vienna, for one thing. She had other things to occupy her than this obsession with getting her only daughter married off that seemed to have taken root of late. For another, the air of excitement that was ever present in Vienna was replaced with a flat and stale atmosphere here in the ballrooms of London. Maybe that was just her own perception though, she thought with despondency.

Another sigh escaped as she looked around at the other guests. It would seem that most everyone else was excited to be there. The couples on the dance floor were swirling in the familiar steps in a kaleidoscope of colours, most of the younger ladies in varying shades of pastel, of course. The smoke from the myriad candles was beginning to create a bit of a haze in the large room, but the evening was not yet so advanced that the ladies' perfumes were overshadowed by the less attractive scents of that many bodies together in a warm room.

She could see another waiter passing by with a tray laden with glasses of punch and sparkling wine. Once more they failed to approach the corner she and her mother had found themselves in. The wallflowers were not deemed to need the liquid refreshment, as they were clearly not exerting themselves overmuch.

Rose finally acknowledged to herself that part of her impatience with the evening was really envy. In Vienna she had never been a wallflower. She would have been on the dance floor from the first note struck by the orchestra. It was only when she needed to overhear a particular conversation that she would sit out a dance, claiming the need to rest her feet.

Glancing down at her lovely new shoes, she reluctantly allowed that there was at least one good thing about being back in London. She would never have been able to find the exact shade of kid leather shoes to match her dress in any of the shops in Vienna. The darling bows and the fact that they were nearly as comfortable as a pair of slippers almost made it worth coming to this wretched ball.

Almost, but not quite, *she thought to herself with another sigh she managed to keep silent. She looked away from her toes and forgot about her impatience when she noticed a change in the air. Her eyes scanned the crowd to ascertain the difference.*

It seemed as though things were about to get interesting. A stir rippled through the gathered revelers, and Rose strained to see what was taking place. A latecomer was being welcomed by their hosts, Viscount Chorney and his lovely wife, Lady Catherine.

From her perspective along the wall, near a corner, she could barely make out who had arrived. All she could see was the back of a head. Obviously he was a tall man, she noted with some interest, as she regularly lamented her own height. And she found it interesting how the light of the many candles glinted off his hair, making it difficult to determine exactly what colour it was.

The excited murmurs of the young women in the room, as well as their matchmaking mamas, made it obvious to Rose that this was clearly a single gentleman of some repute. It was surprising to see the blatant eagerness on the part of the debutantes.

I know this is called the Marriage Mart, but really, have a little dignity, *Rose thought with disgust as the young ladies fluttered and preened around her. She was reminded of the flock of peahens on the grounds of their estate.*

Rose turned to look at her mother when she heard another hiss coming from her. Lady Smythe was gazing transfixed in the same direction she had been looking. Intrigued, Rose turned back to see if she too could catch a glimpse of the gentleman causing such a commotion. She had never seen such a look upon her mother's face. Her infernal curiosity moved her to discover its source.

She could not see his face, but from the erectness of his posture and the lack of gray in his hair she assumed that he was a young nobleman. He walked with a slight swagger that she was surprised to find appealing. Arrogance was not a quality she would normally admire, but on him it seemed somehow fitting. She wished he would turn around so she could see if his face matched the rest of him. Rose held her breath as it seemed that her will was to be rewarded.

Rose came back to the present as the moment stretched. Her lips parted on a whispered "Alex" as she took in the changes the past three years had wrought on her former friend. Time had definitely been kind to him. Gone was any youthful fleshiness. In its place, his cheekbones were much more defined than she remembered, and he had the beginnings of creases in his forehead and around his mouth.

Rose now understood the cooing and fluttering of the many debutantes. The Duke of Wrentham was a sight to behold. His sea-green eyes were even more piercing than she remembered, and she now saw that his hair had darkened to a rich chestnut. He had an air of detached authority that had certainly not existed when they had been friends.

He has changed a great deal and clearly he has been worrying too much, she thought to herself with concern, before she remembered everything else and turned her back on her former best friend.

It had taken great effort to tear her eyes away from him. He had been such a lovely friend to her when she was a child. Her only friend, really, it had seemed at times. It was clear to her that inheriting the dukedom had been a worrisome trial for him. He had never wanted to be the duke, she remembered rather absently, as she marveled over the changes she noticed in him.

Rose didn't have long to analyze her multitude of reactions to seeing him so suddenly. Resolving to think on it later, she had to attend to Mama, who was looking as near to fits as Rose had ever witnessed. Mama's mantra had always been *don't make a scene,* so a sense of consternation swamped Rose at seeing her so close to losing her composure. Finding a reason to be glad they were socially insignificant, Rose managed to take her mother's arm and escort her to a retiring room before anyone noticed their disturbance.

"Can you believe the gall of that man, showing up at a ball where we might be in attendance?" Lady Smythe demanded. She kept her voice low, but the tone's urgency was piercing nonetheless.

Rose glanced around the small room set apart for the private use of the female guests. She was relieved to see that they were alone except for the maidservant in the corner. That young woman quickly averted her eyes when she realized they required her discretion more than her assistance. Smiling politely at Rose, she mumbled something about needing some more pins and scurried from the room.

The dark paneling and velvet-upholstered furniture would have been appealing to Rose if she could have appreciated them in that moment, but all her attention was focused on her mother. Despite being alone in the room, she carefully kept her voice low.

"But Mama, how could he know we would be here? We have been out of the country for nearly two years. He cannot be held accountable to our social calendar." Rose tried to be reasonable, but her own feelings were too divided on the subject; her argument came out sounding weak.

"He should never show his face amongst decent people, regardless of our attendance," Mama declared, her proper tones in strange contrast with the vehemence of her words.

Rose could see that her mother was not going to be capable of thinking coherently at the moment. Even though she, too, resented the duke, her mother's words were going a bit too far. She couldn't rightly say the man was indecent. Instead of trying to reason with her about Wrentham, she merely set herself to the task of calming her.

"Mama, we are guests in the home of Lord and Lady Chorney. We cannot embarrass them or ourselves by causing a scene, no matter the provocation."

Lady Smythe drew a sharp inward breath at her daughter's words. "I never cause a scene. What are you prattling on about?" As she looked down her narrow nose, her pride came to her rescue.

"I know, Mama," Rose tried to soothe, "but you were clearly upset by the sight of Alex."

"Do not speak his name with such familiarity! He is dead to us."

Despite the discomfort she was feeling, Rose could not stop a smile at her mother's uncharacteristically dramatic words. Not wishing to upset her further, Rose tried to wipe it away before continuing. "All right, Mama, but do you think you can return to the ballroom, or shall we fetch Papa and call for our carriage?"

Rose watched her mother's effort to pull herself together, rather awestruck at the woman's transformation. Within a moment she could see no evidence of her mother's momentary distress.

"Thank you, dear, for your concern, but there is no need to disturb your father. I shall be perfectly fine. We cannot leave now; we have practically just arrived. You have not yet set foot upon the dance floor. How are we going to get you creditably established if we return home at the first discomfort? Now come along, Rosamund, quit your dithering, we should be in the ballroom."

Rose stifled another grin at her mother's commandeering of the situation. She would have been happier if Mama had agreed to go home, even though she hated the thought of being a quitter. But this debutante business was deadly dull in her estimation. With another suppressed sigh, she dutifully followed her mother back to the ballroom. Not even the unsettling presence of the Duke of Wrentham could make this irksome event more interesting.

ᗢ ᗣ

Back in the ballroom, Alex let out the breath he hadn't realized he was holding as she had turned away from him. His hand rubbed his chest absently as though to soothe away the ache in his heart. A sense of foreboding rested upon him momentarily. Rose being here for the Season was not going to help him in his quest for a quiet, unassuming duchess.

Clearly, their family feud had not lessened with the passage of time. His mother would disown him if she knew how he felt, but he considered the conflict that had divided their families to be idiotic. He sighed with resignation as he forced his eyes to stop gazing at the beautiful woman moving from the corner of the ballroom.

Her hair was piled up in some intricate, inexplicable way that young ladies so loved. It looked stunning on her; her elegant neck was accentuated by the one piece that dangled down from the complicated knot on top. She had blossomed into a woman in the past three years, he noticed, feeling the tug of attraction. She had always been a pretty girl, but now she was beautiful. As he was greeted and hailed by many in the crowd, the thought niggled at the back of his mind that she couldn't possibly be a wallflower.

"The Smythes are here, aren't they, Your Grace?" his good friend, Wesley, asked him quietly, careful not to look at the subject of his question.

"Have you seen them?" Alex asked, also keeping his voice low so as not to be overheard, but trying not to appear as though he were whispering. Alex was well aware that if it appeared he had a secret the entire *ton* would be agog to know its source.

"No." Wesley grinned. "But I have heard that they are back in Town, and I can tell from your posture that you are even more tense than usual."

"And you attribute that to the Smythes?" Alex was incredulous over his friend's assumptions. "You do not think it is just the atmosphere of salivating mamas trying to sink their matrimonial claws into me for the sake of their darling daughters that has me tied up in knots this evening?"

"But that is always the case whenever you attend one of these infernal affairs, Ancroft," Wesley explained patiently, using his former title as a term of familiarity. "I am telling you, you are markedly different tonight."

With a snort, the duke chose to ignore his friend's observation as he really could not effectively dispute it since the Smythes *were* in attendance and the headache that was beginning to form would confirm that he was, in fact, more tense than usual. He would be willing to argue the subject upon some other occasion, but clearly now was not the time.

With a sigh that he tried to keep to himself, Alex turned back to survey the crowd. "We might as well invite someone to dance. Our hostess will look at us askance if we do not."

Alex was surprised as his friend's grin turned devious. "Which hearts are you willing to set aquiver this evening, Your Grace?" Wesley asked with a suggestive lift of his eyebrows.

"Truth be told, none," the duke answered rather stiffly.

Wesley, surveying the crowd, brought his eyes back to his friend's face with a grin. "Come now, Your Grace, it is not such a trial as all that. Just ensure you dance with a diverse number of ladies, and no one will be able to murmur overmuch."

"They always murmur overmuch," came Alex's plaintive reply, "but never mind about that, you are right. Let us dance."

With that, Alex forced his eyes to stop looking for Rose. There was no way he would be able to approach her in such an environment anyway, even if he wanted to. The fact that she had turned her back on him in such a way made him doubt strongly that she would be receptive to any overtures of peace from him, even if he dared. Not that he had any wish to make peace with the Smythes, he reminded himself as he stopped in front of a lady he had been introduced to on some previous occasion.

"Lady Castleton, might I have the pleasure of dancing with your daughter?" he asked politely, bowing over the older woman's hand gallantly.

The usually starchy matron giggled like a schoolgirl over his courtly gesture. "Get on with you, you young scamp. Of course, my darling Elizabeth would be delighted to dance with you."

Alex noticed the "darling Elizabeth's" slight roll of her eyes at her mother's words, but she turned a welcoming smile upon the duke. Offering his elbow to the young lady, he escorted her to the dance floor as the musicians struck up the next quadrille.

"Thank you for partnering me, Lady Elizabeth." Alex began the conversation with his companion.

"Was I given much choice, Your Grace?" she returned with a straight face.

Alex looked at her sharply, wondering fleetingly if he ought to apologize before he noticed the twinkle in her eye. Relaxing into the familiar steps, the duke allowed a smile to lighten his features.

Ignoring her unanswerable question, he turned the subject. "Are you enjoying your evening?"

Lady Elizabeth tilted her head in slight inquiry as she thought on the subject. With a delicate shrug she replied, "It is passable, Your Grace."

"You do not enjoy events of the Season, do you, my lady?"

"I pray you do not tell my mother I admitted such to you, but no, not overmuch. I would so much rather remain on our estates forever. Not that I wish to remain under my mother's watchful eye for the rest of my life, mind you. I guess you might say this Season business is a necessary evil."

Alex grinned at the young lady before him, wondering if he should admit that he agreed wholeheartedly with her. He pressed for more information. "Then why did you bother coming for the Little Season? Why not wait until the Spring Session?"

"My mother was so disappointed with my lack of success in my first Season. She thought I could use the extra exposure of the Little Season. I believe she thought there would be less competition as some ladies do not come to Town for the Fall Session, but most of the lords who need to be present for Parliament do, thus giving me more selection."

"Your mother is a shrewd strategist."

"I believe all determined mamas are," answered the duke's dance companion, "but it would seem that many of the mamas had the exact same strategy. If you will note, this ball is barely less crowded than one would experience during the regular Season."

"'Tis true, my lady, but one could attribute that to the popularity of Lady Chorney as a hostess, rather than the number of people who have come to Town for the Fall Session."

"She is quite lovely, is she not? Do you know the Chorneys very well, Your Grace?" Elizabeth was glad to change the subject.

"Not that well, but I have been their guest a couple of times as well as hearing the viscount speak in the House upon occasion."

"Last Season I was a guest at the most darling breakfast Lady Catherine hosted. We dined al fresco, which was a novel experience for me as my mama tends to think it is unhealthy. I thought it was divine."

"It does sound novel. Were you not cold?"

"It was near the end of the Season, so we were quite comfortable. It was absolutely lovely despite the challenge of getting ready for a *ton* event so early in the morning. Most of the assembled guests were not used to seeing the day much before noon. I do believe that was part of the amusement, watching how everyone tried to hide the evidence of their excesses from the previous night."

"You do have a perverse sense of humor, do you not?" the duke commented with a wry chuckle.

"Oh, that is exactly what my dear friend Rosamund tells me every time," declared Lady Elizabeth with a smile, causing a sudden hitch in Alex's breathing.

"Would I have met this Rosamund?" Alex asked tactfully, feeling his heart race in reaction as he thought of his old friend, forcing his eyes not to stray to the side of the ballroom where he was sure she was standing. He could hardly fathom his constant awareness of her. Controlling his reaction, he carried on the conversation as though he were unaffected. "She sounds like a sensible woman," he teased.

"I do not know if you have met her. She has never mentioned you. Not that I have known her for all that long, mind you, and we rarely discuss gentlemen, particularly not dukes," she replied pertly before elaborating. "She was not out before she went away to Vienna with her parents. She is just making her debut now, even though she is a trifle old to be a debutante. She is a delightful girl. We enjoy making fun of the Season together. She is finding it nearly as dull as I am, although I believe it is for far different reasons. She says life in London is not nearly as exciting as it was in Vienna, where she has been for the past two years with her father, who is a diplomat."

Lady Elizabeth paused for a moment as she gazed at the duke with rapidly widening eyes. Her mouth fell agape before she shut it with a snap. After swallowing a gulp of air she continued in far different tones. "Of course, you know Miss Rosamund, how silly of me," she prattled as she tried to change the subject. "Is this orchestra not one of the best you have ever heard? I must inquire of Lady Catherine where she managed to find such accomplished musicians for her ball. I know my mama will want to see if she can hire them for our next rout. Do you like to attend routs, Your Grace?"

Alex could not help admiring the young woman's attempts at covering the awkward moment, wondering fleetingly what she would do if he were to ask her why she was suddenly so uncomfortable discussing Rose with him. Of course, a gentleman ought not to put a lady to the blush, one of the myriad lessons he had been taught from the cradle. With a silent sigh he tried to recall what she had last asked him. Oh yes, something about routs.

"At times, my lady. It often depends on who is hosting them, would you not agree? The very nature of a rout calls for it to be quite different from hostess to hostess."

"Quite right, Your Grace," Elizabeth replied with a false little laugh. "I trust you would consider my mama and me to be acceptable rout hostesses. Shall I put you on our guest list?"

"By all means," Alex answered with a tightening smile. Starting to find his companion to be a bit of a trial, he was relieved to hear the end of the quadrille as the musicians wound down to a conclusion.

Escorting his partner back to her waiting mama, Alex gallantly bowed over each lady's hand before making good his escape.

Going in search of refreshments, the duke asked himself yet again why he bothered attending such events. It was not as though at the age of twenty-six he were in *desperate* need of securing his succession. Of course, as he knew only too well, calamities could occur even in someone's prime, but he had several strapping young cousins who would be delighted to take over the house of Wrentham. Well aware that the *on-dit* was that he was ready to settle down to matrimonial bliss, Alex was very much of two minds on the matter.

No, he attended such events on occasion just to be perverse, as he had accused Lady Elizabeth of being. And out of respect for his political connections. As he sipped from the glass he had been handed by a passing footman, Alex wondered if it were too early to leave without causing offense.

With a sigh, he realized that it would most definitely be remarked upon if he departed after dancing with only one lady. He set himself to the task of partnering many ladies so that none would be remarkable.

Across the ballroom Rose watched the duke's antics with a jaundiced eye. He appeared to be having a lovely evening as he led one lady after another onto the dance floor while she remained firmly on the side lines. Not that she would have ever accepted his invitation even if he had asked her to dance, but she so wished *someone* would ask her, she thought with another quickly suppressed sigh. She tried not to notice how very handsome he looked as he maneuvered expertly amongst the dancing couples.

How was it possible that she was left standing on the sidelines when so many other ladies were dancing holes in their slippers? This had never happened to her in Vienna, she thought with wistful longing. In Vienna she had been, if not the belle of every ball, at least rather highly popular. Here in London, she knew almost no one. Of course, she had made a few friends in the weeks they had been in residence, but it was not at all the same as the tight community the expatriates had formed in Vienna. She fervently hoped some of those old friends would soon turn up in the capital.

She was lost in happier recollections when a deep voice pulled her from her distraction. "Miss Smythe? Might I have the pleasure of your company for the next dance?"

Blinking in surprise at the gentleman before her, Rose drew a momentary blank before recognition dawned on her. "Lord Dunbar?" she asked as she dropped a brief, hasty curtsy before her face bloomed into a smile she struggled to prevent turning into a grin. "I would be delighted to partner you in the next dance."

"I was wondering if you perhaps had an injury," the viscount commented, causing Rose to look at him in question.

"I have not yet seen you on the dance floor this evening," he explained.

Rose could see from his contrite expression that he regretted his choice of words, but her own face felt like it was flaming with her embarrassment, so she was unsure how to set him at ease.

"I am new to Town, my lord, and do not know many people," she tried to excuse.

"I wouldn't think that would much matter," he replied, still confused. "A beautiful young woman such as yourself very rarely finds herself standing with the chaperones."

"I have not yet been presented in the Queen's Drawing Room, so that could account for it." Rose tried to put a brave face on it. She was torn between feeling flattered over his compliment and being irked that he was harping on her lack of dance partners.

Rose was almost amused by the viscount's confusion and his look of chagrin as he began to realize that he should never have pointed out a young lady's identification as a wallflower. He tried to turn the matter into a jest. "Did you do something particularly scandalous while in Vienna?"

Rose looked at the viscount sharply as she felt the heat rise once more into her cheeks, but she refused to allow him to get a reaction from her. Keeping her face as straight as possible, she allowed one eyebrow to inch toward her hairline. "Not that anyone ever found out about." She turned the veiled admission into a sly jest.

Lord Dunbar threw his head back and chuckled loudly, causing heads to turn in their direction. Rose struggled to maintain her composure despite her fierce desire to rebuke the viscount. She could hear her mother's words in her mind—*don't make a scene.*

"Come along, miss, our dance is beginning. Do not mind the busybodies staring. You will have to grow accustomed to it, as I am quite certain you are about to become a popular young woman."

Rose stared at the viscount, shocked at his apparent arrogance. "Just because you have paid me a bit of attention?" she asked, incredulity colouring her surprised tones.

"No," he declared with disgust, "because you are a taking little thing and everyone will soon discover that for themselves."

Rose managed to keep her mirth contained to a delicate, low chuckle, but inside she was full of gales of laughter, and she was sure it was written all over her face. Her breath caught as she noticed the look of appreciation on his face. *Is it possible the viscount is about to set up a flirtation with me?* she wondered. His next words disabused her of that idea.

"How is it that you have not yet made your curtsy to our Queen? Surely you were not that far behind us in age," Lord Dunbar probed.

"You are just full of social niceties this evening, are you not, my lord?" Rose asked, sarcasm dripping from each syllable. "Did no one ever tell you it is decidedly bad form to make any reference to a lady's age?"

"But surely you cannot be of an age to be concerned about that?" Wesley defended.

In all honesty, Rose could not prevent the negligent shrug that followed his question. "No, you are probably right. And I truly do not care about such things. But it is strange to be experiencing such a sense of not belonging when I have always felt so comfortable in my own skin." Becoming a trifle flustered over her admission, she hastened to return to the previous question. "I did not come out earlier because we were in mourning. Then we left the country to accompany my father in his diplomatic duties. Now, I am in the uncomfortable position of being rather more experienced than the usual debutantes, but I am confined to all the traditions accompanying making one's debut in London."

"Is it so very terrible?"

Rose hesitated before answering, and the viscount could see indecision clearly displayed upon her expressive features.

"Yes and no," she finally answered, prompting another laugh from Wesley.

"That is so very specific," he chided, his tone dry.

Her colour rising once more, Rose elaborated. "I found the social rounds amongst the diplomats and their families much more comfortable, as we were a smaller group and there was such an air of excitement, as the men were involved in important affairs. Now, being in London, I feel lost in the crowd. And it feels a little awkward to be making my debut alongside seventeen-year-old misses fresh from the schoolroom."

"I can see how that might rub the wrong way." Wesley tried to be sympathetic. "I hear our dance is drawing to a close, so I must bid you good night. I hope the Season becomes more interesting for you."

"It already has," she answered with a smile.

Chapter Two

"I could hardly credit it, Elizabeth!" Rose declared with a touch of disgust in her voice. "No sooner had the viscount returned me to my mother's side than there was practically a queue of men waiting to ask me to dance."

In her agitation Rose got up to pace around the elegantly appointed drawing room where she and Lady Elizabeth were having tea. She usually found the large, sunny room to be welcoming and settling, but today not even the oversized painting of Elizabeth as a young girl could get a smile out of her.

"Are you complaining?" Elizabeth asked, confused.

"Not exactly," Rose had to admit. "The ball was obviously much more interesting when viewed from the dance floor rather than the sidelines with the chaperones. But it was just so surprising that Lord Dunbar had such power over everything. What if he had taken me in disgust? Would I be condemned to obscurity for the rest of my days?"

"My dear Rose, surely you must see that you could never be left in obscurity? It is just impossible for you. There is far too much vitality shimmering around you for you to remain on the sidelines for long. And truly, who cares what makes people tick?"

"I most certainly do," Rose declared with determination. "I want to be accepted into the *ton* because I am witty or some such, not because Lord Dunbar, the famous Viscount of Bracondale, found me mildly amusing."

"But you *are* witty and droll and amusing and lovely. If I did not like you so much, I would find it impossible to be friends with you. You are clearly my competition. So what if the gentlemen were a little slow to discover you? What matters is that they did, and you had a lovely time, right?"

"I suppose you are correct," Rose admitted grudgingly. "Enough about me, did you have a good time at the ball? I was so excited to be finally dancing again that I failed to spend any time talking with you. I am sure you must have also been on the dance floor, but I so rarely caught a glimpse of you."

"That is quite all right. Our mothers would have our heads if we spent too much time with each other and not enough looking over the eligible gentlemen."

Rose's tinkle of laughter followed these words before she resumed her questioning. "So I told you all about my dance partners, now you tell me. Did any of your partners strike a chord for you?"

The strange look that crossed Elizabeth's face caused Rose to intensify her questions. "There *was* someone! Out with it, my lady, who struck your fancy?"

"It is nothing like that, Rose. No one was of particular interest to me, alas." She again hesitated before taking a deep breath and plunging into speech. "I danced with the Duke of Wrentham."

Rose could feel the colour draining from her face at her friend's words. Hating the thought of even her dear friend sensing a weakness in her, she decided to try to brazen it out.

"Was the duke any good as a partner? I must admit I find it difficult to imagine, since I can recall how he hated the lessons his tutor insisted he must endure."

Lady Elizabeth followed her friend's lead and did not refer to the possible awkwardness. "You must make an effort to stretch your imagination then, my dear, as the duke's lessons have clearly paid off. While he was not as skilled as Lord Danbury, he was a wonderful companion for the quadrille we shared."

"But of course, no one can quite match up to Lord Danbury's skills on the dance floor," Rose banter was a trifle weak, but she kept her chin firm and brave.

Elizabeth grinned, continuing, "Well, at the very least all my toes rejoiced over not being trodden upon even once throughout the entire dance."

"I would hardly call that a cause to praise his dance skills."

"Clearly you have not had the misfortune of being partnered with some of the gentlemen I have been paired up with of late." Elizabeth's wry answer was followed by a teasing smile.

"I cannot argue with you there, as I have been sorely lacking in dance partners." Seeing that her friend was about to commiserate, Rose hastened to return to the subject at hand. "I am happy to hear that the duke's title has clearly brought him previously unheard of skills," Rose countered, feeling much more the thing after her momentary lapse of zest.

"He was actually quite a lovely dance partner. Besides not stepping on my toes, he politely conversed with me and appeared to be very kind."

"How lovely," Rose answered in a monotone, not wishing to prolong this particular conversation. "Did you have any other interesting experiences at the ball?"

"Not particularly. While the Chorneys were perfect hosts, I found the ball to be much like any other I have attended and would much rather have been home on our estate curled up with a good book after a long day of riding or visiting our tenants or some such, anything other than being in a stuffy, crowded ballroom listening to bored society matrons rehashing the latest *on dits*."

The two girls shared a look of mutual agreement before Rose answered with reasonable aplomb. "I cannot help but agree with you wholeheartedly, but the trouble is that in order to attain a home of our own we need to marry. And apparently the only way one can marry is to go through this ridiculous charade one calls 'the Season.' So, events such as the Chorney Ball are a necessary evil, would you not agree?"

With a heartfelt sigh, Elizabeth nodded before mustering up a smile and adding, "At least with a friend who feels similarly it is not quite so dreadful."

"Exactly," agreed Rose with a wide grin.

Both girls were distracted by the clatter of approaching people. They had been so engrossed in their conversation that they had failed to hear the knocker. It would seem that their comfortable coze was at an end as Lady Elizabeth had more callers.

"Lucky thing you came unfashionably early," Elizabeth whispered just before the butler stepped into the room to announce the new arrivals.

"Ladies Emmaline and Constance Chadwick to see you, my lady," the staid older retainer intoned.

Rose had to stifle her giggle as she watched her friend put on the airs expected of an aristocratic debutante. She watched in awe as her friend rose slowly to her feet, an air of boredom heavy upon her features.

"Welcome, ladies," she said, her usually cheerful voice dulled by her tones of ennui.

Rose reflected that the *ennui* might not be fully feigned, as the new arrivals were not the most enjoyable company to spend time with. She could feel her own face pinching with a touch of distaste as she observed the two newcomers mincing into the room.

"My darling Lady Elizabeth," Emmaline began in a breathy voice that made Rose wish she could box her ears, "how charming to see you today."

"Yes, charming," echoed her sister without an ounce of originality.

Rose saw that Elizabeth could not maintain her bored façade as this struck her funny bone. "How lovely to see you," the lady lied with a twinkle in her eye she quickly disguised by turning to introduce Rose. "Are you two familiar with my dear friend, Miss Rosamund Smythe?"

Both girls dropped into curtsies that were the barest minimum of politeness, registering Rose's social insignificance as a mere Miss.

"We have not previously been introduced. How do you do?" Emmaline was forced to acknowledge.

Suppressing her amusement as best she could, Rose dipped into her own practiced curtsy, far more experienced than the rest of the girls in the various nuances of social interaction from her years as a diplomat's daughter. Ignoring their veiled jab, Rose offered them a charming smile.

"It is a pleasure to make your acquaintance, Lady Emmaline and Lady Constance. You are the daughters of Lord Chadwick, are you not? I have not been introduced to him, but my father has sung his praises on numerous occasions. As you are here for the Little Season, you no doubt know all about their work on Britain's involvement at the Congress of Vienna."

The two sisters looked at Rose blankly for a moment, unsure how to respond to her. Rose kept her face as straight as possible as she observed their obvious confusion. They clearly thought it beneath their notice to follow politics, but since she had complimented their father, they could not snub her for what they would consider bluestocking tendencies.

Constance gazed at her sister fretfully until Emmaline finally replied. "We and our mother have accompanied him to Town, as he likes to have our company, but we do not involve ourselves in his work."

"No, of course not," Rose replied smoothly as she took her seat, leaving Emmaline to wonder if she had been dismissed by this upstart.

Emmaline and Constance again shared a look of confused chagrin before Emmaline offered a weak smile as Elizabeth invited the two sisters to have a seat.

"Will you two be staying for a visit? Should I ring for tea? This is not my usual at-home day so I am not expecting too many callers."

"How kind of you to offer," Emmaline accepted as Constance murmured her thanks.

Elizabeth tugged gently on the bell pull while Emmaline launched into an explanation of their visit.

"We just had to stop in to compliment you on your *coup* of dancing with the Duke of Wrentham. Was it terribly exciting? Neither of us have yet had the privilege, so we wanted to hear it straight from you."

Rose studiously avoided meeting Elizabeth's eyes as she awaited her reply. She was well aware her friend hated the thought of being the subject of gossip, but it was nearly impossible to completely avoid in the rarified company of the *ton*.

There was a pause as the housekeeper wheeled in the tea trolley. Rose was certain that Elizabeth was hoping that the subject of her dance with the duke could now be avoided, but her wish was not granted.

As soon as they were alone in the room once more, while Elizabeth was pouring the tea, Constance prompted, "So, how was your dance with the duke?"

"I hardly thought it was a subject to be remarked upon. The duke had many partners on the dance floor last night," Elizabeth remarked, attempting to stem the sisters' questions.

"'Tis true," Emmaline acknowledged before turning a quelling look upon Constance, who had blathered, "We already spoke to Lady Anne Austen. She said his dance skills were divine."

Rose saw Elizabeth's lips twitch with her amusement and was hard pressed not to laugh despite her discomfort with the subject of the duke.

"I am sorry to disappoint you ladies. While I found him to be a pleasant enough dance partner I would hardly compare him to anything heavenly. In fact, I danced with Mr. Dylan Mead last night as well, and I will admit to you I thought he was a little more skilled than His Grace."

This resulted in twin looks of disbelief directed at her. "But he is merely an aide in the House," Emmaline said with confusion colouring her tones.

"That may be true, but he is a very good dancer." Elizabeth shrugged with a sweet smile. "And he was particularly amusing. His Grace was pleasant enough, but it struck me that he might have had some weighty concerns on his mind last night."

"Ah yes." The ladies looked relieved with this explanation. "Since his father's death is not so long ago, it is quite likely that as a new duke he has many things to concern him."

Constance nodded seriously. "He is no doubt in need of a helpmate. The *on-dit* is that he is looking about for an appropriate duchess to take over some of the responsibilities upon his estate."

Rose managed not to roll her eyes at this remark but could barely stomach the look of sly pride upon Emmaline's face as the lady commented, "Constance and I have been learning from our mama how to look after the tenants on our estate and run the household and such so that we will be fully prepared when the time comes to take over such duties for our husbands."

"No doubt you will make some lucky gentlemen perfectly lovely wives," Elizabeth replied politely. Rose could detect the effort she made to infuse some sincerity into her voice.

"Is Chadwick a very large estate?" Rose inquired, which gained her a look of pitying disbelief from the sisters. Properly interpreting the look as a result of an arrogant assumption that everyone should be aware of their importance, Rose diplomatically smoothed the moment with her next words. "I have been out of the country for some time, so I am not as familiar with some of these things. You must forgive my ignorance."

This was exactly the right thing to say, Rose could see as the two girls warmed visibly to her at her admission, launching into a detailed description of Chadwick and how important it was. Rose actually was quite aware of many details of most of the landowners in the country, considering it an important piece of information for the role she had assigned herself as a diplomat's daughter. She schooled her features into what she hoped was a look of polite interest and waited out the girls' long-winded explanation.

"How lovely," she finally said, enjoying the flexibility of the expression, gracing them with a charming smile. "Perhaps one day we could see it for ourselves, as it would surely be a treat."

This utterance once again confounded the girls, as they were unsure if associating with Miss Smythe would be to their social advantage or disadvantage. They were saved from needing to respond by Elizabeth smoothly stepping in with a change of subject.

"Never mind about our estates, we are in Town now, let us enjoy it while we can. Which events shall you be attending this evening?"

Rose was again forced to admire her friend's skills, as they had just been lamenting their longing for their estates.

"We have been invited to the Duchess of Westfield's dinner, and then we are going to a musicale hosted by the Duchess of Yorkleigh," Emmaline answered with pride.

"We shall be at the musicale as well," Elizabeth replied as she rose to her feet, signalling the visit was drawing to an end. "It was so kind of you to stop in. We shall look forward to seeing you later this evening."

The visiting ladies were clearly disappointed not to have gotten any juicy details about the duke, but they accepted their dismissal with good grace. Delicately placing their teacups back into their saucers, they too rose to their feet and politely took their leave.

As the door closed behind the Chadwick ladies, Elizabeth and Rose shared a quiet giggle. "Those two are too much," Rose declared firmly.

"But they are perfect specimens of the *ton.* Have you thought about how you are going to handle references to the duke throughout the Season? If what they had to say is true, or even if it is just wishful thinking on the part of many, His Grace is obviously going to be a top subject for the rumour mill. I am certain you do not wish to be remarked upon by being seen to shun him."

Rose appreciated her friend's concern but loathed the need for it. "I had given the matter very little thought." She paused for a moment of reflection before continuing in thoughtful tones. "You are, no doubt, quite correct that it will be remarked upon if I am obvious, but I would like to think I am capable of avoiding him without anyone noticing. I hardly think he is likely to search me out, so it is highly probable that this is a non-issue."

"Perhaps." Elizabeth's tone and dubious expression showed that she was unconvinced, but she did not press the issue. "Have you considered the possibility of ending the feud between your two families? I am sure it is an uncomfortable subject, but has it been discussed in your family?"

Rose knew her friend was trying to be helpful, so she made every effort to rein in the strong feelings that threatened to overwhelm her response. "Their son is responsible for the death of my brother. I do not see how any relationship between our families is possible."

"They lost a son too," Elizabeth answered quietly. "Perhaps you could grieve together."

This possibility had never occurred to Rose, but her feelings were still too raw to consider it, despite the three years that had passed. "It is unlikely my parents would entertain the suggestion. And considering the scene the last time we were all in a room together, I have my doubts either the duchess or her son would be amenable to the idea either. Never mind about that, I know you are just being a good friend, but let us allow the subject to drop for now. You are absolutely right that my parents and I shall have to better prepare ourselves to face them if we are to go about amongst the *ton* this Season. Now tell me, what do you plan to wear to the musicale? I have every intention of sitting with you, so we must ensure our dresses do not clash."

Elizabeth allowed the change of subject, and Rose was happy to feel a giggle coming on at her friend's look of disbelief. "My dear Rose, surely you realize that as debutantes nothing we are allowed to wear could ever clash with each other. All whites and pastels go together rather mundanely in my opinion."

"True enough. But your lovely complexion allows you to wear some colours that would make me look rather sallow. My mother would never allow me to sit near you if I am going to be made to look hideous by comparison."

"Do not be a hen wit, I beg of you. Or are you fishing for compliments? You know full well that nothing you could ever wear or be near could make you look hideous."

Rose reached over and clasped her friend's hand warmly. "That right there is why you are such a good friend. You are the most generous girl I have ever met. You can be sure neither of the Chadwick ladies would have said such a thing."

Elizabeth offered a small shrug. "I merely speak the truth."

Rose glanced up as the large clock chimed the hour. "Well, heavens, I have certainly overstayed any semblance of *politesse,* have I not? I apologize, but my only excuse is that I was so enjoying your company."

"Absolutely no apology needed. I am sufficiently experienced as a hostess that I could have dismissed you had I so wished."

"That I cannot argue with, as I witnessed your skills in that regard just a few moments ago with the Chadwick ladies." The two girls shared a smile before Rose continued, "But I really must be going. Mama will have apoplexy if I am not home in what she considers sufficient time to rest and prepare before this evening's entertainments."

"Very well, you may leave then," Elizabeth laughed. "It is for the best, as I expect you to arrive at the Yorkleighs' with enough time to spare so that we can find seats together before the performances begin."

With that the two girls bade each other adieu, Rose collected her maid, who had been waiting in the kitchen all this time, and the two enjoyed the brisk walk home together.

Chapter Three

T*he Earl and Countess of Yorkleigh will be well able to congratulate themselves on the success of their evening,* Rose mused to herself during a break in the performances, while Elizabeth had taken herself off to check in with her mother. Rose had elected to remain behind, as she was enjoying her mother's good favour for once and had not been commanded to similarly meet up during the intermission. Besides, the girls had managed to find excellent seats, and Rose wanted to guard them lest someone else decided to change seats.

The milling guests were fascinating to watch. Having honed her powers of observation in Vienna, Rose was determined to keep up her skills. She found one could learn so much about a person by watching their interactions. She was gazing about, enjoying herself far more than she would have expected, when she overheard a snippet of conversation that made her feel as though the blood had frozen in her veins.

"Have you managed to secure Wrentham yet?"

Rose was quite sure she had heard that rough male voice before, but she could not place who it belonged to and dared not crane around to see who it was. The voice did not evoke anything good, and a shiver of dread went down her spine. The tone made her well aware that this conversation was not mere pleasantries, and the mention of the duke had her ears on high alert.

Rose's heart galloped in her chest. She was flooded with a tide of conflicting emotions. The familiar but unpleasant voice provoked fear and disgust in her breast, while mention of the duke swept her with a maelstrom of anger and heat. She sat as still as a statue but made every effort to ensure no trace of her thoughts were written upon her face. Rose hoped fervently that Elizabeth would not return and interrupt before she could figure out what was being discussed.

"Not as yet. This type of plan takes time to bring to completion."

"How long can it take to compromise the man?" the first voice demanded harshly. "Your daughter is sufficiently taking. She isn't daft, is she?"

"My daughter is a good girl," the man excused and explained, his voice whining. "She knows what is expected of her and will have the thing tied up nicely very soon."

"Well, see that she does. We need Wrentham for his access to certain quarters, as well you know."

The two men must have realized this was not the appropriate venue for such a conversation as they broke off anything further they might have said and moved away. Rose quickly turned her head to watch them retreat. The first voice she had finally placed, and if it were at all possible her blood had actually grown colder as she realized who had spoken, but the second man, the one with the daughter, she was unfamiliar with. Rose was profoundly relieved to see Elizabeth returning.

"Quickly, Elizabeth, as discreetly as possible, turn around and see if you can identify the short man walking toward the back of the room with the rather wild-looking hair, wearing the puce-coloured waistcoat."

"Do you mean Lord Austen?" Elizabeth asked.

"If I knew who I meant I would not have asked," Rose answered with a waspish huff before apologizing. "Sorry, my dear, my ignorance offends me at times."

"Never mind about that, why did you want to know?"

"I was merely curious about who he was. I was entertaining myself watching people while you were gone, and I was wondering how it was possible he managed to leave the house looking that way." The hastily made-up story did the trick as Elizabeth tinkled with laughter.

"The poor man. That particular shade would look perfectly lovely on someone else, I am sure but certainly not him." Elizabeth paused for a moment in contemplation before continuing, "He is a widower. His wife died a couple years ago. It is just him and his daughter. You might recall the Chadwick girls mentioned that they had called on Lady Anne to interrogate her, I mean, ask her about dancing with the duke."

Rose was grateful Elizabeth was not looking at her while giving her that reminder, as she was certain her feelings were not well hidden, and she did not wish to be making up any more nonsensical explanations at the moment.

Elizabeth was still speaking. "It would seem they are not terribly flush with funds. Perhaps the viscount has turned off his valet. If I recall correctly, I overheard my father mentioning that Lord Austen had made some bad investments since his wife passed. I do believe Lady Anne is in Town trying to make an advantageous match."

With relief, Rose heard the next performance striking up, so no further conversation was possible at the moment. Her mind raced with all the complications. She really should hate the duke, but she had never been able to bring herself to that point. They certainly were no longer friends. However, not that far in the distant past, he was her very best friend. Did that not require a certain degree of loyalty? And then there was the matter of the other man. The one who seemed to be orchestrating the scheme against Alex. Sir Jason Broderick. Another shiver slithered down her back. It was not at all pleasant.

Something really did need to be done about the conversation she overheard. But to whom could she turn? Her father would be blind to the implications because it involved Wrentham. No one else could be trusted with what she knew. Not that she knew very much. And she certainly didn't know very many people, so it was entirely possible she *could* trust someone else. Elizabeth's father perhaps? Rose quickly dismissed that possibility as she continued to feign intense interest in the musicale. While the earl had seemed perfectly kind when she had been introduced to him, she could not imagine herself confiding in the man. Lord Castleton was a pleasant but distant gentleman. She could not imagine him welcoming her confessions.

In this particular case, the fact that someone was trying to entrap the duke, Alex would be the best one to talk to. But if she spoke directly to Alex, he would want to know everything and there were so many details she absolutely could not tell him. Things she knew about Broderick from her time in Vienna. Things the always correct Duke of Wrentham would not welcome hearing from her. Could she manage to brazen it out, telling him only about the attempt to catch him in the parson's mousetrap and leave out the details about why and how she knew so much about the conspirator? Surely his wealth and position as Duke of Wrentham could be explained as reason enough.

Rose sighed in resignation. It was not the best plan ever hatched, but it was the best she could come up with on her own.

"Are you all right?" Elizabeth whispered at her side.

"As right as rain," Rose answered with a grin.

"That is a nonsensical expression, but you sighed just now, it made me concerned."

"Did you not find that musical number to be as moving as I did?" Rose asked, managing to keep a straight face despite her friend's dubious expression.

"Apparently not." Elizabeth's answer was dry before they were hushed back into silence by the other spectators.

Once the musical portion of the evening was complete, Lady Yorkleigh announced that refreshments were being served in an adjoining room. The sound of many conversations swelled to fill the rooms, echoing slightly off the high, ornate ceiling. The crystals in the chandeliers shivered and tinkled with the vibrations.

As the two friends made their way slowly to the other room to have a glass of punch, Rose intercepted Elizabeth's inquiring look.

"Why are you looking at me like that?"

"You seem different since the beginning of the musicale. I just cannot put my finger on what has changed." Elizabeth paused for a moment, gazing at her companion with her head cocked to the side. "You seem tense or on edge. Do you care to tell me about it?"

Rose's lips parted as she thought of a plausible explanation for her distraction or tension, but then she quickly remembered that she had claimed to be moved by the music. Someone moved by the music would not be so quick to be on edge, was her frantic thought, as she tried to come up with something believable to say. Bringing order to her disordered thoughts, Rose forced her shoulders to relax as she turned her face more fully towards her friend with a warm, brilliant smile.

"How could I possibly be uptight at such an event as this?" she asked before lowering her voice in conspiratorial tones. "Aside from the usual reasons of this being a *ton* event, of course," she muttered with a wink. "But did you not think those last couple of numbers were exquisite? I do believe we shall hear those musicians many times throughout this Season, as they shall no doubt be in high demand to perform at other functions."

Elizabeth did not look fully convinced but accepted Rose's words with good grace. "I am sure you are correct. While I did not feel it to be the earth-shattering experience you seem to have found it, many of the performers did do remarkably well. We must find Lady Yorkleigh and express our appreciation."

Rose pulled a face at her friend's words.

"You, of either of us, should be eager to do so, since you enjoyed the performances so very much."

"Are you certain a note of appreciation would not be sufficient?" Rose asked plaintively.

"Quite. Now hurry along if you have finished with your punch, let us go and speak with her now, there does not seem to be much of a crowd surrounding her at the moment."

ଓ ଌ

Rose was mentally castigating herself for her choice of words, as she was strangely reluctant to approach the countess. But in all reality, she *had* enjoyed the musicale and Elizabeth was correct, it was only right that they compliment their hostess in person.

The Society matron smiled in welcome as the girls approached her. Rose admired the deep teal of her beautiful gown; the embroidery on the soft cotton organdy caught the light and nearly shimmered.

"Lady Yorkleigh, thank you so much for your generous hospitality this evening." Elizabeth began the conversation as they neared the countess.

Rose quickly chimed in. "The performances were exceptionally well done. You must have put a great deal of thought into choosing your performers."

"Why thank you, you dear girls," Lady Yorkleigh answered graciously. "I am so pleased that you are enjoying yourselves. I was not certain the younger ladies would enjoy a musical evening as much as a ball."

"Balls are all fine and good, but a musicale is food for the soul," Rose enthused, much to Elizabeth's amusement. Rose had to work hard to control her own giggles as she saw her friend struggling to keep her face from breaking into a grin.

Lady Yorkleigh regarded Rose with elevated eyebrows. "Are you being serious, young lady?"

"Actually, I am. I think music is one of the most beautiful things that was ever invented." Rose had no struggle infusing her voice with full sincerity, as she really did love all things musical. "Of course, at a ball you can enjoy the music, too, but there are added complications that oftentimes interfere with the unadulterated pleasure of a well performed piece."

The countess's smile increased in sincerity as Rose spoke. "How true that is, my dear Miss Smythe. I remember my first Season. There were many distractions to contend with. But are you enjoying the Season despite the complications, as you said?"

"Oh yes, of course," Rose stretched the truth a wee bit for the sake of tact. "Without the Season, I would not have made the acquaintance of my dear friend, Lady Elizabeth, which would have been a sad thing indeed."

The three well-bred ladies shared a smile over these words before their hostess inquired politely, "Have you two had a chance to have some refreshments and mingle with the other guests? There are no doubt some here that you have not yet met, Miss Smythe, as this is your first Season. Would you like me to introduce you?"

Despite her usual composure, Rose felt her cheeks beginning to blush with the pleasure of being thus singled out by the countess. "That is exceedingly generous of you, my lady. I would not wish to impose."

"No imposition at all. Now come along. I am quite certain I have invited some highly eligible young men that you absolutely must meet."

With those words, Lady Yorkleigh set off across the room. With a wry, questioning look exchanged between them, Rose and Elizabeth set off in her wake. Rose wanted to turn away from following the countess when she saw her heading toward a handsome young man who seemed engrossed in conversation. The other man had his back toward them, but Rose had a sinking feeling it was the man she had overheard earlier speaking to Lord Austen. She *so* did not want to talk to him!

"Lord Edgecombe and Sir Broderick, I trust you are having an enjoyable evening," Lady Yorkleigh began, causing the two gentlemen to quickly turn and bow respectfully to their hostess.

"My lady, we are having a marvellous time," enthused the handsome young lord as he bent over his hostess's hand, placing a gallant kiss on the back of her wrist.

"Who are your lovely friends, my lady?"

Rose barely suppressed her shudder at the sound of Sir Broderick's voice. She felt the slither all the way down to her toes. He put her in mind of the snake she had seen at a fair being held in Vienna. The romantic side of Rose had always considered that men with the title *sir* should always be even more gentlemanly than other men of the *ton* due to the origins of the knighthood. It seemed to Rose that Sir Jason Broderick had never been of the same mind. She managed to maintain her composure as the countess performed the introductions.

Lady Yorkleigh began with Lady Elizabeth, but as she introduced Rose to Sir Broderick, Rose could not help interrupting.

"Sir Broderick and I are already acquainted. We attended a few of the same functions while we were both in residence in Vienna, while my father was occupied with the Congress."

"Oh, how lovely," Lady Yorkleigh replied, her tone correctly polite, although her bright eyes seemed to Rose to be looking right into her soul. Rose bolstered the sincerity of her smile as much as she was able. It became less difficult as she turned her attention to the conversation Elizabeth was having with Lord Edgecombe. She hoped fervently that the young viscount was not involved in any nefarious plots with Sir Broderick. Rose could not bring herself to trust anyone she saw conversing with the slippery knight.

"It is a pleasure to make your acquaintance, my lady," he was saying. "And you, too, Miss Smythe. Are the two of you enjoying the Season thus far?"

"Oh, yes," Elizabeth answered promptly while Rose merely smiled politely, neatly sidestepping the question.

Not allowing her off the hook, his lordship probed a little deeper. "I heard you mention you had been in Vienna with your father. Does that mean this is your first Season here in London?"

"As a matter of fact it is, my lord. It has been an interesting experience thus far, I must say."

These words caused the viscount to throw back his head and laugh. Rose was torn between embarrassment over the attention brought to their small group and appreciation of his grasp of her subtle humour. She was relieved when he turned to Elizabeth and questioned her.

"Tell me, my lady, have you found the Season to be interesting as well?"

"Infinitely more so now that I have the enjoyment of the presence of my new friend Miss Smythe," she replied, staunchly loyal, unsure if the viscount was making fun of Rose or not.

As though he were feeling like he was being ignored, Sir Broderick took this opportunity to enter the conversation. "Have the two of you ladies been friends for long? I did not think Miss Smythe had been long returned to Britain's fair shores."

Rose stiffened slightly at the implication that he was aware of her whereabouts but managed not to verbalize her reaction, leaving Elizabeth to answer the question directed at her however she wished.

"In some ways it feels as though we have been friends forever, but you are quite correct, our acquaintance is not of a terribly long standing." Elizabeth either picked up on her friend's discomfort or took the knight into dislike on her own account; Rose could see that her usually sunny smile was noticeably dimmed as she turned it upon Sir Broderick. "Did you enjoy Vienna, my lord? Miss Smythe has been regaling me with amusing tales of her time spent there."

Rose was grateful that the knight had never become aware of any of her involvements in the Congress as he turned and gave Rose a look bordering on pity as he replied to Elizabeth's question. "The ladies, of course, enjoyed the fairer aspects of life in that fine city while we gentlemen saw to the actual work of the Congress. Much of the time I was in Vienna I was far too busy to enjoy what the city had to offer."

"What a shame," Elizabeth answered briefly before turning her attention back to Lord Edgecombe. "Have you ever visited Vienna? I must admit, I am a little envious of my friend as I have really been nowhere."

Rose nearly rolled her eyes as the young viscount hastened to reassure Elizabeth. "But my lady, that is not the case. You have been to London and really, that is all that matters. It is true that I have seen a little more of the world than you, having made the Grand Tour with my tutor after I finished school, but there is nowhere finer than our fair country, and the greatest city in the world is our very own London."

Lady Yorkleigh had remained with the small group during this exchange, and she stepped into the conversation at this point. "Your patriotic loyalty is to be commended, my lord. It is a shame the prince is not here to hear your words. He would, no doubt, be heartened by them. Now if you gentlemen will excuse us, I would like to bear off my friends to introduce them to a few of my other guests."

With those words, the countess swept Elizabeth and Rose off with her. After they were out of earshot, she paused briefly to comment to the girls in a tone low enough not to be overheard by the other guests. She kept a poised smile on her face so no one would be able to guess what they were discussing.

"I apologize, my dears. I had not noticed that Sir Broderick was in company with Lord Edgecombe. Otherwise, I would not have directed you there for the introduction. While I think the viscount is a sweet, charming boy, I cannot quite bring myself to like Sir Broderick and would recommend that you be wary if you ever find yourselves in his company. He is an associate of my husband, which is how he ended up on my guest list this evening. I would normally not be so indiscrete as to tell you of my true feelings in a matter such as this, but I have decided that I like the two of you and thus needed to plant the warning in your ear."

Rose decided then and there that she quite liked the lovely countess. "Have no fear, my lady. You can be sure that neither of us will bandy about your words. And I had already come to my own conclusions about Jason Broderick long ago. You can count on the both of us to be cautious if we find ourselves in association with him in the future." Dropping into a respectful curtsy, Rose continued, "We appreciate your kindness in taking the time to perform some introductions and for having a care about us. But we truly have no wish to monopolize your time, my lady." Glancing around with shrewd eyes Rose concluded, "You have already done us a world of good just by singling us out in such a way, but we should really allow you to get back to the rest of your guests."

With a trill of pleasant laughter the countess grasped Rose's hand in a warm clasp. "You are a dear minx. I shall enjoy furthering our acquaintance in the coming weeks. You really must call upon me at my next at home, which is two days hence. You are probably quite correct that the rest of my guests will not be overly appreciative if I spend too much time with any one guest, so I shall see you back to your mothers."

Lady Yorkleigh took a moment to greet Lady Smythe before she hurried away to speak with others.

"What a perfectly lovely lady she seems to be," Rose's mother commented a moment after the countess left them. "How kind of her to take some time to see to your introductions. You should cultivate the connection if possible, my dear. It could do you well. To be sure, you need all the help you can get as the awkward daughter of a mere baron."

Rose intercepted Elizabeth's sympathetic look and felt the heat rising in her cheeks. Despite her heightened colour, Rose kept her face impassive. She excused herself from her mother's side with a few choice words. "Elizabeth and I had been on our way to check out the refreshments when we encountered the countess. With your permission, we will return there for a few moments."

"Very well, my dear, but see that you do not stray too far. We should be taking our leave before too long."

The two girls strolled away. When they were out of earshot they shared a brief giggle.

"Oh, my dear, I should not laugh as it really is at your expense, but your mother is just terrible at times."

"Laughter is the best way to handle her. But never with her around, of course." The two girls shared another giggle over this before Rose continued. "In her defence, she has faced many disappointments in life and it has moulded her into the lady you now see. It is unfortunate that I did not make my debut before my brother's death. She was a much different person back then. Of course, I was much too young then, but you know what I mean."

"Indeed I do. Now, let us go and see if there are any of those scrumptious-looking pastries left that I had spied earlier."

As the two girls sampled the treats and enjoyed another glass of the punch, they made small talk with some of their fellow guests for a few moments before being left on their own again.

"Do you plan to take Lady Yorkleigh up on her invitation to call on her?" Elizabeth asked with curiosity.

"I do believe the invitation was directed at the both of us."

"Perhaps, but it seemed to me that she took to you much more strongly than to me. And as your mother so kindly pointed out, you need the connection much more than I do."

Rose grinned at her friend's words. "How true it is." She paused in thought for a moment before continuing. "I quite enjoyed making her acquaintance, so I actually do plan on accepting her invitation. It did seem to be quite sincere. Do say you will accompany me."

"I believe that wild horses could not keep me away," came Elizabeth's prompt reply. "Oh dear. It would seem our time is up. I see your mother bearing down upon us. Shall I call upon you tomorrow? I would think it is my turn."

The girls shared one more grin before Rose was borne away by her mother.

As they rode home in their carriage a while later, Lady Smythe took her daughter to task. "You really should be making more of an effort to further your acquaintance with gentlemen rather than always being in company with your friend, Lady Elizabeth. In fact, I saw Lady Yorkleigh introduced you to that attractive Sir Broderick, but you hardly exchanged a few words with him. What is the matter with you, girl?"

Rose just barely managed to keep her jaw from dropping open at her mother's words. How could the older woman possibly find the terrible knight to be the remotest bit attractive, she wondered. Keeping her thoughts to herself, as was her wont of late with her mother, Rose used her mother's own reasoning upon her.

"But, my lady, Elizabeth is an earl's daughter," she explained. "Would you not agree that it is a marvellous connection for me to cultivate? In her company I am much more likely to make the acquaintance of a more eligible *parti* than Sir Broderick."

"Well, I can see the wisdom in your words, but you cannot expect to look too far above your station. As the daughter of a mere baron, you are rather insignificant in our world, and you would do well to bear that in mind."

"Yes, mother," Rose answered meekly, while feeling torn between amusement and pain at her mother's words. She was relieved when they pulled up in front of their townhouse.

Rose dithered in the foyer after saying goodnight to her mother, waiting as Lady Smythe glided up the stairs silently.

"Is my father home, Hartley?" she asked of the butler.

"Yes, miss, he is in his study working," Hartley answered, smiling fondly at his young mistress. "I am certain he would not mind being disturbed by his favourite daughter."

"I am his only daughter," Rose answered dryly before inquiring, "Has he been working long? Do you think he is due for an interruption?"

"He has been in his study all evening. He is more than due, miss. Although, I must say, I am certain he would always welcome your company."

Rose appreciated the faithful old servant's loyal affection and accepted his words with a grateful smile as she headed off down the hall to scratch on her father's door.

"Enter," came Lord Smythe's quick response.

Rose entered the comfortable space with a sniff of enjoyment. She always loved the smell of her father's study. A combination of wood, spice, and old spirits. She was not sure how it was achieved, but this was the only room in the house with that particular scent, and it always felt like home to her whenever she could spend time there.

"Good evening, my darling daughter. Did you have a good time?" He welcomed her warmly before trailing off for a moment. "Forgive me, my dear, I seem to have forgotten where your mother told me the two of you were going this evening."

"That is quite all right, Papa, I am sure you had plenty of other, more important things on your mind."

"Your mother assures me that all this Season business is as important, or even more so, than what I am occupied with."

Rose sighed. "My mother does not appreciate that without the work you, and others like you, do, there would be no Season. There is nothing more important than that. The Season is a bunch of social nonsense, to be perfectly frank."

"We can both agree that that social nonsense played a key role in our work in Vienna."

Grinning, Rose answered, "That is very true, but sadly we are no longer in Vienna and here the balls and such are just for socializing, from what I can see. And husband hunting, of course."

"Well that is very serious, important work, is it not, my dear?"

Rose merely shrugged at this before turning the subject reluctantly. "Sir Jason Broderick was at the musicale tonight."

Her father's face tightened with this news. "Did you talk with him?"

"Very briefly. It could not be avoided."

"You be sure to steer clear of him in the future."

"I will, Papa, you can rest easy on that score. I have absolutely no desire to pursue the acquaintance." She paused for a moment, wondering once more if she could talk to her father about what she had overheard. Deciding to keep it to herself for the moment, she tackled a different, but still uncomfortable, side to the subject. "Mother will disagree with us if she becomes aware of our thoughts on the matter."

"Whatever do you mean?"

"In the carriage ride on the way home tonight she admonished me for keeping my conversation so short with him. She thinks I cannot look any higher than a knight in my social aspirations, and she thinks he would be a handsome choice for my husband."

The baron was a very self-controlled man, a quality that served him well as a diplomat, but these words caused him to come very close to losing his composure. Taking a deep, calming breath, Lord Smythe smiled sadly, but kindly at his beloved only daughter. "Your mother means well, I am sure, but you must remember that she has been through a great ordeal in the past few years and cannot be held accountable for any strange things she may say. She loves you dearly, you know."

"I know, Papa, but sometimes she has a strange way of showing it."

"Rosebud, my darling, you know your papa loves you, do you not?"

"Yes, Papa." Rose smiled through the mist that filled her eyes over her father's endearment.

"And you do trust my judgment, do you not?"

"But of course!" While Rose was aghast at the thought that he might doubt it, a niggle of unease *did* creep into her conscience at the thought that she *was* keeping something from him out of concern for his lack of judgment with regards to the Duke of Wrentham. Pushing the thought from her mind, she looked at her father expectantly.

"Your mother is a good woman and has been an excellent mother, but her own judgment is slightly askew at the moment. I am uncomfortable speaking ill of her, so we shall not delve any deeper into this topic. Suffice it to say that you have my complete trust and I would ask that you use your own good judgment as best you can over the coming weeks. And if you have need of discussing anything with someone, you may come to me at any time. You have quite proven your dependability and soundness of mind many times over when we were in Vienna. The information you were able to dig up was invaluable."

"Thank you, Papa. I just find that life is rather dull now that we are back in England. And everything about the Season just seems so trivial. Everyone gossips all day, and the only thing they seem to be concerned about is the latest fashions or who said what to whom. It is rather grievous, after the excitement of life in Vienna. Is there not something I could be doing to help you here?"

"Oh no, my darling. You did quite enough to help out in Vienna. You must just apply yourself to the task of finding a sensible spouse so that you can set up your own household. It is well past time for that, I would say. We would have seen about it much earlier, if not for our mourning."

Rose was saddened at this reminder and felt a pall fall further over her night. Bolstering her spirits by sheer force of will, she set herself to cheering her father.

"In my mind it is just as well that I have not come up for the Season prior to this. I feel that I am in a much better position to make a sound decision after having had a little bit of experience under my belt, as you would put it. And I would not have wished to miss the time we spent in Vienna. It was something I will remember for the rest of my life. In fact, I have half a mind to find myself a diplomat to marry so that I could follow him about and help him with his work, as I did you."

"I am not so certain that would be a sound choice for you, but take your time and look about at your options. You should be a good girl and settle down to a normal life. I would not want my daughter to be involved with espionage on a regular basis."

Rose could see that her father was ready to have an end to the conversation. While he had been perfectly happy accepting her help when it was convenient, he was not about to countenance her entry into the profession. That, in a nutshell, was why she could not settle in to the rhythm of the Season. She wanted so much more out of her life, she thought with a sad twist of her heart.

Rising from her position in the wing-backed chair in front of her father's desk, Rose took another deep sniff of the much-loved scent, wishing she could somehow transfer that restful, comforting smell to some other room in the house, such as her own sitting room or bedroom. Then she could enjoy it at her leisure. With a resigned sigh over her own silliness, she bade her father a fond goodnight and made her way upstairs to her bed.

It would be some time before she could relax into sleep, as she had many things on her mind to mull over. Her mother's odd behaviour was a matter of some concern, as was her own ambivalence toward the search for a husband. But uppermost on her mind was the conversation she had overheard at the musicale between Lord Austen and Sir Broderick.

Who could I possibly confide in about this? she asked her own reflection as she brushed out her hair, having dismissed the maid. *Lady Yorkleigh was very kind this evening and even seemed to be inviting me to enter into her inner circle. I feel as though I could confide in her about certain things.* Rose gazed at herself with a wrinkled brow. *For instance, I could discuss my marital options with her, or perhaps even ask her opinion about Mama's strangely conflicting behaviour. But I do not see how I could discuss this situation with her.*

There were highly confidential matters at stake. Possibly even matters pertaining to the security of the government, or even the prince. And besides that, there was the matter of a young woman's reputation and the duke's future happiness being in jeopardy.

Rose's reflection turned sadly pensive at this. Alex's happiness was none of her concern. Their families had quite clearly declared a feud. She ought to loath him. No doubt he loathed her. But she still could not bring herself to hate her old friend. And she really could not stand by and do nothing about what she had heard. For the time being, until she could figure out with whom to speak about the bigger issue, or find out more details so that it would be a manageable project to pass to her father, she needed to protect the duke from getting caught in a trap set by Sir Jason Broderick. That duplicitous weasel would not get his teeth and claws into her old friend if she had anything to say on the matter. Once she had the Duke of Wrentham out of the equation then surely she would be able to pass the situation over to Papa.

Thus resolved, Rose set herself to pondering just how to manage protecting the duke from the Austens' clutches. The Alex she knew hated any sort of subterfuge, so she would just have to come right out and tell him. At least, she had to tell him what she had overheard. It would no doubt be best to leave out the details regarding how very unscrupulous Sir Broderick was. He would want to know how she knew, and the entire issue would get murky.

Or even murkier than it already was, she reminded herself as she gazed at her reflection. She remembered the moment where her eyes had locked onto his. Her stomach clenched at the memory. He truly was a remarkably handsome specimen of a man. But not for her, she reminded herself once more. He was a Wrentham after all. She pulled her thoughts back to the matter at hand.

Now all she had to do was figure out a way to have a conversation with the Duke of Wrentham without anyone finding out. Especially her parents. Really, anyone of the *ton* should be kept in the dark about any conversation she might have with the duke, as it could lead to all sorts of speculation. And if she became the subject of speculation, it was sure to reach Mama's ears at some point. And she could just imagine the scene that would ensue if Mama were to find out she had spoken with anyone from the House of Wrentham! It would have to be a public place but perhaps at an ungodly early hour. That would be just the thing. She would make the arrangements tomorrow.

Glancing at the mantel clock, Rose shrugged to her reflection *later on this morning, to be more precise,* she thought with a slight grin. Her grin widened when she realized that she had been brushing her hair all through her mental wrestling. That must be at least a week's worth of brushing. *Perhaps I can take the next few nights off of this wearisome task.*

Chapter Four

Alexander Edward Philip Milton, the Sixth Duke of Wrentham, eyed his former friend speculatively. She looked marvellously delicious this morning with her colour high and her hair piled up on her head in some ridiculous fashion that Alex could never understand but looked lovely on her. But then he surmised that he would consider her lovely even in a burlap sack. And being summoned to a clandestine meeting put him in mind of an entirely different type of girl. Alex reminded himself that she was a Smythe and not to be trusted. He managed to contain his reaction to being in her proximity, continuing to watch her fidget with her art supplies.

Struggling with frustration over the conflicting feelings that had risen in him upon receiving her note the day before, Alex found he did not really want to know why she had demanded he meet her. He fought against a longing to spend time with his old friend and chided himself for the tug of attraction he felt whenever he laid eyes upon her. That was a very new sensation, and he was undecided if it was one he liked.

Watching her as she once again became absorbed in her art, he wondered how long it would take her to realize he was there. It had always amused him how single-minded she could be at times. He obviously could not dither there all day, although it was a welcome distraction from the responsibilities that weighed upon him. Alex decided to get her attention.

ꟹ ꟹ

The light coming in through the tall windows settled nicely onto her page, and the hushed silence almost seemed to echo from the high ceiling. If she had been in a proper frame of mind it would have been perfect for her art. Rose was fidgeting with her sketchbook and pencils rather fitfully when she heard a deep voice just behind her.

"I see your skills have not improved overmuch since the last time I viewed your efforts," he drawled, teasing her.

Just barely managing to stifle a small screech, even though she had been expecting him, Rose felt her nerves were stretched to the limit.

"Oh, Alex, you nearly gave me apoplexy," she chided.

"Did you not summon me to meet you here at precisely nine o'clock?" he asked, perplexed.

"Yes, of course, never mind me." Rose tried to dismiss her nervous start, blushing with her embarrassment.

"I must say I was surprised to receive your summons. I did not think debutantes were accustomed to seeing the day at this hour, nor did I think we were on speaking terms."

Rose had been busily gathering her supplies in order to avoid looking at him in an attempt to overcome her fit of nerves. She had thought it would be a matter-of-fact thing to meet up with him. They had been on the freest terms when she was a child. He had been her very best friend, and she had told him everything in her young life—up until three years ago. Now he was a duke. And he had changed in subtle ways. So had she, obviously. As a child she had never noticed the breadth of his shoulders or felt a flutter in her stomach when he offered her that crooked grin. And of course, there was not the feud to contend with.

Heaving a slight sigh, Rose made herself stop fidgeting and look him in the eye. It did not settle her nerves in the least, as she discovered the remarkable colour did strange things to her equilibrium. Ignoring her own reactions, Rose forced her reluctant tongue into speech.

"Thank you for coming, Your Grace," she began stiffly. "Especially at this hour. I thought it best for us to meet when we were the least likely to run into anyone who would run to tell tales."

"So I take that to mean your parents do not know you are meeting up with me." Alex paused but could not resist prodding her further. "Do you make it a habit to meet men in strange places?"

"Burlington House is not a strange place," she defended with a huff. "And no, I do not make it a habit of arranging meetings with men." Glaring at him, she turned on the offensive. "You should know, I asked you to meet me here for your own sake, not mine. Do you not realize that I have everything to lose by arranging to speak with you and absolutely nothing to gain?"

"Well, I am considered quite a catch."

Rose could see that Alex was prodding her just to see her reaction, but she could not seem to resist it.

She crossed her arms, tapping her foot and keeping the full force of her glare turned upon him. "Not by me," she declared. Simmering down slightly she continued, "But that is actually why I asked you to meet me."

It seemed as though Alex was not quite ready to hear her reasons. He changed the subject. "I was merely teasing when I said your skills have not altered. Those sketches actually looked fairly decent. Have you been practicing?"

Startled by the change of subject, Rose blushed once more over his compliments. "I have had a lot of time on my hands," she answered simply. "Sadly, I am still not that good, but I have been enjoying coming here since we have been in London." She looked to the statue she had been trying to sketch. "I find the lines so fascinating, but so hard to replicate on paper."

Alex followed her gaze and they looked around the room. "I must admit, I have yet to take the time to view these marbles of Elgin's. Do you enjoy them?"

"Oh, very much so," Rose enthused. "The artists did such a magnificent job of depicting the expressions and the musculature. I am amazed by the intricate details. They are a marvel, and I am so grateful that the Duke of Devonshire has so graciously made them available for people to enjoy. It is one of the few places my mother allows me to go on my own."

"You are unaccompanied?" Alex' incredulity brought a blush to Rose's cheeks.

"Well, of course, my maid is about somewhere," Rose excused with a vague wave behind her. After an awkward moment, she returned to the purpose of her visit. "Thank you again for coming. I was not certain if you would. I know this cannot be comfortable for you."

"Curiosity would not allow me to keep away. You have not acknowledged my existence for more than two years, and then I received an urgent request to meet you here. So here I am."

"I was not even certain if you had received my note, as I could not ask you to acknowledge it. My parents would never have allowed me out of the house if they had any inkling I was going to be meeting up with you."

Rose was embarrassed over the boldness of that admission, but it was necessary, so she ignored it as best she could and plunged further into her explanation.

"I overheard a conversation while I was at the Yorkleigh musicale that I felt you needed to hear about."

"Have you taken to eavesdropping, my dear?" he asked, teasing her once more.

Rose knew her face was practically on fire now, but she ignored that as well as his comment. "They were discussing how best to entrap you into marriage," she blurted out.

This finally brought the duke's sober attention to her face. Rose forced herself to meet his gaze as he searched her face before he asked, his tone one of disbelief, "Do you seriously expect me to believe that someone was discussing such a subject in your hearing at the musicale? And if you did hear a couple of silly debutantes having such a conversation, why did you consider it such an urgent matter as to arrange a clandestine meeting with me? Are you perhaps trying to trap me into marriage for yourself?"

She had expected some resistance from him, but she had not thought he would turn on her so completely. Feeling her face smoothing into the stony impassivity usually reserved for uncomfortable social occasions, Rose's voice took on a frigid chill. "I do not care what you believe, Your Grace," she stated, while dipping into an ironic curtsy. "I was labouring under a delusion of misguided loyalty to a childhood friend that caused me to go out of my way to warn you that grown men are conspiring against you and using debutantes to do it. But if you do not care to learn about it, I pray you will forgive me for inconveniencing you by this ill-advised meeting. I wish you a good day, Your Grace."

Unable to maintain her impassive façade, Rose felt tears gathering in her eyes by the end of this speech. Turning away so that the duke could not see, she once more busied herself with her drawing materials, packing them away and making to leave.

Rose heard him make a growling sound low in his throat. She was unsure what it meant, but then Alex grabbed her by the arm and spun her back to face him. "I apologize, Rosie, I meant you no insult. I know you would never stoop so low as to trick me into marriage. Please, I know you went to a great deal of effort to tell me about this, forgive my churlish behaviour and tell me what you know."

Gulping back her tumultuous feelings, Rose mustered her composure and launched into her tale. "It was at the musicale hosted by Lady Yorkleigh two nights ago. My dear friend, Lady

Elizabeth, who I was sitting with, had to go speak with her mother for a moment during a brief intermission in the performances. I remained behind because we had managed to get great seats from which to enjoy the music. I assure you, I had no intention of eavesdropping. I did not even realize the gentlemen were there, as they were behind me and obscured from my view by this strange, sculpture-like object in the room. I really cannot tell you what that object was, and it is the one thing that makes me question Lady Yorkleigh's tastes, as everything about their home is quite lovely."

"Yes, yes, Rose, I know the object you are talking about, please get back to the matter at hand. Quit trying to avoid the ugly part. I have known you for far too long."

Rose felt the colour rise once again in her cheeks, acknowledging the truth of his words. She continued, "I would assume they could not see me, either, or else they would never have said anything in such a location. I am undecided if I am glad they did or not. I feel duty and honour bound to tell you, but I dearly wish I was never involved and that they had never hatched such a scheme in the first place."

☙ ❧

Alex was now over his initial reaction to her words and was again enjoying her company. He had missed his friendship with Rose quite keenly. Hearing her now trying to dither about in order to avoid getting to the truly unsavoury part of her story reminded him of just how deeply he had enjoyed their friendship and what its loss had meant to him. He realized he would happily spend the day listening to her put it off, but clearly it was a serious matter and he needed to get to the bottom of it. He decided to pry it out of her.

"So, who were the gentlemen?" He thought this would be a straightforward question, easy to answer.

"You have to remember that despite my advanced years, I am a debutante and have been out of the country for a couple of years. Unless someone was involved in the Congress, I really am unacquainted with most people. I had to get Elizabeth to identify one of the men for me. He was wearing the most dreadful puce waistcoat. I did not wish her to know about the matter, so I told her that is why I wanted to know."

"And did that help her to identify the gentleman in question?" he prodded gently.

"Yes, she explained to me that the poor man was in mourning for his wife and had lost all his funds and so had no one to tell him that he should never wear that particular shade. It was actually a nice colour, come to think of it. I think you would have been able to pull it off."

Alex could barely contain his grin at her words, but he would not allow her to become sidetracked. "And so this impoverished gentleman with the not-so-terrible puce waistcoat was who?"

"It was Lord Austen, Your Grace," she blurted finally. "I am so sorry if he was a friend of yours. And if you are actually seriously interested in his daughter, Lady Anne, I am even more sorry. But I must tell you, I would really advise against any involvement with them. The other man, I will not say gentleman because he is an affront to the title, was Sir Jason Broderick. I cannot like that man. He reminds me of a snake. Any man who is in cahoots with him cannot be a suitable candidate for an alliance with you."

Alex was taken aback by her words. "Are you absolutely certain of this?"

"I am, Your Grace," Rose insisted with simple sincerity. "Is there a particular part you are questioning?"

"Are you absolutely certain of what you overheard? And are you completely sure of the identities of the people in question?"

"I am absolutely certain of what I overheard, Your Grace. Sir Broderick was asking Lord Austen if he had managed to sew you up yet. Lord Austen said it takes time to catch a duke, but that his daughter was a good girl and knew what was expected of her. To be completely honest with you, it was your name being uttered in hushed tones that drew my attention to their conversation. I cannot tell you what led up to that part of it because I was caught up in looking about the room at the milling people. But when I heard Sir Broderick whispering your name, it caused ugly shivers to run up my spine and caught my attention." Rose shivered again in recollection. "As to their identities, like I told you, I am new to Town so I had to ask Elizabeth about Lord Austen. But this is not her first Season, and she seems to know everybody. Besides, she said she is friendly with Lady Anne, so I am quite certain she would know who her father is."

"How did you know who Sir Broderick was? You have not said that you had to ask about his identity. And it seems to me that you recognized his voice from behind you." He searched her face waiting for her answer. Seeing a multitude of emotions warring across her features, the duke held his breath. He found himself wishing she would drop the formalities and return to the comfort of their shared childhoods and call him Alex. So few people did these days.

଼ ଼

Rose felt like squirming away upon this question. He was getting rather close to all the particulars that she did not wish to discuss. She made every effort to steer clear of them.

"He was in Vienna at the same time as us. We have been introduced before. I have never liked the man."

Much to her relief, Alex took her words at face value as he was clearly distracted by other thoughts. "But I still do not understand why you felt so strongly about it that you felt the need to break a three-year silence in order to tell me about it. Unfortunately, it is not all that rare a thing for me to encounter schemes such as this. Ever since I became my father's heir it has become a fact of my life. Did you not think I could handle it?"

Rose gave a helpless shrug as she contemplated her answer. She was discomfited by his reference to becoming the heir, as it struck so close to her own loss. And she really had not given thought to the fact that he might be accustomed to plots such as this.

"It truly was not that I did not think you could handle it, Your Grace," she began before pausing. "I am sure you could handle any situation you might face, Your Grace," Rose continued, seemingly thinking aloud. "I just remembered how you hated artifice and subterfuge, so I thought you might not even realize such plots might be afoot. I will admit to you that I had not realized that they could be commonplace. Once again, I must apologize if I have inconvenienced you by arranging to tell you about it. I thought it was a terribly important thing. You are a duke now. Someone plotting against you is bigger than just you, if you don't mind my saying so. You are not just another rich nobleman. Being a duke brings this into a matter involving the government, would you not agree?"

Now his gaze sharpened as he searched her eyes. "Are there details you are leaving out about this, Rosie? Did they say anything about the government?"

"No, no," she protested, "I have told you everything I heard. I truly thought you would want to know, Your Grace."

"Would you stop calling me Your Grace?" he blurted out.

"But you are a duke now." She was aghast.

"But you have known me all your life."

Rose shrugged again. "It is not as though we are going to be having many conversations after this anyway. It would never do for me to become overly familiar with you."

"Are you trying to tell me that you are just going to throw this problem into my lap and leave it there?"

"Whatever do you mean?" Rose eyed him, confused.

"You arranged to meet me to tell me about this urgent problem. Surely you must have some ideas about how to solve it."

"Not particularly, Your Grace. We do not associate together. How could I possibly help you to solve this problem? I arranged this meeting to give you the necessary information. What you do with it is up to you."

"Even if it is for the good of your country?"

Now Rose was truly divided. Inadvertently the duke had touched on the one thing that was sure to gain her cooperation. Her desperate wish to do something more with her life, something meaningful, in a grander way than just giving birth to the next heir to someone's estate. She was sorely tempted to take the duke up on his offer. Not that she could trust him, of course.

She still had no idea what to do about Sir Broderick's schemes in the grander scale. She had no idea who she could confide in. Never would she tell Alex about it, but if she remained involved in it with him to a certain extent, perhaps she could gain more information that she would then be able to share with her father. Still on the fence, she asked some questions of her own.

"Did you have anything in particular in mind? I really did not apply myself to coming up with a plan. It was hard enough trying to figure out how I could meet you in order to tell you about it."

"And I assure you, I do appreciate your efforts. I understand you were motivated by loyalty to your country as well as to our old friendship. But do you think that loyalty could help you see your way clear to helping me?"

"Perhaps," was all that she would allow until she got more information.

The two studied each other for a moment, both deep in thought. It was as though they both came up with the idea at the same time.

"Lady Anne," they both blurted out before bursting into laughter.

"Exactly," Alex approved as he got his mirth under control. "Have you met her?"

"Not yet. What can you tell me about her?"

"Not much, I'm afraid. That was why I was rather surprised by your words. I had no idea she had it in her to try to entrap me, nor did I think she had the inclination. We exchanged a few words here and there last Season. I partnered her in a couple dances. That is about it."

"I wonder how she thought she was going to be able to entrap you," Rose mused. "I did hear that you danced with her a few nights ago."

"I danced with a number of girls a few nights ago," was all the duke would say.

"The *on-dit* is that you are hanging about for a duchess this Season." Rose made the statement in as neutral a tone as she could manage, ignoring the flutter in her stomach at the thought, hoping he would divulge some information.

"Is it really?" The Duke of Wrentham met her question with one of his own, not revealing anything. But then the oafish man turned a grin upon Rose and teased, "I never would have considered you to be the type who listens to idle gossip."

Much to her chagrin, Rose could feel heat creeping back into her cheeks. "It is difficult to avoid, Your Grace. It seems that is all anyone amongst the *ton* does with their time." She continued a touch defensively, "And really, it would not be so strange for you to be looking about for a wife. No doubt it is about time for you to be thinking about producing an heir. How old are you now? You must be six and twenty, surely, Your Grace."

Now it was Alex's turn to be defensive. "That is certainly not terribly old. I am nowhere near my dotage, I will assure you."

"Of course not," Rose soothed. "But mayhap you do not wish to have Lady Anne's plot to be interfered with, as it would no doubt make matters much easier for you." Despite her words, Rose felt sick in the pit of her stomach at the thought of her Alex being leg shackled to someone who would conspire with the likes of Sir Jason Broderick, and she had every intention of interfering, no matter what the duke thought on the subject. Not that she had any idea how to go about it, but she was quite certain it would be that much easier if she had his cooperation.

Alex was looking at her as though she had quite lost her mind. Rose had to struggle to contain her grin. She had always enjoyed discomfiting him. "Have you been drinking too much ratafia, Miss Smythe? That is the only possible explanation I can arrive at to justify how you could possibly think I would consider it an acceptable solution to be entrapped into marriage. Not only do I wish to pick my future bride on my own terms, I would also like to actually look forward to spending the rest of my days with her. So in answer to your question, no, I do not wish you to leave her plans undisturbed. Just because I find it hard to believe she is plotting against me does not mean I do not believe you. No matter what our differences might be now, I know you would never lie to me."

Rose's mouth went dry at these words, and she felt another wave of nausea strike her. While she had not told him any blatant lies, she was keeping things from him, and knowing him as well as she did, she knew he would consider that to be the same as a lie. But she was almost certain he would despise her if she revealed those details, so she was absolutely stuck between a rock and a hard place. Refusing to think about those difficulties at the moment, Rose pasted a smile onto her face and brazened it out.

"So, aside from being surprised to hear that Lady Anne is plotting your demise, is there nothing you can tell me about her? She is our best option to try to get more information, and I will be in a better position to pry it out of her if I know what I am working with."

Alex looked at her appraisingly. "Do you really think you could pry information out of someone?"

Rose smiled mischievously but did not bother replying. She was quite certain the duke would not want to hear about her experience with just such activities. She had been rather good at it, if thinking so was not too terribly immodest of her, she thought with another private grin.

"Never mind about that, we need to make a plan. We also need to determine our objectives. Do we merely want to know what the lady and her father have planned for you in order to mitigate the disaster, or do we want to find out what the greater scheme is and how it involves Sir Broderick? I know you hate anything underhanded, so I will fully understand if all you want to do is ensure you are safe from the parson's mousetrap."

ೞ ೠ

Alex was silent a moment as he regarded Rose steadily. He almost grinned as he saw her fidget with her frustration. He revealed nothing of his thoughts on his face as he considered her words.

She was absolutely right when she said that he hated all forms of untruth, but he was no longer a green youth. The lies and deceptions perpetrated by his parents had given him a deep aversion to falsehood. But in the past three years, since his brother died and he became the heir to his father's title, he had learned more than he had ever wished about how the world around him worked. Unfortunately, at times, duplicity was necessary.

He enjoyed Rose's innocent view of him, and he hated to disabuse her of it. However, he could clearly see she was anxious to get to the bottom of the entire plot and so was he. Wishing she would confide in him her reasons for distrusting the knight, Alex was forced to proceed without all the information at his disposal. He couldn't blame her for her aversion to the man. Alex didn't much care for him either.

Drawing out the silence as long as he could, Alex was not surprised when Rose broke it first.

"Well, what do you have to say? I really cannot remain here much longer, Your Grace. If I do not have much drawing accomplished, my mother will wonder why I have been gone so long."

Intrigued, Alex had to ask, "Does she check your sketchbook whenever you return home?"

Enjoying the blush staining her cheeks he had to strain to hear her huff. "Well, of course not."

Letting her off the hook, Alex returned to her question. "I will admit to you that while I do not enjoy anything underhanded overmuch, I really do feel I must get to the bottom of this matter. We need to find out why they targeted me and how Sir Broderick is involved."

"Do you not think the Austens decided to target you because you are a wealthy, unmarried duke?"

Alex felt his cheeks burn over her comment but shrugged indifferently. "I am far from being the only wealthy, unmarried nobleman, and if they were smart, they would have striven for someone a little lower on the social structure, like a viscount. There are several unattached viscounts who have plenty of blunt. It would be far less remarkable for the daughter of an impoverished viscount to become engaged to another viscount, or even an earl, than to a duke."

"That is true, Your Grace, but changes little about the situation," Rose offered. "It could just mean that their ambitions know very little bounds."

"Or that they are stupid beyond belief," Alex could not help adding. "Surely they must realize that a duke has connections and resources they could never imagine in order to prevent any sort of misalliance."

"They could have been relying on your inexperience," Rose countered in a low voice. Alex could see she did not wish to elaborate, but then she continued, "Everyone knows you were not your father's heir for very long."

Alex knew it was difficult for her to refer to their shared loss, so he allowed it to pass without comment. Instead, he continued as though she had said nothing. "It would seem to me that they must be after me for some sort of a political agenda, perhaps something connected to the House of Lords. If it was just an ambitious debutante, I would brush it off and ensure I was never alone with her. But the fact that you heard her father conspiring with someone else on the matter implies there is more to it than just a good marriage for an impoverished family."

"Do you have any ideas who might be after you? Or what they might be trying to accomplish in such a way? If we have some ideas, we will be in a better position to begin our investigation."

Alex gazed at his old friend in admiration. If anyone had ever told him he would be standing in Burlington House surrounded by Elgin's Marbles debating with Miss Rosamund Smythe about who might be conspiring to entrap him into marriage, he would never have believed such a claim. But here they were. And she looked mighty fetching as she gazed up at him expectantly. He had to make an effort to remember what she had said. Oh yes, something about ideas to investigate. He wondered absently what she could possibly know about investigations and clues and all that. But she was right. They needed to have a direction. The only trouble was he was drawing a blank about any possible ideas.

All he could do was shrug helplessly. "I am so sorry, Rose, but I have absolutely no idea where to start. To the best of my knowledge, I have never had any dealings with Broderick. I developed an instant dislike of the man upon first making his acquaintance, but I cannot even tell you why, as we have barely conversed."

The duke was clearly flabbergasted over this development and was even slightly ashamed to not have a ready solution. Rose must have realized this. She hastened to reassure him. "Never mind about that. We both agreed earlier that the best place for us to start is with Lady Anne. That will have to be my job, as you will just be walking straight into their plot if you try to do anything about it. Now, I really must be going, so we must hurry and establish another appointment to meet up to discuss any of our findings. In the meantime, you should speak to your solicitors or man of affairs or whatever you might have along those lines and see if they are aware of any issues Broderick might have with you. Those gentlemen might know more on the subject than you."

"How did you get so smart about such things?"

Alex was intrigued by the blush that spread over her face at this unanswerable question. The only thing she could offer was, "My father is a diplomat," with as much dignity as possible.

Alex allowed the moment to pass and was rewarded by the look of relief on her face. He hurried to make an appointment as they saw her maid approaching. "Would it be remarked upon if you come here again tomorrow or the next day?"

"Probably not," Rose answered. "My mother never rises before noon and is really only concerned with how I spend my evenings. But you had best give me at least one day to try to make the acquaintance of Lady Anne, so let us say the day after tomorrow. That gives me a day and a half to gather as much information as possible. I shall start with my friend Lady Elizabeth. She is a font of knowledge about the *ton,* as well as being friendly with Lady Anne." While she was speaking she fumbled with her drawing supplies, finally tucking them under her arm. "Wish me luck," she concluded as she once more faced the duke.

The duke watched a myriad of emotions chase themselves across his companion's face. He was unable to identify most of them, but he thought she looked rather wistful as she offered him a brief curtsy before she hurried away without another word.

Alex stood in the same spot for several moments, watching her retreating figure, wondering if she would look back before exiting the building. He was unprepared for the profound disappointment that swept over him as she strode away with purpose, never once glancing back in his direction. Slowly bringing his focus back to the statue she had been sketching, the duke allowed the entire interlude to play itself out in his mind. Giving his head a shake to rid himself of the melancholy that had befallen him, he followed in her footsteps and strode from the hall.

Chapter Five

"Good day, Walter," the duke greeted Wesley's butler as the footman held the door for him. "Is the viscount ready to see guests, do you suppose?"

The well-trained retainer did not reveal his surprise at seeing the duke at such an hour. The viscount and his friends rarely saw the morning hours. "If you would care to wait, I will check for you, Your Grace."

"Thank you, Walter. Pray convey my apologies, but it is a rather urgent matter. His lordship need not make himself overly presentable. I just need a few minutes of his time."

"Very good, Your Grace. If you will make yourself comfortable in the yellow room, I shall be but a moment."

Alex could not sit still. He paced about the room while he waited. Gazing about at the walls that gave the room its name, he wondered absently what Rose would think of the colour, remembering with a smile the description she had given of Lord Austen's waistcoat. *Would she refer to it as jonquil or primrose?* he asked himself with a widening smile.

"What are you grinning about, standing in here by yourself?" the Viscount of Bracondale demanded as he strode into the room in his dressing coat. "And what, pray tell, are you doing in my receiving room at this hour? Walter said it was urgent. Can it wait long enough for me to break my fast, or do we need to ride for the border on the instant?"

Alex truly did grin at his friend's choice of words. "No riding will be necessary at the moment. I merely need to run a few ideas past you. We can adjourn to your breakfast room if you would like, but I would prefer to be private, if you do not mind."

"If you can tolerate me in my state of disarray, then I can manage to serve myself. Let us not stand upon ceremony, you can help yourself to whatever you would like as well." Wesley led the way to his dining room where a vast array of dishes had been spread for his enjoyment.

"All this for just you?" Alex asked with surprise. "It would seem to me that my staff is slacking. They do not provide me half this much most mornings," he complained half-heartedly.

"Mayhap my staff knows I can afford more waste than you can," teased the viscount.

"Or perhaps my staff knows I loathe growing fat," Alex countered, laughing over the glower that was cast his way in response.

A few moments later, after the worst of his hunger had been sated, Wesley sat back with a strong cup of coffee in his hand. With a sigh of satisfaction he faced his guest. "Very well, Your Grace, I am sufficiently fortified to hear about this emergency that has struck you so early this morning. What has happened since we saw each other last night?"

"Rosie Smythe has happened," Alex stated without preamble.

Wesley grew serious but strove for levity. "What does Miss Smythe have to do with you arriving at such an unholy hour upon my doorstep?"

"The chit asked to meet me at Burlington House this morning, where she was sketching. She had overheard a conversation involving me and felt the need to tell me about it."

"Interesting," was all the viscount had to say. "What kind of a conversation would be able to make a Smythe speak to a Wrentham?"

"She overheard Lord Austen and Sir Broderick conspiring to have Lady Anne entrap me into marriage."

Now Wesley was at a loss for words. This was but momentary. "Why would she care?" was his first question, dripping with suspicion, as he clearly felt protective of his friend. This was quickly followed by an exasperated exclamation. "And did you really believe her tale? Do you not find it rather difficult to imagine Lady Anne participating in any sort of a scheme against you? And what could Lord Austen and Sir Broderick possibly have to gain by concocting such a plot?"

Much to Alex's amusement, Wesley now rose from the table and began to pace. Not wishing to interrupt his perambulations, Alex forbore to comment as Wesley continued to rant. "I do not think you truly bought into Miss Smythe's tale. You are merely baiting me with this story, are you not, Your Grace? There is no way she would approach you with such a farfetched Banbury tale. You would never believe it, and what could she possibly have to gain by it? No, if the chit did arrange a meeting with you, and you are not merely stringing me along, she must have had some sort of havey-cavey scheme of her own afoot. No doubt in cahoots with her parents. You must be on your guard, Ancroft."

With these impassioned words the viscount threw himself back into his chair, gazing at the duke expectantly. Meanwhile, Alex was still smiling over his friend's use of his former title—in his distress he had reverted to his old form of address.

"I appreciate your concern, Bracondale," he drawled with gentle emphasis, "but I have to admit to you that I do, in fact, believe Miss Smythe. I have known Rosie for most of her life, and I do not think she was lying to me. I really do believe she overheard a conversation between Lord Austen and Sir Broderick in which a conspiracy to entrap me into marriage with Lady Anne was discussed. Whether or not it is as dire a situation as she seems to think remains to be seen. As far as I know, those two gentlemen do not have any sort of grudge against me, and I never would have thought Lady Anne had it in her to participate in any such thing."

"But if what you say is true and Miss Smythe did overhear such a conversation, why would she bother to warn you of it? Would it not be your just desserts in her mind?"

Alex offered a rather wan smile over his friend's weak attempt at humour. "She is a forward little minx who cannot keep her thoughts to herself. She will be the death of whichever man has the misfortune of marrying her. Her managing ways were adorable when she was six. I am not so certain they are nearly as attractive now that she has reached twenty summers."

Seeing that the viscount was eyeing him with marked amusement, Alex gave his head a shake and answered his friend's question. "I believe there remains within her a trace of loyalty toward the relationship we once enjoyed. And she mentioned some sort of nonsense about loyalty to the crown that I could not fully understand. I was sidetracked at the moment and did not ask her to elaborate. I think the poor dear has been overmuch in company with her diplomat father, who would of necessity be at all times concerned with matters of state."

"Well, you *are* a duke, do you suppose there is a kernel of truth to that?" Now Wesley's loyalties, always on the duke's side, swung to include Miss Smythe if she were, in fact, defending his friend.

"She has directed me to discuss the matter with my solicitors and determine if they are aware of any issues those two might have against me personally. In the meantime, she is going to attempt to forge a relationship with Lady Anne in order to see if she can find out anything from that quarter."

Now Wesley was again incredulous. "You mean she is going to help you with the matter? Are you absolutely certain she has no ulterior motives?"

"Quite," Alex answered, his tone dry. "But that is partially why I am here. I am uncertain if my motives are entirely pure. I need to talk the matter out with a trusted friend. I have so few of those these days, there was really only one choice. That is why your butler had to drag you from your bed to see me."

Understanding had dawned in Wesley's eyes during the duke's speech. Alex cringed to see sympathy written in every feature of his friend's face. "Now don't go looking at me as though I have some sort of pox."

This did the trick of bringing a grin to the viscount's visage. "Seems to me that love is worse than the pox, Your Grace."

Alex sighed. He would never have used the L word himself, but no doubt that was what it was.

"You were never reasonable about that chit," Wesley remarked. He didn't bother to await a response. "So when do you meet her again?"

"How did you know we were to meet again?"

"You would not be here with your knickers in a knot if you did not fear you were treading down the wrong road. If you had told the chit to mind her own business or even thanked her politely for the warning and told her you would look after the matter from here on out, you would not now need my assistance, nor would you look so concerned. You would have gone straight to your solicitors as the young miss advised and would be halfway done sorting the matter out by now. Instead, you are here in my dining room, downing my coffee, looking as though you wished it were something more able to steady your nerves. No. You, my friend, have the look of someone who knows he is going to get kicked in the teeth but cannot seem to steer clear to save his own soul."

"You certainly do like to mix your metaphors," Alex grumbled, but did not argue with the truth of the viscount's words. He heaved another sigh before answering his earlier question. "Day after tomorrow, back at Burlington House. That is to give her a day and a half to track down as much information as she can."

"Do you think a debutante is going to be able to gather much information?"

"She is not just any debutante," Alex defended. "When she was still in the schoolroom she was able to ferret out the truth from any of us boys. She always knew everything that was going on at her estate and ours, as well as the surrounding boroughs. No one could keep anything from her. She just had this way of asking questions and looking at you with such interest that you ended up telling her everything she might possibly want to know before you even realized it. It was one of her best and worst qualities all at once."

Wesley's eyebrows had been inching their way up his forehead during Alex's speech, and they had nearly disappeared into his hairline by the time the duke settled into silence, which caused him to burst into a guffaw of laughter.

"Why are you looking at me like that, my Lord Viscount Bracondale?"

"Did you hear yourself as you were talking about her?" Wesley countered with a question of his own.

"All right, Dunbar, you were correct, I did come to you for a reason beyond the actual problem of someone's efforts to entrap me." Alex sighed over his own admission. "You were wrong when you said I have never been reasonable about her. Yes, she was my dearest friend for most of her life, but that does not change the facts of our situation now. Our families cannot tolerate the presence of one another. Besides, she is not at all the biddable sort of girl I picture making me a comfortable duchess. Nothing whatsoever can come of any association between the Duke of Wrentham and Miss Smythe."

Alex paused once more, raking his hand through his hair with frustration. "But I cannot turn my back on the fact that she had the decency to let me know about what she perceived as a threat to me. I cannot reward her loyalty with my own disloyalty. I need to take this threat seriously and allow her to help with the solution."

"Did she offer her help?"

"Not in the beginning. I actually asked her to help. But I know her well enough to know that she would have wanted to be involved."

"Mmm-hmm." Wesley was noncommittal. "So what did the two of you arrange?"

"She is to seek out Lady Anne, possibly with the help of Lady Elizabeth, and try to glean as much information as she can. In the meantime, I will find out what I can about Lord Austen and Sir Broderick. Then, as you said, we will meet to discuss our findings and make a further plan from there."

"So what do you need from me?"

"I might need you to take over the investigation as it connects with Rosie's involvement. I would appreciate it if you would accompany me to our meeting two days hence in order to lend countenance as well as to help if need be. Depending where this situation goes, I might really need your help."

"So you really do believe there is some sort of a threat against you?"

"I do. It is the extent of the threat that is uncertain. It is a fact of a duke's life that there is always someone out to get him on some level. But this seems different. Generally, anyone scheming against me is just interested in benefiting in their pocketbook. On the surface, with Lord Austen, that would be the obvious reason, but Sir Broderick is far from having his pockets to let, so it does not seem so apparent what his motivation might be. This leads me to believe it could be more nefarious than I would wish."

Wesley had to agree. "Unfortunately, anything involving Sir Broderick has the potential of being nefarious. Do you think to keep Miss Smythe apprised of the details as you learn them?"

"It will depend on what those details turn out to be," was all Alex would commit to.

"How is she likely to react if she thinks you are withholding information from her?"

"Not well." Alex grinned. "It would be best if she is not allowed to suspect such a thing." He paused as he imagined her reaction but then shook his head. "Now that I have garnered your promise of help, I must be off to begin my investigations."

Before he was able to take his leave, his host stopped him with these words, quietly spoken. "Did you really think I would fail to come to your assistance, Your Grace?"

"Now don't go getting all starchy with me, Dunbar," Alex protested. "You surely realize it is a tricky situation. And no, it never once crossed my mind that you would fail me. I just did not want to spring it on you in an uncomfortable environment. And truth to tell, I needed a friendly face to talk it out with before I go and face my solicitors."

Now Wesley grinned. "Do you wish me to accompany you on that errand?"

"No, thank you, I am fairly certain I am now up to the task."

"Would you like me to head around to the clubs and ask a few discreet questions about our gentlemen friends?"

Alex was near the door but turned at these words with a look of surprise upon his face. "Thank you, my friend. I did not think to involve you overly much in this affair, but if you did find yourself in interesting company this afternoon, it could be quite helpful. Although we are known to be associates, it may be less obvious if you poke around a little than if I do."

"Very well, then. I shall see you later."

"I am promised at Clairhurst tonight. Will you be joining me there?" The duke could not miss his cousin's ball even if he had little desire to dance attendance upon any more debutantes. It would be a good test of his skills of diplomacy if he could make it through this complicated day without revealing his thoughts to all and sundry.

"Until then," Wesley acknowledged, and the duke finally made his way out of the house.

Chapter Six

Rose's maid had been with her since childhood and knew all of the family's affairs. Rose trusted her more than anyone on this earth. But she did not know if she could confide all the details of this situation and had *not* told her that she would be meeting up with the Duke of Wrentham.

"Did you get much drawing done this morning, Miss?" Mary asked with interest.

"Not as much as I had hoped, but I did find the lighting to be favourable, so I do believe I will go back sometime this week."

"Were there many people about at this hour? I did not wish to disturb you, so I remained in the foyer for much of the time, speaking with the attendant there," the maid explained.

"I appreciate your forbearance, Mary," Rose stated, hoping the degree of her appreciation was not revealed in her tone. "There were not too many people. I actually only noticed one or two. Most who would appreciate those artefacts are either too busy at this time of the day or still in their beds."

"To my way of thinking that is where you should ha' been."

Rose was surprised at her maid's fierce tone and words. "I beg your pardon?"

"Was that the Duke of Wrentham I saw leaving as I came to fetch you?" Mary continued questioning her mistress. She continued on without waiting for an answer, which was good since Rose was undecided what to tell her. "I thought you were mortal enemies. You don't have much place exchanging pleasantries with the likes of a Wrentham, Miss. What would your dear mother have to say if she knew you had been passing time with such as him?"

"Mary, I was not 'passing time' with anyone! I cannot possibly have any control over who frequents Burlington House. I cannot be blamed for who happens along while I am sketching."

Mary's knowing eyes examined her mistress, making Rose squirm. "Seems to me that dukes do not frequent places such as hold statues at this time of the morning unless they have an appointment to be there. It didn't look as though he was carrying any artist's supplies, so I'm thinking he knew he was there for talking or something else, not drawing."

"Mary Singleton, do not dare to besmirch me. I cannot believe my ears! Of what are you trying to accuse me?"

Mary was suddenly contrite. "No, no, Miss, I promise you, I ain't accusing you of anything. But I can't bring myself to trust the duke, you see, and I worry for you. You're keeping something from me, which ain't like you, so it leads me to conclusions. If you'd just come out and tell me what's going on I wouldn't be faced with the dilemma of trying to decide what Lady Smythe needs to know."

Now Rose could not hold on to her ill temper over these words and had to break out into laughter. "Mary, Mary, are you trying to blackmail me?"

Mary grinned. "Maybe just a little. It's really not like you to keep secrets from me."

Rose sighed. "It is true that I usually tell you everything, but I was not certain if I could confide this to you. I had to go straight to the source before I could figure out what to do with it. But I *do* trust you. So, if you would really like to know, I will tell you."

Mary merely gazed at her mistress with another one of her no nonsense looks, causing Rose's grin to widen.

"I shall take that as a yes, then, shall I? All right, you shall have to listen carefully as it may be a bit convoluted, and you have not yet heard of most of these people."

Rose took a moment to compose her thoughts as they walked along toward home. She knew her maid would not break her confidence and had in fact been of much help to her in the past in matters such as these.

"On further reflection, Mary, I do believe I owe you an apology. I should have told you first. You were ever so helpful on occasion in Vienna in sorting certain things out, so I should have expected you to do the same in this situation. So, if you are willing, I would appreciate your help once more."

Now the maid's eyes turned from stern to excited in one blink, and she did a little skip of joy. "Oh Miss, I would love to," she enthused. "It has been deadly dull lately just looking after all your dresses and doing your hair. I don't even get to accompany you as much here since you have made friends, besides Lady Smythe wantin' to go with you most of the time."

"If it is any consolation, I have found it to be deadly dull as well. But this situation is worrisome more than entertaining and rather more complicated than anything we dealt with in Vienna. In Vienna it was easy to conclude which side to take as we were representing the king's interests. Now it is sticky."

Mary merely nodded eagerly. Rose glanced around to ensure they would not be overheard but saw that the streets were still unoccupied as most of the tradespeople were already hard at work, whereas the noblemen and women were still abed or not about for the day as yet.

"Do you remember the musicale I went to night before last?"

Mary nodded, paying close attention. "You did seem a little preoccupied that night, but you said you were just tired."

"I *was* tired, it had been a long evening, but I had much on my mind. I overheard a conversation at the musicale between a gentleman by the name of Lord Austen and none other than Sir Jason Broderick."

Now Mary's eyes widened as her face twisted into a look of distaste. "That one. Does he dare to show his face?"

"It would seem that everyone is keeping his secrets and he is being received, as hard as that is to believe. And I cannot reveal his secrets or my own will get out."

Mary gave a grunt of disgust but continued waiting for the rest of the details.

"Anyhow, I only heard part of their conversation, so I do not know what else was discussed, which is part of the problem. What I did hear was them conspiring to entrap the Duke of Wrentham into a marriage with Lord Austen's daughter, Lady Anne."

Now understanding dawned on the maid's face. "That is why you needed to speak with the duke. You were trying to find out what might be behind it."

"That, and I did feel he needed to be warned if he happened to be unaware of a plot against him. Despite all that has transpired between our families, he has been my friend, or at least my neighbour, for my whole life. I could not stand by and see him get caught up in one of Broderick's schemes if there was anything I could do to prevent it."

"And did he know anything?"

"Not that I could tell. It seemed as though he barely knew the knight. And he seemed genuinely surprised about Lady Anne. He said they have barely exchanged words."

"Words aren't usually what entraps a man, Miss."

"I am aware, Mary," Rose answered, her tone dry. "He asked for my help. And I agreed."

Mary gasped. "You are going to have further association with Wrentham? What if your parents find out?"

"We shall have to ensure they do not," Rose stated, not brooking any argument. "It is the best way for me to be privy to whatever he might be able to find out. I need to know what Broderick is up to."

"What is your role going to be? What sort of help is he expectin' from you?"

"I am to find out what I can from Lady Anne. And if you would like to assist, you could accompany me on my visits and see what you might ascertain from the servants' quarters."

Mary was clearly torn between her loyalties. As a member of the Smythe household she felt it her duty to despise the Wrenthams, but her loyalty to her mistress, who clearly intended to be involved, pulled her toward participation. Her desire for excitement won out. "Of course, I will assist you in any way possible, Miss. When do we start?"

"This very afternoon, if possible. I am to meet the duke again the day after tomorrow, so we must make haste."

"Did you think you ought to tell your father about Sir Broderick?" Mary asked.

"That was my first inclination, as soon as I heard his voice. But I am afraid my father would leave all reason behind when he heard the duke's name in the story. That is why I need more information. If we can get Wrentham's involvement out of the way and ensure he is somehow safe from entrapment, we can pursue the other angle and get my father involved. I wish there was someone else I could confide in who would be able to have a clear mind on the subject because I do fear this is a much bigger issue than just a plot to entrap a duke. And I would rather have someone else involved sooner rather than later. But alas, for now it is us and the duke against the world."

"Not to overdramatize, right Miss?" Mary teased.

"A little overdramatization never hurt anyone," came Rose's cheeky reply. "Although, in all honesty, it feels that way at the moment. I am truly uncomfortable about Sir Broderick's presence in London, let alone knowing of any plot involving him. I can assure you, I would never have approached the duke if it were not necessary."

"Of course not," Mary soothed. "Now we're almost home, please tell me our plan so that I can figure out the rest of my duties."

"Oh Mary, I hope I am not going to be burdening you with this."

"Never fear, Miss. Remember, I asked for it."

"True enough," Rose laughed. "The first place I was going to start was with my friend Lady Elizabeth. I have not yet decided how much I wish to tell her. Certainly nothing about any prior knowledge I might have of Sir Broderick. But she is very well connected socially, so she will be able to introduce me to Lady Anne at the very least. So, if you could accompany me there this afternoon that would be lovely."

"Very well, Miss." As they entered the house, Mary's demeanour returned to her usual role, as befit her station, rather than the role of friend that she sometimes assumed when they were alone. "Shall I take your drawing instruments for you so that you can adjourn to the dining room and break your fast with your mother?"

"Thank you, Mary." Rose glanced in the mirror over the mantle to ensure she was sufficiently tidy before hastening away to join her mother.

☙ ❧

"Rosamund, how lovely to see you this morning," her mother greeted in a weak tone.

"Good morning, Mother. Did you sleep all right?" Rose worried about her mother. She had never been robust, but ever since Luke's death she had become wan and pale.

"Sufficiently well, my dear, thank you. And what about you? You appear to be in fine fettle this morning."

"I was up and about quite early this morning. I took my pencils and went to see some of the artefacts Lord Elgin has brought back with him from the Turks, as they are set up in Burlington House. I so hope the lords can finish wrangling over them, as they truly are a marvel. It is hard to fathom they are so old. I do believe I shall have to return several times in order to get my picture quite right."

"That is lovely, my dear," Lady Smythe replied, clearly not paying full attention. Rose grinned. She doubted she would have any trouble getting out of the house to meet Alex again. As long as she was accompanied by Mary, all would be well.

"Do you have anything interesting planned for your day?" Rose inquired politely.

"Not much, my dear. I have to meet with the housekeeper and perhaps I shall pay a call or two, but I need to conserve my strength for this evening. We are promised to the Charringtons for their ball."

"Oh yes, I have heard they have a reputation for their hospitality. There shall no doubt be a crush."

Lady Smythe gave a delicate shudder before asking, "Are you enjoying your stay in London, my dear? I know you were looking forward to it, but then you seemed rather disappointed when we first arrived."

"I will admit to you that I have very mixed feelings on the subject. I do not enjoy the crowds that most of the *ton* seem to rejoice in. It seems that a hostess is not satisfied unless she has her rooms crammed past their capacity. In Vienna it was much more comfortable to my taste. But of course, here there is a much better mix of people to choose from. In Vienna we were stuck with the same people day after day for a year and a half, which could become tiresome if you did not enjoy someone's company." Mother and daughter shared a smile over this before Rose continued. "With greater choice of people I am able to make more varied friendships, which is lovely. Let us say that the Season is growing on me."

"Do you think," Lady Smythe began hesitantly, "that is to say, have you met any gentlemen that appeal to you?"

Rose allowed a low chuckle to escape her lips. "Ah yes, the real reason behind the Season. No one particularly as of yet, unfortunately."

"Perhaps it will be easier for you once your brother arrives," suggested Lady Smythe.

"Is it really such an urgent matter, my lady?" Rose asked with a touch of worry. "Do I have to make a match this Season?"

Lady Smythe gazed at her daughter with dismay. "Well no, my dear, it is not urgent per se, it is just desirable."

Understanding dawned on Rose. "You do not enjoy the Season overmuch either, do you? Perhaps I could just remain single and return home with you and Father," Rose suggested, hope ringing in her voice.

"That would be lovely, until your father passes on and you are stuck as a spinster living upon your brother's charity. And depending whom he chooses to wed, it could be even more uncomfortable for you. It is much better, for your own sake, for you to find some gentleman with whom you can be happy and set up an establishment of your own."

"Must one have a husband to have one's own establishment?" Rose wondered plaintively.

"It is much more comfortable that way, my dear."

Rose knew quite well that was the way of the world and did not argue the point. Seeing the wisdom in her mother's words she offered this promise, "I will try a little harder to see the merits of the gentlemen I meet. I do not necessarily want to prolong this Season business and would much rather get on with the business of living. Have you met anyone that you thought might be interesting for me, Mother?"

Lady Smythe looked at her daughter, surprised to be asked this question. "Why, thank you for asking, my dear. I did not think you would care to accept any advice I might have on the matter, so I was not paying particular attention, but I will from now on."

Rose felt a twinge of guilt for allowing her mother to feel that way. She resolved to make a greater effort to draw her mother out. "We could make a game of it," she proposed with a grin, gratified to see her mother's smile broaden in return.

Rising from the table, Rose went around to drop a quick kiss on her mother's cheek. "I shall see you later on. Enjoy your day."

Rose dashed up to her room to change into something more appropriate for making calls before heading out to drop in on Lady Elizabeth.

Chapter Seven

"Good afternoon," Elizabeth greeted her friend with a welcoming smile. "I was not sure if I would be seeing you today as we had not discussed our plans."

"Hello!" Rose replied. "I was rather preoccupied when we were taking our leave yesterday. I apologize. Do you have any appointments today? Would you like to make some calls together?"

"That sounds lovely," Elizabeth answered, good natured. Her eyes narrowed shrewdly upon her friend's face. "But what had you so preoccupied yesterday? It seems to me that your mind has been elsewhere ever since the musicale at Lady Yorkleigh's. Are you ready to tell me about it?"

Rose grinned at her friend. "Thank you for not pestering me about it before this. I am sorry that I did not confide in you previously. I could not decide how I felt on the matter."

"Have you come to any conclusions yet?"

"Not really," Rose laughed. "That is why I have decided I need to tell you—so that you could help me decide how I feel."

Elizabeth joined her friend in a fit of giggles. "I shall try. Anything is better than this wretched needlework my mother expects me to work on." With those words, she tossed the offending craft aside and gave her full attention to her guest. "Shall I ring for tea?"

"Perhaps later. For now it is best if we are undisturbed, as I wish for this to remain a secret."

Elizabeth's eyes widened a little with these words, but she nodded eagerly in response.

"At the musicale I overheard someone discussing a plan to entrap the Duke of Wrentham into marriage." Rose did not elaborate, merely stating the bare facts rather baldly, and waiting for her friend's reaction.

"I beg your pardon?" Elizabeth clearly had not been expecting this. "Well, I now understand why you were so undecided on the subject. What are you going to do?"

"I was truly torn, I am rather ashamed to admit. But loyalty to my former friend won out and I met with the duke this morning and told him about it."

Now Elizabeth's eyes were widened to the size of saucers. "Have you gone mad? What if you had been seen? You could have been ruined, as I am fairly certain your parents would not countenance a match with him even if it were to avoid scandal."

Rose had to grin at these words. "My maid was with me, have no fear."

"So why did you decide to tell me now, if you felt you could not before?"

"I need your help to get to the bottom of the matter, in all honesty. I promised Wrentham I would see what I could find out. He seemed genuinely surprised to find out that such a plan was hatched, especially by the parties involved."

"Who was it by the by?"

"The conversation I heard was between Lord Austen and Sir Broderick with regards to Lady Anne."

"Truly?" Elizabeth gasped. "How perfectly extraordinary."

The two girls sat in silence for a moment, both contemplating the implications. Elizabeth broke the silence. "That is why you were wondering who Lord Austen is. So, you must suspect there is something more afoot than Lord Austen wishing to fill his pockets with some of Wrentham's wealth or you would not be so concerned. No doubt young ladies have been attempting to entrap the duke since he left Eton, so I would guess it is second nature for him to avoid stepping into the parson's mousetrap."

"You are very astute, my friend. It was the fact that it was even being discussed that made me first suspect a hidden plot. And the seeming lack of any connection between the two men. I would imagine there are various family members who might discuss such a plan in the privacy of their homes, or perhaps at their clubs when they are in their cups, but this struck me as being particularly odd."

"What did Wrentham have to say?"

"Not much, really." Rose was clearly disappointed. "I got the distinct impression he isn't really interested in my help. He thinks young ladies should be ornamental rather than of any use. He merely thanked me for the information, promised to confer with his solicitors, asked me to look into Lady Anne, and agreed to meet me in a couple days to discuss what each of us have managed to discover."

"So you are going to have another clandestine meeting with the duke?" Elizabeth was incredulous.

"With my maid in tow," Rose protested.

Elizabeth appeared unconvinced but refrained from further comment on that score. "So you are actually here to enlist my aid in meeting Lady Anne, are you not?"

Rose blushed before she could school her features, causing Elizabeth to burst out laughing. "Oh, do not turn missish on me now, my friend. I promise you, I have taken no offense. I understand you have conflicted feelings on this matter. It is perfectly fine that you could not come to me about this earlier. But before we delve into Lady Anne, let me ask you this: are you sure you are going to be all right with any involvement with the duke, even just a little?"

"As right as rain," Rose answered cheerfully.

"That expression does not reassure me. To my mind, rain is always a little melancholy."

"But so necessary for things to grow," Rose countered, which brought a grin to Elizabeth's face.

"You always have an answer for everything, don't you?"

"I try. Now what can you tell me about Lady Anne?"

"Not much, really. She is a pleasant enough girl, a little mousy. I must agree with the duke. I never would have thought she had it in her to be involved in something as complicated as a scheme to entrap a nobleman into marriage. But she and her father are very close—they only have had each other since her mother died—so no doubt it is out of a sense of devotion to him. As I told you the other night, he is rather far up the River Tick so she is probably trying to help him recover the family's coffers."

"Do you like her?" Rose inquired softly.

"To be honest, she does not inspire strong feelings either for or against. She seems pleasant. Rather like many of the debutantes, really. Always proper, never having much of an opinion. She will probably drive you mad," Elizabeth concluded with a grin.

"Excellent, so I shall not be overly sad at upsetting her plans."

"Would you have been otherwise?" Elizabeth was surprised.

"Of course. Marriage is an honourable arrangement. I believe it is a dishonourable way to go about trying to entrap someone, but since she lost her mother and her father is depending on her, my heart does go out to her. If she had set her sights on someone other than Alex and if Broderick were not involved, I would have looked the other way gladly. In fact, if I found I quite liked her, perhaps I would have been inclined to even help. But they *did* pick Alex and Broderick *is* involved, so there is no other choice but to step in and stop it. I just hope it can be done without ruining anybody's reputation."

Elizabeth stared at Rose. "You are one complicated young woman, aren't you? It seems to me that you think too much."

"Mayhap you are correct. Now, I feel a little parched after all this talking."

Elizabeth's tinkle of laughter announced she had taken no offense over her friend's broad hint as she reached for the bell pull. "Tea shall be here momentarily."

After being suitably refreshed, the two ladies set out to call upon Lady Anne.

Rose was surprised as Elizabeth's carriage pulled up in front of a large, elegant townhouse on a very fashionable street in Mayfair. Her thoughts must have been written upon her face because Elizabeth smiled with glee.

"Did I fail to mention that the Austens are staying with Lady Anne's maternal aunt, the Countess of Silverthorne? The countess is sponsoring Lady Anne's Season. She and Lady Austen were sisters and quite close."

Rose was a trifle discomfited by these words. Somehow it made it seem so much more difficult knowing that Lady Anne was well connected. Bracing her shoulders staunchly, she reminded herself that it was a good thing that the lady was well connected. She would be protected from any fallout. And no matter her connections, she should never have set her sights upon Alex. Nor gotten involved with Sir Broderick. Really, when one looked at it from a certain perspective, Rose was doing the lady a favour by attempting to sever her connection with the despicable knight.

Thus resolved, she followed Elizabeth from the carriage and up the stairs to be admitted by the attentive footman.

"We have called by to see if Lady Anne is receiving visitors today."

"Very well, Lady Elizabeth, if you and your friend would like to have a seat in the Green Room. I shall see if Lady Anne is at home to visitors."

The footman escorted them to a lovely room just off the foyer. Rose looked around with interest. The room was aptly named: it was an inviting, cheerful shade of green. Rose quite thought she would like the countess if she were anything like her colour choices indicated. The pleasant smile remained fixed upon her face while there was a commotion in the foyer.

A wispy young woman fluttered into the room. Rose could well see why Elizabeth had described her as mousy. She was very petite and her hair was rather like the colour of a field mouse, a brown that leaned toward grey rather than gold. She looked nervous and fidgety, but it could have just been a trick of her small eyes. At least she was smiling pleasantly enough, Rose observed, avid curiosity about the young woman battling with the conflicted feelings urging her to protect the duke.

Stepping into the room, she dropped a brief curtsy, smiling nervously. "How kind of you to visit me, Lady Elizabeth."

Elizabeth, always poised, smiled graciously and turned to introduce Rose. "Thank you for seeing us, my lady. Please allow me to introduce my friend, Miss Rose Smythe. She is a little late in making her debut and has not yet made the acquaintance of everyone around Town."

"It is a pleasure to meet you, Lady Anne," Rose said as she dipped into a curtsy of her own. "I was just admiring this lovely room. It must be a pleasure to receive people here. It would be impossible to remain out of sorts in such an environment."

Anne looked surprised as she gazed about at the walls. "I never thought about that before. I did think it was a pleasant room," she agreed.

Rose had to stifle her grin as she remembered Elizabeth's words about Anne rarely having an opinion of her own. *How could she not have noticed how lovely this space is?* she marvelled, wondering if the poor girl might not be all right in her head.

"Have you been enjoying your first Season, Miss Smythe?" Lady Anne asked politely after they had all taken their seats.

"I have, thank you, now that I have made a few friends and feel a little bit more at home. I will admit to you that in the beginning I felt a trifle awkward when everyone felt like strangers. It seemed to me as though everyone else already knew each other and I was the only odd one out."

"I know just what you mean. I felt the very same way," Lady Anne agreed once more.

Rose thought of the way to steer the conversation in the right direction. "I never even had a dance partner at my first couple of balls. I feared I was to be a wallflower for the rest of my days."

"Oh yes, that is such a terrible feeling."

Elizabeth could see where Rose was taking this conversation, and she had to bite her lip to stop the quiver as she was swept with an appreciation for how droll the situation was.

"Oh come, now, Lady Anne, you cannot mean to make me think you ever suffered from being amongst the wallflowers. Why just the other night I was so sure I saw you dancing with the Duke of Wrentham."

Anne blushed rosily, making her appear much more animated than was her usual mien. "Well, yes, I did dance with the duke," she admitted with shy pride. "He is such an elegant dance partner. And so kind."

"I have not spent overmuch time in his presence, although I did dance with him that same evening that Miss Rosamund is referring to," Elizabeth said, "Did you enjoy dancing with him?"

"Very much," Anne answered simply with a wide smile.

"Have you danced with him often?" Rose prompted, hoping they did not appear too eager for information, thinking they ought to change the subject for a moment and then bring it back somehow.

"Not yet, that was our first dance, but hopefully there will be more." Anne blushed.

"To be sure," Rose replied, seeing that the young woman seemed sincere. "I am happy to report that while I did not have such an exalted dance partner, I finally did make it onto the dance floor at that very same ball. Lord Dunbar was the first gentleman to invite me, but after that I was kept quite busy. It certainly changes your perspective once you get away from the sidelines."

"Most certainly," Anne agreed pleasantly.

Rose wondered how they could possibly get much information out of the young woman when they heard the door knocker sound. All three looked toward the doorway expectantly. Rose was unsure whether to be disappointed or delighted when Ladies Emmaline and Constance Chadwick were announced. They may be a help or a hindrance.

Lady Anne rose gracefully to welcome the new arrivals. Her bland reception did not inhibit the Chadwick ladies in any way. They strode in energetically, Emmaline chattering away as Constance echoed her sentiments at intervals.

"Oh, how lovely to see you here, Lady Elizabeth, and you, too, Miss Smythe," Emmaline greeted.

"Yes, lovely," Constance parroted as Rose and Elizabeth tried to control their amused smiles.

"Good day to you, as well," Elizabeth replied politely while Rose merely curtsied in their direction, allowing Elizabeth to take control of the conversation with the newest arrivals.

"We were just talking about how we are enjoying the Season. No doubt neither of you have ever spent any time amongst the wallflowers, but we were just discussing how much more enjoyable a ball is when viewed from the dance floor." This was just the conversational gambit to set Emmaline off.

"Oh, yes, my lady, is it not just the very thing? You said the truth, of course, when you mentioned we have not much been sidelined, but I can just imagine it must be awkward if one does not have someone to ensure you have the proper introductions at your first ball."

With those words she glanced in Rose's direction, leaving her to wonder if the look was one of sympathy or gloating. Rose returned her gaze with as enigmatic a smile as she could muster, refusing to be cowed by the likes of her. Undeterred, Emmaline launched into a litany of her best dance partners.

"Lord Dunbar is a dream to dance with, but I must say my favourite dance partner thus far has been the Duke of Wrentham."

"Oh, we were just talking about him," Lady Anne interjected, surprising everyone by volunteering some information.

"Isn't he lovely?" Emmaline asked rhetorically.

Rose made an effort to control her desire to scoff over this statement as she remembered the multitude of times she had seen him standing knee deep in mud with a frog in his hands or some other loathsome boyish stunt. "What do you find to be so lovely about him?" she asked, pleased with the neutral but inquisitive tone she managed to achieve.

"Well, he is handsome and polite," Lady Emmaline began.

"And he has quite a bit of hair," interjected Lady Constance, which caused Rose to have to bite her lip to keep from chuckling. If that was the best thing to recommend him, clearly these ladies had not set their standards overly high. Or so she thought.

"That is an excellent point," Lady Elizabeth pointed out. "So few of the earls or dukes have kept their hair."

Nodding with enthusiasm, Lady Emmaline continued, "And, of course, one cannot discount the matter of him being a duke and rumoured to be as rich as Croesus."

"And he actually listens," Lady Anne added quietly into the silence that had followed Emmaline's words.

Rose blinked with a touch of surprise at this statement. Fearing she was not going to be happy with the answer to the question, she asked it anyway. "What do you mean by that, Lady Anne?"

Anne lifted her shoulder in a little shrug, clearly embarrassed to have said something requiring further explanation, but she finally answered after a moment of thought. "I have only spoken with him a couple of times, but I have noticed that he will ask a question and actually wait for you to answer. It appears as though he listens to your words and how you say them and gives thought to what you have said. Have you not noticed that most gentlemen merely expect you to agree with them or say the same thing as everyone else is saying? Conversations at balls are so rarely original. That is not to say that I have anything original to say, but the duke gave the impression that if you did have a thought, he would be prepared for it."

Rose blinked furiously to rid her eyes of the ridiculous mist that had formed as she listened to Anne's explanation. It crossed her mind that she wished it were *her* that the duke was listening to so attentively. The plethora of feelings she was feeling at the moment were complicated and not ones she would be able to decipher and deal with at the moment, so she shoved them to the back of her mind to be dealt with later.

There was a little silence following Anne's words, which Emmaline cheerfully broke. "Like I said, just lovely." These words were met with a ripple of laughter.

Rose was torn between relief and disappointment when Elizabeth stood, signalling the time for their visit had come to an end.

"It was lovely to see you all today, but Miss Smythe and I must be on our way."

Lady Anne stood to see them out. "Thank you for stopping by. You must come and have a longer visit one day soon."

"Thank you, my lady. That would be most pleasant, I am sure. Why don't you join Miss Smythe and me for a cup of tea tomorrow? I am planning a quiet day without much running around, so having someone come to me would be the perfect thing."

Lady Anne blushed with her gratification. "Thank you, I shall be delighted."

Rose, too, was delighted with her friend's manoeuvrings and was quick to compliment her as they walked away with her maid in tow. "That was very well managed, my friend."

Elizabeth's tinkle of laughter rang out. "That was nothing, Rose, wait until tomorrow. Today we just laid the groundwork. Tomorrow, when we have her on our terms, we shall really dig into the matter."

Rose grinned at her friend's enthusiasm. "The only problem I foresee is that the poor dear appears to be sincere. It seems to me that her life is not a happy one, and her words about the duke listening to her really struck me. What if she truly does have feelings for him?"

Elizabeth looked at Rose seriously. "Will that matter overmuch? Does it change your concerns about her father's machinations?"

"No, but it will bother me more," Rose admitted. "I would prefer that she had a cold heart and was out to hurt him. Then I would have a clear conscience, as I would be rescuing my old friend."

"Have no fear on that score. I firmly believe it is still a rescue mission."

The two girls laughed, linked arms, and made their way home in harmony.

Chapter Eight

That evening, Rose paid particular attention to her appearance, much to her maid's chagrin.

"Miss Rose, whatever is the matter with you? You are never as fidgety about your clothes and hair as this. You aren't planning anymore assignations, are you?"

"Mary Singleton! Of course not, how could you say such a thing?"

"Seems to me like it's a sensible question when you consider the goings on of late."

"You hush, Mary. There are no goings on. I merely wish to look my best. It seems to me to be a reasonable request for a debutante."

"You are perfectly correct, Miss, it is just that you have seemed to hardly care before now."

"Well, now I have friends to meet and the potential of dance partners, so I need to be presentable."

"You have always been presentable, Miss, more than presentable. I think you look better than most of the other girls I've seen. Those two ladies who arrived just before you and Lady Elizabeth left from visiting Lady Anne surely looked like they needed to spend a bit more time with their maids and a hairbrush."

Rose giggled over her maid's words but reprimanded her none the less. "Hush, Mary, I am trying to be friendly with them, so we must be kind even if their hair leaves a little to be desired. Perhaps their maid does not have the skills you have."

"Now you're just trying to turn me up sweet, Miss." Mary grinned at her mistress.

"Is it working? It seems to me that it is terribly important to remain on the good side of the person styling your hair. Else I might not be able to leave the house."

"Oh Miss, I would never do anything to damage your beautiful hair."

"I know, Mary, I was merely teasing you. Now tell me again what you heard while you were waiting for us. I wish to have it fresh in mind before I head out to mingle amongst the *ton* tonight."

Rose could see the maid's assessing gaze in the looking glass and grinned. "Do not be troubled, I have not lost my mind, I remember what you said, I just wish to hear it again."

Mary huffed a little but proceeded to repeat her tale. "Like I told you, Miss, I was sitting in the chair the footman was kind enough to set out for me as I stood in the foyer. Being my first time there, I wasn't about to go wandering down to the kitchens without a by your leave."

"No, of course not, you did just the right thing."

"Anyways, I was just sitting there minding my business, keeping myself entertained by looking around at all the strange decorations they had on the walls, when a couple of parlour maids came along to do some dusting. They were giggling to each other, but they seemed nice enough, stopping to say hello before they went into a room just behind me to do some dusting. They must've forgot I was there or else they didn't care about airing their family's dirty laundry because they started talking to each other about Lady Anne's maid and that she was going to have to be let go because Lord Austen don't have the money to pay her next wages. But then they were saying as the earl might be so good as to hire her on and keep Lady Anne and boot out his lordship as he is just being a drain on the family and isn't even their relative. But then they were speculating that maybe Lady Anne will land herself a fine lord who will fix their affairs all right and tight."

"Thank you, Mary. So none of that was anything we did not already know. You did not hear any mention of Sir Broderick or the Duke of Wrentham. But you did prove that your listening skills are still sharp, so that was excellent work." The two young women shared a grin before Rose continued. "Tomorrow we are going to take tea with Lady Elizabeth. If Lady Anne brings her maid, perhaps you could invite her to go for a walk with you while you both wait for us. It would be absolutely wonderful if you could get the girl to confide in you. Anything you could glean from her would be excellent. If it is true that there is some question of her getting paid, you can be sure she will be happy to tell anything there is to tell. But of course, try not to be too obvious in your inquiries."

"Leave it to me, Miss, I will know just how to go on."

"I know, Mary. It is just that this entire situation has me all at sixes and sevens. A part of me wishes I had never gone to that wretched musicale. But that reminds me that I really must call upon Lady Yorkleigh soon. It seemed to me as though she had a few things to say about the ungentlemanly knight. Perhaps she could be trusted to help me with this situation. I do wish to pass this off to someone more capable."

Heaving a disconsolate sigh, she returned her gaze to the mirror as Mary finally finished tugging and twitching her locks. With a gasp of delight she clapped her hands. "Oh my goodness, Mary, you have truly outdone yourself. I could not have asked for anything better. I do not know how you did it, but I actually look like I could be the belle of the ball. It is miraculous."

"Get on with you, Miss, it ain't no miracle. You're as pretty as a picture every day. I just did a wee bit of enhancing. Just keep in mind that it is much more difficult to do any spying when you're in your looks. People will be remembering you tonight, you can't go sliding in and out of rooms and eavesdropping."

Rose put on a face of disapproval. "Ladies do not eavesdrop, Mary."

"Oh yes they do, Miss, just be careful whatever you are up to."

Rose bounced up from her seat in front of the looking glass and threw her arms impulsively around her maid. "You are a dear and I have no idea what I would do without you."

Mary grinned mistily at her mistress. "Get on with you now, Miss, you do not want to wrinkle up your lovely frock."

Now Rose grinned as she glanced down at her beautiful gown. "You are quite correct. My mother would have my head in a noose if I were to muss it up before we even get to the ball. It is a lovely gown, is it not? I was not completely sure if it would be pleasing when I was picking it out at the mantua makers', but I must say I am well pleased with the result. These puffed sleeves with the darling piping and these appliqued silk fans are really beautiful, but it is certainly a good thing that I will be wearing gloves as this is not the most practical attire for a cool, late autumn evening, I must say. It does make me wonder who decides what is fashionable and why I am such a ninny hammer as to go along with it."

The two girls shared another grin but then Rose thought of something else. "Of course, if the ball turns out to be a crush I will be happy that I am not dressed too warmly. I shall just have to make sure I am not standing in any drafts and all shall be well."

"You will be so busy dancing all night you won't be able to do any of your investigating."

Rose grinned at those words. "Would that not be lovely? I really do not think I could do much investigating at a ball anyway. It is not at all the same as it was in Vienna. There were so few people there, not like here where there are such crowds at every social event. I will of course try to keep my ears open, but I will not mind having a good time." With a girlish giggle, Rose gathered her fan, reticule, and wrap. "I have no idea what time I shall be home and unfortunately I shall probably need help getting out of this beautiful dress without damaging it."

"Of course, Miss Rose, I will be here waiting for you. I will want to hear all about your evening anyway. My only advice is to have a care to your reputation and steer clear of the duke."

"You are a dear," was all Rosamund had as a reply as she hurried out the door.

Lady Smythe was waiting for her at the bottom of the stairs. She was resplendent in jewel tones of crepe. Having managed to keep her figure despite having three children, she looked lovely in the high-waisted style of gown that was in vogue.

"Mama, you look positively smashing this evening," Rose declared with a low whistle.

"Do not be vulgar, I pray of you," Lady Smythe admonished drily.

"I so envy you your colours, Mama," Rose continued, ignoring her mother's obvious ill humour. "This silly tradition of debutantes not being allowed to wear anything other than whites or lights is ill advised, if you ask me."

"Well then it is clearly a good thing that no one asked you, as it is a lovely tradition and one that you will abide by."

"Of course, Mother. I do not have the fortitude to do otherwise, so you need not trouble yourself. I was merely trying to compliment you," she concluded rather airily, trying not to reveal to her mother that her snippity tones actually dented her feelings. "Are you ready to depart?"

Lady Smythe did not reply with words, merely leading the way out of the house to the waiting carriage.

When they arrived at the elegant but large home housing that evening's festivities Rose was slightly dazzled by the blaze of what seemed like a million candles shining from every window. Clearly no expense was being spared this night. She grinned with anticipation before remembering that it would not do to seem overly eager. Glancing around discretely as she followed her mother, Rose admired the paintings on the walls of pastoral settings, possibly the earl's country seat. Feeling a passing sense of nostalgia for the country, Rose bolstered her sagging spirits by looking around in the crowd for Elizabeth.

As her gaze wandered, she felt a prickle climb the back of her neck and knew instinctively that Alex was near and quite probably looking at her. An instant after that awareness, their gazes collided. She felt a wave of heat flow through her body, followed swiftly by one of frigidity. Maintaining her composure with effort, she kept her face as neutral as possible but bowed her head discreetly, acknowledging his presence.

☙ ❧

Alex was amazed that he had known as soon as they entered the room, although the major domo had not yet announced them. His eyes had been drawn to the entrance of the ballroom like a moth to a flame.

He admired the proud tilt of Rose's head as well as the confusing array upon it that was her hair. He never could understand female hairstyles, but this one seemed to be quite fetching. Rose was again dressed in the first stare of fashion. Clearly, the Smythes were not in need of a wealthy match for their only daughter.

But pursuing a match was certainly what they were about this Season. It stood to reason, of course, he realized as he pondered the issue. *Rosie must be twenty by now.* She had missed the chance of a Season a couple years ago due to being in mourning, he thought sadly. Then she traipsed around Europe with her father for a couple years. *Now the Smythes seem set on marrying her off before she gets too long in the tooth.*

She'll do well on the Marriage Mart, Alex decided, trying to be detached on the subject. With her pretty face, perfect figure, and elegant bearing she would make an excellent wife for any nobleman. *And she no doubt has a generous dowry, which would only sweeten the pot. Of course, the fact that she has opinions and doesn't mind overmuch sharing them could be a bit of problem for some gentlemen,* he mused as he watched her wend her way through the milling crowd.

Alex watched as Rose left her mother seated with the other matrons before she strode with purpose in the direction of where he had last seen Lady Elizabeth. He wondered if she had confided in her friend about "the situation." He was not left to wonder for long, when he caught Elizabeth's glance, just as Rose met up with her. Alex had to stifle his smile of amusement as Lady Elizabeth blushed at being caught looking at him. Rose was not so missish. Seeing the look upon her friend's face, she followed her gaze and caught Alex's eye.

Alex felt the contact almost like a physical blow. His stomach turned over, and he felt a prickle at the back of his eyes. He bowed to her in acknowledgement then tore his gaze away from her. This would just not do. He was never so happy to see anyone in all his life as he was when Lord Dunbar turned up at his elbow.

"There you are, Your Grace," Wesley declared jovially. "I was wondering if I would be able to find you in such a crush, but I should have remembered that with your height you are easy enough to locate in a crowd."

Alex, used to comments about his height, managed to keep a pleasant smile plastered to his face as he reconsidered how happy he was to see his friend.

Wesley was continuing to prattle. "I was uncertain if you would even turn up this evening. Thought you might be too caught up in your mystery."

The duke cast his friend a quelling glance, hoping he was not being overheard. He absolutely did not want word to get around Town that there was some sort of mystery surrounding the Duke of Wrentham. He could just imagine the uproar that would cause, and he felt a shiver of dread slither down his back.

"Are you in your cups, my lord?" he asked suppressively.

"Whatever do you mean?" Wesley appeared surprised by the implications.

"Your discretion is even less than usual. I would have expected a touch more discernment from you."

Wesley chuckled. "I have no idea why. Have we not been friends for eons?"

"Good point," the duke replied, his tone dry.

"It would seem all the parties are present this evening," Wesley observed, keeping his voice appropriately low as he gazed out at the sea of well-dressed guests flowing through the countess's rooms. "I just saw your Rosie meet up with her friend, Lady Elizabeth. The Austens were announced not a quarter hour past, and I do believe I saw Sir Broderick in one of the card rooms as I walked by."

"Let the games begin," Alex muttered.

"Are you going to shock the *ton* by asking Miss Smythe to the dance floor?" Wesley was curious.

"You really are daft tonight, are you not? That would be exactly what we do not need for this occasion. I seek information. For that, it would be best if I do not make myself the brunt of every tidbit of gossip to be dissected tomorrow."

"So that would be a no, then, would it?" Wesley drawled. "Very well, then, I think I shall seek out the lady and ask for her myself, if that is the case."

Alex had to clamp his teeth together tightly to prevent from growling his dismay over his friend's treachery. "Judas," he called after his friend's departing back.

Wesley's laugh floated on the heavy air as he waved in acknowledgement but did not stop his progression. "See you later, Your Grace," he called over his shoulder as he walked away.

Alex watched as the viscount made his way through the throng, pausing here and there to exchange greetings. Finally he arrived where Rose and Elizabeth were standing. He could not hear their words, but saw that what was clearly good-hearted banter was being exchanged before Rose accepted his elbow and the two made their way to the dance floor.

Watching them, Alex questioned his own sanity. It was foolish beyond belief for him to torture himself by standing there watching them when there was no possibility of him ever being able to partner her in a dance. But there was a degree of pleasure in the watching as well. She danced with such graceful, economical movements. It revealed something about her that even while dancing she clearly wanted to be in control. She had always been a managing little thing, even as a child, but it would seem that the loss of her brother had made that tendency a bit more extreme. Some might find it charming, he thought, but not him, he reminded himself once more. Finally he turned away, unable to stand the unbearable burden of sadness that pressed upon him for all that they had lost.

With purpose, he turned on his heel and strode further from the dance floor. Finally, he spotted his quarry.

"Lord Austen, what a pleasure to see you this evening." Alex hoped his words sounded much more sincere outside of his head than they did inside.

"Your Grace." Lord Austen's obsequious tone made Alex grit his teeth, but he managed to keep a smile on his face by sheer effort of will. "It is entirely my pleasure to see you, Your Grace. Are you having a good time? Have you seen my lovely daughter? I am certain she would be delighted to dance with you, Your Grace."

"I have not yet had the pleasure of seeing Lady Anne this evening, my lord. I meant to ask you, I have not seen you in the House of Lords very recently. Is all well with you? You used to be so active in the running of our country."

"Oh yes, Your Grace, how good of you to notice. I dearly love being involved with our nation's governance, of course, Your Grace, but I have been so very busy with overseeing my dear daughter's first Season, you see."

Alex smiled at Lord Austen. "I always thought the Season was to complement Parliament, not the other way around."

Lord Austen began to look uncomfortable; perhaps he was embarrassed by Alex's observation. Alex could see his eyes start to dart around as though he were wishing for a rescue from some quarter. Alex hoped his smile did not look quite as predatory as it felt.

"I am sure it must be a huge responsibility to have your daughter debuting at her first Season, especially since she does not have a mother. Of course, no doubt your late wife's sister is of great assistance in such a delicate matter as this."

"Oh yes, the earl and countess have been lovely. They have been most generous hosts. My dear Anne is lucky to have them in her life." Alex watched in fascination as the other man mustered up his composure and appeared a trifle more conniving. "Her connections will make my daughter a remarkably good wife to some fortunate nobleman."

Alex smiled in reply. "No doubt. You will have to be most vigilant to make sure she finds someone who truly appreciates her and all she has to offer."

"That is exactly the truth of the matter and why I have to miss so many sessions, Your Grace. One's only child is a precious thing, and I must take the most care of her that is possible. There are always others who will be able to do as good a job as I ever could in the House of Lords, to be sure."

Alex had to agree with the man about others doing a better job but did not think it seemly to do so verbally, so he merely offered a bland smile. Lord Austen must have taken this for encouragement.

"I do believe my darling daughter would make a lovely duchess, Your Grace."

"Perhaps she would, my lord. There are a few dukes looking about for wives this Season if you can believe the gossips. I happen to not be searching for one myself, as I am of the opinion that I should wait until I have everything in the duchy in order as I would like it. Taking over my father's properties and titles has been a bigger challenge than I had expected."

"Of course, of course," Lord Austen murmured, trying to sound sympathetic, but Alex distrusted the calculated gleam that had taken root in the other man's eyes. The duke feared he had just given added motivation to the scheme against him. But then he reassured himself that he would prefer an attack, the more open the better, rather than waiting around wondering about it. He was not surprised when he heard an oily voice from behind him.

"Well, well, well. What a surprise to see you talking with the Duke of Wrentham."

Alex had to work hard to keep the sneer from his face as he turned to greet Sir Jason Broderick.

"Sir Broderick." It was not in him to lie any further by saying it was a pleasure to see him. He merely bowed his head slightly in greeting.

"Good evening, Your Grace. Lord Austen, how good to see you. I trust you are well. Are you gentlemen enjoying the ball so far?"

"I have yet to spend any time on the dance floor, which I should really give some attention to. I was enjoying a little visit with Lord Austen here." Alex kept his explanation short and opened the way to make his escape.

"Oh yes, Sir Broderick, I am having a fine time this evening. My lovely daughter is off with her aunt. No doubt she is busy dancing. His Grace and I were merely catching up on news from the House of Lords."

"Ah yes, the House of Lords. Is there anything of import going on in the House these days, Your Grace?"

"Nothing that need concern anybody overly. There have been some lively debates over a few issues, but nothing that we cannot handle. Now, if you gentlemen will excuse me."

Alex made good his escape, managing not to allow his sigh of relief to be audible. He felt as though he needed to bathe after being in the presence of Sir Broderick. That man put him in mind of some sort of sneaky creature, such as a weasel or a minx, stalking his prey. He certainly had no intention of being anyone's dupe.

As he had been talking with what he was beginning to seriously consider were his enemies, he had been keeping half an eye upon Rosie and her progress through the room. Having the advantage of height meant he was able to observe the goings on of the ballroom more easily than others. He was glad to see she appeared to be having a good time.

☙ ❧

It had taken Rose a few tense seconds to overcome that moment with Alex where their eyes had met. It had felt like such a significant experience, but she hastened to shove it to the corner recesses of her mind. She could not have significant experiences with a Wrentham, she reminded herself, blinking furiously.

"Is all well with you?"

Rose could hear the sincere concern in Elizabeth's voice and strove to control her features. "Of course, is this not a lovely ballroom? I absolutely adore the size of it and the darling alcoves, such as the one which the orchestra is occupying."

"Now I know you are not all right. You do not use the word darling, especially not in describing architecture."

This brought a genuine smile to Rose's face and a tinkle of laughter escaped her lips. "I will admit to you that I am a trifle nervous this evening. I am unused to playing the role of Bow Street Runner here in London. And all whilst wearing a fancy ball gown."

"Well, you do look smashing this evening, if that is any consolation. And there is not a trace of nervousness showing either. In fact, you look positively radiant tonight. It would seem the role of Runner suits you," Elizabeth teased in an undertone. Rose was grateful she kept her voice low as she did not wish for this conversation to be overheard.

It was very well indeed as just at that moment they were hailed by Lord Wesley Dunbar. Rose was unsure if the duke would have confided in his friend. "Good evening, ladies. You both look lovely this evening."

Both girls dipped into well-practiced curtsies, rising with welcoming smiles upon their faces for the personable viscount.

"How are you this evening, my lord?" Rose asked.

"You look lovely yourself, Lord Wesley," Elizabeth complimented, causing the trio to laugh.

☙ ❧

At that moment another gentleman approached to claim Elizabeth's hand for the waltz that was just about to begin, leaving Rose alone with Wesley.

"Since you are recently returned from Vienna, I am certain you are an expert at the waltz, so I tremble in my shoes lest you cast me in the shade, but would you be so kind as to do me the honour of sharing this dance with me?"

"Oh, my lord, you are a complete hand," Rose countered. Little did she know that Wesley lost his heart to her at that very moment. Never had he met a debutante who was so unaffected or who received compliments with such aplomb. Most debs would simper, bat their eyelashes, and beg for more. Not Miss Rose. Of course, as it was obvious there were unresolved feelings from the duke toward Miss Rose, the viscount kept his feelings familial, but he resolved to assist her in any way he could.

They were silent for a few beats, enjoying the music and getting into the rhythm of the dance, but then Wesley deemed it safe to converse; they could hardly be overheard while on the dance floor. And as long as they schooled their features, no one would know they were discussing anything but the blandest inanities. He trusted Miss Rose would be able to manage that. His trust was well placed.

"The duke has told me of his predicament and your involvement in it," he began.

"Which duke is that, my lord?" Rose asked with an innocent look upon her face that brought a grin to Wesley's.

"How on earth do you manage that?" he asked with genuine interest.

His grin grew as he watched Rose bat her eyelashes. "Manage what, my lord? I assure you there is nothing on my mind save the effort required not to tread upon your toes and count the steps so as to not collide with any other couples on the dance floor."

"Oh, Miss Smythe, now *you* are being a complete hand. You know well and good which duke and which predicament I am speaking of. I can assure you, he would not mind us discussing it. In fact, given the sticky situation of your families' feuding, it would no doubt be best if I act as mediator between the two of you."

"Do you not think it would be best if the fewer people were involved as possible? There are reputations at stake. And we do not wish to cause the very situation we are trying to prevent. No one with any knowledge of this wishes to find themselves in the parson's mousetrap, not even you, my lord."

Wesley was disconcerted by her straight, intelligent stare as she looked him directly in the eye for a beat before looking away with a social smile firmly in place. *This girl is skilled at this sort of prevarication,* he marvelled to himself, wondering how the straight-laced duke would feel about that sort of information.

"I swear to you, I will preserve any confidence you share with me and do my utmost to protect anyone's reputation who might become embroiled in this affair. And I promise you that I do not have designs upon your dowry, as my own pockets are sufficiently well lined."

This was exactly the right thing to say, Wesley observed, as Rose threw her head back and chuckled huskily. He watched in fascination as she brought her sparkling gaze back to his and slowly sobered.

"Very well, my lord, I will bring you into my confidences if that is your wish. You shall soon see that it is not all that exciting but is terribly complicated. I find that I actually like Lady Anne, although she strikes me as being a trifle simple. I have come to believe that she is somewhat innocent in this. While she may be involved in a plot to entrap the duke, I do not believe she means him any ill will but actually considers that he would be a suitable mate. I think she is being manipulated by her father and his friend Sir Broderick."

Wesley watched as a myriad of emotions chased themselves fleetingly across her face before she was again wearing her mask of social behaviour. "Now, that does not really change anything, it merely makes it a little more difficult as she has gained my sympathies. I still have no wish to see the duke entrapped by anyone, least of all Sir Broderick."

"You say that as though you have reasons other than loyalty to an old friend motivating you," Wesley observed.

"Does that matter?" Rose countered.

"Not really, I just find it interesting is all," Wesley answered, searching her face for more information, puzzled by her sweet smile. She turned his attention with her next question.

"Do you know if the duke has found out anything of import? Unfortunately, I have not as of yet, but I have a plan set for tomorrow to gain as much information as possible."

"I have not had a chance to ask him. I know he was planning to meet with his solicitors and man of affairs earlier today, but we did not discuss it since."

Wesley watched in fascination as Rose's eyes strayed toward the duke as they passed him in conversation with Lord Austen and Sir Broderick. Despite her usual grace, she nearly missed a step as the dance turned them away. He watched the colour rise in her cheeks, as she was embarrassed over her misstep.

"I did not expect to see him actually talking to them. You do not think he would confront them in such a place as this, do you?" She was incredulous.

Wesley grinned. "While the duke does hate double dealing, I can assure you that he is perfectly capable of it. Not only would he never wish to cause a scene that would embarrass his hosts, he would also never confront an enemy until he was certain he knew everything about the situation. No, I believe he is merely trying to make sure those two think he still knows nothing."

Rose's eyes flicked back toward the duke, but she quickly recovered herself. "How interesting," was all she had to say, causing the viscount to prompt further.

"Is that all you have to say? From the look in your eyes it would seem you are thinking many more thoughts than that."

He was gratified that this brought a genuine smile of amusement to her face. "Well, it *is* interesting, my lord. The Alex I knew, before he ever had an inkling that he would be a duke one day, hated anything that even hinted at being less than the truth. He would not even play games of make believe when we were children. I find it hard to reconcile that Alex with one who could stand and converse pleasantly with someone we suspect is plotting against him."

"That Alex had to grow up and learn that very few things in life are black and white," Wesley explained, which brought Rose's sharp gaze returning to meet his.

"The two of you have been friends for a very long time, have you not?" she asked quietly.

"We went to school together for many years."

"You are the Wes he used to talk about?" she asked, her eyes again sparkling with interest. "He would regale me with tales of your adventures. I was always so jealous. I was not allowed to do nearly half the things he told me the two of you did."

Wesley chuckled at the pout she displayed briefly before she joined him in a smile of amusement. "If it is any consolation, I was always jealous of the tales he would tell of his Rosie whenever he returned to school from the summer break."

Rose grinned. "It is actually, thank you, my lord."

By this time their dance had come to an end and they were standing on the side of the dance floor. "Should I escort you back to your mother?" Wesley asked quietly.

"Heavens, no!" Rose laughed. "Elizabeth is just over there. I should like to rejoin her."

Wesley bowed over her hand, gallantly placing a kiss to its back. As he stood, he could see Rose was unmoved by his efforts, as her smile was as friendly as previously without a tinge of simpering maiden to be seen. Suppressing his sigh, he wondered if he was losing his touch with the ladies and went off in search of a more susceptible maiden.

Rose was still grinning as she came to Elizabeth's side.

"Why are you looking like the cat who caught the canary?" Elizabeth asked with suspicion.

Rose shrugged. "Lord Dunbar is starting to make me like this Season business. It is not nearly as deadly dull as I had first thought."

"That is good to hear," her friend remarked as she turned to the next gentleman who had come to claim her hand for the dance.

Rose was gratified to see that there were a few gentlemen waiting to ask her to dance. Both girls were kept energetically occupied for some time. Managing to arrange for their escorts to bring them back so they could go in to the late supper together, the two friends had a couple moments to talk as the gentlemen were filling their plates.

"So, were you able to learn anything from Lord Dunbar? Did he make any reference to the duke?" Elizabeth's curiosity had gotten the best of her and she blurted out her questions quietly as soon as they were alone.

"Not much, I'm afraid. But I did see Wrentham in conversation with Austen and Broderick. It turns out the sober duke is able to act the spy when the need arises." Rose was still mulling that discovery over at the back of her mind, wondering if she might actually be able to confide in him. Remembering the feud, she shoved the possibility away once more. "I have realized I cannot discover anything of import at a ball and have decided to just enjoy myself. The investigation can resume tomorrow when we have Lady Anne to ourselves."

The two girls shared a conspiratorial smile before Rose continued, "Have I thanked you yet for your help? You are proving to be a true friend, and I so deeply appreciate it."

Elizabeth looked surprised over her friend's words. "But of course. No thanks are necessary. I can assure you, as this is not my first Season, it is proving to be far more interesting than usual being in London. I shudder to think what it will be like next Season if I do not find a match. I shall be forced to sabotage any chances you might have in order to ensure you are here with me."

Rose chuckled at her friend's words just as the gentlemen returned, so no response was necessary.

As the four of them chatted and ate, Rose felt a prickle along the back of her neck and knew instinctively that the duke of Wrentham had entered the room. Her breath hitched in her throat for a second and she wondered rather frantically if it was always going to be thus. She hated what the Wrenthams had done to her family, but she so missed Alex's friendship and she truly despised this strange awareness that she had developed for him.

It had been so simple and uncomplicated when he was merely the boy next door who tolerated her presence when her brothers demanded that she shoo. She had always lived for the days when he was home from Eton and they could wander through the countryside, climbing trees, fishing, or riding. He had always listened so patiently as she prattled on about whatever entered her head. And he had confided in her all the details of his young life. Even though he was six years her senior, he had been her best friend. She had thought that would last for all her life. Then their brothers had died, and nothing would ever be the same again.

Once more Rose found herself shoving unwanted thoughts to the back of her mind. She felt her lips quirk into an amused smile as she wondered how cluttered her mind must be. One of these days she would have to address all the things she did not wish to think about. But now was not the time. She forced her attention to return to the conversation that was swirling around her, ignoring the fact that she was avidly curious about why the duke had chosen to escort Constance Chadwick to supper.

"This supper is absolutely delicious," Elizabeth was enthusing. "I must say I worked up quite an appetite this evening." She then blushed rosily at making such a forward comment.

Rose could see the relief etched on her friend's face when the gentlemen merely chuckled at her words before turning to her.

"Did you not dance enough to become hungry, Miss Smythe?" one asked. Rose blinked for a moment, drawing a blank at his name. Recognition dawned—it was Lord Terrance Leonard, a young baron who was attending his first session at Parliament.

"Oh, no my lord, I danced plenty. I am just trying to pretend I am a lady," she replied with a laugh. "I will agree with my dear friend, though, that our hosts have been most generous in their hospitality. Their cook certainly knows what he is doing. It is rare that a cook has the skill to prepare such delicious food for a crowd like this."

Everyone nodded agreement and continued enjoying their repast. In an effort to keep her eyes away from Alex, Rose began another topic of conversation.

"Tell me, Lord Leonard, how are you enjoying your participation in the House? Is it as exciting as you had expected?"

"At times, Miss, but there are some deadly dull bits interspersed with the excitement that have made me wonder if this is the right career for me." Rose found his self-deprecating smile to be charming.

"Whatever do you mean?" she prompted.

"Sadly, some of our lords of government seem to like the sound of their own voices more than they actually want resolution to the issues. They can drone on for hours and I lose interest." The young baron blushed over his admission. "I probably should not be telling you this. It certainly does not please my father when I cannot report intelligently on the session I sat through."

"I will share a tip with you that my father relies upon. He said that most of these long-winded speeches are usually written out in advance and the important sentence of each paragraph is almost always the first one. So, try to bring your attention into focus every once in a while and you should be able to get the gist of whatever they are droning on about."

"Why Miss Smythe, that is a most excellent suggestion."

"I hope it will be of use to you. I am sure you will be an asset to our government. Give it a little more time before you decide whether or not to give it up."

"Have no fear, Miss, I have every intention of fulfilling my duties."

This made Rose feel like rolling her eyes. She had not meant to question the young man's dutifulness. Her smile was a trifle wan as she returned her attention to Lady Elizabeth.

Elizabeth was looking amused, so Rose surmised she had heard her exchange with the baron. Rose lifted her shoulder in a slight shrug, keeping her wry grin under control.

"Have you about finished up?" Rose asked solicitously.

"I have, thank you," she replied as the gentlemen stood, taking their plates and summoning an attentive footman.

Lord Kenneth, the gentleman who had escorted Lady Elizabeth, hadn't had much to say over the supper but he now asked Rose to share the next dance.

"It sounds like it's about to be a cotillion. Those are my favourite," he enthused, much to her surprise.

"Thank you, my lord, it shall be my pleasure."

The rest of the night passed in a blur of activity as Rose spent most of it on the dance floor being handed from one gentleman to the next, not bothering to keep track of names or faces, just enjoying the rhythms of the dance. Her mother would be displeased that she was not paying more attention to each gentleman's potential as a possible husband but despite her advancing years, she was in no hurry to commit herself.

Before she knew it, it was the early hours of the morning and her mother was collecting her to escort her home.

"You seemed to be having a fine time this evening," Lady Smythe commented almost cheerfully.

"I did have an excellent time this evening, Mama, what about you? Did you enjoy the ball?"

"I think balls are intended to be enjoyed by the young, my dear," her mother began in a bland tone. "But I did have some interesting conversations with the other matrons lining the walls of the ballroom. Not everyone there is as intolerable as I originally thought."

Rose laughed at her mother's choice of words. "I am glad you were able to tolerate your evening. I must ask you, though, why do you bother attending such events if you find them such a challenge?"

Rose's mother displayed the most emotion she had witnessed there in quite some time, as her features were etched in shock over her daughter's words. "I could never allow you to go out by yourself. It is my duty to chaperone and watch over you."

Now Rose felt truly terrible. "Let us go home to Eastwick, then, Mama. Neither of us enjoy the Season overly. It would be much better to just be comfortable."

"I do believe we have already had this conversation, Rosamund. You need a husband. The Season is necessary to find you one. We shall prevail."

Now Rose grinned at her mother. "I like the picture your words paint. Let us regard it as a battle we must fight and win. That shall add some needed spice to the blandness of the Season." Her mother barely cracked a smile but after a brief pause, Rose pushed on. "Thank you, Mama, for your efforts on my behalf. Knowing what a sacrifice it is for you, I want you to know that I do appreciate it. You were quite correct when you said I would not enjoy being the aging spinster aunt in my brother's home. If I cannot set up my own establishment, marriage is the best option. We shall prevail."

Lady Smythe finally softened and allowed Rose to clasp her hand with affection. "It is what mothers do, make sacrifices for their children. And it is not as bad as all that. The orchestra this evening was rather skilled."

"And was the food not delicious? Elizabeth and I were remarking on how skilled the cook must be to be able to prepare so well food for such a large crowd."

"Speaking of the cook, why don't you sit in with me when I meet with the housekeeper next week? It is time for us to further your education on household management, and you have no experience with running a house in Town."

Rose smiled with genuine happiness at her mother. "That would be lovely."

They had finally arrived in front of their own house and an attentive footman was holding open the door waiting for them to alight. The ladies bade each other a good night and went their separate ways to secure their rest. Tomorrow was going to be a big day.

Chapter Nine

Rose and Mary hurried along the sidewalk up the fashionable street, barely noticing the elegantly clad noblemen and women they passed in their haste. Each had their thoughts full of the respective roles they would be fulfilling that afternoon.

"This is ever so exciting, Miss," Mary exclaimed as they approached Elizabeth's house. "I'm afeared I'm going to give it all away with my fidgets."

"I have full confidence in you, Mary. You are going to be marvellous."

"How can you be sure?" fretted the maid.

"I have known you nearly all my life, for one thing. For another, you have already proven your abilities in Vienna. This is hardly any different."

Mary blew out the breath she had been holding and smiled her relief at her mistress. "You're right, Miss Rosie. Thanks, I needed that confidence booster."

As they climbed the stairs and were admitted by the earl's rather imposing butler, Rose hoped fervently that her words were true. It felt so very different from anything they had involved themselves with in Vienna. She was unsure if it was because they had been in another country or if it was her father's involvement, but in Vienna it had felt like a game. She couldn't shake the sensation that this was so much more serious and dire. It was ridiculous, really, since there were, no doubt, schemes for marriage taking place throughout the Season, but she just could not rest easy about Broderick's involvement. Bracing her mind for the ordeal ahead, Rose smiled bravely, bolstering her own spirits as she was ushered into Lady Elizabeth's receiving room.

"Miss Rose, it is a pleasure to see you," Lady Castleton greeted as Rose was announced. "I shall leave you girls to your giggles. Elizabeth tells me another young lady will be joining you for tea. I wish the three of you a good afternoon. I have some calls of my own to make, but our housekeeper will see to all that you might need."

"Thank you, Lady Castleton. I wish you a good afternoon as well," Rose answered politely, wishing she was better acquainted with her friend's mother, who seemed like such a pleasant woman.

"Come in and sit down," Elizabeth ordered, bouncing a little in her seat after her mother left the room. "We barely had a chance to talk last night."

"I know." Rose grinned. "We were both a little too popular for conversation."

"Are you complaining?" Elizabeth asked with an answering grin.

"Not at all," Rose replied with enthusiasm. "I am very much enjoying being a popular debutante, I will admit freely."

"Did any of the gentlemen catch your interest?" Elizabeth was impatient to find out.

"Not in the least," Rose admitted with a touch of reluctance. "I fear the efforts of the Season will be for naught. My poor mother is going through such a trial to sponsor me, and I cannot muster a drop of enthusiasm for any of the eligible men being introduced to me."

Catching sight of Elizabeth's raised eyebrow Rose grinned and continued. "Nor any of the ineligible ones either."

"Rosamund Smythe, which ineligible gentlemen have you been speaking with?"

"I danced with the Earl of Heath last night. The *on-dit* is that his wife did not die of natural causes. The whispers are that he helped her fall down those stairs. But he is so tragically handsome that I could not resist when he asked me for a dance. Thankfully, although my mother seems to pay no attention to me when we are at a ball, she chose to join me as he was escorting me from the dance floor and glared him away from my presence so I do not have to worry about him trying to call on me."

Elizabeth gave a delicate shudder at her friend's words. "Can you imagine? How would you handle it if he wanted to take you for a ride in the park?"

Rose shrugged and answered with simple practicality. "Well, surely I would be perfectly safe…at least until after the wedding."

This caused both girls to burst into laughter. Rose was the first to sober and bring both their attentions back to the matter at hand. "So, you are going to lead the conversation, I take it, as you are the hostess."

"Of course," Elizabeth answered with pride.

"Have you thought about how you are going to manage to get Lady Anne to open up about her father's plans?"

"We are going to gossip about the eligible gentlemen and how we could possibly get any of them to come up to scratch. You shall lament about your lack of connections and your fears that this will hold back certain likely candidates. Hopefully this will play upon her delicate feelings and she will offer you some suggestions that she has received."

"You, my dear, are brilliant."

"I cannot take the credit. I thought of it last night when you were telling that young baron about your father's suggestions for getting through boring lectures in the House."

"I am so pleased that my father's advice is getting so much mileage," Rose answered with dry amusement. They quickly hushed as they heard the door knocker sound. Elizabeth pulled the bell for the housekeeper just as the butler announced Lady Anne.

"Welcome, welcome," Elizabeth called out, rising to greet the new arrival.

Both girls feigned believable happiness at seeing the younger girl arrive. Lady Anne flushed with happiness, making Rose feel a stab of guilt, which she blithely ignored.

"Thank you so much for inviting me," Lady Anne began shyly. "I find it is rather difficult to make friends as ultimately we are actually in competition, vying for the attentions of the eligible gentlemen."

Elizabeth and Rose smiled at Anne briefly before replying as the housekeeper chose just that moment to arrive. Elizabeth requested that tea service be provided shortly and the housekeeper hurried away. Turning back to Lady Anne, Elizabeth continued as though there had been no interruption.

"It is funny you should say that. Miss Rose and I were just talking about how difficult it is to catch the eye of certain gentlemen to whose suit we might be amenable. I have no wish to appear as though I am competing with any of my friends, but it is a challenge to get any of the eligibles to commit themselves. Would you not agree?"

Rose was nodding to indicate her agreement, although inwardly she was grimacing. What foolishness the Season was, she thought with derision. Variations of this conversation were likely taking place in all the salons and parlours throughout Town as they spoke. This prompted her next words.

"Lady Anne, I never thought of it as a competition, but I fear you are quite correct. Why do we not agree to lend each other a hand instead of interfering with each other's efforts? We could compare notes and share strategies."

"What a lovely idea," Lady Anne replied, although her enthusiasm was a trifle weak. "Do either of you have your sights set on anyone in particular? I saw you went in to dinner with Lord Terrance Leonard. Did you consider him a potential partner?"

Rose did not have to feign her sigh of regret. "Not at all, I am afraid. I think I will require a husband to be a little older. Since I have travelled and seen a little more of the world than the average girl, I think I will require someone with a great deal more experience than poor Lord Terrance. He was pleasant enough, and I am certain he will make some lady a wonderful husband, but I am not certain he is even in the market for a wife at the moment."

Elizabeth took the reins of the conversation back into her capable hands. "My dinner companion was pleasant company as well, but in my opinion he had a little too much to say about his mother. I need a husband who is ready to set up his own establishment, or better yet, one who already has. I do not wish to compete with my mother-in-law for my husband's affections."

"Oh, good heavens, no, that would be perfectly dreadful. What about you, Lady Anne? I did not take particular notice of anyone you were spending time with last night, were any of the gentlemen eligible for you in your estimation?"

Lady Anne still seemed a trifle shy and Rose wondered briefly if they would actually be able to get the young woman to confide in them. Thankfully they were not left wondering for long.

"A few of the gentlemen I danced with last night seemed perfectly lovely," she answered softly with a small smile. "In particular, Lord Dunbar and Lord Edgecombe."

"Oh, Lord Edgecombe, I did not even notice him there last night," Elizabeth answered, not with complete honesty. "How lucky for you that he asked you to dance. I had the pleasure last week. Besides being so handsome, he is also such a great dancer."

"Yes, he is," Lady Anne answered shyly. "And he seems very interesting."

"Interesting?" Rose questioned.

"Oh yes, would it not be dreadful to sit down to breakfast and dinner every day with a dead bore?"

Rose and Elizabeth burst into chuckles at Anne's words.

"Oh yes, I can see your point entirely," Elizabeth agreed while Rose was still giggling too hard to formulate an answer.

Anne continued, much to the other girls' surprise. "Most of the gentlemen I have met only wish to discuss the weather or the Season or their politics. They do not actually wish for you to have anything to say about their politics, though, mind you. As a debutante, you are expected to merely sit and listen to them. If you can muster up awe while you do that, it is all the better. I truly do not think I could playact for the rest of my life, so then where would we be?"

Rose felt her jaw go a little slack over Anne's words. The girl obviously had hidden depths of which she had been unaware. Her predicament grew. She resolved to hold her silence and wait to see how the afternoon developed.

After pouring the tea that the housekeeper had delivered unobtrusively, Elizabeth once again steered the conversation.

"I fear you are absolutely correct, my dear, Lady Anne. But what are we to do? Many of the gentlemen I have met thus far are rather dull and the ones who are not are so highly sought after, I am uncertain how to engage their affections."

"My father has told me countless times that affections can be engaged after the nuptials have been arranged, so really all you have to do is set your mind to the task of which gentleman is best for you and then arrange it." Anne said this with such stark simplicity that both the other girls looked at her, unsure what she was getting at. This caused her to let escape a tinkle of laughter.

"I must confess I am not fully certain what you mean by your words," Elizabeth apologized.

"That is completely understandable. It is a trifle unorthodox, I will agree. But my father has assured me that it will be the best plan to ensure my future happiness. All I have to do is find myself in a compromising situation with the gentleman of my choice. He will arrange everything else. And before you know it, I will be happily wed to a wonderful lord."

Rose just had to ask. "But do you really think you could be happy with someone you have tricked? Would he not be terribly angry? I cannot see how that would be a good way to start off your new life together."

"Surely if he allowed himself to get into the compromising position, he must have feelings for me of some sort, would you not agree?" Anne reasoned.

Rose was not so certain but did not know how to articulate her thoughts on such an indelicate subject. She contained herself to an uncomfortable shrug.

Anne continued. "And maybe he won't even have to find out that he has been tricked."

"Do you think that would be possible to pull off?" Elizabeth asked before she thought of another question. "Have you tried this already?"

Again, Anne let out one of her tinkles of laughter. "Not yet. I have been setting the stage thus far, making sure the gentleman in question is actually to my liking, and laying the groundwork for my plan."

Rose could only look at her in awe, amazed that she was able to present such an innocent face to Society and yet be so devious inside. She had seemed like such a quiet girl, dull almost. Although she felt a level of sympathy for the girl, she no longer felt any compunction about trying to waylay her plans if they still included the Duke of Wrentham. She hoped Elizabeth would pose that question next.

"Is Lord Edgecombe to be your chosen one?"

Rose smiled over her friend's brief hesitation before saying the word *one*. She wondered briefly if Elizabeth had been about to say *victim* but had then thought better of it.

"I thought so. He is so very handsome and so kind. I think he would be a most comfortable spouse. And it would be a pleasure to share coffee with him each morning. But my father has convinced me that the Duke of Wrentham is a far better catch, and I cannot say I disagree. Who would not wish to be a duchess after all?" Anne said this with a matter-of-fact air but

Rose sensed sadness beneath. It would seem Lady Anne did not have a deep yearning to be a duchess. Rose thought to test her theory.

"I am not certain that I would wish to be a duchess. My father is merely a baron, so while we have been comfortable my entire life, we have never lived spectacularly. I think it might be a trifle awkward to go from being a baron's daughter to being a duchess. I have so little experience with running a large house, let alone multiple of them, as I am sure Wrentham must have. And there would constantly be people wishing to curry favour with you for all sorts of various reasons."

Anne nodded her serious agreement. "I agree with you, Miss Smythe, but the advantages far outweigh the disadvantages. And my father would be so pleased. It seems to be very important to him. And I cannot say that I particularly object. The duke would, I mean will, make a very fine husband, to be sure."

Rose, hoping for further revelations, decided not to argue any further. "To be sure," she agreed with unfeigned enthusiasm. Alex *would* make an excellent husband for someone, just not her or Lady Anne, Rose thought with restlessness stirring.

"I must say, I find your plan rather intriguing," Elizabeth said. "Perhaps I could use it for myself. I do not cherish the thought of enduring any more Seasons. I would like to get on with my life without being in the Marriage Mart for another year. Do you not agree, my dear Rose? You do not have too long to spend on the shelf either."

Rose felt her lips twist into a wry smile. Elizabeth was using truth to disguise their deception. "'Tis true," Rose agreed. "My mother assures me that I absolutely must find a mate shortly or I will remain a spinster, and my family will never allow me to set up my own establishment, so I will be confined to being a drain on my brother for the rest of my days. I can assure you that I have no wish to be an unwanted guest in my childhood home. So yes, my dear Lady Anne, I beg of you to share with us a few bits of wisdom as to how we, too, can ensure we get the groom of our choice. And then perhaps we can figure out together who Elizabeth and I should choose."

These must have been exactly the right words. Anne giggled girlishly and launched into her instructions. "You have to be absolutely certain of your choice before you launch your plan because my father has assured me there is no going back once you begin. It is really quite simple. You lure your intended into a sense of security with you, then arrange to be found alone with him, preferably looking compromised, by someone who can enforce the situation, like a parent or brother. In my case, my father will happily play that role."

"Have you thought of what you would do if the gentleman refuses, especially if he does realize it has been a trap?" Rose could not help but ask.

"No true gentleman will refuse— my father has been adamantly clear on that particular subject."

Rose felt her stomach turn with disgust over such underhanded dealings. Hoping it was not written on her features, she carried on. "That seems to be simple enough. Now, though, comes the tricky part. I have not found anyone that particularly strikes my fancy. Do either of you have any suggestions? Or do you have any candidates for yourself, Elizabeth?"

Elizabeth was playing her part remarkably well. She giggled as she said, "This is prodigiously entertaining, I must say. I shall have to think hard on the matter. There are so many possibilities. But you are quite correct, Lady Anne, one must be absolutely certain of one's choice before setting such a plan in motion." She paused for a moment, feigning deep thought over her possible choices. "Tell us, please, Lady Anne, I beg of you, how you could be so certain in your choice. What made the duke so much more appealing than the viscount? Is it merely the more elevated title? Or did you perhaps become privy to know the actual status of their funds? I have heard that

Edgecombe is very comfortably heeled, so I would not see that as a particular factor."

"You are correct, it was not an easy choice. Those factors do all play into it, of course, but the fact is, my father helped me decide. Like I said, my preferences had been leaning in a different direction originally, but my father was quite insistent that the duke was a better choice for me."

"That is interesting. I do not think I would be comfortable discussing this strategy with my parents." There was so much truth in what Rose was saying she did not have to force her reluctant tone. "I cannot think of anyone other than you two ladies with whom I could discuss my options. Do you know what factors your father used to help him decide who would be best for you?"

Rose encountered Elizabeth's gaze and had to fight to control her satisfied smile as she saw the admiring look in her friend's eye. Elizabeth was clearly impressed with that last line of questioning. Rose only hoped it would provide some sort of enlightenment from Anne.

"He said he had received excellent advice from his friend, Sir Jason Broderick, about the circumstances of all the eligible gentlemen when we first arrived in London. My father said it was his estimation that the Duke of Wrentham was my best choice. Since I trust my father and had not truly formed any deep attachments, I was happy to go along with his choice."

"I see, so he did not tell you the reasons. That is really not of much help to either of us, sadly," Rose complained.

"I do believe some of the things that swayed my father have something to do with the duke's acquaintances. My father likes to talk about connections. It seems to be very important. I do not understand it really, but there you have it. The best advice I can give you, according to my father, is to find a man with good connections to marry."

Rose did not fully understand either, but thought she might know much more on that subject than the other two ladies. She did not want to reveal her knowledge, so she feigned ignorance. "Connections. I see, like a good family, right? I can see that might be a good thing to look for. Lord Dunbar comes from a large extended family, perhaps he might be a good match for one of us." She looked at Elizabeth and grinned.

Elizabeth joined in with the fun. "I think the Viscount of Rothsay also has many aunts, uncles, and cousins. And he is quite handsome, and rumoured to be outrageously wealthy."

"I can see that there are many options. I shall have to think on the matter a little longer before I can set any plan in motion," Rose concluded before asking one more pertinent question. "Have you already set your plan in motion, my lady? Are you in need of any assistance from us?"

Anne smiled with genuine appreciation at Rose's offer, making her wish she could bite off her tongue. "That is so kind of you, Miss Smythe, thank you for the offer. I will keep it in mind. I do not think I am quite ready to set it in motion yet. The duke has not asked me to dance at the last couple of balls we have attended, so I do not think he is going to cooperate with my plans just yet. I need to get him a bit more comfortable with me before I can do anything else."

"That would make sense," Rose concluded, hoping her relief was not too evident.

After that, Elizabeth must have concluded they had asked all they could, as she steered the conversation into more acceptable avenues. Before long Lady Anne stood to take her leave.

When the door had closed behind her, Elizabeth looked at Rose and burst into raucous laughter. "Oh my, what have we gotten ourselves involved in?"

"It is exactly what we had feared, so I do not understand your question," Rose replied, puzzled.

"This is just so ridiculous, if you ask me. Can you picture our fathers sitting down together to discuss which gentleman would be the best one to trick into marrying one of us? It just is not done. This leads me to wonder how Sir Broderick is involved in all this."

Rose did not wish to divulge what she knew about the knight so she feigned ignorance. "Perhaps Wrentham will have discovered some plot from him and will be able to enlighten us." She then rose to take her leave. "I should probably be on my way. The hour grows late and we still have to make our preparations for the evening's affairs. Which invitations have you accepted for tonight?"

"My mother and I are going to a poetry reading at the Duke of Yorkshire's home."

"Really? That sounds interesting. I do not think we received an invitation to that." Rose was sorry they would not be at the same events.

"I believe it is to be a small event."

"I hope it is not dull for you. I shall be dancing until the wee hours of the morning at the Rotherham ball tonight. It should prove to be enjoyable."

"Will you be able to call on me tomorrow to let me know how your meeting goes with Wrentham in the morning?" Elizabeth had not forgotten the more scandalous part of the entire situation.

Rose grinned. "I will do my best," she promised as she took her leave.

☙ ❧

That night at the ball Rose again whirled from partner to partner, enjoying each set to the utmost. She was a little discomfited by encountering the gentlemen they had been discussing that afternoon, but amused herself asking the Viscount of Rothsay about his family.

"I have heard your parents both come from large families. Do you enjoy having so many aunts, uncles, and cousins, my lord?"

"I do not give it much thought, Miss Smythe, as it has been a fact of my entire life."

"I suppose that makes sense, my lord. I merely asked because I do not have much extended family to speak of. Neither of my parents have either of their parents still alive. My father was an only child and my mother only had one sister."

"That strikes me as being rather sad, Miss."

"Yes, it does me, too," Rose agreed, wrinkling her brow with perplexity. "I never gave it much thought, but I can see that life would never be lonely if one had grown up with a plethora of cousins."

"It was certainly never lonely, nor was it quiet," the viscount agreed with a smile.

Rose could not quite suppress her melancholic sigh. "It must have been quite lovely. Do you remain close with all those family members?"

Lord Rothsay smiled. "I am, actually. It does make holidays so very chaotic, but it is what I am used to. I think it would be difficult to grow accustomed to for someone unused to the crowds."

Rose wondered if there was an unspoken message in there for her. She was looking at the viscount with interest but then felt that familiar prickle along the back of her neck and knew the duke was present. There would be no more thoughts of potential mates for her until this affair was safely settled. She was relieved when the set came to an end.

The viscount exchanged small talk with her until another gentleman came to request her hand for the next set. Rose was amused to see that it was Lord Anthony Edgecombe. *Am I to partner with every nobleman we discussed this afternoon?* she wondered with strange curiosity.

"You look like you are having a fine time this evening, Miss Smythe," Lord Edgecombe began.

"I am, actually. Thank you, my lord. I had not thought I would ever enjoy the Season, but it is turning out to be remarkably amusing."

"You did not think to enjoy the Season, Miss?" he repeated with surprise. "I thought every young lady pined for the day she could make her debut."

"When I was a young girl, perhaps I did, my lord. And I will admit that I was not dreading the experience at all. But my first impression of a London Season was not all that favourable. Now that I have begun to make friends, it is an entirely different matter."

"Then I am relieved for your sake, my lady."

"I was just discussing with Lord Rothsay his large family. Do you have many relatives yourself, my lord?"

Lord Edgecombe cast her a sceptical look, which caused Rose to feel the colour rising in her cheeks. "Of course, my lord, I am well aware of your family, such as your father, the Earl of Trent, I just meant..." At this she trailed off in confusion and embarrassment.

Lord Anthony appeared to be uncertain as to why she was asking about this, but he seemed to find her confusion perfectly charming. He chuckled. "Have no fear, my lady, I think I understand. You mean to ask how much of my family I am actually close with, do you not?"

Rose, still blushing, was unsure if that was exactly what she meant but nodded anyway.

Lord Anthony still grinned as he continued, "I do have many relatives, but we were not an overly close family when I was a youngster. My mother died when I was a boy and then my father remarried. My brothers and sisters are much younger than me. It is difficult to be close to them when they are away at school most of the time and I am in London much of the year."

"I am so sorry about your mother. That must have been so difficult. Losing my brother was hard enough — I cannot imagine losing a parent at a young age." Rose's soft heart went out to him and it stirred up her own grief. Her eyes brimmed with tears.

"Oh no, my lady, I beg of you. It just will not do for you to cry at the Rotherham ball. I shall never receive another invitation if it becomes known that I made someone weep." Anthony looked so distressed that it brought a watery chuckle to Rose's lips.

"No, no, my lord, have no fear, I shall not weep, I promise you." Rose managed to muster her composure quite quickly, a fact for which she was very proud of herself.

Rose could see that the viscount was reluctant to discuss the matter further, but he kindly asked, "Your grief is still very fresh, is it not?"

"It is," Rose admitted. "It has been three years, but no one ever wants to talk about him with me, so it feels rather raw. My parents especially cannot bear to even hear his name mentioned. And my other brother is away so I hardly ever see him and of course, I cannot discuss Luke with him." Rose could feel her lip quiver so she gave a little laugh to disguise it.

Anthony looked at her with knowing eyes but declined to comment. Rose was relieved when she noticed the set was nearly over. She spied Lady Anne in the crowd surrounding the dance floor.

"Oh my lord, there is my friend, Lady Anne. She would no doubt be a good partner for you to dance with next." Rose felt her cheeks warming over her forward behaviour, but she held the viscount's eye unflinchingly with a slight smile touching her lips.

Lord Edgecombe looked at Lady Anne and smiled just as Lord Dunbar came to invite Rose to share the next dance with him, thus freeing Lord Anthony from the need to keep her company.

Rose watched as Lord Edgecombe swept Anne onto the dance floor. She hoped she was doing neither of them a disservice.

"Is everything all right with you, Miss Rose? You look a little troubled," Wesley inquired with a concerned crease in his forehead.

"All right and tight," Rose replied with as genuine a smile as she could muster. "It has just been an eventful day and I am feeling a trifle overtaxed."

"Would you rather we sit out this number? I would be happy to procure you a glass of punch or ratafia?"

"That is such a kind offer, my lord, but I am perfectly happy to dance this number instead. I am not physically overtired," she explained without going into detail.

She wished she had just accepted his offer, as she could see his thought processes circling around her words, no doubt reading more into them than she would wish.

With a huff of exasperation, she launched into an explanation. "If you really must know, I shall tell you."

"No, no, my lady, I did not wish to pry," he protested, with a gleam of amusement in his eyes.

"You absolutely *did* wish to pry. You were just too polite to do so," she countered with her own amusement rising. "The thing is, I made the mistake of asking a few gentlemen about their families this evening." At seeing the puzzled look upon the viscount's face, she smiled with genuine amusement. "Seems unexceptional, does it not? But Lord Edgecombe told me his mother passed away when he was a youngster, and that reminded me about my brother and how no one ever talks about him and I really miss him. It stirred up a murky mess of feelings that cannot be easily sorted in a place such as this. I do believe Lord Edgecombe will be avoiding me like the plague from now on."

Wesley and Rose shared a small laugh over her last words but then Wesley sobered and made her a generous offer. "I know you probably cannot speak with Wrentham on this subject and I am a poor substitute. But if you would like, I would be happy to talk to you about your brother. At some other time, of course."

Rose grinned. "Did you know my brother well?"

"Not as well as Wrentham and his brother, but we did spend a couple years at school together. And I was there."

He did not elaborate, but Rose knew exactly what he was referring to. She looked at him with widened eyes. "Then I will happily take you up on your offer, my lord, thank you ever so much. When this situation with Alex is sorted perhaps we could meet in some perfectly respectable location. My parents would have apoplexy if they were to catch us in such a conversation, so it would be impossible at my house."

"Very well. I will call around to take you for a drive some time."

"That would be lovely. Thank you, my lord." Rose was grateful for the viscount's offer but at that moment she wished to be alone or at least far away from him, and the sympathy and curiosity she could see shining in his eyes. While she wanted to hear what he might have to say about the day her brother died, she had a strong feeling it was going to complicate her life, not simplify it. But then she gave her head a shake, thinking it was hardly possible for it to get any more complicated than it currently was with her involvement with Wrentham and Broderick's schemes.

Thinking about him must have conjured him, as Rose once again felt the familiar prickle at the back of her neck indicating the duke was present and most likely looking her way. Her eyes were drawn to his. She didn't want to acknowledge him, but the magnetic pull was impossible to resist. All the sounds and chaos in the busy ball room fell away, and for a moment she felt as though they were the only two in the room. She felt her eyes widen as Alex stepped in her direction. Feeling the breath catch in the back of her throat helped to break the spell that had befallen her and she tore her eyes away. The flutter in her stomach was not as easy to control but she was proud of herself as she turned back to Lord Dunbar with a neutral smile upon her face. The buzzing in her ears was hard to ignore and she truly wished this night was over.

Wesley must have sensed her discomfort. "Are you promised to someone else for the next dance, or would you like me to escort you to your mother, or perhaps to procure a glass of punch?"

Rose's smile was genuine as she appreciated his kindness. "A glass of punch would be most delightful at this moment, thank you, my lord."

Walking away from the moment, Rose felt profound relief. Blessedly, the rest of the night slid by and before long her mother came to collect her.

Chapter Ten

It had been a restless, uncomfortable night and Rose was not feeling at all refreshed when Mary gently shook her awake.

"Good morning, Miss Rose, you mentioned you wanted to go sketching again this morning. Have you changed your mind or would you like me to help you dress?"

"Thank you, Mary. While I would dearly love to pull the covers back over my head, I really must get up and go. I would appreciate my chocolate as soon as possible."

"I will ring for it, Miss, and then help you dress. You can drink your chocolate while I arrange your hair."

"You are the very best! Thank you, that is a perfect plan."

Before long Rose was hurrying toward Burlington House with her sketch materials under her arm and her maid in tow. The butterflies fluttering in her stomach made her glad she had not eaten anything more than her morning's chocolate.

She was fairly certain she was the first one to arrive, so she settled herself to do some actual sketching to lend credence to this errand. She didn't think she would be able to concentrate on the art, but before long she was fully engrossed. She could not help the little shriek she let out when she felt a tap on her shoulder. Blessedly, she had a steady hand and did not mar her picture. That would have been difficult to explain.

"Oh, Your Grace, you fairly scared the life out of me," she declared with unfeigned drama.

"Sorry, Rosie, I thought you were expecting me," he grinned, unrepentant.

"Well, of course, I was," she huffed. "I just was unsure how prompt you would be and I will admit I got caught up in this sketch."

"You were always like that — you would get so wrapped up in whatever you were doing, even as a child. Your powers of concentration are admirable. And you really have become remarkably skilled with your art. I am impressed."

Rose bit her lip to prevent the grin of delight that was threatening to break over her face at his awkward compliment. It was truly lamentable that he caused such unprecedented reactions in her. They had always been so comfortable with one another. She really did not think these fluttery feelings had anything to do with their families' feud. It was most disconcerting. She cleared her throat in an effort to dispel the discomfort.

☙ ❧

Alex could see that Rose was uncomfortable with his presence. He was unsure if it were the reminders of their former friendship and intertwined childhood or if it was just him. Knowing she was uncomfortable, he thought he ought not to prolong the moment, but contrarily, he found that he would happily spend more time. He felt such a longing for their former closeness. Stifling a sigh, he got to the point.

"Have you been able to glean any information from Lady Anne?"

"I have, actually. You will be happy to learn that I think the lady is actually a rather sweet young woman who is not maliciously pursuing you. She has been persuaded by her father that her best chance at attaining an advantageous match is to entrap the gentleman of her choice. Lord Austen has convinced her that you are the best choice for her. He and Sir Broderick discussed together the qualifications of various gentlemen, according to Lady Anne. They agreed that you were the best choice because of your connections, she said. Anne is under the impression that her father means your family connections."

"But you are not so sure about that, are you?"

"I really don't think Sir Broderick cares who your relatives are. You are a prize because of your political connections."

The slight emphasis she placed on the word *political* caused Alex to frown. "But I am new to my position in the House and have not been able to make many connections, as you call it. I am hardly a prize. Why would you say that?"

"But you are a duke," she answered simply, which only made his frown deepen.

"But I am not royal," he protested, still confused.

"All the better, as your pockets are decidedly not to let. As a duke, you are high enough on the power scale that people will listen to you, even if you are inexperienced. The fact that you are not royal will not matter. The royal dukes can rarely be bothered to pay any attention to the running of the country anyway. You are the next best thing. Your lack of real connections will probably make you even more attractive for one such as Broderick, as he would like to guide the choices you will make in where you will place your allegiance. Your deep pockets mean you will be able to accomplish whatever you set your mind to. The more I think on it, the more I see that you really would be a prize catch for someone like him."

Alex could hear the sneer that she was obviously struggling to control and gazed at her with wonder as she continued. "It is a wretchedly perfect plan, actually. He will think you are easily influenced because you are young and inexperienced. Now is the perfect time to get their clutches into you. And how better than to do so through your wife?"

"But I do not have a wife," Alex pointed out, still not understanding what she was getting at. He saw her eyes soften as she took in his confusion.

"Not yet, but that is what they are hoping to soon rectify." Rose reached out a tentative hand to touch his. "I am so sorry, Alex, I should say, Your Grace. I wish I could have told you there was nothing to what I had overheard. Sadly, I fear that you are actually in grave danger."

"They would not actually harm me, I am certain. Even if they should try, I am well able to look after myself."

"If it were a fair fight, I fully believe that you could look after yourself. But Broderick would never fight fair. He will use what he considers your weaknesses against you. One of those is the fact that you are a gentleman. That is why it is a perfect plot. All Lady Anne has to do is ensure you are caught in a compromising situation and no matter the truth of the matter, you will feel honour bound to offer for her."

"But what makes them think that even if I fell for the ruse I would be willing to be their pawn?"

"He can be very manipulative," Rose answered with a simple shrug.

Alex felt his eyes narrow into suspicion. "How do you know all this? I am beginning to get the feeling you know a whole lot more than you are letting on. Out with it, Rosie. Tell me what you know about Lord Austen and Sir Broderick."

The colour ebbed and flowed over Rose's face, and Alex was further convinced she was keeping things from him. His frustration grew when she shook her head and refused to answer him. She merely had a question of her own.

"What about you, Your Grace, were you able to find out anything from your men of affairs or your solicitors? Perhaps I am completely off the mark. Maybe they really are after you for revenge for some perceived wrong you might have done one of them."

Alex did not take offense, as he saw the amused gleam in her eyes over her own words. "Unfortunately, none of my advisors could enlighten me in the least. Your words are the only ones that have made even a little bit of sense. Unfortunately, they do not bring me to a complete understanding. You really do need to enlighten me."

"Actually, I do not owe you anything, Your Grace. I have done more than my duty by warning you and then trying to gain more information. The rest will be up to you. I can have no more involvement with you."

"Why ever not, Rosie? You have gone this far, surely you would want to see it to the end."

"It matters not," Rose insisted, verging on belligerence, much to Alex's consternation.

"What has gotten into you? You were perfectly pleasant just a few minutes ago. This would seem to be right in your wheelhouse. With your managing ways, I would think you would love to be involved. Now you look as though you would happily walk away and never set eyes on me for the rest of your days. Have I done something to offend you?"

☙ ❧

Now Rose felt about as high as a toad. She could not reveal all that she knew. She would rather him think it was because of the feud than for him to have a disgust of her. And surely, he would do so if he ever came to find out how she knew all that she did about Sir Broderick.

"I am sorry, Your Grace, you shall have to fend for yourself from now on. I have told you all I know about Lady Anne and her schemes. If you are careful to avoid her and make sure you are never in a situation where she could arrange for the two of you to be alone together, you should be able to avoid this trap altogether."

"But Rosamund, think on it for a moment. For one thing, how can I possibly live with this hanging over me like a guillotine about to strike and leave me headless? And for another, if I manage to escape her clutches and you are correct in your reasoning as to their motivations, will they not simply set their sights on someone else for whatever their ultimate schemes are? Do you not want to foil their efforts completely? If he is as nefarious as you make him sound, should we not endeavour to eliminate him as a threat to our nation?"

Rose felt her gaze arrested upon his words. He had an excellent point. Broderick did need to be stopped, or at least contained. It would be best if someone with some sort of power or ability could ascertain what his ultimate plan was. She had no doubt that the man was up to no good, but she was in no position to be able to do anything about it. And her father would definitely insist on hearing the entire story. But she so did not want to tell Alex about the Vienna part of her tale. And her knowledge of the one was so intertwined with the other.

Her conflicted feelings must have clearly shown on her face because Alex pressed his advantage. His face softened as his eyes searched hers. "Tell me, Rosie, what worries you? Why can you not confide in me on this? I swear to you, I will not reveal any of your secrets."

Rose wavered in her convictions. "I do trust you, Alex, Your Grace," she started, stammering a little as her throat clogged with her feelings. "It is not only my secrets that I keep. And I know you, Alex. You hate secrets and anything that smacks of subterfuge. I cherish the memories of our childhood friendship, despite the difficulty that now exists between our families. If I tell you everything, I fear that our memories will be tainted."

She felt her blush rising in her cheeks and her breath hitched in her throat once more as Alex reached out a tentative finger and tilted her chin to force her to look him in the eye.

"The Rosie I knew would never keep a secret from me, and that was all I ever cared about. I know you, just as you know me. It is true that I hate any falsehood. You know the reasons why. Even though three years have passed, I know you could not have changed overmuch and you are nothing like my father. Any secrets or subterfuge you may have been a party to,

I trust that there was a good enough reason to merit your involvement. You can trust me to maintain a sufficiently open mind that I would not judge you harshly without getting all the facts."

Tears welled in Rose's eyes and she threw herself into Alex's arms. She felt safe and warm as his arms closed tightly around her. She allowed her tears to flow for a moment and basked in the rightness of the sensation before comfort blended into deeper, warmer feelings, and she drew back abruptly as the butterflies took up their fluttering once more in her belly. Feeling her cheeks heating fiercely she pushed herself from his arms.

ശ ಌ

"I apologize, Your Grace. That was highly improper and forward of me. I assure you wholeheartedly that I am not imitating Lady Anne's strategy and trying to entrap you myself."

"Perish the thought," was Alex's dry reply. He let her go with reluctance, gratified to see that the bonds of their friendship were still truly there. It was going to be a challenge, but he determined in that moment that he was going to find a way to preserve their relationship in the future. "Have I reassured you enough for you to unburden yourself?"

"How did you know it is burdening me? I thought I was doing such a good job of keeping my troubles to myself."

"You are," he soothed. "Up until this moment, I was not certain that you *were* troubled. But I surmised your tears were of relief, and while I have a sufficiently good opinion of myself, I do not think your relief was merely due to my promise not to judge you. You have always been of strong enough character that you would defy my thoughts if they were not to your liking."

Rose grinned over his words. "You are quite right, Your Grace." She stuck to formality despite the unorthodox partnership they were sharing. Alex had to struggle to keep from growling his frustration.

"What parts am I right about?"

Now Rose allowed a watery chuckle to escape her throat. "All of it really, Your Grace. I am relieved by your promise to hear me out. But of greater relief is the prospect of sharing my concerns with someone. Particularly someone who is in a position to help, or at least someone who can strategize with me as to what is to be done." Rose heaved a sigh. "The trouble is that it is such a complicated situation, and I do not think I have the time to explain it all."

"I understand. Start with the basics. If need be, we can meet again."

A soft, wistful smile now graced Rose's lips, and it was Alex's turn to feel the breath catch in his throat at the sight. She reached out a tentative hand and placed it gently on his sleeve. "Thank you, Alex. You have no idea how much I appreciate your offer. I know it cannot be comfortable for you to have me around. To offer to spend even more time in my presence is truly generous of you."

Alex kept his smile contained, not wishing to reveal how little of a challenge it was for him to spend any time with her. "You had best get started — your maid will be coming to fetch you before long."

This caused Rose to glance around the large, empty room. "She is the only one I have trusted with this information, to be honest with you, Your Grace, so I have no concerns about her return, aside from the lecture she will no doubt feel the need to give me for divulging my secrets to another." Rose again looked around with concern. "Do you think we will be overheard, Your Grace?"

"I really do wish you would stop calling me 'Your Grace' at every turn," Alex complained, but did not dwell on the matter. "To be perfectly honest with you, at this hour of the morning I do not think we need fear the presence of anyone who would care to eavesdrop on our conversation. I have not seen anyone about the entire time we have been talking."

"All right, if you are sure."

Rose still looked hesitant, so Alex reached out and clasped her hand between both of his. "I am sure."

"After the tragedy," Rose began rather shakily. She paused to gather her thoughts, grateful that Alex gave her hand an encouraging squeeze. After clearing her throat, she tried again. "As you know, my father is a diplomat representing our government's interests in negotiations with other governments. Usually, my mother would remain at home with us children while Father would be away for months on end. After the tragedy, it was decided that we would accompany my father to Vienna. There was to be a Congress of all the great nations to negotiate a means of maintaining peace, instead of the constant warring that has been taking place for the past twenty years or so."

Rose again paused, wracking her brain as to how to continue. Alex encouraged her with his quiet words. "Did you enjoy Vienna?"

"Very much so," she began with more enthusiasm. "It is such a beautiful city. It was a good distraction from the troubles in our family. We had left my little brother at school at first, so it was just my parents and me. My mother was prostrate with her grief at first. It gave me the opportunity to get to know my father a little better, since I had so rarely spent any time with him in years prior.

"He confided in me his worries over the Congress and interested me in the negotiations. I found it fascinating. I so wanted to be of assistance to him as he, too, was weighed down with his grief, besides the weight of the government's expectations. It turned out that so much of the negotiating was done in the drawing rooms and ballrooms of the wellborn Society that had accompanied the negotiators. I finally found a way to be of assistance to my father." Rose blushed and hesitated before continuing. "I imagined that I was doing my part for the king. In hindsight it is rather silly, and I did not have much of an influence on any outcomes, but at the time it felt so very serious."

"What did, Rosie, my dear?" Alex prompted, hoping she would be able to get over her nerves and get to the point.

"I became the ears for my father. So many would clam up if Lord Smythe was in the room, but Miss Rosamund was just a girl with nothing between her ears but the latest fashions or the newest dances. Many things could be discussed, particularly in foreign languages, *sotto voce*, of course, but out in the open. Little did anyone know that languages were my forte, and that I really could not give a fig about the cut of anyone's dress. The dances were another story of course—being in Vienna was marvellous for the dancing. London has nothing on Vienna for that, I am sorry to say."

"What sort of things did you hear and pass on to your father, Rose? Does it have some bearing on our current situation?" Alex was enjoying hearing her ramble but knew their time was running out.

"When Tallyrand arrived in Vienna, the atmosphere changed. He forced his way to the negotiating table for France. That man is as slippery as an eel, and I would not trust him with my worst enemy, let alone my best friend. Sir Broderick became associates with him. I am not sure how Sir Broderick even got involved with the Congress, but he insinuated himself into as many situations as he could. Procuring invitations to every social event and toadying to the hostesses. He became quite popular, especially with the French and the Germans."

Rose took another deep breath to steady her nerves before getting to the crux of the matter. "One evening, at an event much like the musicale, I was again sitting near some sort of a shrubby fern or something, mayhap I was obscured from view, I assure you it was not by design."

"It is all right, Rosie, get on with it. I promise you, I am not disgusted yet, and do not see that eventuality coming."

Rose grinned over Alex's choice of words and did get on with it. "I overheard Broderick and Tallyrand scheming how to ensure France did not have to give over too much territory to England. I cannot tell you how I managed to maintain my composure and not reveal that I was there and hearing what was being said. I have never in all my days been witness to such treachery and I hope to never again be forced to do so. I listened for all I was worth to the scheme they were concocting. After they were gone, I made my way as discreetly as possible to Father's side and indicated I needed to retire for the evening. On the drive to our home I told him all that I had heard. He was able to mitigate their schemes to a certain extent, but Tallyrand still managed to gain so much power for France. And Broderick remains free to concoct more schemes. From what I understand, he argued that he was trying to ensure that we remained fully informed by playing a double agent. I do not believe that for a single second. Double dealing is his favourite game, and he is up to his old tricks here and now, and somehow he has decided to involve you." By the end of this speech Rose was worked up and agitated over the entire messy situation.

Rose could feel Alex's searching gaze burning into her skin and could barely meet his eyes. She knew she was again on the verge of tears and had no idea how to relieve the situation. Feeling she had said quite enough, she desperately wished he would break the brief silence that had ensued. She did not have to wait too long.

"The thing I do not understand is why you thought I would disapprove of this. It seems to me as though you did our government a huge favour." Rose could hear the perplexity clearly in his voice.

"But I intentionally allowed people to think I was empty headed in the hopes that they would reveal information that I could pass on to my father. Basically, Your Grace, I was a spy. Does that not give you a disgust of me? It is hardly a suitable occupation for a lady."

"I fear I must be missing a few details because what you have thus far explained is really much the same as many ladies are involved in here in our own salons and ballrooms during the Season. All the gossiping is really the rehashing of things people have been told or have overheard. It is a highly acceptable activity in our Society."

"But not to you," Rose answered in a soft voice.

"Rosie, my dear, you were not participating in such activities out of a salacious desire to have the latest *on-dits*. You were performing an important service for your father and his negotiations. It is a very different thing in my estimation. What about the various gentlemen who have joined the war efforts but have been redirected towards spying? It is much the same thing. It is a necessary part of information gathering. Unfortunately, those are usually the heroes that go unsung. Just like you. It would seem no one is aware of your involvement, are they?"

"No, of course not." Rose was horrified at the thought.

"Not even Broderick?" Alex probed.

"Oh heavens, no. Can you imagine if he did? He would have been out to get me for sure. And he would be sure to use the information to ruin me. I appreciate that you have made the effort to see the positive side of my activity, but surely you see how it could be twisted into something else altogether."

"I do. But you will have to put that from your mind for now, my dear. It seems to me that the information you have shared with me today merely reinforces the fact that Broderick needs to be stopped. If we merely thwart Lord Austen's plan to entrap me into a marriage with Lady Anne, I do not doubt that they will just set their sights on someone else. We need to ensure all gentlemen are safe from whatever Broderick is after."

"It would really help if we knew what he was trying to accomplish. Do you think it could be anything to do with the French? Tallyrand has continued to reinforce his position now that Bonaparte is finally locked up." Rose nibbled on her lip with concern as she contemplated the possibilities.

Alex forced his eyes not to focus on her lips. "We shall have to do some digging to find out. Now that I am more fully informed of what we are looking for I will ask my man of affairs to look into it. Previously, they were merely looking for threats toward me and could find nothing. But as you have pointed out, it is nothing personal between Broderick and me, I am merely expedient."

Rose grinned at this. "Please do not take that to heart, Your Grace, I mean Alex," she stumbled before carrying on, "You would not want Broderick after you personally anyway."

Alex returned her grin. "You have a good point there, my dear."

Rose's smile turned wistful. "You have no idea how relieved I am to share this burden. When I realized Broderick must be up to something once more, I was so worried about it. I wanted to tell my father but…" At this she trailed off.

Alex's understanding smile nearly broke Rose's heart. "But you were afraid he would be unable to see beyond my involvement in the matter."

Rose nodded. "That was my fear, yes. That is why I thought to help you ensure you were safe from their plots, then when you were out of the situation, I could get my father involved."

"Do you not think he would want to know how you came by this information? No matter what happens with me, you cannot change the fact that you found out about it because of the conversation you overheard with regards to their plot to entrap me."

"I know. I have not yet come up with a solution to that dilemma—thus my great relief in being able to unburden myself to you. Mayhap I shall not have to involve my father at all if we can manage to solve it on our own."

"Do you have any ideas as to how we are going to do so? I will admit to you that I am woefully inexperienced in the skills needed to thwart someone scheming against the government."

Rose wrinkled her nose at Alex's words and chewed her lip again in concentration. "I think at this point we really need more information. It would be most helpful if you could find out more about Broderick's associates — who he is involved with could tell us a lot. I will also speak to Lady Yorkleigh. The night of the musicale she seemed to indicate she had information about Broderick and was endeavouring to warn me away from him. I do not wish to involve any more people, so I will try to find out what she knows without revealing what I know. I have a plan in mind, but it does involve a bit more subterfuge." She said this last bit with a tone of apology. Alex was quick to protest.

"My dear, I have already assured you that this is clearly in the defence of our country. Spy away, if you think that will help."

"Thank you, Your Grace." Rose could feel her face stretching into a smile that revealed her dimples. She felt so light and happy after unburdening her soul and finding that Alex did not turn away in disgust from her. The relief she felt was truly profound and she felt as though she could fly home. Then she remembered her promise to Elizabeth and her face fell.

"What is the trouble now?" Alex asked, amusement and exasperation both showing in his tone of voice.

Rose shrugged. "I just remembered that my friend Elizabeth knew I would be meeting you today and wanted me to come to see her afterward. She helped me gain the information from Lady Anne so I feel as though I owe her, but I do not want her involved in the situation with Broderick any more than she already is. I shall have to skirt around some of the facts, which makes me a trifle uncomfortable."

Alex grinned at her with far more amusement than sympathy, which caused her to pull a sour face at him in return. He was still chuckling when Rose's maid arrived.

Eyeing the duke suspiciously Mary asked, "Are you nearly finished, Miss? We should be getting on our way pretty soon."

"Thank you, Mary, I just need to gather up my things. Could you please help me finish up?"

Mary kept a suspicious eye on Alex while she hurried to tidy Rose's drawing supplies. "You didn't get much done today, Miss," she scolded, much to Alex's amusement and Rose's embarrassment.

"The muse did not strike me today, Mary. Now, we should be on our way. Thank you for your help." Turning to Alex, Rose dipped into a respectful curtsy, suddenly feeling bashful.

Alex took her small hand into his much larger one, placing a kiss delicately on the back of it. "Until tomorrow," he said with a questioning lift to his voice.

Rose shook her head. "You had best give me an extra day to see what I can gather. Let us say two days hence."

"I shall make every effort to contain my impatience," Alex replied with complete honesty, feeling a deep disappointment that they would not be seeing one another for a couple of days. For a moment, he wished fervently that their friendship did not need to be kept a secret, but now there were even more reasons why that was necessary.

He stood watching as the two girls hurried away from him. He was gratified when Rose stopped at the entrance and turned back to look at him. As their eyes met and held for an inexplicably long second, he felt his heart rate pick up as though he had been running. Trying to remain unmoved, he lifted his hand in a small wave. She looked slightly flustered as she turned back to hurry after her maid.

Alex looked around the room at the fragmented statues that Elgin had inexplicably brought back to England. He shook his head over the folly of men and then strode from the room. He had things to learn and places to be.

Chapter Eleven

"Miss Rose, are you certain it's fittin' for you to be meeting with His Grace, the duke? You know how your parents would react were they to find out. Not only about who he is, but about you meeting up with him. I know you've been arguing that it's a public place and no harm will come of it, but it don't seem so public when there's not a soul stirring at the odd hours you've been going there."

"I pray you, do not scold me, Mary. The situation is troublesome enough without you lecturing me. I do realize my parents would have apoplexy or disown me or some such. That is why we must ensure they never find out. I trust Alex, I mean the duke, and I truly need someone I can trust right now. You know how Broderick is. He needs to be dealt with. And because of how I heard about it, I cannot trust my father to be reasonable. This is the only way for the moment."

"If you are certain, Miss," was all Mary would allow with a slight sniff of disapproval.

Rose grinned. "Thank you, Mary. I would never be able to do it without you. You are the important factor in all of this. You always are. Now be a dear and hurry along. I promised Elizabeth we would stop in today, and I really must return home to break my fast and look in on Mother."

"Oh Miss, I plum forgot you hadn't eaten. You must be near to perishing."

"My stomach was too nervous this morning to be able to eat anything. But you are quite correct that now I am absolutely ravenous. I certainly hope the kitchen has not completely cleared away the breakfast dishes."

"If they have, Miss, I will make sure you get something, have no fear."

"Thank you, Mary." Rose smiled her gratitude at her trusted maid just as they reached their stairs.

"Hello, Hartley, how are you on this fine day?" she greeted the butler as he welcomed them home.

"You seem chipper this morning, Miss Rose. It does not strike me as being that fair today."

"No day really is in London, is it, Hartley? That is why one must ignore the day and decide that one's contentment is dependent on their state of mind. I have decided that today is fine and I am happy with or without the sunshine."

"Very well, Miss," Hartley replied with an indulgent smile.

"Is anyone else about yet today?"

"Your father has already left to go about his business and your mother has not yet left her rooms. Can I do anything to assist you, Miss?"

"I would dearly like to have something to eat. Do you know if breakfast has been cleared away as yet?"

"I do not believe it has, Miss."

"Thank you, Hartley, you just made my day." With a grin, Rose handed the rest of her pencils to her waiting maid and hurried to the dining room to assuage her hunger.

A short while later, after eating, changing, and having her hair tidied by Mary, Rose made her way to her mother's room. After scratching on the door, she was admitted by Lady Smythe's personal maid.

"Good morning, Priscilla, how are you this morning?" she asked kindly.

"I am fair to middlin', Miss, thank you for asking."

"Is my mama up and about yet?"

"I was just about to do her hair," the maid answered as Lady Smythe called out, "Priscilla, who are you dithering with? If that is the maid with my tray, bring it in."

"Good morning, Mama, it is me holding Priscilla up, I am sorry to admit. And I do not have your chocolate or toast. Would you like me to run down to the kitchens and get it for you?"

"Good morning, Rosamund. No, that is quite all right. Priscilla has already rung but it was kind of you to offer." Lady Smythe went through the motions of living her life, but her heart was clearly not in it as she spoke with a melancholy, put-upon voice.

"I wanted to check with you if you needed me today. I was going to go visit briefly with Lady Elizabeth, but I could not remember if we had any plans."

"No, no, Rosamund, you go right ahead. It is nice that you have found a friend to help keep you occupied. You have so much more energy than I can muster, so it is good for you to have others your age about."

Lady Smythe's tone made Rose feel as though this were an accusation rather than a compliment and she struggled for a reply. "Well, if you are certain you shan't miss me, then I will scamper over to Elizabeth's for a wee spell." Rose's flippant chatter made her mother sigh, which Rose chose to ignore as she continued. "I will take Mary along with me as I might make some other calls before I come home. I have some correspondence to take care of this afternoon, and then it will be time to get ready for the evening." Rose could see that her mother's attention was not fully engaged, but she persisted nonetheless. "Do you not find it droll how we seem even busier than we are at home and yet we get so little done with our days here in Town?"

"What is that, my dear?" Lady Smythe asked distractedly.

"Naught of import, Mama. I shall wish you a good day and I will see you this evening." With that, Rose gave up trying to engage her mother in conversation and made good her escape with a faint sigh of her own. It was a tragedy that she had, in essence, lost her mother at the same time as losing her brother.

Returning to her room, she collected her own maid. "Come along, Mary, I am fairly certain I shall have need of you."

"Very well, Miss," the maid answered with a grin. "Are we going spying again?" she asked, with a skip in her step and her voice hushed.

Rose had to giggle over the other woman's enthusiasm and attitude, which was so different from her own. "Most likely," she answered, annoyingly vague.

"Will you at least promise to tell me if you find out anything that could be of use to us?" Mary asked, not bothering to keep the plaintive tone from her voice.

"That is a promise I can keep," Rose answered with conviction. "I always find it useful to discuss everything with you. You have a good head on your shoulders, and I know you will not run and tattle."

"Of course not, Miss."

The two hurried along and once more found themselves in front of Elizabeth's parents' lovely townhouse. Just before they climbed the stairs, Rose thought to tell Mary, "I have no certain idea how long we shall be here. I am hoping to not have to tell Elizabeth everything about my meeting with the duke. I think it is in her best interests to remain ignorant of the details. I hope my playacting skills are up to snuff, as I would hate to harm the friendship over this nonsense."

Mary gave her mistress's arm a squeeze of reassurance. "I know you have your reservations about your involvement with these shenanigans, but your skills are still sharp, Miss, and you are actually good at this kind of thing, which is not what one would expect of a well-born chit like yourself."

The two conspirators shared a grin as they climbed the stairs. Mary went off to join the servants below stairs as the butler went to announce Rose.

"The Honourable Rosamund Smythe to see you, my lady," he intoned properly.

"Thank you, Francis, please show her in," Elizabeth replied, keeping her excitement in check.

Once the door was closed behind her guest, Elizabeth bounded up from her place on the settee. "I have been pacing a trail in the rug all morning, as I have been running to check the window every few moments. Did you see him? Was your meeting a success? Do we have a plan to proceed with?"

Rose grinned over her friend's words. "I am so sorry for keeping you on tenterhooks. I was so nervous this morning that I could not eat before my arranged meeting, so I had to go straight home afterward in order to not faint on your front stairs upon my arrival."

"You would not have been the first to do so," Elizabeth dismissed with a wave of her hand.

Rose laughed. "I would not think Francis would be so accepting of that idea."

"Well now that you are finally here, please hurry and sit down and tell me all about it! Was the duke able to shed any light on the matter? Did you tell him what we found out? Did you make a further plan?"

Rose could not help laughing again. "Slow down, my lady, I pray you. Unfortunately, I do not have much solid information to give you. As far as Wrentham could find out from his solicitors and his man of affairs, there is nothing that either Austen or Broderick have against him. So, on the surface it seems as though it is as Lady Anne said—he is just a prime catch for various reasons and they set their sights on him."

Rose could see the disappointment clearly etched on her friend's face. "So, there is nothing further for us to do?" she asked, her tone plaintive.

"I did not say that. I passed along all that we found out from Lady Anne, and Wrentham is determined to be vigilant. It saddens me a trifle because Lady Anne really does seem to be a charming young woman who is merely misguided. I cannot agree with her father's idea. It seems to me that it is a recipe for a disaster of a marriage. You would not think any father would wish that for his daughter."

Now Elizabeth looked pensive about the matter. "So, what can we do?"

"We can be vigilant over the next weeks while out and about. I still cannot feel easy in my heart that Broderick is not up to something. It strikes a strange chord that he would be scheming with someone to entrap a husband for that someone's daughter. Wrentham pointed out that if it is not a love match on her side, they might just set their sights elsewhere. I cannot think this will lead to a happy life for Lady Anne. I propose that we should make an effort to dissuade her from her plans. She should set about getting to know some nice gentlemen and hope one of them makes her an offer that she can be happy with."

Elizabeth nodded her agreement. "It may not be as exciting as sneaking around to find out some information, but it is a sound course of action. And do you think we should keep an eye out for the duke in case we need to defend his honour?"

Now Rose could feel her face shifting into a sceptical expression. "Do you think that would be possible?"

Elizabeth laughed. "I was jesting you, ninny. Although, now that I think on it, I do believe the idea has merit. It would keep him from the parson's mousetrap. Eventually he has to marry someone, but I can tell that your old friendship is still important to you, so I would think you would at least wish it to be a happy union."

"You are absolutely correct on that score. I was just wondering how we could defend him."

"By keeping an eye out for scheming hussies who are trying to entrap him," Elizabeth stated, as though Rose had lost her mind. This led to great hilarity between the two girls, and the subject was slowly changed to other matters.

After a short time, Rose stood to take her leave. "Thank you for being such a great sport on this matter, my dear lady.

Your help was invaluable. I certainly could not have done it without you."

Elizabeth shrugged, dismissing Rose's compliment. "I barely did anything. I am absolutely certain you could have done it on your own—I merely sped up the process. I shall be sure to keep my eyes and ears open for anything pertinent tonight. We are going to the theatre, so there might not be too much to find out there, but there is always lots of gossip floating around at the intermission." Her eyes glinted with excitement. "I have always enjoyed the gossiping because I love to be up to date on the very latest *on-dit*, but now it takes on an entirely new meaning when there could be actual useful information in it."

Rose laughed once more. "You are a dear. I shall see you soon. We are going to a ball this evening that is being held by one of my father's ambassador friends. It shall be anything but dull, although I cannot quite say that I am looking forward to it."

The two girls parted from one another on the best of terms and Rose left, collecting Mary on her way out the door.

"Did you manage to extricate yourself, Miss?" Mary asked, as soon as they were out of earshot of the house.

Rose giggled at the maid's terminology. "I did at that, Mary. Elizabeth is a dear and not at all a suspicious sort. She has no reason to think there would be anything more sinister than a young lady determined to make a good match. No doubt their scheme is not even all that original. We agreed that we should still keep our eyes and ears open for any mention of Broderick and his activities, as well as trying to steer Lady Anne into a more honourable method of making her match."

"That was well done of you, Miss," Mary congratulated. "Where are we off to now? This is not the way home."

"We are going to stop in and see if Lady Yorkleigh is at home to visitors. If she does not have anyone else there, I am going to try to find out if she knows anything of use about Broderick. The fateful night of the musicale she seemed to indicate to me that she had her own reasons for distrusting the man, and it felt as though she were warning me away from him."

"Oh Miss, this is so exciting!" The maid almost squealed before sobering to add, "But you must have a care for yourself, Miss. I fear this could end up being an unsafe situation for your person or your reputation. I know this is important and all, but shouldn't you be keeping in mind that you are here in Town in search of a husband for yourself?"

"Do not fret, Mary. I will have a care, have no fear. Besides, having you along will help to preserve my reputation in whatever situation I might find myself." Rose sighed before continuing. "As to my search for a husband, that is another matter altogether. I know it will need to be done eventually, but I do not think I am in dire need as of yet. Surely my little brother is not about to marry any time soon, so I shan't be the spinster aunt before at least a few years have passed."

"I don't mean you any insult, Miss, but you ain't getting any younger."

"Mayhap not, but I am quite certain that at twenty summers, I am not yet nearing my dotage," Rose huffed.

"True, Miss, but I was trying to say that you should at least keep it in mind."

"I know, Mary, you are quite correct. And I promise you that I shall give it some thought at my earliest convenience. In fact, you could help me, if you so choose."

"How ever could I do that, Miss Rose?" the maid asked, clearly intrigued at the thought.

"You know me better than anyone—you could help me decide what I should consider important traits in my future husband. The rest of my life is a rather long time to live with someone, so I would hate to make a bad choice. My parents will, of course, ensure that he is well enough established to properly support me, so that is not what I wish to concern myself with. I want to look for a man I can respect, and with whom I will enjoy spending time. So many of the gentlemen I have met thus far make me think that a few weeks spent in their company would bore me to tears, never mind the next several decades."

Mary was looking at her mistress with wide, eager eyes. "I will put my mind to it immediately, Miss."

"Thank you, Mary." Rose smiled her appreciation. She congratulated herself on her skilful change of the subject, which also would help her tackle a tricky task that was necessary but intimidating. "I look forward to hearing your insights."

The young maid barely acknowledged her mistress's comment, so engrossed was she in her own thoughts, her mind engaged in the important task.

Rose had a genuine smile of amusement still creasing her face as the door to Lady Yorkeligh's home was opened by an attentive footman. He could not help his answering smile at the pretty young woman on the doorstep.

"Good afternoon, I was wondering if Lady Yorkleigh is at home to visitors today," Rose asked politely.

"May I tell her who is calling?" the footman asked formally.

"The Honorable Rosamund Smythe."

The footman widened the door for her to step into the foyer. "Would you care to have a seat here while I check with her ladyship?"

"Thank you," Rose replied simply.

A moment later, the butler came to collect her. "Her ladyship will be happy to see you. Might I take your wrap for you? Your maid could either wait here for you or go to the kitchens, if you think you are to be a while."

"Thank you." Rose turned to Mary to allow her to choose. "It is up to you, Mary. I might be a while. If you would like, you could make yourself comfortable in the kitchens."

"Thank you, Miss, but I have a lot to think on. If it's all the same to everyone, I'll just sit myself down right here and ponder while you are visiting."

Rose grinned and left her to it, following the butler to a lovely, welcoming receiving room. As he opened the door, Rose could see that it was decorated in the warmest shades of cream and ivory, and while it passed through her mind that it must be terribly difficult to keep clean, she did find it extraordinarily attractive.

"Welcome Miss Rose, it was such a pleasant surprise to hear that you were asking to see me."

"I hope I am not disturbing you, my lady."

"Not at all, I was actually just wishing that I had arranged something to amuse me today, and then I heard the knocker and was hoping it was somebody interesting. To my delight, it was you."

Rose could feel a slight blush of delight rising in her cheeks over the older woman's pleasant welcome.

"That is so kind of you to say, my lady," she began with deference.

"Oh, do not be so starchy with me, young miss. I am determined that we are to be friends. Now come and sit down, and let me ring for some tea so that we can be comfortable."

Rose did as she was bidden and perched delicately on the settee, fearful because it looked too fragile to be useful. Thankfully, its appearance was deceptive and it turned out to be remarkably comfortable. She soon settled in for her visit.

The two ladies exchanged idle chitchat about the weather and what amusements they had attended the evening before while they waited for the tea trolley to be brought in. Once the housekeeper had brought it in and served her mistress and guest and then bustled from the room, the countess sat back comfortably with her teacup and eyed her guest carefully.

"Now, Miss Rosamund Smythe, what brings you to my parlour on this fine fall day?"

"Well, my lady, you did mention at your musicale that I was welcome to return at any time," Rose began, a little flustered.

"Indeed I did, and I am delighted that you have acted on that sincere invitation. But it strikes me that there must be a reason, as it has been about a week since I uttered it. If it was merely to cultivate our developing friendship, I would think you would have turned up sooner."

Seeing that her guest was becoming even more flustered by her words, the countess hurried to add, "I am not complaining or censuring you, my dear girl, I am merely stating the facts as I see them. I am delighted that you have finally turned up at my door. I am merely curious what has prompted it."

"My dear Lady Yorkleigh, since you were so kind as to invite me to visit, I was looking forward to speaking with you further. I apologize profusely that I did not come a couple days ago, as you invited, for your at-home."

Lady Yorkleigh waved away her apology so Rose promptly continued. "But you are correct that there has been something that has prompted the timing. It is a rather delicate subject and I hesitate to impose upon you."

"Please, my dear Miss Rose, I welcome your imposition, or rather, it is no imposition at all. I am ready to be of service."

Rose now felt a touch more relaxed over the countess' droll words and so, smiling, she launched into her tale, very nearly telling the truth. "At your lovely musicale I had the dubious pleasure of becoming reintroduced to Sir Jason Broderick. I have taken the gentleman in dislike and did not relish cultivating the acquaintance. Unfortunately, my mother has decided that she thinks he might be a fine catch for me, that as a baron's daughter I should not think to look too highly for a mate and that a knight might make me an excellent husband."

Lady Yorkleigh refrained from commenting at this point, and Rose continued her explanation. "Now do not get me wrong, my lady, I am not opposed to a knight. I am not overly concerned with a gentleman's status or trying to improve my own through my marriage. I am perfectly content to be a Miss or Mistress. The trouble is with Sir Broderick himself. He strikes me as being a rather repellent man. But I do not have any facts to back this up in an argument with my mother. Since you, yourself, warned me away from him at your musicale, I thought that perhaps you could share something useful with me."

The countess had continued to look at Rose steadily throughout this speech, holding her own counsel and not betraying much of her thoughts by even the twitch of an eyebrow. Rose was admiring her ability to keep herself contained, but then was distracted by the lady's words.

"I mean no offense, my dear, but is your mother daft?"

Rose burst into raucous laughter. After a moment, she was able to control her mirth. Wiping the tears that had escaped during her hilarity, Rose finally was able to reply. "My lady, I have on occasion wondered that myself but, no, I do not believe she has lost her wits, she is merely of a different mind than I am."

"But, my dear, this is far more serious than just a matter of taste. I can, if I make a concerted effort to be unbiased, see that some might consider Sir Broderick to be handsome, but the man is a snake under his skin. Clearly your mother has not taken the time to even have a conversation with the man or she would have disabused herself of the notion of marrying you off to him. Not that he would want you."

At Rose's faint gasp over this surprising statement, the countess finally found her smile. "I can assure you, I did not just insult you. The man has no taste for ladies with any thoughts of their own in their head. To be honest, I strongly doubt that he is in search of a wife for himself, but from what I have observed, the only ladies he ever dances with are very fresh from the schoolroom, with very large dowries to recommend them."

"You have partially set my mind at ease in that case, my lady. I have found a reason to be happy that I am becoming a trifle long in the tooth."

"You are nowhere near being on the shelf, so do not be a ninny," Lady Yorkleigh countered, with a wry twist to her lips.

"But if my mother insists that I set my cap at the man, do you know anything that I could use to dissuade her?"

"You could always just be very unskilled at cap setting," the countess suggested with a twinkle in her eye. "But in all seriousness, Miss Rose, there are a few things. Is your mother in the habit of gossiping?"

"Not overmuch," Rose replied, puzzled.

"The reason I ask is because some of the things I am about to tell you I would not want to be bandied about Town."

"Aside from my mother's questionable taste, I do believe her discretion can be trusted if she is asked to keep a confidence."

"Very well, then I will tell you a few things. I do trust *your* discretion. I quite took a liking to you when we were introduced. You may decide for yourself what you tell your mother after we are finished with our visit."

"Thank you, my lady, you have no idea how much I appreciate your help."

"Think nothing of it, my dear. Would you care for some more tea?"

Rose had prepared herself for the countess to launch into a tale of the knight's depravities, and was thus surprised by the prosaic offer of tea. She allowed a nervous giggle to escape her lips. "Thank you, my lady, that might be a good idea."

"Tea is always a good idea, my dear," the older woman stated with conviction. "Now where should I begin? There are actually many things to tell you. Some I am not certain are suitable for a young girl's ears. I will be a little vague on some of those details, I am afraid. Your mother will appreciate that, I am sure."

Rose was still puzzled and wished fervently she would just get on with it. The suspense was making her feel edgy.

The countess dithered for a couple more minutes, fussing with the teapot and getting herself settled comfortably once more in her seat. Finally, she launched into speech.

"Sir Jason Broderick should not be trusted by anyone, in my estimation. Young girls are not safe from him because he is rumoured to have ruined a couple young women of good families and then refused to marry them. Not that anyone would wish their daughters married to him, as he also has a violent temper and has been known to express his anger upon his servants and animals, so I would not put it past him to be a wife beater. So, to get your mother to smarten up about the highly unacceptable knight, you shall just have to tell her about the rumours and I am quite convinced she shall set her sights elsewhere."

Rose struggled to contain her disappointment. She was absolutely certain that Broderick and Austen's schemes involving Wrentham had nothing to do with the sullied reputations of unsuspecting debutantes. She had *so* wished that Lady Yorkleigh was going to be of help, but she could not divulge her involvement with the duke, so all she could do was smile and nod as sincerely as she could muster.

"Thank you so much, my dear Lady Yorkleigh. I am not entirely certain I know what you mean, but no doubt you are correct in surmising that it will be sufficient to get my mother to change her mind on considering a possible match between us." Rose was quite proud of how that had come out. She wondered briefly if she should rise to take her leave. She wasn't left wondering for long, as Lady Yorkleigh began to speak once more.

"I would not normally discuss this next bit with a regular debutante. However, you seem to be a wise young woman, and since your father is a diplomat, I would expect you should have a little more knowledge of the ways of the world than some."

Rose felt as though she had frozen in place, wondering how close to the truth the countess was about to get. As she was looking expectantly at her, Rose forced the corners of her mouth to lift into what she hoped looked like a close approximation of a smile and nodded her head, praying she did not look like a simpleton. It must have passed muster, as Lady Yorkleigh continued.

"I believe some of the reason for your late debut is because you and your mother accompanied your father to Vienna for his politics." Lady Yorkleigh again looked at her closely, so Rose hastened to reply.

"That is correct, my lady. It was a lovely time. I do not regret going with him for a minute, even though it means I am rather older than the other young ladies making their curtsy to Society."

"Youth is not necessarily the asset everyone purports it to be, my dear. You are absolutely perfect the way you are and shall make a brilliant match. I am certain of it."

Now Rose's smile was much more genuine as she appreciated the lady's words. "Thank you for that kindness, my lady."

"I am not being kind, I am merely speaking the truth. Now, let me get on with my tale. Your maid will be nodding off in the foyer."

Rose smiled but did not interrupt as she was now on tenterhooks to hear the rest that Lady Yorkleigh had to say.

"Did you meet that scoundrel, Tallyrand, while you were in Vienna?" At Rose's nod, she continued. "His argument is that he always has France's interests at heart, and one cannot fault him for doing what he considers his patriotic duty, I suppose, but he is just so conniving and crooked while he is doing it. Broderick is a close associate of his. While one can excuse Tallyrand by considering his motivations, Broderick is another matter altogether. His motivations are always what is best for Broderick, not anyone else, and certainly not the nation.

"It concerns me to see him actively running about amongst the *ton* once more. I fear what he might be getting up to. You see, he is a terribly smart man and plays upon other people's weaknesses. For example, Prinny has a weakness for anything to do with Bonny Prince Charlie, of the Stuart dynasty. This can be exploited, and I have heard Broderick has been making attempts to do so. As well, his relationship with Tallyrand is highly suspicious. They should be on opposite sides, as Tallyrand is trying to dispute with some of England's claims for territory. These were settled to a certain extent in Vienna, but I have heard that those boundaries are currently being disputed still."

Rose gazed at her hostess, feeling rather awed. She had no reply for the lady's words but knew there was quite likely a high level of truth in them. She had a lot of information to take to Wrentham at their next meeting, but she was unsure if he would be in a position to help her with it. Rose wondered if she should confide in the countess about their situation, but she resolved to ask the duke about it first. Since he was her primary co-conspirator she owed him her primary loyalty at the moment, but her utmost concern lay with finding out what Broderick was up to and if he was trying to harm their country. If he was, all other allegiances would have to take second place to making sure he was stopped.

Realizing she was dithering and that something needed to be said, Rose remembered that her pretence for speaking of these things with the countess was her mother's strange words, so she marshalled her thoughts and came up with something to say, she only hoped it made sense.

"My lady, I so appreciate your confidences. You are quite correct, as a diplomat's daughter I am quite well aware of the ramifications of what you have just told me. I will not betray your confidences to my mother, although I do trust her discretion, but I do not think it will be necessary. These things just give me added incentive to ensure my mother's ideas do not come to fruition."

"That is very well, my dear girl." As Rose stood to take her leave, the countess quickly spoke up. "Oh, my dear, do not say you have to go as yet. We have not had any pleasant conversation. I know you came here with the express purpose of learning how to avoid the knight and all that, but surely you could stay and visit a wee bit longer."

Rose was gratified by the older woman's invitation and sank back down onto the settee. Glancing around at the well-appointed receiving room, she said the first thing that popped into her head. "I absolutely adore the décor in this room. Did you have it done recently, my lady? I wish my parents would consent to make some changes at our home, but they will not even consider the idea."

Lady Yorkleigh smiled widely at Rose's compliment. "Why thank you so much for your kind words, my dear. We had this room changed before the Season last year. I agree with you that sometimes a freshened room is just the thing. I find it helped change my perspective completely."

"My family could certainly use that," Rose offered in a low tone. "Ever since my brother died the entire family has become frozen. My father is going through the motions of his work, of course. But coming to London for the Little Season is the first original thought my mother has had. I was so hoping it was an indication that things were about to change, but sadly I have found my hopes dashed."

"Oh, my dear girl, I am so sorry. I had heard about your loss, but as we were not acquainted at the time I did not express my condolences. It must be so hard for your parents to lose their firstborn."

"It is. I am sure it is wholly unnatural for a parent to be predeceased by their child, but *their* lives are not over. I fervently wish my parents could get out of the doldrums they have sunken into. They have two other children that need their attention, and who are very much alive."

"Your mother seems to be attentive, at least to a certain degree. She is chaperoning you about Town for the Season." The countess was trying to be kindly reasonable.

"Mayhap, but keep in mind the original purpose of my visit. She *did* suggest that Sir Jason Broderick would be a good match for me," came Rose's dry reply.

Lady Yorkleigh could not suppress her grin. "That cannot be argued with — it does make one wonder where her thoughts are." The countess paused for a moment but then continued in an earnest tone. "I know we are still newly acquainted and I would never presume to take the place of your mother," she began, while Rose burst in, "Besides the fact that you are not nearly old enough to have the role naturally."

"You are too kind, my dear, but as I was saying, I would be happy to be somewhat of a surrogate for you in these coming weeks. A young lady's debut can be a perilous, confusing time if she does not have sound advisors. I beg you, please feel free to stop in at any time to discuss any issue you might care to have an experienced perspective upon."

"That is such a kind offer, my lady, and I promise you I *shall* take you up on it. I so appreciate your condescension, but I fear that I shall not be able to reciprocate in any way to demonstrate my deep appreciation."

"No thanks are necessary, my dear. Lord Yorkleigh and I were not blessed with any daughters, and our sons are now at Eton. I am sadly bereft, and while I enjoy accompanying my husband to Town when he wants to take his seat in the House, I would dearly love to be occupied in a more meaningful manner. If I could in some way smooth the way for you, I would feel as though I had a role to play. You would, in fact, be doing *me* a favour, rather than the other way around."

Rose laughed at the countess' droll words. "Now you are truly being too kind, but I shall accept your offer nonetheless. You must be sure to tell me if I transgress or overstep the bounds of your offer, though, my lady."

"Very well, we have a deal," the countess declared before she fixed shrewd eyes upon her guest. "Now perhaps once we have become better acquainted you will find your way clear to tell me the real reason why you were asking about Sir Broderick."

Despite her best efforts, Rose was quite certain that her surprise and chagrin were clearly displayed upon her expressive face. She tried to brazen it out but did not want to lie to her new friend. "My mother really did express the opinion that he would be a good choice for me."

"I did not think you were lying, my dear. I merely am of the opinion that you would have been well able to come up with reasonable arguments on your own, or rather, you would have just ignored your mother's ridiculous suggestion." At seeing Rose's discomfort the countess hastened to add, "I pray you do not trouble yourself over it, my dear girl. That is why I said that I hope in the future you will confide in me. I do not expect it at this time. And I do not mind telling you what I can, even without full disclosure."

Rose grinned at the countess. "Thank you, my lady. I promise you that I will. And now, I really should be on my way."

As Rose took her leave and collected her maid, the countess accompanied her to the foyer, chattering about social niceties and arranging a date for them to take tea the next time. Walking down the front steps of the Yorkleighs' elegantly attractive home, Rose could feel Mary's inquisitive eyes burning into her back. She grinned, as she could feel the maid's impatience. She was impressed that the other young woman managed to hold her tongue until they reached the nearest street corner.

"Well, Miss, how did it go?" she demanded with impatient curiosity.

"Very well, Mary, thank you for asking," Rose answered maddeningly, causing Mary to expel an impatient breath. Rose could not hold onto her chuckle. "I am merely funning with you, Mary, although it was a very good meeting. The countess was most helpful." Lowering her voice and glancing around, Rose beckoned the maid closer and recounted what Lady Yorkleigh had had to say about Broderick. At the conclusion, Mary's eyes were wide with concern.

"What are you going to do about all of this, Miss? Surely you're going to have to go to his lordship, your father."

"I wish I could, Mary, but I still fear that he will have difficulty being reasonable about this, especially as the duke is still involved. And just this morning my mother was mentioning that Papa has to go away again, this time to Paris. They were wondering whether or not Mama and I ought to join him, but they decided it is too important for me to continue with my first Season." At this last bit, Rose could not help the tone of disgust that crept into her voice and the roll of her eyes that accompanied her words. "Can you believe I shall be missing out on Paris, Mary?"

"But do you not think it is wise, Miss? For one thing, the Season is important for one such as yourself, and for another, if you cannot confide in your father, then you have to sort this situation with Broderick out yourself."

"You are quite right, Mary, but I still wish I could go. Mayhap, from what we have learned about Broderick, he will be going to Paris as well, and I could investigate him from there."

"Or he might be just waiting for an opportunity such as this, when many of the government gents are out of Town to act on whatever nefarious plot he has cooked up."

Now it was Rose's turn to have widened eyes. She gazed at her maid with concern. "You have such a good point there, Mary. You are quite correct, I certainly must be vigilant. It is a good thing I have already arranged to meet with Wrentham. I so wish I had stuck with the duke's suggestion of meeting tomorrow instead of the day after," she mused, staring off into the near distance. "Do you think it would be remarked upon if I were to be seen speaking to him in public? If we were to find ourselves at the same entertainments this evening, do you think I could talk to him without my mother catching wind of it?"

Mary looked at her mistress with worry clearly etched in her face. "I don't rightly know, Miss. Do enough people know about your families' issues for it to become an item for the gossips if it was noticed? Because if it is, your mama is sure to find out."

"You are quite correct, as usual. But if an opportunity arises, I will take the chance and tell him to meet me tomorrow. I do not think I could bear to wait an entire day. Or perhaps I should send him a note." At catching sight of Mary's dubious expression, Rose answered her own unspoken question. "No, of course not, none of the footmen would be able to keep that to themselves, and then I would definitely be in the suds."

"They say patience is a virtue, Miss."

Rose could not resist sticking her tongue out at her maid. "You and I both know that it is not one I possess. But you are quite right. I shall have to pretend that I have some if I cannot contrive a way to speak with His Grace this evening." Rose resolved to put the matter from her mind for the time being. "Now we are nearly home and I have been gone for far longer than I had expected. It is nearly time for me to begin my preparations for the ball I am to attend this evening. I hope I have not kept you overly from your duties." She was quite contrite.

"Well, Miss, considering most of my duties revolve around you, I'm thinking you didn't keep me from anything." Mary grinned at her mistress in a fine humour.

The two girls climbed the front stairs of their own home and the door was opened swiftly.

"Welcome home, Miss."

The rest of the afternoon passed in a blur of activity as Rose bathed and primped in preparation for the ball. She shared a light repast with her mother before they each returned to their chambers to conclude their dressing. It had been a quiet meal with rather stilted conversation. Lady Smythe was even more distant than usual, so Rose found it difficult to engage with her. She chalked this up to her father's departure. Even before the tragedy, her mother had always hated it when her husband travelled, but since it had become almost a phobia. Rose hoped her mother would be able to cope because she would be rather too occupied over the next few days to be able to assist her. It was one more worry to buzz around at the back of her mind, where she pushed it in order to concentrate on the upcoming evening.

Looking into the mirror as Mary put the finishing touches to her hair, Rose could not help but appreciate her own reflection. She was not an arrogant girl, but she could see that her excitement had put a flattering blush into her cheeks, which was thankfully complementary to the shade of her gown.

Chapter Twelve

Lady Smythe seemed to float next to Rose as they descended into the crowded ballroom after having been announced and greeting their host and hostess. Rose could see that it was going to be a successful event. Their hostess would be gratified by the number of people who had accepted her invitation and were cramming themselves into the elegantly appointed, but not overly large, room. Rose hoped that meant she would be able to ever so discreetly seek out Alex and arrange to meet up on the morrow, if he were indeed present.

Slowly descending, Rose gazed about at the milling multitude, struggling to distinguish faces in the crowds. Plastering a pleasant, social smile onto her face, she turned to check on her mother, hoping she would be all right on her own. Feeling a niggle of worried guilt, Rose solicitously got her settled amongst her friends before going off to pursue her own activities.

Bumping into Emmaline and her sister, Rose exchanged pleasantries for a moment before Emmaline was swept off to the dance floor by a pleasant gentleman. Unfortunately, Constance was rather more difficult to carry a conversation with once her sister was absent. Rose made the effort, deciding it was excellent practice for her future life as a Society hostess.

"Have you been having a pleasant evening, Lady Constance?"

"Very pleasant, thank you, Miss Rose."

"Good, good. Did you do anything particularly interesting today?"

"Not particularly, Miss."

"That is unfortunate. I made a few lovely morning calls this afternoon. It was most pleasant."

"Oh, how pleasant."

Rose began to find it to be an amusing game and persevered. "You look lovely this evening, Lady Constance."

"Thank you so very much, Miss Rose." For a moment, Constance looked gratified by her compliment, but then she again looked confused and slipped back into vacuity. "You look lovely this evening, too."

"Why thank you so much, Lady Constance. I cannot say that shopping is my favourite activity, but I am pleased with this particular purchase. I think my modiste did a smashingly good job." Rose tried to keep her grin within bounds but feared she failed miserably. Gratifyingly, Constance responded to her conversational gambit.

"How could you possibly not enjoy shopping, Miss Rosamund? Just this afternoon my sister and I spent an enjoyable few hours on Bond Street. It is one of the very best parts of coming to Town. You should see the darling gowns I ordered. And Emmaline bought a perfectly scrumptious hat to go with her new riding habit. The dressmakers here are so much better than the ones in the village near our estate. I do declare I would happily shop every day."

"Lady Constance, I had no idea. Perhaps I ought to accompany you on a visit to Bond Street and you can show me how to have an enjoyable time there."

"That would be my pleasure any time you would like, Miss Rose."

Rose was happy that she had managed to have what amounted to a real conversation with the other young woman, but blessedly, Lord Kenneth came to claim her hand for the dance before she had to come up with any more conversational efforts.

"Thank you, my lord, how could you possibly have known that I most particularly wanted to dance the quadrille?" Rose asked playfully.

The young lord looked slightly embarrassed by her question, but manfully responded, "Does not everyone love the quadrille, Miss Rosamund? I thought you looked particularly fetching this evening and wanted to twirl you around the dance floor for this number."

"Well, I thank you kindly for the invitation, my lord."

For a moment the dance took them apart from each other, but they were able to resume their conversation as they re-partnered.

"Are you enjoying your evening, Miss Rose?" he asked pleasantly.

"I am, very much so, thank you, my lord," she replied, smiling as she heard the surprise evident in her tone. He must have noticed and was not such a dullard as to ignore it.

"Why do you sound so surprised, Miss Rose?"

"In all honesty, the Season has not been my idea of a rollicking good time up until now. I cannot say that I particularly enjoy the large crowds of people, and the constant need for gossip wears on my ears. On the other hand, I love the dancing and I have met some lovely people that are fast becoming good friends, so I think it is turning out to be a good experience. But I sounded surprised because just a week or two ago I would not have been able to fathom the possibility of having a good time at an event such as this."

"You are not the usual sort of debutante, are you?" he asked, with a tease in his voice.

"I think perhaps many debutantes find the Season is not quite what they had anticipated, they just manage to hide it better than I do," Rose replied with a cheeky grin.

They were again separated, but when they returned to their places Rose asked her partner, "Have you had much opportunity to talk with Lady Constance? I had a lovely conversation with her just before you invited me to the dance."

"I apologize if I interrupted," he began before he answered her question. "But no, I cannot say that I have ever managed to have a conversation with Lady Constance. In all honesty, I thought I was rescuing you when I asked you to dance."

"Well thank you ever so much for the gallantry." Rose grinned. "But you may be surprised to know that if you try hard enough you can get a conversation out of her. I asked her about shopping and was shocked nearly speechless by the results. You should try it, my lord. She really is a lovely girl."

Rose would never have considered herself to be a matchmaker, but she found she quite enjoyed the prospect of matching up various of her acquaintances. Neither of these two were wordy talkers but they both seemed to be kind individuals. Rose thought Lord Kenneth's quiet kindness and strength would be a lovely match for Lady Constance's shyness. Rose could almost see the wheels turning in his lordship's thought processes as he mulled over her words. She was not at all surprised when he escorted her back to Constance and then invited that young lady to the next dance.

Rose was standing on the side of the dance floor, momentarily alone, smiling happily, when she heard a quiet voice behind her. "Why are you grinning like the Cheshire Cat?"

It took a great deal of will power to control her reaction as she felt a shiver creep up her spine and her skin break out in gooseflesh. "Good evening, Your Grace," she replied, without turning around or looking at him. Anyone watching would not even know they had acknowledged one another. At least not yet. Rose plied her fan to hide the movement of her lips.

"You look lovelier than ever, Miss Rose," Alex complimented from behind her, keeping himself obscured by an artfully placed potted fern.

Rose could feel a blush creeping up her cheeks but steadfastly kept her gaze upon the dance floor, waving the fan more vigorously in an attempt to stem the rising tide of her blush. Ignoring his comment and keeping her voice just above a whisper she muttered, "I really need to speak to you quite urgently."

"There is a broom closet just beyond the retiring rooms. Go get yourself a glass of punch and then, if no one is watching, head toward the ladies' retiring room. If still no one is around, I will whisk you into the broom closet for a moment of speech."

"Your Grace, I am absolutely certain that is a terrible idea," she stated with a laugh sounding in her voice. There was no reply from behind her as Alex had already left.

Glancing around, Rose saw that it did not appear that anyone had taken any notice of her. To be on the safe side, she took a turn about the room slowly, keeping her eye on the dance floor, watching out for her friends and glancing around to check on her mother. Seeing that everything seemed to be in its place for the moment, Rose thought that she just might be able to pull off such a questionable stunt. She set off for the refreshment room at a brisk pace, reasoning that no one would stop her if she looked like she knew what she was doing.

A sudden attack of nerves made her mouth dry and she was grateful for Alex's suggestion that she have a glass of the delicious punch. Rose was surprised by the quality of the cool drink. So often it seemed barely more than flavoured water. She dithered for a moment over the punch bowl, wondering if she should abandon the idea of trying to speak to Wrentham this evening. And worrying about the consequences if they were caught meeting in a broom closet. And wondering if the duke had already arrived. Giving herself a silent scold for being so missish, she forced some steel into her backbone. After looking around to ensure no one was looking at her, she eased her way toward the retiring room. Stepping just past the door to that room, she almost squeaked as she felt a large, warm hand haul her from behind into a small room, and then all was darkness.

"Alex?" she asked in a shaky whisper.

"Of course it's me, you silly widget, who else did you think it was?" he teased her mercilessly in the darkness.

Rose took a gulp of air as she struggled to deal with all the conflicting feelings she was experiencing in that moment. The nerve-induced adrenaline that was coursing through her veins was leaving her legs feeling jiggly and weak. But the thing uppermost in her mind was the unexpected sensation of being pressed up against the firm muscles of the Duke of Wrentham's chest. He had certainly changed since their childhood days, and she was struggling to sort out her feelings on the matter.

"What are you doing, Your Grace?" she hissed at him as she felt him rubbing her back in a soothing gesture. It was obvious to Rose that he had picked up on her attack of nerves. She was comforted by the gesture and had to remind herself that he was her enemy and that they had only teamed up in order to deal with an even bigger enemy. She put her hands between them and shoved against his chest. In the confines of the small space he could not go far, but at least he was no longer touching her.

He was still disconcertingly close, and it was as though being in the dark made it that much more intimate. He smelt surprisingly fresh despite the warmth of the ballroom they had just left, as though he had just bathed with some sort of lemon soap. His breath, which wafted by her in the close confines of the closet, carried hints of the glass of port he must have enjoyed recently. She even noticed the rich scent of his highly polished leather shoes. She could not understand why even the sound of his breathing made her breathless. She was left feeling strangely impatient.

"Why did you arrange for such an unorthodox meeting, Alex?" she demanded, sounding angry.

"I apologize, Rosie, I thought you wished to speak with me urgently." He finally spoke and his voice sounded strange to Rose's ears. She thought it must be from the strain of whispering. She hoped to put an end to this ridiculous episode as quickly as possible.

"You are right, I do need to speak with you, but surely we cannot be in this closet for very long or we are sure to be discovered. Then we will be in the suds for certain."

"Have you discovered something of use to us?"

"Yes, Lady Yorkleigh was most helpful when I visited her today. But there is so much to tell you and I cannot bear to be here in the dark," she whispered urgently. "Could you arrange to meet me early in the morning tomorrow instead of the day after like we had planned?"

"Sure, yes, no problem. That could easily be arranged. You were right—this was not one of my wisest moves. You should probably go. I will stay here. If anyone sees you emerging, just say you mistook the door to the retiring room. I will wait a sufficient while before I follow suit."

"All right, Alex. Are you quite well? You sound rather strange." Rose was now concerned.

"Yes, yes, quite well. Perhaps there is rather too much dust in the broom closet. Now out you go."

Rose could feel that her face was displaying how dubious she was about his statement, but as there was only the faintest sliver of light coming in from under the door, it was quite obvious the duke could not see it. She refrained to comment and merely opened the door a sliver, peeked out, and hurried to leave. Luck must have been on her side that night as no one was about when she made good her escape. She decided to adjourn to the ladies' retiring room for a moment to collect her thoughts before rejoining the crowds in the ballroom.

☙ ❧

Alex was left to stew in the broom closet.

This was certainly not his brightest move, Alex mused to himself as he willed his rioting feelings under control. He should not be having any sort of warm feelings for Miss Rosamund Smythe. Nothing could come of them, despite the love he had felt for her the past sixteen years.

He had been ten years old when four-year-old Rosie had stolen his heart. He had been sitting behind the garden sheds, crying over some hurtful thing that had occurred in his family. At this point, he could no longer remember the exact cause of his grief, as it had not been a rare thing. What had been the rare thing was the tender compassion clearly visible in the little girl's eyes.

"There, there," the little Rosie had said as she patted his back gently, "It's best to let it all out for a couple minutes and then stop. If you don't let it out it stays all inside you, but if you cry too long your eyes will hurt." Her four-year-old wisdom had been indisputable and his tears had instantly dried. As a ten-year-old he hated anyone knowing that he could possibly give way to tears, but since she was barely more than a baby it didn't really matter. She probably cried all the time herself.

He had been wrong about that. The sweet-natured little girl so rarely gave way to tears. But of course, she didn't have as many reasons to cry as he had at that time. Her parents still appeared to care about each other and, as far as he could tell, no one ever lied to his Rosie.

Alex gave his head a shake to rid himself of the bittersweet memories. It mattered naught how delightful he had always found her. It was no longer possible for a Wrentham to pursue any sort of a relationship with a Smythe. Perhaps if he reminded himself about a million more times he would be able to convince his heart to stop racing every time he caught sight of her.

If she would just stop looking more beautiful every time he laid eyes upon her it would no doubt be an easier task for him to accomplish. And if he could stop finding her earnest concern for the strange situation she had discovered so endearing, surely he would be able to put her from his mind once more.

If they could get this Broderick nonsense straightened out quickly he could get on with finding himself a duchess and retire back to the country. Once Rose found herself a husband there would be no need for their paths to cross very often in the future. That thought should have brought him a measure of happiness rather than the sinking feeling he was experiencing in that moment. A grunt of frustration escaped him, which he quickly stifled lest someone hear him. After another moment of hesitation, he too stepped from the closet.

Alex was not as lucky as Rose. The moment he had shut the door he heard an incredulous voice behind him. "Is there something amiss, Your Grace?"

The duke gritted his teeth to prevent the vulgarities that threatened to slip through his lips at being caught out. It would certainly not do to tell off one's host. Alex gritted his teeth and did his best to brazen it out. As he was turning to face his host it crossed his mind how ironic it was that Rose had been so concerned about his feelings toward subterfuge and here he was, about to play as big a part as any she had. Alex was uncertain what his face was revealing but from the look on the ambassador's own face it must have been convincing, as his lordship looked truly concerned.

Because of the worry on Lord Chatsworth's face Alex wondered idly what the poor man was thinking. This struck his ready sense of humour and he had to struggle to suppress an inappropriate urge to chuckle. Now was certainly not the time. He would have to remember to tell Rose about it in the morning, he thought to himself as he opened his mouth to address the ambassador.

"My Lord Chatsworth, naught is amiss, thank you so much for your concern. I was in need of relieving myself." Alex couldn't help the blush that he could feel creeping up his cheeks at this revolting conversational gambit. Remembering that the man is an ambassador, Alex hoped fervently that the man was not into spying as well and did not see through his ridiculously thin excuse.

Now Lord Chatsworth looked appalled. "And you thought to relieve yourself in the broom closet?"

Alex felt his lips twitch with amusement over his host's tone of voice, despite the awkwardness of the situation.

Mustering a degree of dignity, Alex strove for the jovial tone of one who had imbibed a little too much. Forcing a chuckle, Alex waved the other man's words away. "Of course not, my good man. I was merely looking for the appropriate location. How was I to know that was a broom closet? I thought it an ideal spot for a water closet."

Lord Chatsworth was clearly torn over how to address the tipsy young duke. His respect for the duke's title won out. "Your Grace, we have not yet gotten around to upgrading the entire house with plumbing. We do not have a water closet on this floor, but if you would care to follow me I will show you to the room that has been set aside for such a necessity. In the future, should you have such a need again, feel free to ask a footman to direct you."

Alex was impressed with the other man's words. They implied that at least some of the house had been upgraded with plumbing. Most of his properties had, of course, seen such upgrades, but he was a duke. He knew that most of his associates were still trying to decide whether or not the upgrades were necessary. Alex wondered how he had ever lived without plumbing before and grimaced at the thought that he would now have to relieve himself with his host in attendance.

Stifling his sigh, he rolled his eyes in disgust with himself. If he hadn't had the hare-brained idea of pulling Rose into the broom closet in the first place he would not be in this current predicament. He consoled himself with the lopsided reasoning that it could have been much worse. If the ambassador had been just a moment or two earlier he would have seen Rose exiting the broom closet and if he had investigated at all, they would have all been in the suds, as Rosie had said. But then again, from what she had told him, Alex could imagine that Rose would be able to brazen her way out of the situation even more skilfully than he had. And no doubt the affable ambassador would have been happy to escort a giggling debutante to the ladies' retiring room.

Within a few moments the questionable ordeal was over and Alex was able to make his way back to the ballroom. He was just in time to see Rose in conversation with Lady Anne and Lord Edgecombe. The duke found himself consumed with curiosity over what they could possibly be talking about. It crossed his mind that he should be trying to hide his interest, but he could not tear his eyes away as he watched Rose animatedly talking while the other two looked on in fascination.

Chapter Thirteen

Rose had hurried away from the broom closet as quickly as her skirts and propriety would allow. She had wanted to pick up her skirts and run, but fear of observers held her to a more sedate pace. As soon as she was away from the closet, she whisked herself into the ladies' retiring room, where a mirror had been conveniently placed for the guests' use.

Surprised to see how flushed she was, Rose hastily glanced around the room, hoping she was not being observed. A maid sitting in the corner was paying her very little attention and the rest of the room appeared to be unoccupied.

Turning her attention back to the mirror, Rose was glad to see that despite her close encounter with Alex, Mary's hard work on her coiffure had not been laid to waste. There wasn't much she could do about her flushed cheeks, so with a slight shrug she turned away from her own reflection and headed back to the ballroom.

Well aware that it was her excitement making her colour so hectic, Rose determined to set her mind to other things. Remembering her and Elizabeth's plan to aim Anne in a different direction, she determined to try her hand once more at matchmaking. Scanning the room for her quarries, her eyes lit upon one. Grinning, she headed across the room with purpose.

"Lady Anne, you look lovely this evening."

"Oh, Miss Rosamund, how kind of you to say so," came her soft reply.

Rose suppressed her amused smile and tried hard to keep the conspirator's glee from her face. She had never considered herself to be a busybody, but she was so excited about the meddling she was about to do.

"Are you enjoying your evening thus far?" Rose asked gently, pleased that her tone came out just how she would like, not too bored but not invasive either.

"It is not as crowded as some of the balls I have been to, so that is pleasant, to be sure."

Rose was puzzled over Lady Anne's lukewarm response. "Is everything all right with you, my lady?" she asked in a low voice, making sure not to draw undue attention to them but concerned about the young woman.

It was apparent that Anne was trying to put on a brave face. "You recall the conversation we were having, do you not?"

"About suitable husbands and how to acquire them?" Rose asked, as neutrally as possible.

"That's right," Anne replied with a slight smile over Rose's wording. "My father has decided that I have dithered long enough and wishes me to proceed as soon as possible."

Rose was glad for the experience she had in maintaining a straight face despite this provocative statement. Keeping her composure with effort she prompted discreetly, "And you are unsure if you want to proceed, is that the problem?"

Anne's nod was miserable. "What you said about a husband not wanting to be trapped really made me think. What if Papa is wrong about affection being engaged after the marriage is arranged? What if my husband were to take me in disgust if he were to find out that it was all a trap? I do not want to be miserable for the rest of my life."

Feeling her heart go out to the other woman, Rose was glad that she had already determined on her set course. Lady

Anne could not have Alex, but she deserved to be happy. Clasping Lady Anne's hand warmly in her own, Rose reassured her quietly. "Have no fear, my friend, we shall ensure you find happiness. Let us find you an uncomplicated husband who will be delighted to make you happy."

Lady Anne brought her eyes to focus on Rose's face. "Are you sure that is even possible?"

"Absolutely," Rose replied with as much conviction as she could muster, grinning as she saw hope dawn in the other woman's eyes. "Good, it will not do for you to look as though you are heartbroken. Men do not find that terribly attractive for the most part, in my experience."

This brought a rather watery chuckle to Anne's lips, but she did manage to look a little happier. Rose again gazed about at the milling crowds and was delighted to see the object of her search. Ignoring the vulgarity of her forward behaviour she raised a hand and beckoned for Lord Edgecombe to join them.

"What are you doing?" Anne asked in a low but urgent voice.

"I am looking for your happiness. Lord Anthony is a kind, delightful young viscount who strikes me as a likely candidate to make any lady a wonderful husband. And in any case, it looks to me that he is a good dancer. If you do not think he is a good choice for husband, you can at least enjoy being on the dance floor."

Anne looked a little confused over Rose's managing ways, but could not argue with her logic. Rose felt her amusement rise as she watched Anne muster up a welcoming smile when the kind viscount arrived, looking at the two ladies questioningly.

"Is everything all right with you two?" he asked solicitously.

"All is well, thank you so much for asking, my lord," Rose replied briskly. "We just needed you to settle a dilemma Lady Anne and I were having."

Rose watched with delight as Anne looked at her askance, but Lord Anthony bowed slightly. "I would be happy to help in any way that I can," he answered gallantly.

"I am rather embarrassed to admit to you that we were discussing your dance skills, my lord." Rose struggled to contain her blush at this bold statement, but was amused to see the stain creeping into the viscount's cheeks as well.

"My dance skills," he repeated with surprise. "Whatever for, Miss?"

"Because you are a delightful dance partner. I was telling Lady Anne that I think you are better at the waltz, but she was insisting that she thinks you are more skilled at the country dances." Rose paused, while her two companions looked between her and each other. At the perfect moment, she could hear the orchestra striking up the next number. "How lucky is that? It seems to me that they are about to play a waltz. Why don't you be a dear and prove me right, my lord? Show Lady Anne what a marvellous waltzer you are."

Rose nearly giggled over the look of incredulity that crossed Lord Edgecombe's face. *He is looking at me as though I have lost my mind*, she thought, controlling her expression with effort. *He might not be that far off from the truth*, she answered herself as she watched him pull himself together and reply diplomatically.

"I do not think I need to prove anything to either of you ladies, but I would be happy to dance the waltz with you, Lady Anne, if you would do me the honour of being my partner."

Blushing, Anne accepted before shooting Rose a dubious look of censure, which Rose chose to ignore, merely grinning at the departing pair. At that moment, Lord Dunbar appeared at her elbow.

"You look decidedly pleased with yourself, Miss Rose. What have you been up to?"

Batting her lashes vigorously, Rose tried to put a confused look onto her face. "I have no idea what you are talking about, my lord."

"That I sincerely doubt, my dear. But would you do me the honour of dancing this waltz with me?"

"That would be a delight, my lord, thank you." Rose grinned at Wesley with pleasure.

As the strains of the waltz swept them into the rhythms of the dance, Rose happily followed the viscount's lead while trying to ignore his searching glance.

"Is that your strategy then, Miss?"

With a soft sigh, Rose saw that the man would not be put off, although she tried once more. "Whatever do you mean, my lord?" she asked, with as much innocence as she could muster.

Now Wesley could not prevent his chuckle but he managed to contain it so as to not cause a scene. "You really are a minx, aren't you? I can see now why Wrentham cannot get himself to cut his ties with you despite the convoluted family history." Seeing the stricken look upon Rose's face, the viscount hastened to make his apology. "Forgive me, my dear, that was inexcusably crass."

Rose managed to maintain her composure and with impatience she waved away his apology and returned to the subject she had previously been trying to avoid. Now it seemed like a welcome diversion. "You were asking me about my strategy, my lord?" she reminded him.

Grateful for the change of subject, Wesley was quick to jump in. "Yes, it would appear that your plan is to save the duke by means of diverting the lady's attentions elsewhere."

"You are only very partially correct, my lord," Rose replied primly before breaking into a smile. She could not hold onto her offense with the pleasant viscount. "For one thing, I am quite convinced that Alex is fully capable of saving himself, if the need should arise. But in this instance, I do not actually believe that merely redirecting the lady's attention would save him. It strikes me that there is more afoot than entrapping a wealthy mate for Lady Anne, and I do believe she is as much a potential victim as the duke. I think she is a sweet young woman who will be in need of a suitable mate if this situation goes sideways, as it is sure to. I think Lord Edgecombe is a lovely young man, who would treat her well. I merely thought to ensure that the two of them have an opportunity to look at one another in a different light. There is nothing quite like taking a turn on the dance floor to the tune of a waltz to put one in a suitable frame of mind."

Now Rose could see the light of teasing enter into Wesley's eyes. "Oh good, so does this mean that if I were to approach your father, you would be amenable to my suit?"

Rose rolled her eyes drolly. "If you had been trying to engage my interest, surely you would have seen fit to direct the conversation into more appropriate avenues than censuring me for my managing ways."

Wesley was quick to protest. "I did not call you managing."

"It was surely implied by your questions, my lord."

Rose giggled at the look of confusion covering the viscount's face and quickly gave way. "Never mind, my lord, we are co-conspirators at the moment, and that pushes all other thoughts from our minds. You are perfectly safe dancing the waltz with me, I shall not be misconstruing your intentions, have no fear."

Blissfully unaware of Wesley's conflicted feelings, Rose was happy to finish the dance and return to the sidelines. There she was handed off to another gentleman waiting for her hand for the next song.

Feeling bemused, Wesley went off in search of Alex.

"That chit is a menace, Wrentham," he declared without preamble after ascertaining that they were not within easy earshot of anyone else.

"Who might you be speaking of?" Alex asked absently.

"Surely you know full well of whom I speak. Miss Rosamund Smythe," Wesley declared with fervour, causing Alex to look at him rather askance.

"What has happened?" Alex's concern was clearly evident. "From where I am standing, it looks as though she is having a good time, dancing and visiting with her friends."

"She has absolutely no idea of the power she wields!" Wesley declared with conviction. "She thinks that because we are conspiring there is no way I could possibly view her in an amorous light."

Alex could feel his features tightening and tried to keep his tone unthreatening as he demanded, "Do you see her in an amorous light?"

"No! Yes! That is hardly the point," Wesley replied hotly.

"Then what is the point, because I do not see one clearly evident, my lord."

Wesley must have realized the error of his ways as he quickly back pedalled. "Do not get up in your high ropes, Wrentham. I am not about to poach on your territory. I am merely concerned for the both of you in this situation. She is a highly attractive girl and she has no idea of that. I think that puts you both in grave danger. Her heart is too tender for one thing. She is feeling sorry for the Austen chit and wants to ensure she is well matched before this situation blows up in our faces. Can you imagine? She has no care for her own wellbeing, but she feels badly that she is interfering with the lady's plans for you. She wants to ensure the girl has a second option in place. She was playing matchmaker just before I asked her to dance."

Alex looked at his friend with confusion on his face. "And how does that make her a menace?"

"She told me that she thinks the waltz is the most romantic dance. That is why she wanted Edgecombe to dance with Lady Anne for the waltz. But she thought neither she nor I were at risk of warmer feelings because we are too involved in the conspiracy to be so distracted. If that is how innocent she is, she is at grave risk of getting hurt in all of this. Despite your families' feud, the two of you are going to fall in love, and it is going to be a big mess." Wesley ended this statement with rather melodramatic flare, which brought a reluctant smile to Alex's face.

"It is a big mess already, so there is naught we can do about that. But you are right, Rose is an innocent and that does need to be kept in mind. I hold no ill will toward her as a person, but her parents are another matter altogether. The words that were exchanged when my brother died cannot be overlooked. For Rose's sake, I have resisted pursuing justice for my family, but there is no way I can allow our names to be bandied about. I am most certain she feels similarly on the subject, so I believe your fears are not well founded. Was there anything else you wished to tell me?"

Wesley looked at Alex, studying him to verify the sincerity of his words. "I am just surprised to find that I quite like the chit. From what I know of her parents, I didn't think to like her."

"Why not?" Alex was incredulous. "Just because her parents are intolerable does not mean she has to be."

"It most often follows that way, does it not?"

"I would like to think that I am nothing like my parents," Alex huffed.

"With that very look on your face, I am sorry to inform you that you quite put me in mind of your father." Wesley barely managed to suppress the laughter that wanted to pour from him at the look of disbelief that crossed the duke's face.

"I am nothing like my father," Alex insisted, feeling the colour rise in his cheeks in his fierceness. "I often wonder if the duke even was my father, if you must know."

Wesley rolled his eyes. "There are many things that can be said about both of your parents, but surely, when you look in the mirror you must realize that, despite either of their reputations, you are most certainly a legitimate Wrentham."

"Sometimes I wish it was otherwise," Alex sighed, but then allowed the subject to drop. Looking back to the dance floor he smiled. "So, Rosie is playing matchmaker now, is she? I wonder if that is why her earlier dance partner went to dance with that Chadwick chit after speaking with her. It is dashed difficult to know what goes through a girl's head." Alex shook his head and Wesley couldn't help agreeing with him. "I just hope she is not distracted from our ultimate mission here. While I would not want to see Lady Anne hurt either, it is far from uppermost in my mind at this point."

"It seems to me that ladies are able to keep more than one thing in their mind at a time. It is an admirable quality, I must say. One that I envy them often," Wesley commented while Alex looked at him strangely. "What, Your Grace? Do you not think it would be helpful when playing whist with the likes of Lord Ashcombe?"

"I do just fine, thank you very much. I certainly do not need the mind of a woman to keep track of my cards. Nor do I think it an asset to keep so many things uppermost in mind. It makes one easily distracted," was Alex's final comment on the matter, before he shook his head at his companion and bade him adieu. "I must be off. I promised I would look in at Worthington's rout this evening. And speaking of Lord Ashcombe, I do believe I shall stop in at the club and see if my feeble brain can manage a hand or two."

Lord Dunbar pulled a face at his highborn friend. "Mayhap I shall meet up with you there myself. It would not do to allow you to be plucked too cleanly, if your mind should be distracted by thoughts of our fair maiden."

Alex's ready sense of humour prompted him to laugh at his friend's gentle ribbing. "Mayhap I shall see you there," was all he had to say as he turned and strode from the room.

☙ ❧

"Your daughter does not appear to be keeping up to her end of the bargain, Austen," Sir Broderick was snarling in a low voice.

"These things take time, my lord," whined Lord Austen. "My Annie is a good girl."

"She should be making an effort to catch the duke's eye and dancing with him, rather than spending the evening with every other young buck there is."

"Young girls get these ideas in their heads, my lord. It takes a steady hand. Besides, catching a duke's eye takes time." Lord Austen was plaintive.

"It doesn't take more than a minute to catch the eye of a red-blooded man if you know what you're doing," argued Sir Broderick. "What kind of ideas are you talking about?" he demanded in a rough voice.

"Naught but young girls' fairy tales, my lord, nothing for you to trouble yourself with. I will talk to her some more and forbid her from talking with those other girls."

"Which other girls?" Broderick persisted. "And what ideas? You do not tell me what to trouble myself with. I will be kept informed of every development."

"She was visiting with some young ladies recently, and they were talking about making a love match. The chit thinks she might be made unhappy if her husband discovers he was tricked into marriage," Austen excused.

Broderick managed to keep in mind that they were in the ballroom of a fashionable, High Society home with all the *ton* about them hungry for any tidbit of salacious gossip. He did not let loose with the tirade he wished to unleash upon the feckless lord before him. Taking a deep breath to stem the flow of words and think of the most effective way of handling the situation before him, Sir Jason finally responded. "How did you allow such an idea to take root in her head, Austen? You are not keeping up your end of the bargain from what I can see. Your only responsibility was to ensure your daughter managed to catch Wrentham. It should have been an easy task."

Lord Austen had visibly paled as he listened to the knight hissing his words. He had never been on the receiving end of one of Broderick's retaliatory rebukes, but he had heard about them and was willing to do all that was necessary to avoid it for himself. Nearly cowering before the smaller man, Austen begged, "My daughter is a good girl, sir, she will do what she has been told, I will see to it, I can assure you."

"Never mind your assurances, I can see with my own eyes just how well she is following your instructions. But I also now have an idea of the culprit. Keep your daughter away from the Smythe girl. She is nothing but trouble. I will handle the rest."

Lord Austen turned bewildered eyes to the dance floor, surprised to see how happy his daughter looked in the arms of Lord Edgecombe. He did not comprehend how this tied in with Miss Smythe, but if that was all that was required of him, he could surely manage to keep his dear Anne away from her. She was a good girl and would do just as she was bidden, he assured himself once more as he wiped the sweat from his brow as surreptitiously as possible.

It was none of his business if the knight was looking with evil intent at that other girl. Lord Austen was just relieved it was not his Annie that had triggered that particular look. Feeling a shiver of dread slither down his spine, the viscount felt a moment of shame for his involvement with the wicked man, but there was very little one could do when their pockets were to let and such a one came around with the promise of funds for what had seemed like such an easy task. He reminded himself again that this task would in fact provide a ready solution to all his woes. Trying to brace his weak-willed spine into order, Lord Austen refused to look at the other man as he stalked away on a mission of vengeance.

ଓ ଈ

Alex had always been a keen observer. *Stupid skill to have when one is a boy in a family such as the one you grew up in*, he thought dourly. *But it turns out to be terribly handy once one is an adult. You still end up seeing things you wish were not true, but at least a duke has a certain power to affect a change. Now what am I going to do about the fact that the awful Sir Jason Broderick is looking with such evil intent at my Rosie?*

Striving for discretion, Alex kept his attention focused on the wicked knight while making every effort not to be obvious to anyone, especially not Broderick himself. *It would not do to have the hunter realize he had become prey*, Alex thought with a sinister twist to his lip. *No doubt the man has noticed that Rose has been introducing Lady Anne to eligible gentlemen. I wonder how observant Rosamund is. As a child, she could be so single-minded that the house could burn down around her and she would barely notice if she were absorbed in something she thought was interesting. I shall have to put a bug in her ear tomorrow to curb her matchmaking efforts with regards to Lady Anne, if she does not want to draw the ire of Broderick down around her head.*

Nodding to various friends and connections as he made his way through the crowds, he was able to keep his eyes upon the goings on of the various parties. Alex was impressed to see how Rose handled herself with whomever she encountered. Her poise would make her an excellent duchess. Alex was shocked by that stray thought, but it was true nonetheless. Just not a Duchess of Wrentham, he reminded himself as he continued to keep his eye on her movements and tried not to notice how pretty she looked this evening in her pale primrose gown, with the light from the myriad candles shimmering in her chestnut hair.

Aren't you just so poetical this evening, Alex thought to himself in derision. With relief, he saw Rose approach her mother. He was most certain Lady Smythe would be able to keep Broderick at bay.

Chapter Fourteen

"How did you enjoy the ambassador's ball?"

Rose gasped as she heard the low voice near her ear. The shiver that slid its way down her spine was not unpleasant, although she was undecided how exactly she felt about it.

"Alexander Edward Philip Milton Wrentham! You fairly scared a year off my life," she declared heatedly, covering her confusion with playful anger.

"You really need to learn to pay more attention to your surroundings, my dear lady. I noticed last night that you seemed to be playing matchmaker with Lady Anne. Have you lost all your senses? Sir Broderick took note and did not look at all pleased. You are supposed to be making every effort not to draw attention to what we are up to." Alex hadn't meant to rile her up, but when he saw her it seemed he couldn't help himself.

Rose could feel the heat rising into her cheeks and her temper rose with it. "I was not drawing undue attention to myself, Your Grace," she insisted with emphasis, as she stuck her chin at a stubborn angle.

"Then why in heaven's name would you be visibly thwarting Broderick's plans by trying to set her up with other eligible *parti*?"

Rose felt goose bumps break out on her skin as she sensed the duke's conflicted feelings toward her. She focused on his anger as he ground his teeth in frustration.

"Think on it, Your Grace," Rose demanded with impatience. "Why would Broderick think anything of my actions? He has no way of knowing what I overheard. Do not all the young debutantes share their giggles about the eligible lords and gentlemen wending their way through the salons of the *ton* during the Season? Why would anyone remark upon my introducing Lady Anne to anyone?"

"Mayhap no one else would, you impertinent little chit, but Broderick did. I saw him watching you with his eely eyes. You are the one who told me you have a history with him. He may not be as ignorant of that history as you had thought. He seemed quite aware of the fact that you were trying to match Lady Anne up with that viscount, Lord Edgecombe. And as despicable as I think he is, I would never accuse him of being daft. He might be fully aware of your reasons for doing so."

Now Rose laughed, although it was not a sound filled with mirth. "Sir Jason Broderick would never understand my reasons for trying to help Lord Anthony and Lady Anne see that they would make a perfectly lovely couple."

"What are you talking about? He will no doubt consider it an attempt to foul up his plans."

Rose shrugged as nonchalantly as possible, which clearly irritated the duke. He growled low in his throat at her display of disregard.

"Your Grace, do you also think that is why I was doing it?" she asked in a low voice.

Alex's eyes grew wary at her tone. "Is that not what you were about?"

"Not at all," she insisted swiftly. "We have every intention of fouling up his plans as you said, by other means. But I feel badly about it because Lady Anne is a sweet young woman who deserves better than her father intends for her. I am sure he means well, thinking he is killing two birds with one stone as it were, but since I cannot allow her to marry you, I feel duty-bound to ensure she finds someone suitable in your place."

As they were arguing, Alex and Rose had come toe to toe and were glaring at one another fiercely. Rose could feel her chest rising and falling furiously and cared not a fig about the flags of colour flying high in her cheeks. She could hardly believe the duke was being so daft. She would never have thought it.

Rose's passionate defence of her choices must have affected Alex. She could see his gaze darkening as his focus strayed from her eyes to her lips. Rose felt the most profound desire to lick them as her mouth suddenly dried with nerves. She felt frozen in place, her heart racing with a maelstrom of emotion as she watched his unsteady hand reach toward her. Searching his gaze, she could see that Alex was unconvinced of the wisdom of his next action, but he was doing it anyway. It was startling how heat curled in her belly in concert with his warm hand curling around her nape as the duke pulled her face toward his own.

The few chaste kisses Rose had previously experienced had done nothing to prepare her for this moment. The warm brush of his breath just before their lips touched was but a prelude to the multitude of sensations that inundated her senses as their lips met and held. A warning sound was clanging at the back of her mind that this was a terribly bad idea, but for this moment Rose was determined to indulge in the sensations coursing through her.

All her senses were heightened and they were all sending an overload of messages. She could hear his intake of breath, sharp in the hushed silence of the great room. He smelled of the shaving soap he had so recently used and tasted delicious as his lips expertly parted hers and his tongue teased at the entrance of her mouth. She would never have thought tasting someone else would be a nice experience but in that moment, it crossed her mind that she would happily do this all day.

She wasn't quite sure what to do with her hands, but she was terribly glad she had not worn gloves as she reached up and ran her fingers through his silky hair, glorying in the springy thickness. Her other hand found its way to his cheek and she caressed him mindlessly. The eyes she had closed briefly in the moment opened slowly to better take in the sight of him and they connected yearningly with his intense stare. Seeing the familiar sea-green shade brought a shaft of clarity to her befuddled mind.

I am standing in Burlington House for all the world to see, kissing the Duke of Wrentham, of all people. Horror dawning, Rose pulled herself wrenchingly away from Alex. Without conscious thought, her hand pulled back and cracked loudly against his clean-shaven cheek, while her other hand slapped over her own open mouth.

The momentary inertia that had seized her finally released its grasp on Rose, much to her relief. She could feel the heat ebbing and flowing from her cheeks as they flooded with colour and then paled as she thought of all the ramifications of their interlude. Once again, her eyes darted around to make sure no one was watching them or had seen what had transpired. Relief flooded her as she realized they were alone.

"Whatever were you thinking, Your Grace?" she demanded.

"I was thinking that you looked delectably adorable in your righteous indignation," Alex explained with a drawl, biting back his grin as her ire rose as if on cue.

"You are truly as despicable as my parents have been saying the Wrenthams are. I did not want to believe it, but you have just proven that it is true." She barely recognized the soft breathy voice that was issuing from her lips and cringed at the lack of certainty and the utter disappointment she could hear.

☙ ❧

Alex could hear the crack of her hand still ringing in his ears, and he was fleetingly surprised at the sting her little hand had managed to produce. The sensual haze he had momentarily been in quickly dissipated as he took in the horror and terror etched on Rose's beautiful face. It was highly inappropriate, but he felt like smiling, seeing her rosebud mouth scrunched up into such a look of bitter distaste. It did not sit right on her usually open, smiling face.

Alex refused to be cowed by this slip of a girl, he was a duke for heaven's sake, but it required a great deal of effort. Straightening himself to his fullest height and gathering all his dignity around him, he looked down his nose at her. Keeping a tight rein on his own temper and trying to keep in mind that she was no doubt labouring under a plethora of emotions, he hoped he would not say something he could not take back because clearly thinking before she spoke was not of much concern to his Rosie.

"Pull yourself together, Rosamund," he bade her in as authoritative a tone as he could muster. "I have not accosted you in any truly dastardly way, as you are clearly thinking at this moment. Naught is amiss here. I thought a girl with your experience would comprehend and be able to handle the heightened senses that a situation such as this can cause."

Feeling like a toad as he saw the myriad of emotions that crossed her expressive face, Alex hated himself for playing upon the worries he was well aware concerned her. He could not help the awe he felt as he saw her pull her dignity and composure around herself like a cloak.

☙ ❧

Rose's pride stiffened her spine and she was able to look Alex in the eye as she coolly began speaking, obviously deciding to just ignore the entire personal situation and merely address the whole reason they had met up in the first place.

"Thank you for meeting up with me, Your Grace. I had a very enlightening conversation with Lady Yorkleigh about Sir Broderick yesterday and it became more obvious why he would be so intent upon controlling you. He is out to control the government. You are high enough in the House of Lords for his needs. According to Lady Yorkleigh, Sir Broderick has had his sights set upon The Prince for quite some time."

"Prinny?" Alex asked, incredulous. "Whatever for?"

"While, if I understand correctly, although his authority has been drastically curtailed, he is still the regent of our country and will one day be King. He may not have as much power as his father or grandfather once did, but he is still the monarch. As such, he has the most authority in all the land."

"If you believe that you are far more naïve than I ever thought," Alex scoffed.

Rose could feel her eyebrows spring into her hairline and her jaw unhinged inelegantly. "Now you are just being ridiculous, Your Grace," she huffed.

"No, I am not, my dear," Alex explained rather condescendingly much to Rose's disgust. His snide smile made her palm itch to slap his face again, but she managed to keep it firmly at her side.

☙ ❧

Alex saw her clench her hands and had to exert an effort over his features to keep a grin from breaking over his face. *The lovely young woman is so easy to goad if you know her well enough.* He could see that the situation between the Smythes and Wrenthams was going to have to be straightened out as soon as possible, because there was no way he was going to be able to stand by and watch this treasure be married off to someone else. He would learn to live with her managing ways. He now knew the quiet girl he had envisioned as his wife would bore him to tears. And while he missed his brother, the circumstances of his death did not need to dictate Alex's own future. Chastising himself that such thoughts were not at all helpful at the moment, he shoved the idea from his mind for the time being and returned to the subject at hand.

Realizing it would not do to have her stomp off in a huff as they still needed to work together amicably to clear up the Broderick situation, Alex tried for a placating tone. "You were, of course, correct in stating that the Prince Regent holds the highest office of authority," Alex began, placing slight emphasis on the word *office*. "But as you also said, much of his power has been curtailed. The man who wields the most authority is actually the Prime Minister."

Alex could see Rose's eyes widening in surprise as he began his explanation and had to bite back his amusement. It was clear that he had been paying attention to his lessons in school and had been working hard in the government over the past few years. He had never had interests like this when they had been friends.

She finally waved him to silence. With a sweet, conciliatory smile upon her lips she offered an apology. "Your Grace, I am sorry for calling you ridiculous. Clearly you know much more than you ever let on. But please recall that I am fairly well educated in these matters as well. We are wasting our precious time by standing here debating the politics of the situation. It matters naught. The fact is, your very speech reveals even more why Broderick would be wanting to control you. As the Duke of Wrentham you are, by birth, highly placed in our government's affairs. And by the words you just spoke you displayed a degree of knowledge and involvement that make you dangerous to anyone not on the same side as you."

Alex blinked at her in surprise. Rose's lips twitched with her amusement, and she was clearly taken aback to see his answering grin.

"How can you find this funny?" she asked with confusion.

"Another perspective is always so helpful," he explained rather vaguely. Now it was his turn to wave for silence as he could see that Rose was about to launch into speech. "You were absolutely right—we must not waste any time. We really need to ensure that we are not seen together. I fear that Broderick may have taken notice of you, and I do not want you in harm's way. It would be most helpful if we could ascertain what *exactly* he is after. Do you think he wants to be Prime Minister or some such position, or is he after something more specific?"

"Men that seek power are so often after both more power *and* something specific," Rose answered pensively. "In Broderick's case, I have never taken the time to try to figure out the workings of his mind, but in Vienna he was involved in fouling up the land divisions. I am uncertain how that benefits him, but you can be sure it does somehow, whether someone was paying him handsomely or if the land in question was his. Now there are to be more negotiations taking place in Paris shortly. My father is about to depart."

"Your father is leaving town," Alex repeated in surprise. "But that shall leave you without protection."

Rose blinked at the duke with surprise, clearly unsure how to respond to his remark. "I do not know whether I should remind you that I do not require protection or to explain that my father's absence will not leave me unprotected," she said with a small laugh. She then looked around at where they were, and Alex could see she was remembering what had transpired between them. A tide of warm colour rose in her cheeks. "Well, maybe I do need protection," she conceded with another small laugh. "But my father's presence or absence will not make much difference in that regard." Seeing the arguments written on Alex's face she continued, placating, "My brother is to arrive in Town on the morrow, so I shall still have a male family member about, have no fear."

Remembering her brother as a towheaded little boy did not reassure the duke as to his friend's safety. "Your brother is a boy, Rosamund, what good will he be?"

"Time does march on, Your Grace. He is just about to turn nineteen. He has finished his schooling and he has even been on the Grand Tour for some time. It is hard to imagine, but he is practically a man."

They shared an amused smile before Rose continued. "Once again, we have strayed from our topic. I do declare, Your Grace, we are rather useless at this. It would seem we could fritter the day away mumbling nonsense at each other and we shall have nothing accomplished. I must be leaving shortly or my absence will be remarked upon. Do tell me if you can think of anything we ought to be doing."

Alex grinned at his companion and then wrinkled his brow. "You are right, it does seem like we could easily spend the day together."

Rose grew flustered. "That is not what I was trying to say, Your Grace," she insisted with discomfort.

"I know, I know," Alex soothed. "I was merely funning you. Now, do you have any ideas? Do you think it might be best to put a bug in your father's ear at this point? It would seem that neither of us is fully equipped to thwart the knight in whatever nefarious plot he might have. If it does have something to do with the treaties being negotiated in Paris, since neither you nor I are going, there is nothing we can do to stop him."

Rose chewed her lip as she thought on his words, oblivious to the intent expression descending upon the duke's face as he watched her, licking his own lips hungrily. He tried to wipe all expression from his face as her attention returned to him.

"Are you quite all right, Your Grace?" she asked solicitously. "You look a trifle unwell."

"I am perfectly fine, thank you for asking," he declared with aplomb. "What have you decided?"

"I think you are quite correct. We do need my father involved now. There is no avoiding it. But this might be the last time we can talk."

Alex found the earnest look she cast his way to be utterly endearing and felt his heart swell with emotion that he made every effort to keep within bounds as she continued.

"It is quite possible that I shall be banished to our estate if I cannot find the perfectly correct words to convey the seriousness of the matter to my father. Even if I do find the right words, if I have to tell him of our involvement, that will most likely still be the outcome. Or mayhap he will take me with him to Paris, although he no doubt is fully aware that would be a reward, not a punishment," she mused with a grin.

When Alex made to protest, she waved away his concerns. "Do not trouble yourself, Your Grace. I cannot say that I am truly attached to this Season business. It does not suit my disposition to be placed on the market for matrimonial bidding. As you yourself have remarked, I am not the biddable sort of girl most noblemen want to take as their wife, and I so wish to be useful. I will be perfectly happy to go back to the country, or better yet, to head off to Paris with my father. I am not averse to the idea of marriage—it is just that the silliness of catching a husband drives me mad. Perhaps my father will marry me off to the nearest statesman and that will suit us all perfectly well."

Alex could see that her wobbling smile did not quite reach her eyes, but there was nothing he could do as she bolstered her spirits and ploughed on bravely. "I am not telling you this to make you feel sorry for me, Your Grace. I am just wanting to warn you that you might be on your own to deal with Broderick if I do get banished. And in the event that his schemes do not involve Paris, you shall have to be vigilant to thwart him. I know you do not enjoy these sorts of shenanigans so you must be sure to enlist whatever help you might need. If I am well away from the situation, you need not fear for my reputation, so it is not as necessary to keep matters secret."

☙ ❧

"You look so tragic right at this moment, Rosie. I cannot believe that you are as unmoved by the thought of banishment as you say."

Alex's concern caused the tear she was valiantly trying to suppress to spill over and slide slowly down her cheek. "I truly would not mind going back to the country," she explained as she brushed the offending moisture impatiently away. "I just wish I could be around to finish this thing. I am the one who uncovered the problem. I would dearly love to be around to see its resolution."

"Well then, do not borrow trouble, my dear," Alex declared with confidence. "I do believe you are a sufficiently resourceful girl that you will be able to tell Lord Smythe about this without getting yourself banished. Have you thought about what you will say? Think it through, and if you would like, you could even practice on me. I could play the role of your father."

If it had been the duke's intention to make Rose's mood lighten, he did the exactly right thing as she burst into a fit of giggles that was difficult for her to control.

"Oh Alex, you are a complete hand," she declared after she managed to get her mirth within bounds. "I do not think I could remain serious if you were to try to pretend to be my father, but I do appreciate your suggestion. And you are absolutely correct—if I think on it enough I should be able to muddle my way through. My main concern, even more than the fear of banishment, is to ensure that my father takes this threat seriously and does not merely dismiss it because of your involvement. It might be best if I leave you out completely. This would ensure I get to stay in London to keep an eye on the scoundrel, if he does not head to Paris, and would also keep my father focused on the problem. If I can skip over certain details without Papa noticing, I just might be able to pull it off." She concluded this statement with a cheeky grin.

Alex returned her grin cheerfully. "You were always good at pulling the wool over everyone's eyes when you were a slip of a girl. I am perfectly sure that you are even better at it now than you ever were. If anyone can get Lord Smythe to miss a detail or two, it is you."

"But your statement reminds me that my father scarcely ever misses a detail, so I shall have to be alert and diligent." She paused for a moment, deep in thought. "All right, Your Grace, I really must go. This is the best course of action we can take at this point. I will do my utmost to get a message to you as to my father's reaction, whatever the outcome. If he has anything helpful to share I will endeavour to pass it on to you as discreetly as possible, even if I have to leave Town." On an impulse, she grabbed for Alex's hand. "Promise me you will be careful, Alex. Broderick can be a very dangerous man. Do not do anything foolish, and enlist whatever help you might need."

He must have felt the slight tremble in her hand despite her brave words because Alex squeezed her hand between both of his. "I promise you, little one. I will take care of myself and keep that upstart from causing any trouble for our beloved country. Now you promise me that you will take care of yourself. I know your parents love you and would never harm you, but they are not completely rational when it comes to the subject of the Wrenthams. You have repeatedly expressed concern over my hatred of double dealings, but in this case, I absolve you of any need for guilt. Lie if you must. I would dearly love to have you remain my partner in this particular endeavour."

Rose pulled back in surprise, gratified by his concern, but chagrined over his words. "Your Grace, I could never lie outright to my papa. I would like to avoid mentioning any explanation of our particular involvement, but if I cannot avoid it, I will not lie about it. That is where I draw the line in my life of spying."

She could not quite decipher the flicker of emotions that crossed Alex's face, but Rose felt another wave of goose bumps rise on her flesh, as she thought he was about to kiss her again. She took a step back from him; he allowed her to pull her hand from his grasp, and the moment passed.

Alex summed up their conversation. "Very well, Miss Rose. I will trust your judgment and await word from you. I promise to remain vigilant regardless of what transpires between you and your father. And I will wish you luck," he finalized with another wide grin.

Rose appreciated his lightening of the mood. She was glad their interlude was about to conclude. His presence had been unsettling to her the last few times they encountered one another but this time, with that kiss at the beginning, it was nearly more than she could handle. She was grateful they had managed to have a coherent conversation despite the swirling emotions she was experiencing, but she was also glad their time together was coming to an end. It would not do for her to fall in love with the Duke of Wrentham, she scolded herself for what felt like the millionth time, as she hurriedly took her leave of him and gathered her things.

Without a backward glance, she strode to the open doorway, but before exiting the room she could not resist turning back for one last look at the handsome nobleman. With an upraised hand, she waved goodbye and forced her reluctant feet to bear her away.

☙ ❧

Alex was left staring at the empty doorway, his arm still elevated in the small wave they had exchanged. With rueful regret, he took a deep breath and turned away. Looking about, he decided to leave by another way. His usually alert senses were somewhat preoccupied with thoughts of Miss Smythe. He wondered if they would ever again be able to share such easy camaraderie. With renewed determination, he reminded himself that he was a duke, and he would have to make it possible. All of a sudden, though, his dulled wits sharpened as he realized someone was watching him. From the quick glance he got before that *someone* got up and tried to hurry away, it looked as though they might have become comfortable watching him for a while. That meant that he had been watching *them.* That is when Alex's blood ran quite cold, and his previously dulled wits truly came into focus.

Endeavouring to appear nonchalant, he turned his head in the direction he was walking, toward the back entrance of Burlington House, while keeping an eye on the character out of the corner of his eye. *Who are you?* he asked inside his mind. *And are you watching me on the orders of Sir Broderick? And if so, how am I to ever get word to Rose?* was his last anguished thought as he hurried toward his waiting carriage.

Glad to see his tiger on the ground on the far side of his team, the duke hastened to join him, forestalling the young man's leap onto the back of the conveyance.

"Pete, come here. I have another assignment for you today." With a quick glance over his shoulder, he could see that the observer was still in sight and had, in fact, paused to see if the duke was still watching him. Hidden as he was behind the horses, Alex did not think the other man could see him. "Do you see that squirrelly looking man by the last pillar?"

"The buck with the brown coat, whose hat looks like someone stomped on it?" Pete asked eagerly.

"The very one. I want you to follow him as discreetly as possible and then let me know what you find out." Alex paused to regard his young servant seriously. "I must warn you, this could be dangerous. I will not turn you off if you refuse."

"Get on wit' you, yer Grace. I can look after meself. And danger ain't nothin' but excitement with a different name."

Alex grinned at the young man's words. "Very well then, do not let him notice you, and you absolutely must not be caught. Run away if you are in the least bit of danger. Whatever you might find out is more useful to me than a dead tiger."

"Discreet is my other name," Pete responded with quiet dignity as he peered out from between the horses' legs. "I'll have all the info you could want and more before the end of the night, yer Grace. Don't you trouble yer mind none about me."

With those words the young man scampered quickly away from the carriage and took up an advantageous position close to the large building.

Alex made a show of checking his horses' harnesses and then climbed up into the vehicle in order to make an explanation for his disappearance from view, hoping the scoundrel watching him would not realize he had been set upon. With a mental shrug, despite his myriad of misgivings, Alex drove away leaving his tiger to gather as much intelligence as he could.

Hoping he was wrong, Alex feared that his Rosie was now in much more danger than he ever would have thought, and the duke wracked his brain for any ideas on how to mitigate the danger.

As soon as he arrived at his large house in Mayfair, Alex summoned several footmen to his study as he contemplated how Miss Smythe would react were she to realize just how capable of duplicity he had become. He had found it quaint to realize how innocent she truly was despite her protestations otherwise and could not bear to disabuse her of her ideas. *But how could she possibly believe that a duke could remain as innocent as she thinks me? Clearly the poor dear has no real experience, despite her protestations to the contrary.*

"Thank you, men, for your quick response to my summons," Alex began, addressing the three large men assembled in his study, dressed in the Wrentham livery. "I have a job for you."

"All right, guv'nor," declared the most vocal of the three, happily. "Not to be rude about your hospitality in providing us with work, but being a footman is deadly dull."

Alex grinned at the man's words. "This job might not be that much more interesting, I am afraid, Craig. I need the three of you to rotate shifts watching Miss Rosamund Smythe."

The three men looked at each other before turning blank looks on their master. Craig, always the spokesman, answered for the three of them. "Are we watching her to keep you informed of her activities, yer Grace?" he asked as politely as possible. Not that he really cared what the duke was up to, but he needed to know the scope of their duties.

"That is not exactly what I meant, although I would be glad if you could manage to keep me apprised of her whereabouts. I fear she might be in danger, and given the current situation between our families, I cannot warn her or her father of the danger. I need you three to watch over her as discreetly as possible, and keep your eye out for anyone else that might be watching her or her house."

"Ah, I see. Right-o, yer Grace. That should be right easy. If that will be all, we'll get right on it."

The young men made to leave before one of them thought of something. "I'm assumin' we oughta change out of our uniforms, right, yer Grace?"

"That is an excellent idea, Thomas, yes. Try to be as unobtrusive as possible. My livery being spotted near the Smythe residence would give rise to comments and conjecture, I am quite certain, and would no doubt get you chased away as quick as a wink, too."

Grinning, the three men exited the room, hurrying away to fulfil their duties. Alex could hear them grumbling as they went down the hall, arguing over who would be the first to take a turn at the task. He was happy to have such a reliable staff and hoped it would be enough. He really needed to get a warning to Rose, but a note delivered by one of his footmen would be impossible, and even a hired urchin would be noticed by her parents.

With fortuitous timing, Alex thought of Wesley, just as he heard the knocker on his front door. Jumping to his feet, Alex hoped it was his friend coming to pay a visit. Not waiting for the butler to announce him, the duke strode toward the front of the house.

"My Lord Dunbar is here to see you, Your Grace," the butler announced redundantly as Alex entered the foyer.

"Excellent, William, thank you," Alex answered cheerfully as he walked past both the butler and Lord Dunbar, expecting the viscount to follow him as he entered the front receiving room. Glad to see Wesley close on his heels, Alex shut the door firmly behind him after instructing the butler, "See that we are not disturbed for at least a quarter of an hour."

"Very well, Your Grace," the butler tried to answer, but the doors were already closed on him.

"You look in fine spirits this morning, Your Grace. I was unsure if you would even be up and about at this hour of the day," Wesley declared to his good friend.

"Whatever do you mean?" Alex was confused.

"It is still a couple of hours before noon, Your Grace. Despite your early call upon me the other day, I know it is not your usual habit to be about so early," Wesley stated with a grin.

"Is it really still that early?" Alex asked, surprised. "I would have thought it was halfway through the afternoon," he mused. "Well never mind about that. What are you doing here, if you thought I would not be about? Is it something urgent, or can it wait, because I really have need of you."

"That is why I am here. I awoke this morning remembering your concerns last night over Broderick, and I thought to offer my services this morning, such that they are. Keep in mind that I am a novice, but I am willing to do whatever is in my power to assist you and our fair country."

"Those are truly noble sentiments, my good man, but right at the moment, I need your assistance for the fair Rosamund."

"Rosamund?" Wesley asked a trifle blankly.

"We met this morning to discuss the situation, and I fear we were being watched. I failed to notice until she had already left, so I was unable to warn her. And of course, I cannot call on her to deliver the news myself."

"Nor can you send round a discreet note," finished the viscount, catching the duke's idea. "So, you would like me to call upon her and apprise her of this development. Well, that shan't strain my skills overmuch. I would be happy to. How urgent is the delivery of this news? Should I set out immediately or wait until the socially acceptable hour? And is there anything else you might need me to do?"

Alex grinned at Dunbar's willing offer of help. "Thank you so much, Wes. I truly appreciate it. Part of me wants you to rush right over there, but it will draw the least amount of attention if you call at a more acceptable time, of course. And I am fairly certain she should be safe for the time being. She was planning to return home and tell her father about Broderick's plots, or what little we know about them, at the very least. She could be closeted with him for a while. And she is afraid she may be banished after that interview, so if she gets sent back home to their estate, she should be reasonably safe there."

Wesley had a thought. "You say you were observed together. Do you think the person who was watching you heard your discussion?"

"I think it highly unlikely, but it is possible. I was not paying very close attention to our surroundings, I am ashamed to admit, and did not notice him until after Rose had left, like I said. When I saw him, he was far enough away that it is doubtful he could hear our words, as we were speaking in low tones anyway. But under the circumstances, if he is one of Broderick's men, just the fact of us being together is damning, especially when coupled with her matchmaking efforts last night. Broderick will most certainly come to the conclusion that we are onto him. I have no way of knowing how that will affect him, but I must admit I am relieved that someone with knowledge, authority, and ability shall soon be involved in this convoluted affair."

Wesley was nodding in sympathetic understanding. Alex continued on when it became obvious his friend had nothing further to ask or add. "I set my young groom to follow the one who was watching us. You may tell Rosie that so she knows more information might be forthcoming. But I pray you do not tell her that I have set my men to watching her. I am unsure if she would be receptive to this idea. She has the ridiculous notion that she is capable of looking after herself."

Seeing Wesley's face screwed up into an objection Alex laughed and carried on, "I do not mean to disparage her abilities, do not get me wrong here. She is an intelligent young woman, fully capable of all sorts of things that I probably cannot even fathom, but one cannot get around the fact that she is a girl, and as such, a man such as the likes of Broderick is quite capable of doing her a great deal of harm.

"And if she is labouring under the delusion that he is unaware of her involvement, she will not be alert to any dangers. Even once she is made aware, I still cannot be easy about her safety. Even though it is she who brought me the information that has led to this situation, I cannot help but feel that it is my fault she may be in danger." He paused before adding as an afterthought, "And possibly even banished."

"All understandable sentiments. But I must ask you an impertinent question, Your Grace." Wesley paused while Alex looked at him fully with his left eyebrow quirked in haughty inquiry. "What are your intentions toward Miss Smythe? Given the state of affairs, as you called them, between your two families, I should think you would be delighted to see her in danger or banished."

"Why would I ever wish to see her in danger?" Alex was shocked at his friend's suggestion. "Even with the difficulties between the Smythes and the house of Wrentham, I would never wish to see any of her family in danger, least of all Rosie." Alex paused as he attempted to bring his temper under control and thought more about Wesley's words. "And I would dislike her to be banished, as well. I am hoping to find some way to bridge the breach between our families, if you must know."

Wesley grinned. "That is excellent news, Your Grace." Seeing the warning look being shot his way by the duke, he hastened to add, "News that I will, of course, keep to myself."

"See that you do," Alex warned before beginning to pace. "How soon do you think you could call on her?"

Wesley chuckled over the duke's obvious concerned distraction. "Did we not just agree that I cannot arrive before the fashionable hour? I thought to take her riding in the park. That way we can be assured of privacy for our discussion. I could, reasonably speaking, arrive a little early, even an hour or two, but that would still be a couple hours from now. It would actually be wise for me to do so, then the park will not be overcrowded, and we will be guaranteed privacy for our conversation."

"Yes, yes, of course, I apologize, Dunbar, my wits have gone begging," Alex excused with a wry grin. "It is just as well if she is to be closeted with her father for some time—no doubt her explanations will require more than a few minutes. I just fear that if she is unsuccessful in keeping mention of me out of her story, she may be in hot water with her parents."

"Understandable fears, Your Grace," Wesley acknowledged before reasoning, "But even if they do send her packing back to the wilds of their estate, they would have to allow her a little bit of time for packing. And I would imagine they would not send her off when she is bound to end up driving in the dead of night, so she would have at least until tomorrow morning. Surely, not to place too fine a point upon my own importance, but I *am* a viscount—they would allow me a few moments of her time, no matter how frustrated they might be with their errant daughter."

Alex finally found reason for mirth, and he let out a loud guffaw over his friend's words. "You are a complete hand, my lord. Thank you for that reminder. Lord and Lady Smythe might, in fact, view you in the form of a saviour, and they would be delighted to bundle her up into your carriage for a ride. That is, as long as they do not remember that we are such good friends."

Wesley waved away the duke's concern. "I am known to be a highly sociable creature, one who has many varying friendships. They shall not dwell overmuch upon our connection, I am sure."

Alex was not fully convinced, but they lacked any other plan so there was naught he could do. He had plans to ride around to visit his solicitors once more and engage their assistance in finding out Broderick's schemes, now that it was determined they were not directed at the duke personally but, in fact, the entire government. Alex bade a hasty goodbye to Lord Dunbar and hurried about his own preparations.

"I shall wish you luck, then, Your Grace," Wesley said jauntily before making his way to the door.

"And you as well," came the heavier reply.

Alex stood watching the door as the viscount left nearly as swiftly as he had arrived. Thanking the heavens for the comfortable friendship, the duke pulled the bell for his butler as he strode from the room.

"See that my phaeton is brought round and ready in fifteen minutes, I have to go out forthwith."

"Very good, Your Grace."

Chapter Fifteen

Rose had collected her maid from the foyer of Burlington House, where Mary had been happily flirting with a footman.

"I beg your pardon, Miss, I should have been more attentive to you," Mary was stammering, hurrying along in Rose's wake, mistaking her haste for anger.

Rose stopped abruptly. "No pardon is needed, Mary, I can assure you. I am certainly not angry with you, whatever gave you that impression?"

"You are very quiet, Miss Rose, and going as fast your skirts will allow. Besides, the pinched look about your mouth made me think you weren't in the best humour."

Rose had to laugh over her maid's words. "I apologize, Mary, if I was going too fast. I have a task ahead of me that I am not at all looking forward to, and I would like it to be over and done with. But that very same task requires some planning and I am worried about it, thus my quietness and perhaps a pinched look that I did not realize I was sporting. Thank you for reminding me that my feelings write themselves upon my face. I really must make a greater effort at being stoic."

Now Mary laughed. "Oh no, Miss, you certainly do not owe me any apologies, to be sure. What has you so troubled? Is there anything I can help you with? Does it have anything to do with the duke, Miss?"

"Yes and no, Mary. I do not think there is anything you can do to help me with this one. The duke and I agreed that this is a far greater problem than the two of us can handle on our own, and now is the time to apprise my father of the situation. I fear you will be assigned to help me pack my bags when my parents ship me back to the estate in disgrace over my association with Wrentham."

Rose could not even bring herself to say his name at this point as all her tumultuous feelings came back to the fore and she remembered the brief kiss they shared before she smacked his face. Hoping her face was not once more displaying her confused feelings, she shoved the thoughts to the back of her mind to be mulled over later. Now she had to concentrate on what to tell her father. She was relieved that they were nearly home.

"I cannot say I am sorry that you will be telling his lordship about this mess, Miss. I have not been easy with you traipsing around with the Duke of Wrentham messing with the likes of Sir Jason Broderick. Much better it is for Lord Smythe to be involved."

"You are quite correct, Mary. Now we had best hurry along. My mother mentioned that Papa is to leave for Paris. I dearly hope I have not missed him."

"But surely he would not depart without saying farewell to you," Mary protested.

"My father is far too busy to be concerned about such things, Mary."

"Yes, of course, Miss. Let's hurry along then," Mary agreed simply, lifting her skirts in order to be able to keep up with the long-legged strides of her mistress.

Endeavouring for decorum, Rose refrained from taking the stairs two at a time and took a deep breath before opening the door to their home.

"Has my father left yet, Walter?" she asked as the butler was helping her with her coat.

"No, Miss, he is in his study. He is getting everything ready for an early morning departure for Paris, Miss. He asked that he not be disturbed, as he has so many things that need to be done before he leaves."

"Thank you, Walter, I will try my best not to take too much of his time, but I really do need to speak with him on a matter of some urgency." Rose would not be deterred despite the sinking feeling in her nervous stomach.

Feeling as though birds had joined the butterflies fluttering in her stomach, Rose tried to ignore her shaking limbs as she made her way to her father's study. Taking another deep, steadying breath before she knocked, Rose waited to hear her father's summons.

"Enter," Lord Smythe called distractedly.

"Good morning, Papa, I hope I am not disturbing you too terribly. Walter mentioned that you asked not to be disturbed, but if you have a couple of minutes, I need to speak to you about an urgent matter."

Lord Smythe looked at his daughter in surprise. Her tone must have conveyed the pent up anxiety she was feeling, even though she had striven for an air of light inquiry. Putting down his pen, the baron rose from his chair and came around his desk to grab his daughter's hand.

"I know I am often preoccupied, my dear, but I will never be too busy for you. Please, have a seat here beside me and tell me what concerns you." He seated her in one of the two chairs situated in front of his desk and he perched himself on the edge of the other one, keeping her cold hand in his as his worry mounted over the look in his daughter's eyes.

"You are making me nervous, my dear. Will I have need of my brace of pistols?" he asked, hoping to lighten the mood.

"I dearly hope not," Rose replied with a shaky laugh.

Now that her father was near and willing to take on her burdens she felt an overwhelming urge to throw herself in his arms and cry. Bracing her backbone and reminding herself she was a fully competent woman, Rose lifted her chin proudly, took another deep, fortifying breath, and then launched into speech.

"It is about Broderick, Papa. I fear the scoundrel is up to no good and he has designs on the government."

The baron looked at his daughter with amazement. "Whatever do you mean, my dear?"

"Remember I told you that I have seen him about a little this Season? A new friend of mine, I am not sure if you know her, Lady Yorkleigh, warned me away from him."

"She is a good, sensible woman in that case."

"Yes, she does seem to be. She told me that he wishes to gain control over the Prince Regent. I do not know exactly what he is about, but I thought that you should know since you are leaving Town. I am not sure if he means to attend the Congress in Paris or if he will remain here, but you know so much more about these things than I do. I did not feel that this was a matter that I could look after any longer."

Lord Smythe was looking at his daughter with puzzlement clearly written upon his features. "I feel as though I have missed something in your explanation, my dear. I pray your forgiveness for being daft, but none of this is anything new. The knight has been a scoundrel for years. It is a wonder he is accepted in polite Society, but there is so rarely proof of his schemes. But proof or not, we have always known of his designs upon poor Prinny and his aspirations to control the government. Why does this have you in such fidgets at this time?"

Rose had so wished she did not have to go into any more details, but she realized now that was a futile dream. She took another deep breath and pushed on with her explanations. "I overheard him one night at a musicale I was attending, scheming with someone."

Lord Smythe gazed at his daughter, clearly expecting more details. Rose could feel heat rising in her cheeks and made herself plod on with her story. "He was speaking with Lord Austen. As far as I can tell, the man is a dunce and needs to make better choices in his companionship, but he is fairly innocent when it comes to conspiring against the government. He is just another pawn for Broderick to use. But it was very obvious to me that they were up to no good."

"When was this, my dear," Lord Smythe prodded. "And why did you decide to do the investigating on your own, without keeping me informed of these developments immediately? I still feel as though you are trying to withhold some pertinent details."

Rose realized it could be avoided no longer so she blurted out the full facts. "The two of them were plotting to entrap the Duke of Wrentham into a marriage alliance with Lord Austen's daughter, Lady Anne. I did not want to tell you right away because I feared you would dismiss my concerns about his schemes due to Wrentham's involvement. I was hoping to discern if there was truly a threat to anyone other than the duke himself before I came to you with this."

There was a heavy silence for several heartbeats while Lord Smythe regarded his daughter steadily. "I see," he finally said heavily. "And how did you come to the conclusion that there is a greater threat?" he asked, ignoring the truth that his daughter had skirted—that he did not care a fig for any threat against Wrentham.

"I spoke with Lady Anne and realized that they had targeted Wrentham for reasons other than his wealth and title."

"Some would probably consider the cur to be handsome," the baron replied dully.

"True, but that still does not seem to be the situation here, Papa. I truly feel as though this threat is not about Alex," seeing her father's reaction to the use of the duke's name, Rose hastened to cover her verbal tracks. "It would seem that Wrentham is taking his responsibilities seriously and has gotten involved in the House of Lords. Lady Anne says he is well connected. When I pried a bit deeper into her words I believe that, although she thinks this has to do with how many relatives he has—it was a term her father used. You and I both know that the Wrenthams are not an overly large family, so this must be tied in with the activities he has been engaging in politically. Lord Austen does not care about such things, so it can only be Broderick up to no good."

"And what do you propose I do about it? You were quite correct when you surmised that I would not give a fig for any threat toward Wrentham," Lord Smythe reminded his daughter testily.

"But that is just the thing, Papa, I do not believe the threat is really about the duke or even his wealth. I think Broderick merely sees him as a means to an end, a tool as it were, a means of getting to the Prince and influencing the workings of our government."

The baron eyed his daughter askance. "Are you aware that I need to be leaving at first light for very important negotiations in Paris?"

"Yes, Papa, that is why I felt the urgency to tell you now, before you leave. I did not know what else to do. I do not trust anyone else's discretion, knowledge, or intelligence, Papa. I needed your advice before you left. Do you think this is a serious threat, or am I full of feathers?"

The baron smiled over his daughter's choice of words and scrubbed his hand over his face as he thought about all the complications she had just thrown in his lap. Sighing heavily, he finally replied. "You did the right thing, daughter dear. I know this could not have been easy for you. You are right in thinking Broderick is a threat. He pretty much always is. Have you told anyone else about this?"

Rose started slightly at his question and tried to hide her guilty blush. She *so* did not want to tell her father about her meetings with the duke. She attempted to sidestep the question with half-truths. "I enlisted my friend Lady Elizabeth to help me in making contact with Lady Anne. Elizabeth is an earl's daughter and made her debut last year, so she is far more socially connected than I am. She was able to perform the introductions and help me tactfully question the other girl.

"I also spoke with Lady Yorkleigh, but I did not tell her why I wanted to know about Sir Broderick. I told her that my mother thought he would be a good match for me and I needed something to tell her to put her off. That wasn't untrue, but I did not think I ought to confide the true motivation behind my questions. I am accustomed to only telling you things, Papa. It has been troublesome to try to work this out without your help."

"Now we are getting to the crux of the matter, are we not, Rosamund? Why did you not come to me with this straight away? There is really very little I can do with just one night. Have you thought of the problems that could ensue if Broderick does not come to Paris? How can we set up safeguards so quickly?"

Rose hung her head dejectedly at her father's series of questions. "I am truly sorry, Papa. I thought for sure there would be proper safeguards in place, even without a specific threat and that once you were apprised of the situation you would know just who to tell and it would all be right and tight. I held onto my silence before now because I worried that you would be glad of a threat upon Wrentham and would not look beyond it to the potential larger danger. I wanted to see if I could find out whether it was just to the duke or if there was something more afoot."

"So, you did not trust me?" her father asked quietly, searching her face for her true feelings.

"Of course I trust you," Rose insisted hotly. "There is no one on this earth that I trust more than you. I just was unsure if you could have unclouded judgment when it comes to Wrentham. I truly am sorry, Papa, I should not have questioned your ability to be open minded."

"No, you shouldn't have, but I am man enough to admit that there is merit to your fears. If you had not done some digging, I might have been disposed to dismiss the possibility just because I do not care for the duke or the knight. But now something must be done. I shall make a few inquiries and send some messages to the proper quarters. It is good that you were not planning to accompany me to Paris. Now you can stay here and keep your eyes open for Broderick if he stays in Town. I shall have some protocols set up for you to follow before I leave."

Impulsively, Rose leaned forward and threw her arms around her father's neck, giving him a squeeze and placing a brief kiss upon his cheek before pulling back sheepishly. "Thank you so much, Papa. I am truly sorry for adding to your burdens, but I am so relieved to be able to share it with you."

"Anytime, my darling daughter. Please know that you can come to me anytime, but for the moment you really must run along and leave me to sort through a few things. I will be sure to reserve a few moments to discuss whatever is necessary before I leave."

Rose bounded up from her chair and hurried to leave her father in peace. She ran up to her room, not bothering for decorum, taking the stairs two at a time. She reasoned that inside, where no one but family and the servants could see, it would do nothing to sully her reputation.

With a grin, she tripped into her room and sprawled onto her bed.

"I am uncertain if you look as though things went well or not," Mary mused from the other side of the room where she had herself immersed in Rose's wardrobe, where she was searching for anything that needed mending.

"It went marvellously well, Mary. I should never have questioned otherwise. I have the most wonderful papa in the world. I didn't even have to tell him about speaking with Wrentham," she declared happily as she lifted her head to smile at the maid.

"I'm not so sure that you should have gotten away with it so freely. I worry this will embolden you to continue with such scandalous behaviour."

"Oh Mary, you fret too much. I can assure you I will not be meeting with the duke anymore. This problem has been handed over to those more equipped to handle it, and my days of clandestine behaviour are over. For now, anyway," she added as an afterthought. "Now I shall be free to apply my mind to deciding on a suitable groom for myself." She smiled cheekily at the maid before asking, "Speaking of that, were you able to give the matter any thought, or have you been as preoccupied as me with other matters?"

"I did, as a matter of fact, Miss," Mary began but then they were interrupted by a knock on the door.

Mary hurried over to see who was there.

A footman was standing there with a message. "A gentleman is here to see you, Miss Rose. He wishes to take you for a ride in the Park."

"A gentleman?" Rose repeated. "Does this gentleman have a name, Gregory?"

Blushing to his roots, the young servant answered, "Yes Miss, Walter says as it is Lord Wesley Dunbar here to see you, Miss. What should I tell him, Miss? Are you welcoming a ride with Lord Dunbar or should Walter tell him you are not at home to visitors this afternoon?"

The young Gregory needn't have finished his questions as Rose was already off the bed and next to Mary, pawing through her gowns to find suitable attire for a ride in the park. Running over to the window and looking down, she let out a little squeal when she saw the conveyance that surely belonged to the viscount standing in the street.

"Oh Mary, he brought a high-perch phaeton. I shall be the envy of all the ladies this afternoon," she declared with glee while glancing at the clock with a frown. "Although, it does seem rather early for a fashionable ride around Hyde Park. Mayhap his lordship plans to go elsewhere and that is why we need to have an earlier start."

Now Rose thought of another thing, and she turned wide eyes upon her maid. "Do you think it's acceptable for me to go out for a drive with the viscount right now? What if my father needs to speak with me? Has the footman left? Perhaps we should have him take a message to Lord Smythe and see what he has to say about my going out for a little while."

The footman was still waiting. In her excitement, Rose had failed to properly answer the poor lad. He was standing waiting for her reply. It did not take long for a reply to come back. "Your father says you are to carry on about your business and enjoy your afternoon. He will not have much to tell you before this evening, or maybe not even until early in the morning before he leaves."

It was the answer she had been hoping for. She was already half changed into a pretty gown of sprigged muslin that perfectly matched the darling parasol she had recently purchased to keep the still warm, late autumn sun off her face. "I shall need a spencer, too, Mary. The sun might be warm right now, but in a carriage such as a phaeton I am sure to catch my death from the breeze if I am not careful to cover myself up."

Before too many moments had passed she was ready to descend to greet the gentleman caller.

ଓ ଛ

Lord Dunbar was pacing in the Smythes' front receiving room, hoping earnestly the young lady was not going to keep him waiting for too many moments longer. The suspense was eating at him and he was anxious to be on the way. He heard a commotion in the foyer and turned to look toward the door to see what was going on.

His mouth opened on a quiet gasp of surprise. "Miss Rosamund, you do look ravishing this afternoon. I shall surely be the envy of all the gentlemen we encounter this afternoon," he complimented.

Rose blushed prettily at his compliments, but maintained her composure sufficiently to ask primly. "And where might we be going, my lord? I thought it a little odd for you to be calling round at this hour."

"Can a gentleman not just be that anxious to see you?"

Rose's tinkle of laughter filled the air between them. "Now, that is a bouncer if ever I heard one, my lord."

Wesley could not resist the twinkle in her eyes as she gazed at him merrily. He fully understood why his friend the duke was so tied up in a knot over this young lady. He sincerely hoped Wrentham would be able to straighten out all the complicated twists and turns their lives had taken of late.

He hastened to answer her reply. "'Tis not a bouncer at all, Miss, I can assure you. I was most anxious to set my horses to their paces today and I thought it would be lovely to see if you would like to join me. I hope I have not inconvenienced you by arriving a trifle earlier than is the fashionable norm, but I thought we would have all the more opportunity for conversation if the Park is not overcrowded." He concluded his statement with a look of significance, and Rose returned his gaze with her own eyes wide and focused.

With her mouth agape in the shape of a silent *oh*, Rose nodded slightly. Recovering swiftly, she pulled on the gloves she had been holding and neared the viscount to grab his arm. "Now would be a lovely time for a ride in the Park, and I am completely ready to go. We ought not to keep your horses waiting much longer, should we, my lord? If you are ready, we could be on our way."

Wesley laughed over her turning of the tables on him and allowed her to usher him from the room. Before many moments had passed they were high up in his phaeton, making their way swiftly toward the Park. The traffic was thin and they were able to get to a rapid speed. He was glad she did not squeal at the pace, but he was forced to control his amusement as she grabbed onto the seat with both hands.

"Your team seems to be wonderfully matched," she said with as much composure as she could muster.

Wesley laughed again. "You are a downy one, Miss. Most young ladies would be demanding to be put down at the nearest corner if I were to drive like this with them in my phaeton."

Rose managed to keep an innocent look upon her face as she gazed steadily at the viscount. "Whatever do you mean, my lord? Surely you would never try to intentionally put me to the blush, would you, my lord?"

Wesley had brought the phaeton down to a slower pace by this point and was able to look into her dancing eyes as she had made this sally. "No, Miss, I would never do such a thing," he drawled sarcastically.

Rose batted her eyelashes at him in response, and Wesley barked with another laugh. "You are a complete hand, Miss." Wesley applied himself to pulling his matched bays through the entrance of the park and letting them take a sedate pace as they meandered along the well-travelled lanes.

After a few moments of silence, Rose turned to Wesley. He enjoyed seeing her eyes dancing with merriment once more. "So, my lord, I am waiting on tenterhooks to know what we shall be conversing about. You did hint rather heavily that you had something to discuss with me, did you not?"

Wesley smiled as he answered. "I admire your forbearance, Miss Rose. I am impressed that you managed to hold onto your silence for this long. Most ladies would have been badgering me long before we made into the park."

"Really, my lord?" she countered. "I would think most ladies would have been too busy yelping at you to slow down and all thoughts of any conversation with you would have fled from their minds, swept away with the wind created as your horses galloped through the streets of London."

"Now you are exaggerating," Wesley chided.

"Not by much, my lord, but never mind about that. I am not most ladies, but I do find that I am growing impatient over your teasing. Did you have something you wished to discuss with me or not?"

"As a matter of fact, I did," Wesley teased but then quickly launched into his explanation as he saw that his companion was about to lose all semblance of patience. "I actually bear a message from Wrentham."

"The duke? Is everything all right with him?" Rose's dismay was evident in her tone.

"All is well. He is just concerned over something that occurred this morning while you two met."

ന്ദ ജ

Rose blushed over this reminder of her questionable conduct, as well as her memories of the sweet kiss they had exchanged that morning. Her eyes flew to meet those of the viscount as she wondered frantically if Alex would have told his friend about that. Struggling to maintain her composure, Rose asked in as neutral a tone as she could muster. "What is he concerned about, my lord? Did he tell you all about it?"

"He did, in fact. And he wanted me to pass the information on. It only came to his attention after you had already left, so he could not tell you himself. And of course, he cannot simply call upon you for a myriad of reasons."

"Of course," Rose replied a little faintly, as she realized it was not what she had feared. Her relief was short-lived.

"The duke has reason to believe that your meeting was witnessed. He does not think you were overheard, but he does believe someone was watching the two of you together. He had very little information when I was speaking with him earlier today, but he did want you to know as soon as possible so you could be on your guard. He fears you may not be perfectly safe."

"His Grace worries like an old governess. What could there possibly be to threaten my safety even if we were observed?" Rose demanded in counter argument. "'Tis true that my reputation could be in tatters were it to become known that I have met with the duke at Burlington House, but since it is a venue open to the public, and I had my maid in tow, there is very little that could come of anyone speaking of it."

"It was actually not your reputation which concerned him, although, of course, as a gentleman, he would want to ensure that no scandal were to be attached to you. But rather, he is concerned that the man watching you could have been a follower of Broderick, and that dastardly fellow could now view you as a threat to his plans, in which case you could be in serious danger indeed."

Rose remained silent as she absorbed Lord Dunbar's words and all the possible ramifications. "I now understand the duke's concerns," she finally mustered before quickly rallying with a shrug. "Even if Broderick were to figure out that we were onto his schemes, I am most certain he would not think to threaten me. I have already passed all my concerns about Broderick on to my father, and it is out of my hands. I am no threat to Broderick on my own. Surely he will not trouble himself with a mere slip of a girl."

Wesley once again threw back his head and laughed. "If he knows what kind of a girl this particular slip is, he will be very troubled, Miss. But perhaps you are right and there is no danger, however Wrentham was most insistent that you be told that it is a real possibility. He was trying to find out more information, but he wanted you to know as soon as possible. I would suggest it is best if you do not arrange any more clandestine meetings but instead try to speak in a crowded ballroom where you will be sure to be fully safe."

"Surely you realize that I cannot be seen speaking to him. We are sworn enemies."

"You cannot be serious," Wesley declared with chagrin. "You have spent much of the past two weeks in each other's company, working to solve a common problem. That does not sound like the behaviour of sworn enemies."

"Be that as it may, we are, or rather our families are, which is pretty much the same thing. We cannot be seen to be speaking. Our parents would have apoplexy."

"This is the daftest situation I have ever heard of. You should all be sharing your grief, not blaming each other for it." Wesley's words made Rose realize he would never understand.

"You do not know what you are talking about, my lord," Rose dismissed his comments and tried to turn the subject. "Anyhow, you have fulfilled your duty and passed me the duke's message. I will be on my best behaviour and do my utmost to be on guard lest the devilish knight should be after me."

"I beg of you, Miss Rose, do not make light of this. You really could be in danger."

"Mayhap you are right, my lord, but my father is now aware of the situation. He will come up with a solution before Broderick can do any of the nefarious things he might have had planned."

"But did you not say that your father is leaving on the morrow for Paris? If he is not here, how will you be protected if Broderick does not follow him to Paris, or if he sets some sort of action against you?"

Rose could see that the viscount really was quite serious and was concerned for her safety. A niggle of doubt crept into her consciousness. She really ought to take offense at the man for doubting her ability to take care of herself, but his concern for her was endearing in an overbearing sort of way. She made an effort to be conciliatory. "Have no fear, my lord. I assure you I will be careful. And I promise to call on your help should the need arise."

Seeing that he still looked uneasy, Rose shrugged. "There is not much else I can do, my lord. My father has promised to look into the situation, and I am quite certain he will not leave me here in danger or unprotected. I appreciate your concern over me, but I really do not think there is a need for you to be overly anxious on my behalf."

With relief Rose saw that Lord Dunbar finally looked appeased and allowed the subject to drop. They rode around the Park in companionable silence, breaking it periodically to make various innocuous comments about the weather or the people they encountered. Finally, as they neared the gateway that they had entered, Rose finally spoke.

"This has been lovely, my lord. Thank you so much for inviting me for a drive, but I do believe I ought to be returning home."

Wesley blushed slightly. "I guess I should not monopolize any more of your time."

Rose laughed with glee. "You, my lord, are the most entertaining gentleman I have met. You endeavour to appear so manly and unconcerned, but deep inside you are the sweetest man around."

Wesley's blush deepened, and he pulled a face at her. "I beg of you to keep your voice down, or you shall leave my reputation in tatters." He quickly spoiled the effect by grinning at her, which she swiftly returned.

"Shall we see you tonight at the Rotherhams' ball?" Wesley changed the subject by inquiring politely.

"Are you wanting to watch over me to ensure my safety?" Rose teased. When he merely shook his head at her she continued. "I am uncertain about my plans for the evening at this point, my lord. I had been planning to attend, but now it depends on my father's actions. I am most eager to know what has been decided."

"If you do make it to the Rotherhams', would you save a dance for me?" Lord Dunbar asked politely.

Rose now looked at the viscount searchingly. "Are you trying to turn me up sweet, my lord?"

Wesley again barked out a laugh he could not contain. "I am merely trying to ensure we have an opportunity for conversation this evening. If you cannot speak to Wrentham yourself, you could pass a message to him through me."

Rose felt the heat rising in her cheeks and she stammered out a reply. "My apologies, my lord, I did not mean to be so forward."

Wesley grinned at his companion. "Absolutely no apologies required, my dear girl. I suspect we are of the same mind that we need to ensure this matter is taken care of before we can concentrate on other things. I know this has been more your and Wrentham's situation, but I feel tied up in it, too, since I know about it." He paused for a moment as he steered his team around a crowded section of street. Rose was unsure how to read his expression when he looked back at her. "Mayhap when this is all said and done I shall call upon you again."

Rose was undecided how she felt about the possibility of the viscount "calling upon" her so she made light of his comments. "And mayhap I shall be at home to visitors when you call, my lord."

The viscount chuckled deeply. "Now you are the one who is a complete hand, Miss Rosamund Smythe."

Rose grinned as they neared her home. "You are a good friend, my lord."

Wesley smiled ironically. "That I am, miss, thank you for noticing."

Rose couldn't help the girlish giggle that escaped her lips just before he handed her down in front of the Smythes' townhouse. "Thank you, my lord, truly. I had a lovely afternoon and it helped to pass the time so I did not lose my mind completely while I waited for news from my father." Rose looked toward her front door and then back up at the viscount. "I promise I shall do my best to share that dance with you tonight."

Wesley squeezed her hand before letting her go. Rose was glad he did not bother to comment. *What is there left to say?* she asked herself ironically.

Lifting her skirts, Rose dashed up the stairs, eager to see if her father had any news to share with her.

Chapter Sixteen

"Good afternoon, Walter. Is my father home?"

"He is not, Miss, but he did leave a message for you," the butler intoned importantly before pausing, leaving Rose to prompt.

"What is the message?" Rose was near the end of her patience.

"He said for you to go about your regular activities and to just leave a message here for him if you are to go out. He was unsure how long he would be, but he was quite clear that he wishes to speak with you before he leaves for Paris."

Rose was deeply disappointed. Now that she had shared the information with her father she was terribly anxious to find out what she should do next. Even if the direction was that she was to do nothing, she dearly hoped she would at least be informed about what others were going to be doing, otherwise she would not be able to rest easy.

The thought of going to a ball this evening, with this all hanging over her unresolved, was not at all an appealing prospect. With a mental shrug, she reminded herself that it had been this way in Vienna as well. *It seems to be the lot of lady spies*, she thought wryly, which brought a smile to her face, and she was able to leave the butler in peace without badgering him for any more information.

"Thank you, Walter. For now I shall be in my chamber, if my father should return and want to speak with me. Later I will be going out to attend the Rotherham ball."

"Very well, Miss."

Now sober, Rose climbed the stairs deep in thought. She wished fervently that she could summon Alex. It was such a pity their two families had fallen into such a state. Mayhap Wesley and Elizabeth were right and they should be mourning together instead of blaming each other. Really, what did it matter if it was their son's fault that her brother was dead? Had he not paid the ultimate price by dying as well? Rose shook her head sadly at her thoughts. Even if she could convince her own heart to forgive the Wrenthams, she was most certain that her parents would not be swayed. It would matter not a jot that she was losing her heart to the duke.

"Now, where did that thought come from?" Rose asked herself, speaking aloud in her shock.

"What thought, Miss?" Mary asked, as Rose had already reached her room by this point.

Rose could feel the heat rising in her cheeks as she glanced quickly at her maid. "I was just thinking out loud, Mary, never mind me."

"It sounds as though your thoughts were surprising even to you, Miss," Mary commented.

"Indeed they were, Mary. But never mind about that, do you know anything more since I left?"

"I am sad to report that, no, I don't, Miss. You are the only one in this family who confides so thoroughly in me. Seems to me as though your father don't confide in anyone if he can help it, so I never expect to hear too much from him."

Rose grinned. "I suspect you are right in your assessment of my father. He does like to hold his own council. I guess he realizes he is the smartest man he knows."

"I'm not disputing how smart he is, Miss Rose, but it does seem to me that everyone needs to bounce their ideas off someone else every now and again."

"That is very true indeed, Mary. Speaking of that, have you had a chance to think much more on who you consider might be a good suitor for me?" Rose was happy to change the subject. Debating her father's secretive disposition would accomplish nothing except frustration, and she really did need to get on with the main reason for coming for the Season.

Rose's words accomplished their purpose as Mary squealed and did a little dance. "Oh Miss, thank you for asking me. I was uncertain if it was my place to bring it up, but I surely have been thinking on it."

"Mary, my dear, you know we are friends. When we are alone you need not concern yourself about whether or not it is your place to discuss any subject, I can assure you, but on second thought, it is good that you kept it to yourself. I might not have been in the right frame of mind to consider your words on another day. But right now, I need to put my mind to something, and this seems as good of a time as any to consider my matrimonial prospects. So tell me, is there anyone in particular that you think would be my perfect match?"

"Now, before we start I want you to know that I have given this a great deal of thought. I have known you since you were a girl and I dearly want you to be happy."

Rose impulsively threw her arms around the older girl, giving her a warm hug while they both grew misty eyed. "I know, Mary, and I truly appreciate it. There are very few people that I trust as much as I do you."

"Then you will pardon me for saying that I think the Duke of Wrentham would be the perfect match for you."

In the blink of an eye the warm camaraderie dissipated. Rose's blush reached her roots as she launched into speech. "How could you possibly say that, Mary?" she demanded heatedly, ignoring the fact that that thought had already crossed her mind more than once. Having someone else say it made it terrifyingly real.

"Hear me out, Miss. I know everyone is angry about the young master's death and you all blame the Wrenthams for it, but what if you're wrong? What if it wasn't Milord Maxwell's fault? And even if it was, why does that have to condemn the rest of you to being sworn enemies for the rest of your days? You all were the best of friends for eons, before the two scallywags went off to the war." Mary paused a moment before she continued in a softer, kindly voice. "And I've seen you with him, Rosie. Your face is so open and happy when you are in His Grace's presence. You get along so well, and he's one of the most handsome men I've ever seen, besides being a duke. Seems to me as though it would be the perfect match for you."

"I thought you were just as dead set against the Wrenthams as the rest of the household, Mary," Rose protested, without disputing the truth of Mary's words.

Mary shrugged. "I was, but when you asked me to think on who would be a good match for you, I tried to be as honest as I possibly could be. This is the conclusion I came to."

Rose took a deep breath and held it for a couple of beats before replying. "Well, I appreciate your honesty, Mary. Did you by any chance come up with a second choice because I am quite certain I shall not be able to follow your advice with your first suggestion."

Mary smiled sadly. "I figured as much, Miss Rose so yes, I did think of a few other options." Pausing to collect her thoughts, Mary continued. "The young gentleman who came to take you riding seemed to me to be a good, solid second choice."

"Lord Dunbar?" Rose asked in surprise. "Why do you pick him for me?"

"His servants speak highly of him, Miss, which is a rarity these days. His horses appear well cared for as well. This tells me he is a kind man who does not mistreat those in his control, which if you don't mind me saying so, is what you will be as a wife."

Rose nodded soberly as she mulled over her maid's words. She had made a good choice when asking her maid to think over this subject. She obviously had a much different perspective than anyone in Society, but it seemed a lot more useful than someone commenting on the cut of a gentleman's coat or the shine on his new carriage. Mary's observations actually spoke to how a girl might expect to be treated should she accept a gentleman's proposal. Rose admitted to herself that she had never thought about that before. Her main concerns had been whether or not the gentleman was a good conversationalist. While that was still a factor for her, she really ought to consider what else Mary had to say.

"Thank you so much for sharing your views with me, Mary dear. Was there anyone else?"

"I actually did not come up with a very long list, Miss, I am sorry to tell you. It is surprising how few gentlemen stand very high in their servant's opinion. And of course, I was rather picky. I wanted only those gentlemen who were known to be heavy in the pocket. I also only looked at those with titles. And I didn't want anyone too long in the tooth either."

Now Rose found something to laugh about. "Why Mary, I had no idea you were so exacting in your tastes."

"When it comes to you, Miss, I would say no one is quite good enough, but I set myself a set of standards and I stuck to them. The only other name I could come up with was Lord Dunkirk, the Earl of Strathgowan."

"Really? I have not yet had the pleasure of making his lordship's acquaintance. I am impressed with how thorough you have been, Mary, although disappointed in the scanty results. I shall have to see about finagling an introduction to the earl as soon as possible."

"Or you could just apply your mind to making peace with the Wrenthams," Mary argued.

"I think learning to fly would be easier," Rose answered tartly. "Mayhap you ought to be a trifle less discerning in your tastes. I do appreciate your concerns for my welfare, but I should remind you that I do not currently have a title and am just fine with that. I am quite convinced that being a lord does not guarantee that a man will make a good husband."

"No, I would have to say that I agree with you on that, but wouldn't you like to have a title to pass to your children? I heard you say that the Season is a wee bit of a drudgery when you are only a baron's daughter."

"'Tis true, Mary, I did say that." Rose sighed. "I guess you are right. Well, now what shall I do?" Seeing her maid's significant glance Rose laughed. "No, Mary, I do not think I can take you up on your suggestion of negotiating peace between the Smythes and the Wrenthams and then setting my cap at the duke. I do believe we are going to have to rethink the options. Just as soon as I ensure this situation with Broderick is cleared up."

Feeling as though she were quite finished with this conversation, Rose strode across the room toward the wardrobe containing her newest gowns. "Now Mary, although I cannot fathom preparing for a ball while I am in such a state of mind, I think it is best if we get started. Mayhap a bath would help me relax and feel more the thing."

"Very well, Miss." Mary wisely chose to hold onto her own council for the moment, merely turning on her heel and ringing for a footman to start bringing the water.

Chapter Seventeen

Rose stood on the sidelines of the dance floor, feeling as though all the ballrooms in London looked very much the same. It was uncommon to see new faces at any of the balls she attended. It really was a rarified society she was circulating in, she thought drolly to herself as she scanned the crowds around her, looking for a friendly face.

Her gaze had just met that of her dear friend Elizabeth when a cold hand on her arm stopped her upraised arm from waving. Her attention snagged and her blood turned to ice in her veins as she heard the dreaded voice near her ear.

"Miss Smythe, what a pleasure to see you here this evening. Might I have a word with you?" The words were polite, but the grip on her arm belied the request. Rose winced as Sir Broderick tugged her toward the back of the room.

Rose glanced around rather frantically, calculating the damage to her reputation should she make a scene, wondering if she should cry for help, or see the situation out and take it from there. Broderick took the decision out of her hands with his next words.

"Do not bother calling for help, my dear girl." His low menacing tone brought a shiver to Rose's stiff spine. "My associates have your mother in their control and will not hesitate to hurt her if you do not cooperate with my requests."

With an effort of will Rose managed to control the scream threatening to crawl up her throat. She felt as though her features had turned to stone as she hurried along beside the ungentlemanly knight. Her ever active imagination wondered fleetingly what others might see if they really looked at her. From her frantic gaze, it did not appear as though anyone were noticing that aught was amiss. She castigated herself for not ensuring her mother was safe. They should not have ventured out this evening. Alex had tried to warn her that there might be a threat, and she had thought she knew better.

Giving her head a shake, Rose forced the recriminations from her mind—they were not at all helpful at the moment. Hoping to buy a little time, she dug in her heels and slowed down. "My lord, I beg of you, I cannot in all decency run after you. If you do not wish to be remarked upon, it will not do for us to be seen dashing from the room."

Broderick's grip on her arm did not lessen, in fact, his grip tightened painfully, but he did slow down his pace somewhat. Rose wracked her brain for ideas as to how to extricate herself from this predicament, but the threat to her mother curtailed any of her schemes. She would have happily shredded her reputation and screamed at the top of her lungs in order to get away from the slimy Sir Jason Broderick, but the thought of his henchmen harming her mother kept her lips firmly clamped shut.

Before she could formulate any executable plan, they were treading down a hallway and the knight tugged her down another dimly lit passage. Rose's terror heightened as she realized she was about to be escorted from the house entirely. She could see no way of escape and wondered fleetingly if her parents would ever find out what had happened to their only daughter. Rose decided not to just meekly go to her death.

Digging her heels in once more, Rose tried to come to a standstill. "This has gotten ridiculous, my lord. I wish to know the meaning of your actions. I do not appreciate your threats toward my mother. I have accompanied you from the ballroom as you requested. I assume you wish to have words with me. Very well, my lord, have your say, but then I insist that I be reunited with my mother. I must be reassured of her welfare."

Broderick's smile put Rose in mind of a weasel as he looked at her steadily through his small, dark eyes. "You are in no position to be making any sort of demands, Miss Smythe, are you? There is no one about to aid you in enforcing them, but in fact, just around the next corner several of my friends are waiting for us, so if you should start to struggle or call out, they shall be here to aid me in the blink of your pretty green eyes. So screaming shan't do you a lick of good."

"What do you want, Sir Broderick? Why have you accosted me in this ill-bred manner?"

Broderick grinned. "I know you think I am lower than the dirt beneath your dainty little feet, Miss Smythe, but you are not the one in control here." He tugged on her arm once more, but again Rose resisted. His words implied to her that there were other undercurrents in play, but her scattered wits could not quite get a grip on any of her ideas. She determined to try further speech.

"I refuse to go one step further until you tell me what is going on, Sir Broderick. You know it is not at all the thing for me to be accompanying you anywhere unchaperoned. If you were wishing to spend time with me, you ought to call upon me at my home at the prescribed time like any other gentleman."

Despite her fears, Rose had to exert an effort to suppress her amusement over the look of incredulity that flitted across the knight's twisted features.

"I am not trying to fix your affections, Miss Smythe," he declared with disgust. "I am trying to keep your meddling ways from interfering with my plans."

"What plans have I been meddling with, my lord?" Rose inquired, trying to ascertain the depth of her danger.

"Do not play coy with me, Miss Smythe. I have been well aware of your meddling ever since Vienna. Did you think I would find it difficult to figure out that it was through you that your father and his cronies always seemed to be one step ahead of me? You might have been able to thwart me in Vienna, but you are not going to be able to do so this time. Prinny *will* sign the territories over to me, and there won't be anything you or your interfering father can do about it."

"What are you going to do with me, my lord? Surely you are too smart to be able to be thwarted by a mere girl, so you need not trouble yourself with me." Rose was becoming truly terrified as she examined the maniacal look that had settled itself upon Broderick's features as he spoke of the Prince Regent and his land. She could not contain the yelp of pain that escaped her as his fingers dug deeper into her upper arm.

"You are far more trouble than you ever let on, aren't you? Now quit resisting, Miss Smythe. If you give me anymore trouble I will not hesitate to bash you over the head and carry your insensate body quietly from this house. I highly doubt you would enjoy that experience though it would not bother me one little bit. In fact, I do believe I would enjoy it immensely."

Now Rose could see that he was looking at her rather lecherously and her fear ratcheted up another notch, threatening to choke her. Looking behind her frantically once more, she realized there was no one coming to her aid. She needed to keep her wits about her and figure out a way to rescue herself. She could not afford to have him deprive her of her senses. She stopped resisting and forced her feet to move once more, but she could not make herself stop questioning him.

"Where are you taking me, my lord? And why? What do you hope to accomplish by taking me? Surely you must realize that it will merely draw attention to your intentions if a hue and cry is made over me." Rose was hoping to appeal to the greedy little man's logic.

"But that is where you are wrong, my dear Miss Smythe," the awful man replied with an oily grin. "No one noticed our departure and there is no reason to associate your disappearance with me in any way. In fact, if you disappear it will keep your father far too occupied for him to even consider going to Paris and interfering there. And all the *ton* will be too abuzz with speculations over what could have possibly happened to you to be bothered with matters of government. It is an absolutely brilliant plan."

"But if my mother is missing as well, surely it will become obvious that something nefarious is afoot."

"Ah, Miss Smythe, you really do need to learn not to trust what everyone tells you. The last I saw of your mother, she was happily sipping punch and listening raptly to something old Lady Rotherham was jabbering away about." Broderick chuckled cruelly over the look of disbelief he saw on Rose's face. "And soon, you will write a note to your parents telling them you have run off with a seaman you met in the park, so that will give them some direction in their thrashing about over you. It should buy me just enough time to accomplish my ends."

"And just what might those ends be, my lord?" Rose could not resist asking.

"Never mind about that now, you have wasted enough of my time, hurry along or I shall be happy to carry you."

Rose did not doubt he would enjoy knocking her unconscious so she did as he had bade and forced her feet to a quicker pace. By now they reached a small door and had been joined by two other unsavoury looking characters.

"Where are you taking me?" she squeaked as she saw the dark carriage through the open doorway.

"I'll tell you when we get there," was Broderick's unhelpful reply.

Rose's teeth began to chatter from a combination of her nerves and the cool night air. She clenched them together to hold back the screams of alarm that were clawing to be heard. After taking one frantic glance back at the large house before ducking into the carriage, she could have sworn she saw Alex at one of the brightly lit windows, but she chastised herself for conjuring him in her fear. And besides, even if it was him, there was no way he could see her in the dark gloom from within the brightly lit room.

Taking her seat across from Sir Broderick, Rose stared at him stonily.

☙ ❧

Elizabeth was in a quandary. She had been so certain that Rose was about to approach her, in fact Elizabeth was sure Rose had been raising her arm to wave to her when she was approached by Sir Broderick. Because of the distance that had separated them Elizabeth had been unable to see clearly what was taking place, but she was absolutely certain Rose would not happily accompany the knight anywhere. But what should she do about this information? She had not spoken with Rose in a day or two, so she was unsure of the latest developments. As far as she knew, Rose's parents were still unaware of the association Rose had been having with the Duke of Wrentham and why she had been doing it, so it would require too much explanation if Elizabeth were to seek out Rose's parents and tell them what she thought she had seen. And there was part of the trouble, she was unsure of what she had really witnessed, but now Rose was nowhere to be seen in the ballroom and Elizabeth was growing increasingly uneasy.

She took one more turn around the dance floor, looking around as innocuously as she could manage, then she headed toward the ladies' retiring room, thinking Rose could perhaps be there. When Elizabeth could not locate her friend there or in the refreshment room, she was truly concerned and starting to verge onto panic. With relief, she spied the Duke of Wrentham in the crowd.

"Your Grace, I am terribly sorry to disturb you, but might I have a word with you?" She tried to be as discreet as possible but her urgency must have conveyed itself clearly as she gained the duke's full attention.

☙ ❧

The hairs at the back of Alex's neck stirred uncomfortably as he heard the young woman's voice at his side. He recognized Rosie's friend, Lady Elizabeth, and wondered at her nervous tone. "What can I do for you, this evening, my lady?" he asked solicitously.

"I have a concern I would like to discuss with you as quietly as possible." Elizabeth glanced around as she spoke, heightening Alex's awareness of the young lady's distress.

"Is everything all right with you, Lady Elizabeth?" Alex asked, as he offered her his elbow and guided her toward a small alcove that was momentarily abandoned.

Elizabeth did not bother with beating around the bush, merely launching into her explanation. "I apologize for disturbing you, Your Grace, and please excuse my forward behaviour, but I did not know who else to turn to."

Alex blinked over the girl's words, but merely nodded encouragingly, unsure what this was leading to.

Elizabeth took a deep breath and began her tale. "I was standing on the side of the dance floor waiting for my next partner when I saw Rose for the first time this evening. She looked preoccupied, but when our eyes met she smiled a greeting and looked as though she were about to wave and come towards me. But just as she was raising her arm, I saw Sir Broderick grab it. He said a few words to her and then they left the room together. She did not struggle or anything like that, but I cannot believe she would have voluntarily left with him. Rose really does not like him."

At the lady's mention of Broderick, Alex felt all the air rush out of his lungs and he felt lightheaded for a brief moment, but he managed to contain himself and listened to whatever she had to share.

"I thought to tell Rose's parents, or at least her mother, who I saw sitting with the other chaperones across the room over there, but there would be too much explanation required. Do you know what I should do, Your Grace? I am terribly afraid that something bad has just happened to my friend."

Lady Elizabeth finally stopped talking and stood before him wringing her hands. Alex didn't wish to terrify her, but he very much feared the same thing. Keeping his voice as calm as possible, he asked her a few questions.

"How long ago was this, my lady?"

"I cannot be certain, but I believe it is no more than fifteen minutes ago, although it feels longer because I have become increasingly scared. But it was just before the waltz, then there was a quadrille, and now they are just striking up the cotillion."

"Very good, my lady, now are you absolutely certain it was Sir Broderick who approached Miss Smythe?"

"Yes, Your Grace, I am absolutely certain. I would recognize his distinctive face and short stature anywhere. Besides, the look of distaste upon Rose's face was also very recognizable." Despite her nerves, Elizabeth smiled over this thought.

"Thank you, my lady, you are being most helpful. Now, are you certain no one else noticed this exchange between them?"

Elizabeth shook her head. "Not completely certain, Your Grace, but even if anyone remarked upon it, there was no evidence of anything. Rose did not struggle or call out, and aside from his grip on her arm, there did not seem to be anything he was doing to force her. If I did not know her feelings about him, I would not have thought much of it. But I *do* know. And that, coupled with the fact that I cannot now find her, leads me to believe that he has taken her somewhere."

Alex could see that Rose's friend was getting worked up and he tried to soothe her to avoid any attention being drawn to their predicament. "Perhaps we are getting worried over nothing, but I will look into the matter. Can you remember which direction they went?"

He was relieved as Elizabeth pulled her fraying wits back together and looked out from the alcove. Pointing toward the orchestra she said, "I was over there, facing toward the dance floor, with my back toward the musicians. Rose was almost directly across from me. When they turned away I could see their backs, so they went in the direction of the retiring rooms, but I already looked there."

"Very good, thank you. That was an excellently detailed description. I am going to go and do some discreet investigating of my own. Could you find Lord Dunbar and tell him what you have just told me?"

Elizabeth appeared to be grateful to receive an assignment and without another word hurried away to do as he had asked. Alex stood looking around, glad for his height as he was able to get a better idea of what was around. Seeing a few doors and passageways at the back of the ballroom in the direction Elizabeth had indicated, he set off at once. Passing the wall of windows on his way by, Alex glanced toward them, but there was nothing he could see except the reflection of the dancing crowds.

It was so very difficult to hurry in a crowded ballroom, especially when one was a duke. Alex tried to keep a pleasant expression on his face and made every attempt to avoid being drawn into any conversation as he made his way through. With a smile and a nod to whoever hailed him, he finally reached his destination. The first door he reached was locked. He hoped Broderick and Rose had had as much difficulty getting through the crowds as he had, he thought distractedly, *or else they will have an even greater lead on me.*

Next to the locked door there was a hallway that was not lit welcomingly like the rest of the space opened up to the Rotherhams' guests. Alex set off down that passage, hoping he was not chasing a dead end. There were a couple of doors off this passage, but his investigation proved they were merely closets and storage areas, not large enough to be containing a missing lady and a wayward knight.

Alex finally reached a door at the end, he surmised from the turns he had taken that it might lead outside. It was not locked. Opening the door, he stepped out into the cool night, angry and terrified to see a carriage in the distance as it pulled out onto the street. Even if it contained his Rose, there was nothing he could do to stop it from this distance. With disgust, he turned back to the doorway and nearly collided with Wesley.

Cursing in his frustration, Alex gritted his teeth to stem the flow of his vitriol. He was glad to see the viscount and it was not his fault they were too late to save the lady.

"Thank you for coming, Dunbar. Unfortunately, I think we just missed her. If Broderick has taken her, they just drove away in that carriage."

"Are you sure? Did you see her?"

Alex had not seen Elizabeth and was surprised to see her stepping out from behind Wesley.

Alex's look of disbelief directed at the viscount merely produced a sheepish shrug. "She would not be denied the opportunity of looking for her missing friend. I did not wish to waste my time arguing with her when I could be helping you with the search."

"I do not think a search will produce anything but causing a commotion. If at all possible, we shall have to try to retrieve Rose without anyone amongst the *ton* finding out that she has gone missing. I am quite certain they have left the premises, so we shall have to formulate a plan to figure out where he might have taken her. And why."

Alex looked at Lady Elizabeth, feeling sorry for his next words. "I am so sorry to have to tell you this, my lady, but you will not be able to accompany us. You will have the difficult task of getting through the rest of your night pretending as though nothing is amiss. I will try my best to keep you informed as soon as we know anything, but it most likely will not be before tomorrow. Do you think you can manage that? We might need to call on you soon in order to preserve Rose's reputation."

"I will keep myself in readiness, Your Grace. Do not trouble yourself about me. I am not in any danger, except that of boredom. I do believe I shall soon find my mother and plead a headache, as there is no way I will be able to enjoy the rest of the ball. But you two hurry along and do whatever needs to be done."

Alex was about to dismiss her from his mind as he had so many things to do, but then Elizabeth continued with another thought. "Your Grace, did I do the right thing in telling you instead of her parents? Do you not think we should tell them? Now that you are chasing after her, should I find Lady Smythe and let her know what is going on?"

Alex hesitated. He knew Rose had planned on telling her father about Sir Broderick, but he was unsure if she had managed to keep his name out of the situation. The fact that she had been at the ball this evening proved she had not been banished as she had feared. But did that also mean she had not had a chance to tell her father anything?

"Clearly Lady Smythe has to be told something, or else she will cause a scene when she cannot find her daughter," Wesley pointed out reasonably.

Alex laughed. "Lady Smythe does not cause scenes. It is her abiding motto. But you are quite correct. She must be told something. I would prefer to deal with Lord Smythe myself. Do either of you know if he is here this evening?"

"I did not see him, Your Grace," Elizabeth replied, while Wesley merely shrugged and shook his head.

"All right. I will collect my servants and try to glean as much information as possible. The good news is I had already set someone to the task of watching Broderick, so hopefully we will know something very soon. I will go and try to speak to Lord Smythe, if you two could try to get Lady Smythe out of here without her raising a hue and a cry over her daughter."

Wesley cast a sceptical glance at his friend. "Are you quite certain you are up to the task of facing Lord Smythe on your own?"

"There is very little other choice, my friend, but thank you for your concern." Alex grinned at the viscount. "I actually am of the opinion that the two of you have the harder task. At least in the privacy of his own home the baron can react however he sees fit."

"Thank you, Your Grace, for your help in this matter. I will speak with Lady Smythe, and then perhaps Lord Dunbar can escort her home. I will collect my own mama and wait at our home for any news. I dearly wish that I could be helping in some way."

Before he left, Alex squeezed the young woman's hand comfortingly. "Do not mistake the matter, my lady, you have been a great deal of help. If not for you, we would not even realize that anything was amiss until it was much later. Now we might be able to get this all straightened out before daybreak."

Chapter Eighteen

Rose still had her teeth clenched together to control the chatter they wished to make. She could see very little through the carriage's dirty windows. Being unfamiliar with the part of town they were driving through anyway, she would not have been able to figure out where they were, even if she could see well. She tried again to reason with her captor.

"Where are you taking me, my lord?"

"Somewhere where you won't be causing me any more grief," came the flat reply.

"Are you planning on killing me?" she asked with as firm a voice as she could muster.

"You really aren't the usual sort of Miss, are you?" Broderick stated, with a glimmer of respect showing in his tone. "Any young lady I've ever had the misfortune of dealing with would be screaming blue murder by this point, or else prostrate in a dead faint."

"Have you had much experience in abducting young ladies in the past, my lord?" Rose asked tartly.

This brought an amused twist to his lips. "Not overmuch experience, Miss, but I do find your sort to usually be much less in control of their wits than you."

Broderick finally looked straight at her, which caused a sense of foreboding to descend upon Rose. She tried valiantly to ignore it.

"How did you find out about my plans for the Duke of Wrentham?" he asked almost pleasantly.

She didn't see any point in avoiding the truth. "I overheard you speaking to Lord Austen at the Countess of Yorkleigh's musicale. It was during the intermission. The two of you were sitting a couple of rows behind me. You obviously did not notice me, or else you thought I was too far away to hear you. In fact, I did not hear most of what you were saying as I was distracted by watching everyone milling about, but when you mentioned Wrentham's name my ears perked up."

"And so then you had to run out and tell him about it, didn't you?" Broderick sneered.

Rose shrugged, refusing to be cowed by the likes of him. "It seemed like the best course of action at the time."

"What did you hope to gain by telling His Grace?"

"I hoped to save him from your clutches," Rose brazenly replied.

"But instead it is you who is in my clutches," Broderick taunted.

Again Rose shrugged, although this time it was a bit forced. "I am most certain my father will save me."

"Your father will not even know of your disappearance for a few more hours yet, and then when he does, there will be the note you are going to write to explain it all away."

"What do you hope to gain by all of this?" Rose inquired, ignoring his reference to any note writing. At the back of her mind, she was busily trying to compose a note that would send a message to her father without alerting Broderick to her plans.

"I guess there's no harm in telling you. If I can keep your father distracted and you out of the way, I plan to get the Prince to sign over to me control of the lands he is about to regain during the negotiations in Paris."

"But why would he sign them over to you? Are you even acquainted with His Majesty?" Rose was puzzled over the knight's ambitions.

"Of course I am acquainted with Prinny. And he is going to sign them over to me because I have been working studiously at convincing him that I would be the best man for the job. I would have had the duke's influence to seal the deal if not for your interference, but if your father isn't around to sway him otherwise, I should still be able to make it all come about."

"So, then you are going to kill me, aren't you?" Rose concluded.

"What makes you say that?"

Rose could see that her outward calm was disconcerting to her captor. It gave her a strange sense of satisfaction, but she could not keep the tremble completely from her chin as she answered the creepy man. "I cannot imagine you wish to go to the trouble of keeping me locked up for the rest of my days, but if you let me go you cannot be certain that I will not broadcast your dastardly deeds to everyone who will listen."

Broderick looked steadily at his captive, surprise flickering in his wicked eyes. "You don't seem overly troubled by the prospect."

"I refuse to entertain you with my hand wringing," she replied frostily, as she also thought to herself, *and I refuse to beg you to do otherwise.* Turning her head toward the window, Rose set herself to the task of ignoring the despicable man. She wished fervently that she could tell where they were going.

As the carriage began to slow, she was unsure if she was happy or not that her wish was about to be granted. Not that she had any idea where they were, but she was about to find out what type of destination they had been bound for. She had lost track of time so she was unsure how far they had travelled, but as she took a deep breath the scent of brackish water led her to believe they were near the river.

"Are you taking me out of the country?" she gasped with fear.

Broderick's diabolically amused grin did not reassure Rose, but he finally responded directly to her question. "I have no current plans of taking you, or having you taken, out of the country. I am quite sure you can be convinced to behave properly so that we shan't have to go to such extremes as that, nor of killing you as you previously suggested. I have a lovely little place near here that will do quite nicely for keeping you out of the way for the time being."

As the carriage came to a stop, Rose gathered her wits thinking she might be able to make a break for it somehow. She had no idea of where she was nor of how she could find her way home, but for a moment she thought anything would be preferable to being in Broderick's clutches.

Her intentions must have been written upon her features, as evidenced by the knight's next words. "Do not do anything so foolish as to try to get away, my dear. I know you do not relish my company, but I can assure you that you will be far safer with me than you will be wandering about the stews on your own at this time of the night. Or at any time, for that matter. This neighbourhood is not accustomed to the presence of one such as you, and I will not vouch for your safety if you venture abroad."

Rose gulped down the knot of fear his words had brought to her throat. She was well aware that he was trying to terrify her, but she also knew quite well there was truth in his words. Although she was supposed to be a sheltered Society debutante, as a diplomat's daughter she was privy to some of the tales of the darker sides of city life. She was not safe whichever way she turned. Resolving to do her best to stay alive and whole until morning, when it would be safer to endeavour to escape, she forced herself to look steadily at her captor.

"So what now, my lord?"

Broderick stared back at her coldly, clearly displeased with her lack of obvious fear. Rose remembered Lady Yorkleigh's veiled warnings about the knight's rumoured entertainments and felt a shiver of dread drift down her spine. Valiantly suppressing her fears, Rose lifted her chin proudly and returned Broderick's cold stare.

"Now, Miss Smythe, you are going to get down from this carriage, slow and steady like, and then you are going to follow my friend, Squint, into that building just yonder. You aren't going to do anything so foolish as to try to run, and you certainly aren't going to draw any attention to the presence of such a pretty young thing being in the vicinity by screaming."

Rose could feel her blood turn to ice in her veins at her words, but she did not give in to the fear coursing through her. As the door opened she could see a henchman with a disfiguring scar next to his eye, unsurprised that the despicable knight would refer to the disfigurement in the man's nickname. Ignoring his offered hand, Rose gathered her skirts and stepped delicately down. She was followed by Broderick's voice.

"I will be right behind you, Miss, and will not hesitate to give chase or use force if you do not behave yourself."

Rose kept her chin firm and steadily ignored the hateful man, hurrying to follow Squint through the gloom of the dockyards to a dilapidated building. Fearing it might fall down around her, Rose kept darting her eyes around looking for different ways to escape. It was little more than an overgrown shed, from what she could see in the dim light cast by the shuttered lantern the knight's partner was carrying. Rose was certain she would be able to break free so long as she was left alone come daylight. She comforted herself with that thought as Broderick drew near.

Grabbing her arm and tugging her to a chair near the corner of the room, Sir Broderick pushed her down and pulled her arms behind to tie them. Rose began to struggle in fear at being thus confined. He struck her with a stunning blow.

Blinking the black spots from her eyes, Rose managed to retain her consciousness, but had not been able to contain the squeal of pain the back of his hand had inflicted upon her cheekbone. As her vision cleared she could see him grinning at her. Rose scowled. "You are despicable. Do you really think to get away with this?" she demanded, not bothering with polite address.

"I absolutely do. Now that you are all trussed up, I can be on my way. See that you behave yourself or Squint here will be happy to crack you for your troubles."

Rose eyed them both with distaste as she pulled on the ropes Broderick had deftly tightened around her wrists while she had been briefly stunned by his blow. She struggled against the despair rising in her chest at the thought that her own rescue depended upon her wits and resources.

The two men walked away, leaving her in the dark. Rose strained against the ropes at the same time as she frantically listened to the silence, wondering if anyone would return to watch over her or what might be hiding in the dark near her. She did not think she would be able to tolerate with equanimity the presence of any rodents at the moment. Hopefully they were otherwise occupied, she thought, nearing hysteria.

Before long, she was regretting her wish for light as Squint returned with his lantern and his eerie presence. She had not yet heard him speak. Rose wondered if she should plead with him for her release, calculating how much she should offer to pay him for safely returning her to her home. Her frantic thoughts were soon put to an end as her rough looking captor spoke for the first time.

"Don't be bothering to have yerself any ideas, Miss, I ain't listening to you. Jest sit yourself in your chair and wait until his lordship comes back and tells us what we're doing next."

Rose did not bother offering a reply, sitting in stony silence. She hoped the night would pass quickly.

ଓ ଃ

Alex stood on the street at the bottom of the stairs that led to the Smythe residence. It was taking him an inordinate amount of time to gather his gumption to go and knock on the door. He did not even know for sure if Lord Smythe was at home, but the duke was dreading the upcoming conversation. Chastising himself for being such a lily-livered ninny, he forced himself to climb the stairs and knock on the door.

The well-trained butler did not reveal his shock at discovering the Duke of Wrentham on the doorstep, merely ushering him into the receiving room with the promise of returning shortly with the information if milord was at home to company.

Alex cooled his heels in the elegantly appointed room, gazing about at the ivory wall hangings, wondering if Rose enjoyed this room. He rather thought she might hate it. Ivory did not seem to be the type of colour his Rose would enjoy overmuch. He was interrupted in his mental ramblings by the arrival of the diplomat baron himself.

Not bothering with the formality of the butler's presence, Lord Smythe barged in. "You have a rather high level of audacity coming here like this, Wrentham," he almost snarled. "To what do I owe the displeasure?"

Alex almost smiled at the older man's choice of words but managed to contain his ill-timed amusement. "Please, accept my sincere apologies, my lord. I am well aware that I am not a welcomed guest in your home, and I do not bring glad tidings. I will not waste your time with social niceties, as you do not wish to suffer my presence for any longer than necessary."

His words seemed to pacify the irate baron, who seemed a little less growly as he asked Alex to sit down. "You might as well have a seat if you have something you need to say. It cannot be anything good if it has made you come here. Do you need a glass of something before you get to the details?"

Alex could not contain his smile at his host's words. "That would be very much appreciated, my lord, thank you very much."

Lord Smythe made short work of pouring them each a glass of brandy. He seated himself across from the duke and took a big gulp of the strong spirits. After releasing his breath, he prompted the young man before him. "Well, you had best get on with it. It isn't going to get any easier the longer you put off telling me whatever was so urgent as to bring you to my door."

"No, you are quite correct, my lord, and time is of the utmost importance." He took a quick sip from his glass and another deep breath before he finally launched into his tale. "I have reason to believe Sir Jason Broderick has abducted your daughter from the Rotherham Ball."

Lord Smythe nearly blew brandy through his nostrils as he exhaled in his shock over Wrentham's words. After a choking cough he demanded, "What are you yammering about, Wrentham? What possible reason could Broderick have for abducting my Rosamund, and what would cause you to come to such a daft conclusion?"

"Did Rose tell you about Broderick and his schemes?"

"I cannot say why you think this is any of your business, you rapscallion, but yes, just today Rose told me what she had overheard at the Yorkleigh musicale."

"Well, it would seem Broderick has become aware of her interference in his affairs and he has decided to make off with her."

"What has led you to this conclusion? I am quite certain you are being ridiculously foolish, Your Grace. The girl is probably right this moment dancing a hole in her slippers at the ball she was to attend this evening." He glanced at the clock on the mantle. "At this late hour, she should actually be winding her way home at some point soon."

"Her friend, Lady Elizabeth, saw her speaking with Broderick at the ball. Since then she cannot be found. The only logical conclusion is that he has taken her."

"But why on earth would he take her? It doesn't make a stitch of sense."

Alex could see that Lord Smythe could not conceive of anyone threatening his darling daughter. His instinctive fear for her safety was clouding his usual formidable logic.

"It is possible that he might know of her involvement in trying to thwart whatever schemes he has gotten up to."

Lord Smythe had finally marshalled his logic and looked at the duke with a cold, assessing stare. "How does it come to pass that you have knowledge of this situation and that you are the one who is coming to me with these suspicions of my daughter's absence? Perhaps it is you who has made off with her. Are you trying to perpetrate another Smythe tragedy at the hands of a Wrentham?"

Alex felt the anger rising in the back of his throat at the baron's words. Making every effort to rein in his temper, he repeatedly reminded himself that getting into a brawl with the older man would solve nothing, even if it would relieve some of his pent up frustrations.

Through his gritted teeth, Alex tried to speak as respectfully as possible as he said, "It was not my brother's fault that your son was killed in battle, my lord."

Seeing the baron was about to protest hotly, the duke hastened to continue. "In any case, that is far from the point of my visit. I can assure you that I would never do anything to harm your daughter. Rosamund was my dearest friend before our mutual tragedies. Despite the estrangement, I would still never intentionally hurt any lady, let alone her. I would do anything in my power to ensure her safety, which is exactly why I have bothered coming here to tell you about my concerns. If you do not wish to listen to what I have to say, that is your prerogative, my lord, and I will leave you to your own devices. But as soon as I leave here, I have every intention of searching for her. I will tear apart this entire city if I have to, but I will ensure the safe return of your daughter."

The duke's impassioned declaration arrested the baron's attention and he was again eyeing his guest speculatively. "I am once again prompted to ask why you are so very concerned about this matter. She may have been your best friend once upon a time, but that is surely no longer the case."

Alex did not want to get into the details of the meetings he and Rose had been having with her father. "I feel as though I am partially responsible for her predicament as her interference with Broderick was somewhat motivated by her concerns for my welfare."

"How could you possibly know that?" Lord Smythe demanded.

Alex felt the heat rising in his cheeks, but he tried to avoid the subject. Making as if to rise he began, "If you do not wish my presence in your home, I will be glad to take my leave. I merely came by to tell you that I am very much afraid for your daughter's safety."

Before the baron was able to respond to Alex's words, the gentlemen were interrupted by a commotion in the foyer. Lady Smythe could be heard demanding of the butler, "Is my lord husband at home? I must speak to him at once."

The butler must have hesitated momentarily for she repeated herself, "At once, I tell you!"

The baron went to the door of the receiving room. "I am here, my lady, what seems to be the trouble?"

Lady Smythe hurried toward her husband. "You must do something, my lord. I am near my wit's end. He has taken my baby girl."

Lord Smythe looked beyond his wife to see that she had been accompanied by Lord Dunbar. Gathering his wife into the crook of his arm, the baron said calmly, "Perhaps we ought to all adjoin to the receiving room. Won't you join us, my lord?"

The trio made their way back into the room Lord Smythe had just vacated but they were brought up short by Lady Smythe's shock at seeing the Duke of Wrentham in her front room.

"What is he doing here, my lord? Surely this night has enough drama in it without adding a Wrentham to the mess."

Lord Smythe smiled at his wife and urged her to a seat. "It would seem he is here with the same concerns as you have." Looking at Lord Dunbar questioningly, he continued speaking to his wife. "I am curious to know how you have arrived at your concerns."

"Oh my lord, Rosamund's friend Lady Elizabeth and this dear gentleman, came to me at the ball to say that our daughter has gone missing. They are under the impression that Sir Broderick is somehow involved. I am unsure why they would think that nice man could have anything to do with anything bad happening to my daughter but anyhow, she was nowhere to be found at the Rotherhams.

"Of course, we did not do as thorough of a search as I would have liked, but the nice young people assured me that alerting everyone to her absence would be harmful to her reputation. Lord Dunbar was quite convinced that we shall be able to recover her before anything irrevocable is done to her and no one needs to be any the wiser. I am unsure if you will think that it was acceptable to leave the ball without her, but his lordship was quite convinced that it would be best if I was to return home and discuss the matter with you."

Lord Smythe patted his wife's hand soothingly. "You did just the right thing, my dear. Perhaps you ought to go lie down now. I am sure this has been quite the shock for you."

Lady Smythe began to rise from her chair to do as he suggested but then thought better of it and instilled a bit of iron to her drooping spine. "I do believe, my lord, that it would be best if I remain here and wait to see if there is anything I can do to help in this strange situation." Looking toward the duke for the first time since her initial shock, she continued,

"And I really must know what Wrentham is doing in my receiving room."

The baron appeared nonplussed by his wife's words, and Alex could see that Wesley was not going to step in to cover the awkward moment, so the duke stepped forward to explain his presence. "I know I am not an invited guest in your home, my lady, however, I came to inform you and your husband about your daughter's abduction."

"But how do you come to be involved? Are you here to make demands of us?" Lady Smythe was clearly struggling to keep the shrill from her voice but it echoed slightly off the high ceiling despite her efforts.

"Of course not, my lady. I merely have information to share. I suspect Broderick thinks he has snatched her without anyone being the wiser, so we might have the advantage. If we can manage to find her tonight we should be able to keep her safe and still thwart whatever schemes he is plotting."

Lady Smythe gazed at the duke rather dazedly. "But I really do not understand any of this. Why would Sir Broderick do something so dastardly? He seems like such a nice man. Surely he must realize that if he wanted to pay her his respects he would be more than welcome."

The baron and the duke both gazed at her with amazement before sharing a remarkably companionable look of commiseration. Lady Smythe's look of confusion was changing once more into an accusation. "I think you are just trying to divert our attention from your own dastardly deeds and placing the blame on poor Sir Broderick. What have you done with my daughter, you despicable rake?"

Alex was struck silent by his surprise over the lady's misguided opinions. His shock grew to new levels when Lord Smythe stepped in to his defence.

"My lady wife, I am amazed that you would even consider thinking about allowing Sir Broderick to call upon our daughter. He is the dastardly fellow in all of this, not His Grace." At the look of incredulity written upon his wife's face, the baron could not help laughing slightly. "Yes, yes, I know, I would normally have nothing good to say about Wrentham, but under these circumstances, I do believe him. I do not wish to get into all the details with you at this time, but I am already aware of Rosamund's involvement with Broderick and his schemes.

"She had gleaned some information, which she passed onto me just this afternoon. If His Grace tells us that she has been abducted by the knight then, unfortunately, I am inclined to believe him. And in that case, we need to be as polite as possible in order to gain his assistance in retrieving her as quickly and safely as possible."

Seeing that his wife was now beginning to look mutinous, Lord Smythe continued. "If you do not think you can manage to be civil to His Grace while he is in our house then it might be best if you retire to your room and wait until he takes his leave."

Lady Smythe looked flummoxed by her husband's declaration, but aside from casting a glare in the direction of the duke, she did not add anything further. She daintily sank back down onto the settee and clasped her hands in her lap. Plastering a reasonably pleasant smile onto her face, she looked back at her husband and asked, "What are you planning to do to ensure that we do not lose another one of our children, my lord?"

The three gentlemen in the room shuffled their feet uncomfortably for a moment before Alex finally took control. "Thank you for hearing me out, my lord. I took the liberty of arranging for some of my men to report to me here, as I wished to inform you of all that I know at the earliest possible moment. Earlier today I had set a couple of my runners to watching Broderick, so I am confident we shall soon be receiving word of where Rosie might be being kept." He did not even notice that he had slipped into referring to her in such a familiar way, but when he caught the baron's sceptical look he felt the heat rising in his face.

Wesley finally stepped forward at the perfect moment to relieve the duke of his discomfort, drawing attention to his presence. "I am unsure if Wrentham has explained this to you yet, my lord, but I have already told your wife what Lady Elizabeth saw this evening."

"Yes, yes, my lord, his grace already told me about it before you got here. I do believe he is right and this is an urgent matter. We ought not to sit around here dithering. Your Grace, when do you expect to hear word from your men? I too had set men to watching the knight today after I had spoken with my daughter. Hopefully they will be able to report something useful before too very long."

"That is most excellent, my lord," Alex responded. "I cannot say for certain when I will hear from my men. If they cannot leave their post, it might be difficult for them to get a message to me. It might be best if we set out on a search ourselves. I cannot be comfortable with the thought of Miss Smythe in the clutches of that man for a moment longer than necessary."

"It has already been longer than necessary," Lord Smythe grumbled. "I am still trying to understand why the girl took so long in coming to me with her information. Perhaps we could have prevented this entire scene from even happening."

"Hopefully you will have all the time in the world to discuss your questions with her after we have gotten her to safety, my lord. I would like to demand what she was thinking to go off with him in the first place. According to Lady Elizabeth, it does not appear as though the dastard used force."

Lord Smythe again gazed at the duke with a look that bordered on empathetic. "Surely you realize, Your Grace, that my daughter is not one that enjoys being told what to do. If you did anything so foolish as to tell her not to speak with the knight then that could explain this entire scenario."

Alex grinned. "I am becoming aware of that tendency, my lord. However, the blame for this cannot be placed at my feet. I did not tell her anything, nor did I try to tell her what to do, aside from be careful, which I think is innocuous enough that it should not lead her to go off in the company of the villain of the piece."

Lord Smythe nodded. "It is possible that he threatened her or someone she loves in some way in order to secure her cooperation. There is no blame to be placed, Your Grace. At least not in this particular instance," he interjected darkly.

Seeing his friend Lord Dunbar twitch as though he wished to defend the duke, Alex caught his eye and shook his head slightly, quelling the impulse.

Getting to his feet, Alex turned to face his baron host. "Thank you for seeing me, my lord. I hope I shall soon have gladder tidings. I am not sure what you intend to do but I cannot bear to sit here waiting to hear what my runners have gleaned. If you shall be home, would you be so kind as to interview them and send word to my house if there is anything pertinent to the search? I am going to swing by my house and see if any messages have arrived there, and then I am going to pursue a few leads that I can already think of from research I have previously completed."

The baron, too, had risen to his feet during this speech. "I feel as though I ought to accompany you, but perhaps if we were to divide our efforts, we could get twice as much ground covered. I also feel that I cannot just stand here waiting. Since you have arranged for some of your men to report here, why do we not agree to meet back here in a couple of hours and share whatever we have been able to find out? Then if your men are here we can speak to them together and decide how best to proceed from there."

It was obvious to all in the room that Lord Smythe was doing his best to be cordial and make the most of an uncomfortable situation. He, no doubt, appreciated the duke's offer to help despite the tensions between their two families. Lady Smythe was not so accommodating.

"He cannot return here, my lord," she hissed.

Alex controlled his amused smile over the uncomfortable look that descended upon the baron's face at his wife's words.

"I have spoken, my lady. It is best to be done this way." At her continued mumblings of disagreement, Lord Smythe looked at her sternly. "He is a duke. Even though he is young and inexperienced there will be doors he can open that are closed to me. It shall be a productive cooperation. We will be able to accomplish the most in the shortest amount of time if we work together. Do you not want our daughter home as soon as possible?"

"Well of course I do, do not be ridiculous."

"Then don't *you* be ridiculous, my lady. We need His Grace's help, so make an effort to be gracious about it."

Lady Smythe's colour was high and she looked uncomfortable to the extreme when Alex made good his escape from the room with Wesley in tow.

As they rode away Lord Dunbar whistled low. "I can safely say I have never seen such a scene as I just witnessed. I never would have thought I would see the day that the mother of a young, unwed girl would be so rude to an unmarried duke. It just isn't done." He chuckled before asking, "What could you have possibly done to put you so beyond the pale in their eyes?"

"Surely you knew about the feud between our two families," Alex replied, not bothering to explain any further, intent upon the task at hand.

"I did, of course, although I think it completely daft, but I had no idea it was to such an extreme. The woman wanted to have you tossed bodily from her home." Wesley was incredulous.

"Never mind that for now, we have more important things to think upon right now. Are you sure you are up to this adventure tonight?"

"I am shocked you would even ask, Your Grace. I would be loath to be anywhere else."

"Thank you, my friend. I so appreciate your help. Now, since we are both dressed for something other than the low adventure we are about to face, I propose that we each head home and quickly divest ourselves of our finery and meet at my house as soon as possible. Hopefully there will be some word to give us direction from there."

Wesley saluted smartly and headed off to his rooms without another word. Alex urged his mount to a faster pace and within a couple of minutes pulled up in the mews behind his house. Tossing his reins to his waiting groom, Alex began striding purposefully toward the door before he thought better of it and turned back to exchange a few words with the groom.

"There is a strong possibility I shall need your help tonight. How many strong, sharp, discreet men could we muster from the household staff for what could be a rough fight?"

The groom did not so much as blink over this question, quickly replying, "I should think we have at least twenty that could fit that description, Your Grace."

At the back of his mind Alex wondered what kind of adventures his father had gotten up to that the staff would be so sanguine about what he was asking. Hiding his misgivings, the duke replied to the waiting servant. "Very well, thank you. I require more information before we need to summon everyone. Please, keep yourself in readiness, but it would be best if the others get their rest while they can."

When the duke entered his house, he was surprised to see his butler pacing with his tiger in tow. Alex was glad to see the youngster whom he had set off in pursuit of the man watching him at Burlington House.

"Pete, am I ever glad to see you! You two look troubled, which tells me you have information for me."

The butler looked relieved to see his master arrive. "There have been a few messages for you, Your Grace."

"Excellent. I need to change and I need to hurry. Could the two of you accompany me to my chambers so that we can kill multiple birds with one stone?"

"Your Grace, I do not think that would be entirely proper," the butler huffed.

"Mayhap not, but a lady's safety is very much in jeopardy. I do not think we can afford to be overly fastidious at a time like this. Come along." Alex did not await a response. He was amused and relieved to hear his butler's heavy sigh, closely followed by the sound of his footsteps following the duke up to his chambers.

Alex was reminded of how happy he was that his valet was not the usual highly strung sort as he walked into the room with the other two in tow. He barely showed a reaction as the duke started stripping off his elegant clothes. The valet was a little more flustered when Alex demanded his roughest clothing to be readied.

"But Your Grace," he began to protest then quailed under the duke's stern glare. "Very well, Your Grace."

Alex grinned. "All right, Pete, out with it, what do you know?"

Pete quit gazing about at the rich surroundings and brought his attention back to his master. Gulping back his nerves he launched into his tale. "That bad man what was watching yer Grace and his lady friend, he knew all the trails there was to find and took me on a merry chase. But I managed no problems, yer Grace, cuz I used to hunt with me pa before I came to work for yer Grace."

Holding onto his patience, Alex smiled encouragingly as his valet fussed around him. "I am glad you managed so well, Pete. Were you able to find out anything useful?"

"I did, yer Grace." Pete grinned. "The first bad man met up with another bad man and he says to him, 'tell his lordship that the chit met up with who I swear was the Duke of Wrentham.'"

"Wait a minute, Pete. So the bad man was actually watching Miss Rose, not me."

"Would seem so, yer Grace."

"Were you able to find out anything else?"

"The second bad man flipped him a coin and he went off, so I figured he wasn't going to be of much more use, so I followed the second chap as he left their meeting. I hope that was all right, yer Grace."

"I am quite certain you made the right choice, Pete. Where did the second man go?"

"He was a fair bit harder to keep a track of since the first thing he went and did was to climb into a hack, but I was able to grab onto the back just as it took off so I managed just fine, yer Grace."

"Would you be able to show me where the places were that you have been?"

"I'm fair and certain that I could, yer Grace. But I knows for sure where we was when the hack stopped so I don't have to show you. The chap runs up the stairs to a fairly posh house and goes in. I waits and waits and not much happened but I did ask one of the kids what were running around who lived in that there house. They says it's Sir Jason Broderick, yer Grace. You would know where he lives, right?"

"Yes, thank you, Pete. I do know where that is. And that just confirms what I already knew about Broderick. But I might need you to help me find the men you saw. They might be in a position to help us find the lady."

"The lady? Has something happened to yer friend, yer Grace?"

"Yes, Pete, I guess I failed to tell you that bit. We believe that Broderick has abducted her. And we need to find her as quickly as possible. She might be in grave danger."

At this point, the butler stepped in and shared the messages he had received. Alex was finished dressing and Wesley was waiting impatiently to know what was going on. The two set off in search of Rose.

Chapter Nineteen

Rose was beginning to despise this particular adventure. She had been so excited about sharing in the intrigue, trying to figure out what Broderick was up to. Now that she had saved Alex, she felt as though she had gotten herself in way too deep. She could feel the warm trickle of blood as she struggled once more against the ropes binding her wrists.

The loud snores of the henchman guarding her were annoying and yet reassuring. Rose was frustrated by the passage of time. She had hoped to have freed herself before daybreak so that she could escape and make her way home before too many were abroad. It would not do to be seen arriving home in her gown from the night before, especially not looking the worse for wear as she surely did. But it would matter very little if she could not get herself free. She had very little confidence in Broderick's desire to keep her alive.

Endeavouring to reassure herself, she reminded herself that if he had wanted her dead he could have just done it the evening before. Why bother going to the trouble of tying her up and having her guarded if he planned on killing her? Of course, there were fates worse than death, her wayward imaginings reminded her unnecessarily. Her struggles to free herself of the bonds resumed. *Why did he have to tie the ropes so tight?* she wondered wretchedly, trying to decide if they had budged at all or if it was just her wishful thinking. *Or maybe I have just worn off a layer of my skin with my struggles and that is why it suddenly feels a little looser.*

A giant yawn surprised her as she continued to twist and tug. She had been too terrified to sleep at all during the night, besides the discomfort of her position. A faint sound in the distance stilled her actions, and she tensed in anticipation. The footsteps drew closer.

"Squint, you lazy lout, what good are you to me if you are going to sleep on the job? The girl could have gotten away," Broderick bellowed, waking the guard with a hard kick to his midsection.

Rose winced in sympathetic reaction, flinching in fear as Broderick approached her before she could quell the telling motion. He grinned at her reaction, making her stomach turn. She raised her chin defiantly.

She sat very still as the knight approached her, keeping her eyes trained on his every move, cursing her inability to escape before his return.

Broderick circled her, most likely just to ratchet up her fear another notch. He chuckled over her injured wrists. "I see you did not sit as demurely as you would like me to think through the night, did you? That must not feel too good," he observed dispassionately. "Perhaps you shall get an infection and die. It would save me a great deal of trouble."

"I do not aim to be that helpful, my lord," Rose answered sweetly, causing her captor to laugh once more.

"I am glad to see my knots held up. I shan't be tarrying here, I merely wished to ensure the guttersnipes had not made off with you. There is some cheese, bread, and ale for you if you would like to break your fast."

Rose thought of defiantly rejecting his offering but thought better of it as she heard her stomach growl indelicately. Lifting her chin proudly she politely thanked him before asking, "How am I to eat with my hands bound in such a manner?"

Sir Broderick grumbled under his breath something unfit for a lady's ears but stepped forward to untie her. She almost wept from relief as she brought her arms back to their natural position. She had to struggle to maintain her composure when she caught sight of her mangled wrists, though. Biting the inside of her cheek, she was exceedingly proud of herself when she detected that her lips did not even quiver.

She reached forward and grasped the flask he was holding out to her and took a slow draft. The cool slide of the liquid as it went down her parched throat was such a relief that she easily ignored the fact she didn't even like ale. At the moment, it tasted like the sweetest nectar. She took another slow swallow, savouring the moisture and refreshment. Putting the flask down, she slowly reached for the chunk of cheese he had laid out for her, delicately taking a bite.

Huffing with disgust, Broderick spoke up. "I do not have time to wait for you to meander your way through a meal. I have places to go. I will have to tie you back up before I leave."

Rose could not prevent the protest that moaned through her lips. "No, please, I beg of you. I really am terribly hungry."

"But you're taking too long, Miss."

"Why don't you jest tie her hands in front of 'er, milord," suggested Squint, speaking for the first time since the knight's arrival.

Rose had nearly forgotten he was there, she had been so focused on the food her captor had brought. She eyed him askance. Though she could barely tolerate the thought of being tied up again, if her hands were in front of her she thought she had a much better chance of being able to escape. She hoped her face did not reveal how excited she was at the knave's suggestion.

She could feel Broderick's eyes upon her and avoided making eye contact with him. He stood there studying her for a few heartbeats. Rose finally released the breath she had been holding when he spoke.

"As much as it would be a relief to have you off my hands as quickly as possible, I do not want you dying of blood loss before your possible usefulness is at an end. If you rip some strips off your gown, you can wrap your wrists with the cloth before I tie your hands back up."

Rose could hear the grudging reluctance in his voice and hastened to follow his suggestion, although she was unsure if she would be able to do so with her hands in their weakened state. Feeling the heat rising in her cheeks as she reached down toward her skirts, she made every effort not to lift them above her ankles as she struggled to find a suitable section, thankful for the fullness of the style she had chosen to wear. Realizing her petticoats would be made of softer, more absorbent material, she thought to start with that. Blessedly, it did not take her overly long to tug two chunks of fabric from her underthings. She sent up a quick prayer of thanks that her maid always insisted that she wear multiple layers.

She quickly wrapped the fabric around the worst of her wounds, hoping that she was not doing them more harm than good. It certainly couldn't be any worse to have the fabric protecting her flesh, as she anticipated struggling against the ropes once again as soon as Sir Broderick left and Squint took his eyes off her. Taking a deep breath against the anticipated pain, she offered her hands to her captor.

Rose wondered if she were being too compliant when Broderick shot her a suspicious scowl. She strove for nonchalance. With a shrug she said, "I am hungry. I would like to get back to my meal."

Broderick grinned and Rose cringed inside at the evil she saw in his eyes but she refrained from further comment. He made short work of tying her hands back together, and Rose bit her lip not to cry out, relieved that she still had movement.

Before long, Broderick was gone after a brief exchange with Squint and an admonishment to Rose to "behave." Rose smiled weakly at Squint and went back to her meal, concentrating on chewing slowly and imagining that she was elsewhere.

She had been wondering how her parents were handling her disappearance. Rose was surprised but grateful that Broderick seemed to have forgotten that he had wanted her to write a note telling her parents that she had run off with a seaman. She had been trying to come up with some sort of message that would tell her parents where she was but that Broderick would not be able to see through. She had not yet been able to come up with anything that made much sense. Thinking about her family made the bread feel like sawdust in her mouth, so she thought of Alex instead.

Despite the feud, thinking about the duke helped to steady her nerves and inspired her with hope. She allowed herself to imagine the scold he would give her for being so foolish as to allow herself to get into this predicament. Her imaginings were so real to her that she almost laughed out loud as the scene played itself out in her head. Rose shook her head at herself. *Mayhap this ordeal is making me mad. I shall be a candidate for Bedlam before this is through*, she mocked herself.

But the daydream had done the trick, she had fortified herself with the simple meal Broderick had provided and her nerves were fortified, too. She was resolved once more to get herself out of this mess. Steeling her backbone, she thought to herself, *If I survive this, mayhap I shall follow Mary's advice and see about brokering peace between the Wrenthams and Smythes.* She smiled slightly as she tested the strength of the latest knots.

Squint had gulped down the provisions Broderick had left for him and settled himself back into his chair. Despite the knight's violence and threats, Squint looked as though he were preparing himself for another nap. Rose held herself very still and did not utter a peep, hoping he would soon be fast asleep. Before too long his reassuring snorts and snores were filling the air and she got back to work on freeing herself. As she struggled, she wondered absently what time it was.

☙ ❧

Alex was cursing the time that was passing. The sun was fully up in the sky and the city was bustling with activity. He had not been able to discover the whereabouts of Broderick or his captive. He was ready to go and confront the man himself.

"That will not be at all useful, Your Grace," Lord Smythe tried to soothe him. "If we lay down all our cards, we will lose any advantage we might have. As long as he thinks we don't know anything, we have the element of surprise on our side. If we confront him, he will merely deny it and be all the more careful. We could even endanger Rosamund by doing so. I am hoping that he will have her guarded somewhere and is feeding her. If he feels endangered, at best he will abandon her, at worst he might kill her. I think we should keep searching as quietly as possible."

"But this infernal delay is driving me mad," the duke declared.

"I cannot conceive of why this is of concern to you, Your Grace," Lady Smythe complained. Catching her husband's censorious glance she interjected, "Not that I am complaining about your help, of course, Your Grace, I am merely surprised that you would seem to be so invested in it."

Alex was feeling frantic for Rose's return but was unwilling to explain himself to her mother. He knew the answer he was about to give was weak, but he gave it anyway. "I am involved, my lady, and I hate feeling thwarted."

It seemed to be a sentiment all in the room could relate to, as no one dismissed it and most nodded their head.

Lady Elizabeth had come by to see if there was any word. Since there was no good news and very little she could do to help, she stood to take her leave. "My dear Lady Smythe, I do not wish to be a burden for you to entertain at this time, so I shall leave you for now. Please know that I am ever ready to be of any assistance to you."

"Thank you, my lady. We sincerely appreciate that. Hopefully we shan't need to, but we will call upon you if needed. And I promise you we shall send word as soon as we know anything."

The assembled gentlemen all bowed to her as she left but had little to say. Lord Dunbar escorted her from the room.

Lady Smythe had resumed her seat and was absently wringing her hands. "This wretched waiting is what makes it so awful, my lord. Why have we heard nothing? Do not most abductors make demands of some sort so that you can pay a ransom and be done with it?"

"Can you not find something to occupy yourself with, my dear? I do not think it is healthful for you to sit here worrying yourself into a state." Lord Smythe was in no position to comfort his wife as he too was nearly beside himself with worry.

"No, I cannot occupy myself with something, my lord. What would you have me do? Take up my needlework?" She laughed mirthlessly.

"Perhaps you could go and make some calls, act as though naught is amiss, lest anyone wonder what has become of Rosamund."

"There is absolutely no way my acting skills could stretch that far, my lord, I can assure you. But you do raise a good point. What are we to do if we cannot recover her shortly? There will be talk, and she shall be ruined."

"We shall have to invent a story. Maybe you really should go and call on someone who gossips. Come up with a story that she has gone to the country to visit a friend or a relative and spread it about."

"Nobody would believe that a debutante is going to leave Town at the height of the Season, my lord," Lady Smythe declared, panicking, and becoming more shrill the longer she spoke. "My darling daughter is going to be ruined through no fault of her own. And then where will we be?"

Alex could not bear the older woman's distress. "Have no fear, my lady. Rosie will never be ruined. I shall marry her and restore her to Society. No one would dare to whisper about the Duchess of Wrentham."

Stunned silence descended upon the room for a moment before Lady Smythe burst out with inflammatory words. "I would rather she be ruined than be a Wrentham," she spat. "Your family shall not steal another child from me."

"My lady, please, how can you speak thus?" chastised Lord Dunbar, disbelieving the words he was hearing.

"The previous Duke of Wrentham was responsible for the death of my firstborn, I will not let the current duke get his hands on my daughter." Lady Smythe looked like a vengeful angel with her pale skin and her dove grey gown flowing as she paced in her wrath.

"But how could the Duke of Wrentham have had anything to do with your son's death? He was so happy to be off to the war. It had nothing to do with Wrentham."

Lady Smythe gazed at Wesley, her expression arrested. "What could you possibly know about the matter?" she demanded.

"I was there. I was in the same regiment as both your son and Wrentham's brother." Wesley looked between the Smythes and Alex, amazed that they were all gazing at him searchingly. "Surely you all realize how much they both wanted to be there."

"My son never said anything about enlisting. He must have just gone because he felt such a loyalty to his friend. The last duke was such a wretch, no doubt his son thought the only avenue of escape was to enlist. My dear boy had to go, too." Lady Smythe muffled her sob with the handkerchief she hastily held to her face.

Gently, Dunbar sat next to her and took her other hand. "I am loath to contradict you, my lady, but I have to tell you that both the boys joined up without telling each other. They both thought the other ought not to, but they each wanted to do so quite urgently. They were so happy to discover they were both there independently, and despite the trials and privations of being in the army's camp, they both thought it almost a lark right to the very end. They were so eager for an adventure."

"But why would my dear son want to join up? And why would he not tell us that he wished to do so?" Lady Smythe was clearly bewildered.

"I cannot rightly say why he did not tell you. I do know that Luke thought you would be proud of him for doing what he thought as his duty to his country. He felt that it would put him in better stead to follow in his father's footsteps as a diplomat if he fully understood what they were battling over. It seemed as though he felt very strongly on the matter, but he did not wish Wrentham's brother to know because your son felt that it was Maxwell's duty as heir to a dukedom to remain at home, and Luke did not want to make his friend feel divided in his loyalties."

Turning to Alex, Wesley continued his tale. "On the other hand, your brother really *did* wish fervently to get away from home. He felt terrible for leaving you behind, and he did not wish to tell either you or Luke that he was going for fear that you would wish to accompany him. Someone had to stay home and be the responsible heir," Dunbar explained with a lopsided grin.

There was a pause as everyone absorbed the viscount's words, but then Alex prodded for more information. "But you say they were happy?"

"Oh yes, Your Grace, very much so. Both of them were delighted when they discovered that each of them was there without any prompting from the other. They acted like boys. In a way, I do not think either of them realized the gravity of the situation, nor do I think they thought there was any possibility of them getting injured, let alone killed. But they most definitely were happy. They took to the regiment life like naturals. They acted as I would imagine they did when they were away at school. It was often hard to believe that they were men and soldiers, not the schoolboys they resembled."

Lady Smythe let out a watery chuckle as Wesley's tale wound down. "They always were such rascals when they were getting into mischief together."

Lord Smythe had come to stand behind his wife. With his hand upon her shoulder to offer her comfort, he looked at the duke sitting in his receiving room. "While I cannot condone some of the words your father said to us at the time of our sons' deaths, I realize now that none of this situation was any of your making, Your Grace. Please, accept our apologies for any rudeness we may have subjected you to, as well as our condolences at the loss of your brother. Over the past couple of years many have told me that we ought to be sharing our grief with your family instead of blaming each other. I can see now that they were right."

Alex smiled sadly at the older man. He was glad that relations between their families could warm, but it did not change the fact that the young men were dead nor that Rose was still missing. "Thank you, my lord. I do appreciate that. We shall have to get Dunbar here to visit my mother when this situation is cleared up and retell this story to her. But in the meantime, I feel as though I must do something. Are you absolutely certain there is no one else you can speak to who might have some information that could be pertinent?"

Alex had stood up and begun to pace as he was speaking. "Why does no one have anything new to tell us?" he demanded in frustration.

Just then there was a knock on the front door and the butler ushered in a rather scruffy looking man. "Jim is here to see you, Your Grace."

"I apologize for appearing in your front room in all my dirt, my lady, but I figured as you'd all rather hear what I have to say rather than see me clean."

"Yes, of course, pay it no mind," Lady Smythe quickly urged.

"Have you found out something useful this time, Jim?" demanded the duke, harsh in the face of his frustration and exhaustion.

"I do believe so, Your Grace. Pete and I were able to track down the man who was watching you and Miss Smythe at the museum."

"What did you just say?" Lady Smythe interrupted.

"Never mind that now, my dear. We shall sort it all out later," her husband urged as the poor man before them blushed to the roots of his hair.

Clearing his throat bashfully, Jim carefully kept his eyes on the duke's face, not looking at any of the other occupants in the room. "As I was saying, Your Grace, we tracked him down in a seedy tavern near where Charlie saw him. He was rather bosky, so it wasn't too difficult getting information out of him. He said as his employer has a bunch of sheds down by the docks. I was going to set out to search it, but I thought you would want to be along and maybe we would need help in case things turn dicey."

"That was excellent work, Jim, thank you. Were you able to get a description from him so that we can narrow down our search? I am perfectly willing to search the entire dock area, but in case they have someone on lookout, it would be best if we could be as specific as possible in our search." The duke was already on his feet heading for the door, eager to begin.

"Indeed I do, and I'm ready to take you there, Your Grace. I also took the liberty of getting some of your men together—they're waiting in the mews."

"Excellent." Alex was glad to see that Wesley was right behind him. He turned to Lord Smythe. "Are you ready to join us, my lord?"

"I am, Your Grace. But come through the back way here. I wish to stop in my library on the way by, and it would be best if we exit discreetly now that the day is well advanced. Who knows if we are being watched?"

"Good thinking, my lord," Alex complimented politely as he urged the men forward. They couldn't be gone fast enough to please him.

Much to Alex's relief, before long they were nearing the wharf and he could see the warren of buildings and sheds, relieved that Jim had some sort of description to go by. Jim went in front and led them to a section of dilapidated sheds huddling together near the shore of the river.

Quietly giving directions, Alex sent the small group of men to fan out in their search for Miss Rosamund.

Chapter Twenty

Rose had once again lost all track of time as she struggled with her bonds. As quietly as possible, she had wiggled and tugged, this time using her teeth to assist as she tried to untie the knots holding her captive. She almost sobbed with relief when she got her hands free. Striving for silence, she turned in her chair to fight with the rope holding her to it. She made short work of that, too, and was soon free.

But now she faced the question of what to do next. If Squint woke up and discovered her freed, she might really be in the suds then. She dithered for another couple of moments looking between the filthy window closer to her and the doorway just beyond the sleeping Squint. The window would be a safer bet on the one hand, but there was no way of knowing if it would even open. Then she remembered that her supposed guard had not woken until Broderick had kicked him, so she thought he must be a terribly heavy sleeper. She decided to take her chances and tiptoed quietly past him. Holding her breath, she opened the door, praying there would be no squeak to give her away.

Within the space of a few heartbeats she was out the door and sighing with relief. She gave up on tiptoeing, picked up her skirts, and ran for her life. Rose must have made too much noise for she could hear Squint clambering after her. She saw a door at the end of the hallway and burst through it out into bright sunlight. Looking around, she was stunned to see Alex in the distance along with Lord Dunbar.

Running as fast as her feet would carry her, she dashed toward him. "Alex!" she screamed as he turned toward her. She threw herself into his waiting arms. Sobbing with relief she clung to him as Squint, rather dull in intellect, ran after her, not realizing that he was endangering himself. Wesley quickly subdued him while Alex was occupied with soothing the young lady on the verge of hysterics.

"I cannot believe you were so close," she was babbling. "I could have waited for you and you would have found me."

"It is not in your nature to wait around for rescue, though, is it, my darling?" Alex used the endearment without either of them noticing. "Besides, it is just as well that you did rescue yourself, as it seems we were slightly off in our directions. We had reason to believe you were in the set of sheds next to the one you were in. It would have taken us some time to get to yours."

"True, but Broderick would have never been able to come for me with you and your men searching the area."

"Speaking of Broderick, have you any idea what he is up to? Now that you are safe, we should probably see about thwarting him once and for all." Alex could not make himself let go of Rose, but he did lift his head to look about.

At that moment, Rose's father approached. "What is the meaning of this, Your Grace? I would ask that you unhand my daughter this instant."

Rose felt the rush of embarrassment heating her face as she tried to pull away from Alex. In the fierce emotions that had dogged her during her escape, she had failed to notice that she was still clinging to the duke. She realized he must have felt the same as he was slow to release her. After a moment, he let her go and she ran to her father.

Lord Smythe engulfed his daughter in a fierce hug before holding her away from him and examining her closely. "Did that wretched man hurt you in any way?" He gasped when he saw the bloodstained cloths wrapped around her wrists. "Good heavens, child, what happened?"

Rose followed his gaze to her wrists and blushed guiltily, trying to hide them from sight as she realized that all the men were staring at her, awaiting an explanation. "Perhaps we could be getting along home now, Papa. I would dearly love a bath and perhaps a meal. And a change of clothes would not be amiss either."

"Yes, yes, of course, my dear, but pray tell, what happened to your wrists? Did Broderick cut you?" Lord Smythe tried not to be demanding, but he wanted to disembowel the cretin who had so harmed his only daughter.

"No Papa, I did this to myself, actually."

"How could you have possibly done that to yourself?" Alex demanded, incredulous.

"Through the night, my arms were tied behind my back. I had hoped to escape at first light and make my way home before my absence would be noticed. I struggled against the ropes for hours. This is the result."

"Well, it cannot be said that you did that to yourself. You did not tie yourself up. Any right-minded individual would do their best to escape. Broderick did this to you. For that he will pay."

Alex looked so fierce as he said those words that Rose could not help the grin that broke over her face. "Could we please leave, Papa? Your Grace? I have no wish to remain here another moment."

Those last words were not as strong leaving her mouth as she would have wished and to her chagrin she felt her legs giving way weakly. In the blink of an eye Alex was there, scooping her into his arms, disregarding Lord Smythe's objections.

"Never mind your protestations, my lord. Clearly, she is worn out and needs to be escorted home. Let us see her there safely, and then we will deal with the rest." Turning to Wesley he gave him an assignment. "Dunbar, could you remain here with a couple of the men in case Broderick returns? If you capture him, send word. We will see Rosie home safely and then spread out through the city to capture him. Rose had been about to tell me what he was scheming."

Rose chose that moment to revive herself. "He is trying to get the Prince to sign over the lands being negotiated from France to him. That is why he wants to keep Papa occupied, so he cannot thwart his plans. He was hoping to ensnare the backing of the Duke of Wrentham to assist his efforts. But when that did not work out as planned, he decided to prevent Papa from going to Paris for the negotiations." Looking into Alex's eyes shyly, she whispered, "You can put me down now, Your Grace. I am fairly certain that I can walk under my own steam."

"Never," he whispered back with a smile. "You need to rest."

Rose relaxed slightly, enjoying the shiver of pleasure that shimmied up her spine at his masterful ways. Within minutes, they were in a carriage and on the way to the Smythe residence. Alex had had to relinquish his hold on her when he placed her on the seat and the baron had been quick to take his seat next to his daughter. He sat glaring at the duke for the duration of the ride. Alex ignored the hostility, smiling calmly as they drove. Rose looked between the two men curiously, wondering how they came to be cooperating together, but she was too tired to ask about it.

Things moved quickly as soon as they got home. Rose was bundled into the house through the servants' entrance at the back. Her mother cried and fussed over her, as did her maid. A bath was quickly drawn for her and her wounds anointed with ointment. The gentlemen took themselves off to avenge themselves upon her captor. Before long, Rose was tucked up into bed to sleep off the rigors of her ordeal.

଑ ଒

Some hours later, Rose groggily climbed from the bed, facing the eager attentions of her loyal maid.

"Oh Miss, I am ever so glad to see you alive and well. We were all so terribly worried about you. It has been awful being stuck here, not being able to do anything. At least the men were able to dash about searching for you. All we could do was sit about wringing our hands and worrying."

"I am so sorry that everyone was put to such trouble over me."

"Don't be daft, Miss Rose. You didn't ask for this trouble and, of course, we would worry over you. Everyone loves you."

"Thank you, Mary. Do you know how my mother is? I was so tired when I got home I could hardly see straight, but I did notice that she looked rather drawn."

"She stayed up most of the night waiting for word. His Grace and your father were in and out throughout the night searching for you and waiting for news from their different sources."

"Does it not strike you as strange that my father and the duke have been cooperating over this?"

"Somewhat, yes, Miss. But maybe you won't have to be the one to broker the peace after all. Perhaps it has already been negotiated."

"Now that I find hard to believe, Mary."

As they were talking, Mary had helped Rose to dress in a simple day gown of pale yellow sprig muslin, with long sleeves to nicely cover her bandages, despite the early evening hour.

"Surely Mama has sent our regrets to whichever entertainments we were supposed to attend."

As Mary was just putting the finishing touches to her hairstyle, there was a scratching at the door.

"Come in," Rose called, admitting her anxious mother.

"You look remarkably lovely, my dear," Lady Smythe said with a lightness that Rose had not witnessed in her in years.

"Thank you, Mama," Rose said with a smile.

"Looking at you, no one would ever believe you have just escaped the clutches of a madman."

Rose blinked at her mother. "You seem remarkably sanguine about the entire affair, Mama."

"I, too, had a nap and it did me the world of good. It is so wonderful to have you home safe and sound."

Looking into the mirror, the two shared a look of warm companionship. Lady Smythe inquired politely, "Are you truly as comfortable as you look, my dear? Should we have called for the doctor to attend to your injuries? Are you certain there is nothing else hurt on you?"

"I am quite certain. My main concern at the moment is how very hungry I am. Even my wrists are not causing me much discomfort. The housekeeper's concoction has worked wonders for my scratches. Now all I can think of is to eat."

"Well then you are in luck. The kitchen staff has been expending themselves all afternoon as you slept making all your favourite dishes. If you are ready, they will be serving it momentarily."

The two Smythe ladies made their way down to the dining room in companionable silence. Lady Smythe had her arm around her daughter, reluctant to take her hands off her. Rose was surprised at the display of affection. Her surprise was to exceed its bounds as she entered the dining room to see the Duke of Wrentham seated conversing quietly with her father. Rose gazed wonderingly between the two men.

Lord Smythe stepped forward to kiss her gently on the cheek and Alex winked at her when no one was looking. When no explanation of his surprising presence was offered, she smiled crookedly at them both and allowed her mother to guide her to her seat.

Dinner was a quiet affair. Just as they sat down Lord Smythe assured his daughter that Sir Jason Broderick was safely confined, no longer a threat to her or the Prince, but everyone at the table silently agreed not to discuss it for the duration of the meal. It would be much safer for everyone's digestion if they stuck to innocuous topics such as the latest *on-dits* or which play they had enjoyed most this Season.

"We have received word that your brother should be arriving later this evening. Apparently their crossing was rough and it took longer than expected." Lady Smythe seemed so excited at the prospect of welcoming her son home. Rose attributed her altered manner to that and relief over her own safety.

Rose was highly amused at the politeness everyone was displaying. The last time she had seen her parents in the same room as a Wrentham, cutting words had been hurled from both sides. She assumed the truce had to do with their mutual efforts to save her and thwart Broderick.

So, she was stunned into silence when the dishes were removed and her father turned to her to say, "It would seem the duke has some things he wishes to discuss with you, my dear. The two of you may sit in the receiving room for a few minutes while your mother and I go to my library to enjoy the fire I am sure the footmen have started there."

Blinking in confusion, Rose did not resist as Alex pulled her seat back for her and offered his elbow. She wondered if she were still dreaming as he escorted her to the ivory room at the front of the house.

Settling herself on the settee, Rose blushed with pleasure when Alex sat closely beside her and did not release her arm. Instead, he held her hand gently and stared at the bandages covering her wrists.

"I am so sorry for the pain you have had to endure these two days," he began earnestly.

"Oh Alex," Rose sighed, "This can hardly be considered your fault. I should never have gone off with Broderick, but when he said he had my mother, I could not think fast enough to resist as he escorted me from the room."

"Ah, so your father was right. He figured some sort of a threat must have been made against a loved one to make you cooperate."

"How did you know something had happened to me? And how has it transpired that you and my father are getting along so well? I thought we hated each other."

"I never hated you, Rosie, and I dearly hope you do not hate me either."

Rose blushed and looked away, not answering his question.

He did not pursue it at the moment, instead answering her first question. "Lady Elizabeth alerted me almost immediately. She had seen you leave the ballroom with Broderick and right away was suspicious that all was not right. Unfortunately, by the time I was able to discover your whereabouts, I was just in time to see his carriage leaving the Rotherhams' property. I had already had men posted to watch your house, hoping to keep you safe, so I came right away to tell your father what had happened and to see if my men knew anything."

"But how did you manage to get my father to be so pleasant to you? And my mother? She seems to be a different person than she has been in ever so long. It is lovely, but strange."

Again, Alex ignored her questions. He had one of his own that he was burning to ask and he wanted to know her truthful answer.

"Rosie, my dear, your father told you I have something to discuss with you." Seeing her stifling a yawn, he was quick to ask, "Do you feel up to a conversation now, or should I let you get some sleep? I could return tomorrow."

Rose was exhausted, but she could not bear for this particular dream to end just yet. She clung to his hand and shook her head. "I am perfectly fine, Your Grace, thank you for asking."

Alex smiled into his beloved's eyes. "You lie very sweetly, my dear. I will try not to keep you for too long, but I am relieved that you will not make me wait until the morrow. I do believe I would expire from the suspense."

Rose grinned at his foolishness. "Well then, get on with it. I highly doubt my parents will leave us alone for overlong anyway."

"Rosie, my darling," he began haltingly as Rose grew serious. Noticing his use of the term of endearment, her eyes grew round with her amazement. "You have been my dearest friend since you were four years old. It is true we have barely spoken for three years, but our association in the last several days has shown me that you have not changed. I have loved you since you were in pigtails and short skirts. Would you do me the great honour of becoming my duchess?"

Staring at him with her mouth slightly agape in her shock, Rose could not answer immediately. The first thing that popped out of her mouth was, "But Alex, I am neither gracious nor graceful, how can I possibly be a duchess?"

"While I disagree fiercely with your assessment, when you are my duchess it will not matter, for everyone will have to call you 'Your Grace' regardless."

Rose grinned at his words, but still stared at him as though he had lost his mind. "How could you possibly love me, Alex? Wrenthams hate Smythes. Your mother would never allow it and your father would roll over in his grave. Besides, my parents. Did they know what you wanted to discuss with me?"

"They did, as a matter of fact," Alex replied, leaving her speechless once again. He took advantage of her silence to prod further. "It matters not what anyone else thinks. How do you feel about it?"

He began to worry at her continued silence, so he began to bargain with her. "I know you have not been enjoying the Season and you feel that settling into domestic life will be a letdown after the excitement you have experienced in Vienna. Would you agree to be my duchess if I promise to find us more adventures?"

Taking a moment to entertain the thought, Rose allowed all the feelings that had been growing in her heart over the past weeks, but that she had been fiercely suppressing, to flow over her in waves of warmth. Looking at her dearest friend beside her, she knew her love was undoubtedly beaming from her eyes.

"After the events of the past two days I suspect I may have had enough adventure to last me for a while, Your Grace," she replied drily, "although that is a highly romantic offer." She paused for a moment, clasping his hand tight. "I have loved you for as long as I can remember, Alex. When I was a little girl it was hero worship, but as I grew older it has changed. I would love nothing more than to be your wife."

She was about to say more, expressing her doubts about their families' reception to his proposal, but he crushed her words by pulling her into his arms.

The brief kiss they had shared previously, although thrilling, held nothing in comparison to the warm embrace they now shared. Alex poured all his feelings into the connection of their lips while Rose accepted and returned them with fervour. Although inexperienced in matters of love, she made up for her lack of skill with her enthusiasm to demonstrate her feelings. They broke apart at the sound of footsteps in the hall.

Blushing and laughing, Rose gazed at the man before her with wonderment. "Have you truly asked me to be your bride, or am I dreaming? And are you certain my father will accept this?"

"You worry too much, my darling. You are soon to be a duchess. Everything will work itself out."

And it did.

The End

About the Author

I've been writing pretty much since I learned to read when I was five years old. Of course, those early efforts were basically only something a mother could love :-). I put writing aside after I left school and stuck with reading. I am an avid reader. I love words. I will read anything, even the cereal box, signs, posters, etc. But my true love is novels.

Almost ten years ago my husband dared me to write a book instead of always reading them. I didn't think I'd be able to do it, but to my surprise I love writing. Those early efforts eventually became my first published book – Tempting the Earl (published by Avalon Books in 2010). There were some ups and downs in my publishing efforts. My first publisher was sold and I became an "orphan" author, back to the drawing board of trying to find a publishing house. It has been a thrilling adventure as I learned to navigate the world of publishing.

I believe firmly that everyone deserves a happily ever after. I want my readers to be able to escape from the everyday for a little while and feel upbeat and refreshed when they get to the end of my books.

When not reading or writing, I can be found traipsing around my neighborhood admiring the dogs and greenery or travelling the world with my favorite companion.

Stay in touch:

www.wendymayandrews.com

www.facebook.com/WendyMayAndrews

www.instagram.com/WendyMayAndrews

www.twitter.com/WendyMayAndrews

Find out what happens to Elizabeth after Rose is kidnapped from the ball in the exciting sequel,

The Countess Intrigue

Engaged to a rumored murder. What's a lady to do?

During her second Season, Lady Elizabeth Castleton is found in a compromising situation with Lord Justice Sinclair, the Earl of Heath. Despite her attraction to him, she is dismayed to find herself betrothed to the man who is rumored to have killed his first wife. Her parents refuse to lend credence to the rumors, so she is soon married and on the way to her husband's estate.

She cannot decide what to make of the handsome earl but after an attempt is made on her life, Elizabeth is terrified that history is about to repeat itself. She determines to find out once and for all if she is married to a murder.

Can she stay alive long enough to find her happily ever after?

Available now on Amazon

Made in the USA
Las Vegas, NV
30 November 2025